THREE RIVERS

Roberta Latow

BALLANTINE BOOKS • NEW YORK

Copyright © 1980 by Roberta Latow

All rights reserved. No part of this publication may be reproduced, stored in a retrieval system, or transmitted, in any form or by any means, electronic, mechanical, photocopying, recording, or otherwise, without the prior written permission of the publisher. Published in the United States by Ballantine Books, a division of Random House, Inc., New York, and simultaneously in Canada by Random House of Canada, Limited, Toronto, Canada.

Library of Congress Catalog Card Number: 81-066653

ISBN 0-345-29446-7

This edition published by arrangement with Desmond Elliott Publisher Ltd.

Manufactured in the United States of America

First Ballantine Books Edition: August 1981

Acknowledgments

My initial thanks must go to Peter Menegas, who unselfishly gave me his friendship, expressed confidence in me and at critical moments reassured me that I would, after all, survive my anxiety over a first novel in print. To my publisher, Desmond Elliot, I must record how heartened I was by his enthusiasm and support of my work. A special word of appreciation must go to Donald Munson, who expressed to me in a few words a verbal portrait of true love and introduced me to the works of Miguel de Unamuno.

For sheer hard work and expertise, I am most grateful to Lydia Galton, who painstakingly edited *Three Rivers*, and also Joanna Miller Seymour for her assistance and typing. Also, many thanks must go to the staff of Arlington Books, who worked tirelessly checking up on us all.

Lastly, acknowledgment is due to The Hogarth Press and Harcourt Brace Jovanovich for permission to use the poem, *Return*, by C. Cavafy, translated by Rae Dalven, at the beginning of this book.

*For Peter and Desmond,
and then came Mike*

Return often and take me,
beloved sensation, return and take me—
when the memory of the body awakens,
and old desire again runs through the blood;
when the lips and the skin remember,
and the hands feel as if they touch again.

Return often and take me at night,
when the lips and the skin remember . . .

Return by Cavafy

I

SHE HEARD.

"Isabel, Isabel. Oh, she's gone off again. What *are* you thinking about, Isabel?"

The three friends at the table laughed kindly at her. Teasing her to let them in on her journey away from them. She gazed beyond them to the room. Solid, rich, delicious and soft—an easy way to describe the dining room of The Connaught. She was having a very good time. They all were. Isabel smiled, picked up her knife and fork and looked down at the plate covered over with paper-thin, silky slices of smoked Scottish salmon.

Their silence made her look up and say, "You would never believe it." She thought that she had better answer them. They all knew her too well. Any little lie would never do. Any big one, impossible.

"Actually, I was thinking about my mother's funeral."

"Your mother's funeral, are you mad? Your mother isn't even dead."

"I know it's mad, but that is what I am thinking about. I think about it all the time. It haunts me. I don't know what I am going to do about my mother's funeral."

The positive atmosphere around them was stronger than the madness of Isabel's journey. It vanished so quickly, she might have said she was thinking of her dirty laundry. But her mother's funeral—ah, that was always with her. The ladies laughed about something or someone in the restaurant, lifted their glasses in a toast to the birthday lady and went on with their lunch.

Isabel took a sip of the delicious Montrachet, turned to the friend next to her and answered her question; they all laughed. The waiters drifted around the table, picking up the first course plates; another of the ladies at the table had them riveted with a very funny story about a man who tried to pick her up in Shepherd Market. She told it

1

very well, but not well enough to stop Isabel's mind from drifting back to the fantasy funeral of her mother.

But would it really happen that way? Suddenly she thought to herself as the waiter ground fresh pepper over the Scottish salmon, *Why don't I ever just think about my dirty laundry?*

Lunch over, the group stood at the entrance of The Connaught, watched over by the smart-looking doorman, who managed to take on the image of a painted piece of Coalport china. After much cheek-kissing between the four of them, two of the women went off in one direction. Isabel and the other woman, Caroline, decided to do a stint of extravagant window-shopping, and how much more extravagant window-shopping can one do than Mount Street, Mayfair?

One went mad over the show of shoes. The other went mad over the Bill Gibb dresses. They remarked how marvelous Allen the butcher's window was. Isabel said it was a copy of a Rembrandt painting come to life. Caroline said Bailey's window of stuffed pheasant, partridge, grouse and baskets of quails' eggs was another painting, asking Isabel who she thought could have painted that. She answered, "Only England! That's some chicken shop." They laughed, linked arms and went on their way.

They were now standing in front of John Sparks's window. The one window in all London that never, ever misses and always leaves Isabel speechless. She stood there in that state, completely absorbed by the perfection of the ancient Chinese table; the Han horse glistening in all its glory had her enraptured. She tripped and almost fell over as they passed silently to the next window. An exquisite chest, probably very early Korean; on the top a Celidon bowl filled wildly with dozens of cream-colored lilies. She was looking through the glass, but could smell them. Isabel was the table, the bowl, the lilies, the scent. The scent, the lilies, the bowl, the table were Isabel. They were fixed in that moment.

Isabel stood there, glued to the spot.

Caroline asked, "Are you thinking about your mother's funeral again?" with a very concerned look on her face.

Isabel turned, coming back to another reality with a thump. She smiled and told her that she guessed that she was.

"But, Isabel, is it true, do you always think about your mother's death?"

"No, I don't ever think about my mother's death. I think about what I should do about her funeral."

"Oh, not her death. Well, that seems so odd to me. Isabel, you are the only American friend I have, so you are my only frame of reference. Is it an American thing to think about funerals?"

"Well, let's just say that I have been trained to it, you know, the way one is toilet trained as a baby, taught to walk as a tot, taught to talk as a child, trained to be a good girl and not a bad girl. All those things happened to me when I was a child, and after those were managed, the next lesson after 'Love Thy Mother and hate everyone else' was supposedly mastered, was a series of instructions across the years of what to do about my mother's funeral. She trained me very well for, as you see, I walk and talk and have fine bathroom habits and I still worry about my mother's funeral."

What a good girl.

"You are putting me on, aren't you? Are you serious? I never know when you are serious, or is it just your droll sense of humor?"

"I suppose I am being dead serious, if you will forgive the pun."

One of the things that Isabel enjoyed most in life was to sit under the trees in Berkeley Square. That is what she did on that afternoon with her friend. They smoked a few cigarettes, chatted on about their lives, which were so different. Then Caroline left.

There were but a few people in the square, and they were at a great distance from Isabel. It was a half-cloudy, half-sunny day and a bit on the windy side, but she liked it. The wind moved the mass of leaves above her head and brought her visions of patches of sky every now and again. The traffic, as if in another world, was whirling around and around the square. Up Davies Street, round the top of the square, taking off up Bruton Street, others to the bottom of the square, shooting out at Berkeley Street.

She was sitting on a weatherworn wooden bench, facing the string of Georgian buildings that were once the most elegant town houses of Mayfair. One had been lovingly and magnificently put together by Clive of India. Still magnificent, though the glamour and romance of the great days of the Raj were gone. And now, well, now in the hands of one of those worthy organizations—missionaries (to wherever missionaries are still allowed to go). One looked in wonder at the stillness of the house and secretly hoped that the ghost of Clive came out at night, wandering through his home, leaving just a drift of the scent of his forbidden pipe. Just enough so that when the first of those do-good ladies opened the front door, a sweet whiff of Clive met her.

Just two doors up there is the Clermont Club. Not many goody-two-shoes there. But it was fun to look at that grand and wonderful building, and every now and then some Arab would drift out of the door; some smart Mayfair gamblers with their Saville Row suits and quick, sharp eyes; a couple of very pretty ladies, all dressed down so that one felt they were very dressed up, on the arms of their sugar daddies. The Rollses all lined up, the chauffeurs bored and dull-looking, waiting to be mechanized by their employers, who do just that by simply appearing on the pavement, raising their chin and looking straight into their car.

Annabel's, just downstairs from the Clermont, all locked up, just waiting for nighttime to come.

Then there were two other houses filled with Merchant Banks, hiding behind polished brass knockers on heavy wooden doors. Those wonderful brass plaques that gave their names in half-inch-deep, discreet lettering. It made one feel when walking by and reading off those names, how solid, how secure, how honest. Well, maybe not honest, but certainly reputable. Oh, yes, a great deal of solid security going on behind those window boxes. And then, scrunched in between those more grand buildings, one more simple, almost plain, but still grand for its period and location as well as its simplicity—the wonderful Maggs Brothers. Rare books, in this wonderful old building with rare people as well as the books. The subtle spark of life and speciality issuing forth by way of Persian Primitives in one window and an illuminated page of a rare book in the other.

How she loved to look at all this, to watch it all go by and to even be a part of it.

It was shortly after four o'clock when she left the square and walked the short distance to her house. As Isabel unlocked the street door, she thought to herself what a lovely afternoon it had been, how silly she was to be preoccupied with those strange thoughts about her mother.

Isabel awoke from a luxurious, deep sleep and lay in her bed daydreaming, all warm and cosy, her dogs at the foot of the bed still asleep. The room was dark and when all the cobwebs of nighttime moved away and the daydreams became boring, she got up. She switched a small light on next to the bed to see the time: 9:18 A.M.

Isabel sprang out of bed and went to the chaise to snatch up her dressing gown—a heavy, white, raw silk galabia lined in the finest of peach-colored silk, which felt so wonderful on her naked body. As she moved to the windows, the fine silk sensuously touching her breasts, thighs and buttocks as she took each step made her nipples harden in response. She stretched and shook herself like a wet puppy dog, hoping to dispel this morning sexiness—and succeeded. She pulled the cords of the draperies and the room sprang to life as the light poured in. Winston, her pug, raised his funny, pushed-in face, gave a not very silent yawn and a few pug snuffles, rolled over and went back to sleep; Rita, the Shi-tzu, seemed to nuzzle her head deeper into the eiderdown, wagging her tail as she did so; Arthur, the tabby cat, never moved at all—he lay cuddled up in his favorite place—a deep feather cushion next to the wood box on the hearth.

Isabel moved to the mirror, ran her fingers through her hair and looked deep into her face, hoping that she had not aged much through the night. She hadn't. Isabel at forty-three looked more like thirty-two. She stepped back a bit and saw herself in the reflection of the mirror. Her quick, intelligent eyes rapidly took stock of herself: Her statuesque five feet eleven inches were devoid of any excessive weight, and her sensuously large breasts only helped to emphasize the elegant slimness of her long waist and spare but rounded hips. Her huge, deep, dark eyes carefully checked the silky chestnut hair, the flawless and very white skin, the long Grecian nose and the happy mouth with a lower lip that could pout so beautifully when necessary. Isabel knew she was beautiful, that the bits and pieces of her face were put together in just the right way; but it would not have mattered much if some of the bits and pieces were askew because, with Isabel, it was all in those enormous, intelligent, yet innocent, dark eyes. Everything Isabel was, or ever would be, was set in those eyes. It was Isabel's eyes and her soul that drew people to her and kept some of them at her side forever. One of those quick, brown eyes winked at her from the mirror, and she smiled back at the familiar, beautiful face and turned to look at the room she loved.

A very large bed lay in the middle of the enormous room; the twenty-one-foot ceiling was deeply carved with swirls of acanthus leaves and simple flowers that reminded one of hollyhocks and morning glories. It was all the color of desert sand—the walls, the ceiling, the carpets, the silk at the windows. A Louis XIV fireplace in fleur-de-peche marble and the great, carved, full-length, mother-of-pearl mirror from Damascus were the only highly decorative things in the room. Between the fireplace and the mirror there was a chaise covered in woven rag of the same pale sand color, looking not unlike an old-fashioned rag rug. A long, low Japanese table, of great age and pure line, sat in the middle of the floor, between the wall with the mirror and the foot of the bed. On it were piled helter-skelter a half-dozen books that Isabel was reading at the present time and a bowl of peach-colored tulips fully blown, their stems twisting and turning up and around, pretending to be swans, bending their necks to an imaginary soft, warm wind. When made up, the bed was covered with a large, luxurious, soft and silky lynx rug that swept onto the carpet. A multitude of handwoven cushions of various sizes, and in all shades of beige and white soft wool, which had been hand spun in Morocco, the Niger, Afghanistan and Scotland and then hand woven under Isabel's instructions, were the only things that broke the effect of all the deep fur on the bed.

As she walked toward the back of the room, she bent down and picked up a few coins that must have fallen out of Max's pocket the night before. She dropped them in an empty ashtray and went out onto the balcony to gaze at her garden below and remember the pleasures of last night and of Max. She tingled as she relived their passions.

"Are you all right?" Max had asked at one point, and she had replied: "I feel wonderful, I'm just fine. I feel full and empty at the same time. Rich, beautiful and full of the power of being me, and yet I feel humble. Ten feet tall and oozing out of everywhere with sparkles of something, I don't know what. But most of all I feel lucky. Do you know how lucky we are, to be able to have such gorgeous sex together? How many times in a woman's life do you think she finds a man that she can be as free and as happy with sexually? Oh, Max, being with you has made me realize I haven't had sex as good as we have now for a long time. I guess that I feel humble that I have found it again."

She paused and looked at him deeply.

"You know what? Having sex with you, tasting you all the time, the smell of you, the smell of us, makes me realize that only once before in my life did I ever have great sex. I was very young then and didn't realize how great it was. Only now, through you, have I learned to understand how great that sex was and how great sex is. All those years ago I didn't understand what it was all about and how important it was to one's life, so I ran away from it. What strange, dumb tricks people play on each other. I was very young, he was middle-aged; I was stupid and he was wise. As a matter of fact he never forgave me for leaving him. Now I am much older and you are very young. I hope *you* won't run away."

"Slide a little closer," Max demanded. "You're so soft and warm, always the way I want you to be."

"Did he love you the way I do?" Max asked as his hands roved across her pulsating flesh. "Did he always want to bury himself in you? His fingers, his tongue, his face? Tell me about it. Did he love you, did he make love to you the way I do? Tell me about him."

"He's dead," she said flatly.

"Well, if he is, he was once alive, and from the little that you say I have the impression that you had one hell of a happy sex life together. Tell me about that sex life, Isabel. Hearing you talk about it turns me on. Come on, talk about him while I hold you. Turn me on."

"I don't suppose that you want any of the side details that went along with that gorgeous sex we had so many years ago? You know, the little details like the wife, the children, my being twenty-one and thinking that I was in love with him. Even today I don't know if I *was* in love with him or in love with the sex that he gave me and I gave him. It took you, all these years later, to make me realize how that man turned me on sexually and gave me greater sexual experiences than anyone before or since.

Until now. How peculiar, lying here next to you, Max, lying here just inches apart from each other's faces, sort of all intertwined and our bodies all moist and that lovely smell of sex and talking about a man who turned me on long ago. What can I tell you? That it was exciting? Do you want the details, darling?"

Max murmured that he did.

"OK. He wanted me every time he saw me. Anywhere, any time, any place. It was a little difficult, you understand—his wife being my friend. But after a while that didn't matter much either. If she was in the kitchen cooking dinner and I was a dinner guest in the house, just the three of us—the children put to bed—he would simply tip me over on a chair, raise my skirt, spread me apart and slip his fingers inside me. Or if I were sitting on the arm of his chair he would simply stop thumbing through his magazine, pull me onto his lap, raise my dress, and he would thumb me until I came. Then, of course, being a good, clean, suburban husband, when his wife called 'Dinner,' he would disappear to the bathroom and wash his hands.

"Or would you rather I told you about the times his wife was not quite ready, busy and late putting the children to bed at those times when the three of us were going out. To save time he would pick me up. Oh, he knew how to use me, even in the car. Those were only the little times. Then there were the big times, you know, those times when we would make it, rarely, but sometimes, in a nice big bed. That was, of course, when he was supposed to be playing golf. Those sneaky little sex acts on Saturday afternoons and Sunday mornings were very exciting. Even if a little uncomfortable on that floor in his office. But he did want me and did know how to get me and keep me. He got me to the point that I was open and ready for him at all times. I gave up thinking about anyone else and was always naked from the waist down under my skirt so I would always be ready. I couldn't get enough of his wanting me."

"I think I get the rounded picture; now let's have one scene," Max begged.

"Listen, Max. It's a long time ago, and I only remember the scenes as all similar; only the positions and demands varied. He was a man who took me to bed and made love to me. It all started out very easy. The very first time he had me, he undressed me, spread my legs apart, examined every detail. No man had ever done that to me before. He took each layer of flesh and slowly separated them and played with those red-pink layers. I remember I was lying on my back, my ass on the edge of the bed and my legs spread out and up. He had great control. He did it to me slowly and hard for a long time.

"That was the beginning. It was always beautiful and tender and sweet like that. As time went on he used to like to turn me over and put me on my knees, the way you like to, and enter me from behind. Then, after a time, that was not enough. He wanted me to have another man with him. Still not enough. He started little games: Sometimes I would wear long black stockings and garters with high-heeled black shoes and nothing else. That would really make us both very sexy, and we would do it in every possible position, in any possible place. And I loved it, I loved it all.

"Max, how big and hard you have become in my hand. Let me kiss you."

"Oh, yes, yes, Isabel," he entreated. "Oh, that's great. . . ."

Ah, Max, Isabel thought as she shivered in the cool October London air. Such a fine architect, too fine in fact to be successful financially or commercially. He is what is called an architect's architect. Fortunately for Max he had been born well, brought up well and educated well, coming as he did from English aristocracy, more country than city, more eccentric than flashy. He was financially secure in his own right simply by being born Maxim Aspinal.

At the age of thirty, this tall, six-foot-four, extremely thin, ash-blond-haired, blue-eyed, handsome young man had been having a sexual life with Isabel for the past three years. He was in partnership with another architect in a small office in Knightsbridge. They had a few draftsmen, an engineer and a secretary who kept the office in order in the day and Max in order at night. She was his mistress, his housekeeper, his laundress, his lady. She knew that there was another woman, but her fear of loss kept her quiet most of the time, rationalizing away the smell of jasmine, rose and lily of the valley that faintly lingered on his body and that he claimed was Johnson's baby powder.

In the three years that he and Isabel had been together, they had never been out to a restaurant, a pub, a friend's house, or for a walk. They had been all around the world together in bed. Max was mean about money—his mistress paid her own way and all but supported him. He lived simply, dressed Saville Row until threadbare. The most extravagant thing in Max's life was his sexual life with Isabel. He had never brought Isabel a flower, a bottle of wine, a trinket or a jewel, never sent her a letter, a note, a postcard—oh, yes, once he sent her a postcard because he wanted her so much he had to make contact.

He periodically brought a few friends to have a drink with her; the visits were always rather brief, the visitors always men. Max would then leave with his friends, and return within the hour.

When Max came through the door everything became electric. It had been that way from the first and had never changed. The one thing that Max was never mean about was giving himself completely to Isabel while they were together. He had the overwhelming desire to give her everything. No matter how much pleasure he gave her, he always wanted to give her still more, and he knew it was the same for her. It was this incredible sexual feedback that kept them tirelessly together and always wanting each other, always ready for each other.

They never spoke about their work, art, politics, or themselves, the past, the present, the future. They were into each other without any outside influences except one: music. Occasionally Max and Isabel lay naked and entwined together, not speaking, but floating off with Pink Floyd, George Harrison, Vivaldi, Rachmaninoff or Segovia.

Unassuming, but such a special man, this Max Aspinal.

Isabel returned to the bedroom. There was a nip in the air; she closed the doors on the chill air and the memories of Max and went to her dressing room and bathroom.

By the time she left the bathroom she had completed the first stage of her morning ritual, and she arrived back in her bedroom cleansed and thinking about her day. Endo, her Japanese houseboy, had placed her morning tray on the Korean chest near her bed. The paper, a large glass of her morning drink—consisting of yogurt, orange juice, protein powder, raspberries, peaches, four almonds (to keep the cancer away) and Redoxon (to keep the colds away)—a small saucer with half a dozen vitamins, and a few garden roses in a small silver bowl were on the tray, as usual; and Isabel climbed into bed to read her paper and drink her drink slowly, and relax before another hectic day.

Creative in her work, clever in survival, and with an amazing degree of innocence about both, whatever Isabel did she did to the best of her ability and always to completion. Isabel was intelligent enough to use herself sparingly, something she could do now at forty-three only because she had burnt out so much by the time she was thirty-three.

Isabel was both devoted to and successful at her work —art and design consultant; it was creative, interesting, exciting, rarely boring. Each job has its own demands, its own rewards. Jobs such as the six months she spent at The Louvre when she was hired to rearrange the interior spaces for the Decorative Arts Department, and the two days' work selecting the colors for a Texas millionaire's offices in Dallas, and the six-week trip to Ethiopia assembling art and artifacts for the Brooklyn Museum, or the three years she spent in Algeria assembling the finest collection of Punic art in the world, now housed in several private collections and museums around the world. All were stimulating and challenging. She advised on the designs of handmade carpets in Portugal, on the interiors of a house in Hampstead, and three times a year arranged the current exhibitions for a small museum in the south of France. In addition, she had written three books and collected thousands of others for her library.

Half an hour later, Isabel once again climbed out of bed, turned some music on and dressed. The next twenty minutes were spent making up her face. These would be the last private twenty minutes of Isabel's day. She remembered once reading something of Carlos Casteñeda's about energy spots. This place where Isabel sat every morning was her energy spot: It was here that many flashes of inspiration came, many good thoughts, many bad ones as well; it was here that she gathered up her energy to face the world, or at least the day.

Dressed in a beautifully cut Ralph Lauren tobacco tweed suit and raw silk blouse, Isabel left the room and went downstairs to greet Endo and the birds, who were singing away in their cages hung among the leaves of the

Ficus benjamanas, huge dracenas and yucca trees in the drawing room. Isabel took a chair near the windows where Endo had placed her morning tea and the mail. As she went through the post, the date revolved in her mind. *Someone's birthday, that's it, it's someone's birthday today. Of course!* Her sister's birthday. She must call her sister to wish her a happy day. Even if she disliked her sister, she still wished her well, especially on her birthday, otherwise, why would she have sent that gift a week ago? Yes, she must call her and wish her well.

It was 11:15 A.M. now. Isabel started making her phone calls of the day.

These were especially happy days for Isabel because she was just completing a lucrative and exciting job, she had enough money to keep going on for a few months, and two really interesting jobs coming up in the near future. This was the most security she had ever had in her life; enough to give her some leisure, but not enough to make her lazy.

On the phone constantly for the next few hours, she forgot about the birthday call. Her driver was scheduled to pick her up at 1:30. They would go to Sotheby's, where she would bid on a Mirandi for a client in New York, then to The Tate, where she was doing some research for the book on which she was now working. A whodunit written under her pseudonym, Meredith Montague, that must go to the editor no later than February.

Endo appeared at one o'clock with a tray for her lunch, which she asked him to bring to her studio at the top of the house.

Isabel took the tiny open lift to the third floor. The glass roof was just sliding back as she stepped out of the elevator into the studio that took up the entire top floor. Joy, her weaver, poppped out from behind one of the trees in the room and greeted Isabel. Although the sun was not very strong that day, the wind was almost nil, and it was still warm enough to have the roof open for an hour or two.

As they stood over the loom, they worked out the pattern of the weft for a piece being woven for a pair of Louis XV chairs owned by the Aga Khan. Endo appeared with another tray for Joy, and the two sat down at Isabel's marble worktable, lunched and chatted until Endo rang up to say Jim, her driver, was there and waiting.

By five o'clock the Mirandi had been secured. On the ride between Sotheby's and The Tate, one Isabel was dropped off and the other Isabel—in the form of Meredith Montague—collected. The two hours at The Tate were well spent, and by the time Jim had driven the Mercedes up to the house on Hill Street, Isabel had gathered the missing links that she needed to get on with her book.

Sitting in the back of the car as they rounded Berkeley Square, she sorted out the remainder of her day: *Fifteen minutes with Joy to check the weaving, twenty minutes for disposing of the day's phone calls, if there are any, must remember the happy birthday call, half an hour with Joanna to check over the last pages written on the novel. After that, work on the book.*

As Isabel let herself into the building she met the Japanese cultural attaché, who lived in the ground floor and the basement of the house. Isabel had been entertained there many a time. It was a famous and sought after invitation among the very social world of diplomats in London. A charming man, Mr. Hayakawa asked Isabel to tea the following day. He made a point of telling her that there would only be two other people, for he had been quick to realize over the years that his neighbor rarely accepted invitations for large social events. When Isabel accepted, he gave her a slow smile and told her how pleased he was because he had something of great beauty that had just arrived from Kyoto and he wanted her to see it.

Isabel called for tea in the drawing room, went upstairs and kicked off her shoes, changed into a beige wool kaftan, brushed her hair and went back to the drawing room.

Endo had placed the tray on a table near the windows and Isabel's favorite wing chair. The room was the entire width of the house and had a very high ceiling. The walls were covered in fine seventeenth-century paneling broken only by two fireplaces, one at each end of the room, and five arch-shaped windows twenty feet high, with French doors set in them and hung with deep-buttercup-yellow silk tied-back draperies. These were rather like grand peepholes on the purest of Japanese gardens beyond.

Endo had lit one of the fires and was just touching a match to the second. The fires gave a warmth to the room, making one forget the grayness of late afternoon. Isabel sat quietly sipping her tea. There was a huge bowl of late garden roses on the table. The tea, flowers, crackling fires, the room, all gave Isabel much pleasure, peace and a great sense of tranquillity.

Some time went by before she reached again for the telephone on the table. She dialed through to Athens, but no line was available. No sooner had she put the phone down than it started to ring. She took a sip of tea, sat back very relaxed and picked up the telephone.

"Hello."

"Hello, I have a call for you from Saudi Arabia."

"Operator, I am afraid that you must have the wrong number."

"Sorry, madam, but is your number 499–7899?"

"Yes, that is this number, but I think there must be a mistake."

"Well, that is the number that is being called from Saudi."

"Well, they must have made a mistake when they wrote down the number."

"Excuse me, madam, I will check again. Will you hold?"

The operator came back on the telephone. "Madam, I have checked with the caller in Saudi Arabia, and he does have the correct number. I am putting you through now."

"But, operator, there must be a mistake. The only person I know who could possibly call from Saudi Arabia is at this moment in the United States."

A different voice said, "Yes, you do know someone in Saudi Arabia, Miss Wells."

"Oh, dear."

The voice on the other end of the line laughed.

"Oh, dear, I am embarrassed."

"Please, do not be embarrassed and let me introduce myself. My name is Alexis Hyatt. You probably do not remember me. We met at a reception and later dined a few seats from one another at the Chicago Arts Institute more than six months ago. It has taken me a long time to find you again."

"Well, as a matter of fact, I do remember being introduced to you, but very briefly." (But Isabel thought to herself: *I remember our eyes met and he fancied me, but I couldn't be bothered. Oh, I do wish I could remember what he looks like.*)

"Ah, well, that at least is something. Now, may I explain how lucky I am today, for it is here in Saudi where I am visiting the king and his brother that at last my search for you has ended."

"Mr. Hyatt, I don't want to be rude, but even though I met you six months ago I don't know who you are."

"Then, Miss Wells, permit me to tell you. I am an Egyptian and have long been a minister in my country. By my own request I no longer hold an official position but act for my government and, indeed, for other governments whenever I am needed. My family's history makes it natural for me to work for my country. I am a collector of art and artifacts and over many years have added to my family's collection. These are the two things that occupy my life, and since one day I shall give them to my country, the two are almost one and the same."

"But, of course, *Hyatt.* I have been privileged to see some of your things scattered around the world, Mr. Hyatt. You have a fine collection."

"Miss Wells, I wanted so much to speak to you that night and have thought about you ever since."

Isabel suddenly became very nervous about this man. It was all very flattering, but what did he look like? She remembered now, quite vividly, that their eyes had met and she had known that he wanted her very much. Knowing Arab men, she knew better than to look him in the eye again.

"Mr. Hyatt, how did you get my number?"

"Ah, at a reception last evening here at the palace. One of the guests was the curator who introduced us all those months ago. We were discussing the problems I am having with the cataloging and housing of my collection—what should be kept in my private premises around the world, what will be selected for the museum I am building for the collection. I told him how much I admired the new wing in his museum and suddenly remembered that this was the man who had introduced me to the woman who has haunted me. I tried to explain to him who you were when suddenly he said, 'But, Alexis, that is the very woman you must commission to work with you. She was one of the advisers hired by our directors.' And at last I knew your name. Since he did not know where to reach you, I had him call his office in Chicago and he produced your number within hours. So here I am, and I want to see you as soon as it is possible for you."

"This is all very flattering and you are very kind, but I don't know you."

"You sound frightened. I know that this may all seem strange to you. I don't mean to push you."

Oh, damn, she thought, *he sounds so terrific, but is he another short Arab with tiny eyes, thick glasses and a banana-colored suit? He certainly doesn't sound it, but all this sounds too good to be true. Is he my prince, going to sweep me away and love and adore me, or is he going to want to give me an uncontrolled bad fuck and finish, or is he going to hire me?* These thoughts flooded Isabel and made her very nervous. All she could think to say was: "Well, when you are in England next, you must come for tea."

There was a moment of silence, and then Alexis Hyatt said, "Miss Wells, I do not want to have tea with you in London."

Isabel heard a very strong tone of authority in that voice and realized that the voice obviously had been educated in England but had a trace of what seemed to be a French accent. *Oh, dear,* thought Isabel, *it doesn't sound like a banana-suited type,* and pulled herself together to say, "Mr. Hyatt, what do you want?"

"Miss Wells, I want to hire you to come to Egypt for one week to discuss the possibility of your working on a project with me. When are you available?"

All trace of anything intimate was gone from his voice. The charm was off and the business was on; well, Isabel had her answer—it's a job—and her heart fell. Just another job, a good one nonetheless. It could be just for one week or might be a very large and interesting one. She made up her mind in a split-second.

"Mr. Hyatt, I can get my diary now and we can discuss dates, or I can send a selection of dates and my fee for the week tomorrow."

"Miss Wells, please go and get your diary. I will hold the phone. I should like you in Cairo as soon as possible, and as for your fee, there is nothing to discuss—whatever it is, you will please send a bill and how, when and where you want payment. After we have settled on the date my assistant will call and give you all the relevant information."

A bit nonplussed by his sudden switch of tone, Isabel went to the library, looked through her diary, picked up the extension and said, "Mr. Hyatt, how soon do you really need me?"

There was a pause, and he replied, "The very first day that you can be there."

"I could leave in three days if I can get a reservation. Is that too soon for you?"

"Three days' time is perfect. You need not bother about the reservation, Miss Wells. I will send my plane for you. My London representative will be in touch with you within the next twenty-four hours. Again, Miss Wells, I am very happy to have found you." She thought his voice softened ever so slightly. She thanked him rather formally and said good-bye.

As Isabel hung up, she thought about her new job and how extraordinary life was.

She knew she should call Athens again, but then she decided to find out more about Alexis Hyatt. She picked up the phone and called Cecil Davenport, a most famous and renowned *antiquaire*. The phone went on ringing for quite a long time as Isabel tapped her foot on the marble floor, thinking, *Please be there, Cecil. I do hope I haven't called too late and he has gone for the day*. The phone went on ringing, no answer.

"Damn," she whispered, none too softly.

Isabel rang Athens again.

Her sister Ava answered the telephone and appeared to be in a very rare "up" mood.

"Isabel, I received your gift this morning, and I loved the book! You know how hard it is to buy best-sellers here in Athens, and I am such a Le Carré fan! Thanks so much! It's been such a busy day—lunch with mother, who sends her love of course, and tea with the girls. Alfred has planned a wonderful dinner with friends, and I can't wait for his gift."

Isabel knew that when all attention was on Ava, she was as pleasant and quiescent as possible for a usually sharp and hard lady who demanded the limelight no matter how small the beam.

Isabel took advantage of the easy moment between them to wish her well, and was so happy that Ava was in a kindly humor that she made the great mistake of telling her about Alexis Hyatt's phone call. "That's a very strange story you are telling me, Isabel. Of course he doesn't fancy you. Just because a man makes a phone call doesn't mean that he's in love with you."

"Then, why did he call?" demanded Isabel.

"Well, he called because he probably wants something from you for nothing, or a favor. Ask yourself, why else would he call you? Don't be so vain. Are you so desperate for attention that you have to make these love stories up? Stop fooling yourself. You've always lived on fantasies."

Isabel was furious with herself for falling into the same old trap. A few sentences of normal, friendly conversation from Ava and there she was, talking openly about herself and being attacked by Ava.

Only weeks before, when Ava had humiliated her so much in front of friends, Isabel had finally admitted to herself that Ava's unconscious dislike for her and her conscious politeness towards her were no longer bearable. Too many years of letting things go by in order to keep some kind of peace and the little tyrant quiet had done no good for either one of them. Being catered to and pacified in every way had only added to Ava's psychopathic narcissism and Isabel hated her for it.

After Ava hung up on Isabel, she went over to the bar, poured herself a large Scotch, and as she lifted her glass and tossed back the drink, she saw herself in the mirror. Putting down the empty glass she began to admire herself. Ava was totally enthralled by her own tiny five-foot, well-trimmed figure, her very short, well-cut, ash-brown hair, her large piercing brown eyes and tiny, turned-up nose, all set in that still flawless, still unwrinkled face.

She looked deep into her face and thought, *I am so lucky I'm wonderful to look at, but intelligent and practical too.* She ran her hands over the body of her dress, tucked the pink silk shirt into her skirt until every fold fell into its proper place, ran her hands over her hips and turned sideways to look at her profile; she pressed one hand against her flat stomach, the other hand over the flat of her buttocks; then she took a handful of the fleshy part to feel how nice and firm they were. She turned full front into the mirror again and thought, *How well I deserve my beauty; how hard I've worked for it all my life.* Then, smoothing a hair that was out of place and examining her fingernails for any slight chip in the enamel, she left the bar and the mirror. As she walked away she thought briefly of Isabel: *foolish, vain Isabel, living in dreams of men who might come along and make a life with her.*

She thought of Isabel as beautiful and intelligent. But intelligent only because she had managed to pay her own way all of her life. Lazy Isabel, who sometimes stayed in bed until midday. Lazy Isabel, who never jogged, who didn't work out in the gym four times a week. Lazy Isabel, who would never apply herself long enough to learn a second language perfectly and who got away with living in foreign countries merely with her personality and bits and pieces of the local language. Lazy Isabel, who made her money from other people's laziness and lack of intelligence in being able to create things that Isabel was hired to do, and all in the name of Art. No. Money was the thing that Ava admired about Isabel. She at least earned her own way, but to this day Ava never quite knew how Isabel got away with it. Imagine anyone hiring someone because they had good taste! To Ava that was the height of tastelessness. No, she could never figure out how anyone could hire a design consultant. Why, even the title revolted Ava.

Vain, selfish Isabel, with her jobs for the rich and sometimes famous—famous in whose eyes? Isabel, with her over-sophisticated, so-called beautiful home that was never, by Ava's standards, quite clean enough; her clothes were just a bit too individual. Her animals belonged in a zoo, or at least in a country house—not in London! How sad that Isabel lived under the delusion that she had a beautiful and glamorous life.

Ava looked around her living room at all the clean, practical Danish furniture with its simple cotton covers in bright primary colors; the photographs of herself and Alfred taken on their various trips around the world; the paintings, all original oils on canvas by Alfred or Ava—a flower, a bird, a tree, two fish kissing—in the same primary colors as the furniture; the tiny sculptures in clay, painted in bright, white enamel by Alfred; and, of course, the books—two hundred copies of *A New England Childhood;* two hundred and sixty copies of *Essays by a New England Girl*, which Ava had written and had privately printed in Athens. She sold them to friends or even strangers who read Ava's cleverly written ad in the *Athens News*. Both she and Alfred believed that the only reason the publishers would not buy them was that they were too well written to make money. The fifty copies on the shelves in the living room of the March 1970 edition of the *Reader's Digest* with Ava's story—"The Sicilian Baker"—was proof enough to them that Ava was a writer and a success.

Ava and Alfred could write, paint, sculpt, design and decorate as well as or better than any of the professionals, except maybe a few who had been dead for at least two hundred years. So they backed themselves instead of Art.

Oh, yes, this is more like it. She and Alfred had a neat package of a marriage. *Nothing phony about me or our life,* she thought. *Up at six in the morning and work, work, work, keeping this package together.*

Isabel had never been able to find a husband. Ava was convinced that Isabel's selfishness had never allowed it. Ava thought Isabel incapable of sharing a life with another human being and even if she had once had the chance, she was certainly too old now.

So, what if she does have a great many friends who love her very much, and what did it matter if she had lived with some men on and off all her life. She was never clever enough to make a husband out of one of them. Now the years had passed her by, and where was she? Still dreaming that a man will come along with whom she can make a life. She lives extravagantly, impractically, and if her health goes we will all have to support her. There are only three years between us, and why is it I am the one that has to think and act for the family? She is the older, but I am the wiser. While she plays the artist, I, at least, am the success.

Ava changed into a swimsuit, went out into the garden and dived into the pool, where she swam fifty laps without stopping.

She lifted herself out of the pool with almost more energy than she had entered it. Wrapping herself in her terrycloth robe, she went back to the bar and poured another large Scotch, drank it down in one go, looked in the mirror, smiled and called her hairdresser. She put down the receiver, jogged into the bedroom and dressed in her newest dress.

Two hours later a pretty little lady with a snappy figure, sheathed in a pink, pure silk shirtwaist dress, stepped out of the salon. Heavy gold jewelry set off her dark tan and brought a sparkle to her pretty face. Her terrific-looking legs with their trim little ankles were shod in pink, calfskin pumps that clicked away on the pavement as she wiggled provocatively up the street to meet her husband. Any man over sixty would have looked at her and thought, "That is some hot ticket"; any man under forty would have thought, "That gal is looking for a good fuck." Both would have been right.

While Ava was arrogantly flirting her way across Kolonaki Square, Isabel was working on *Ashanti Sun,* her fourth Meredith Montague to go to press in three years.

While Ava was belting back Scotch at a smart Greek restaurant bar with her husband and friends, Isabel was dining alone on a perfect *soufflé*, a salad of endive, and Scottish raspberries, all prepared and served by Endo.

And when Ava was blowing out the candles on her birthday cake and taking bows to a room full of strangers for being born, Isabel was lying in bed being ravished by Max's tongue. He brought her to orgasm a few times, and when he could hold back no longer, he entered her, and they made love slowly till they came together.

After Max left, Isabel, feeling glowing, lay in a deep, hot bath smoking a joint and listening to *The Dark Side of the Moon.*

Late the next morning Isabel was propped up among the pillows in bed with pad and pencil, her personal telephone book and a box file with last night's Meredith Montague pages that had to be gone over for corrections before Jo-anna arrived. The first thing to be done was to organize herself, arrange the work schedule for her absence and give Endo instructions on what she wanted done in the house.

Isabel had been at this for about ten minutes when she remembered to call Cecil Davenport. She was put through to him immediately. She gave little away when she asked about Alexis Hyatt. And Cecil gave even less away. What he did do was to ask her to lunch at Wilton's, which he said was better than talking on the telephone.

"One-thirty all right for you, Isabel?"

"Yes, lovely, Cecil. But are you sure you have the time?"

"Yes. Have you had your first pheasant of the season yet?"

"No, I haven't and it will really be nice to have it with you."

"Well, it will give me great pleasure to take you to lunch; we'll talk then. By the way, Isabel, it isn't quite right to call him Alexis Hyatt. Once he was called Hyatt Bey, then there was a time when he was called Excellency, and now he is *Sir* Alexis Hyatt. His title was bestowed upon him by the queen for his services to the Court of St. James and the Arab world, which he well deserved because he is a brilliant diplomat and as pro-Arab as he is pro-West. I'll send the car around for you."

An American in the know who thinks he is chic and very cosmopolitan would include Wilton's high on his list of London restaurants. Down through the years Americans have loved Wilton's because they believe it is the height of English chic. It is, without question, the English gentlemen's restaurant. Not far from their tailors, just around the corner from their clubs, down the street from Fortnum & Mason's, right in the heart of St. James.

A Frenchman dining in London, on the other hand, would go to Wilton's because it looks like an Englishman's French restaurant, with Edwardian cooking.

An Englishman dining at Wilton's would very likely be of the aristocracy, a stockbroker trying to look like English aristocracy, a property developer trying to look like a stockbroker, or an industrialist trying to look like a country gentleman with an O.B.E., who in fact looks like a property developer or a stockbroker, but never an aristocrat.

A world-famous antique dealer whose club is Brooks, who is married to a duchess, is as much a scholar as a dealer and is an honorable gentleman would dine at Wilton's because it is a great restaurant and a habit.

As Cecil and Isabel entered the restaurant, they were warmly welcomed by the owner, who graciously called for a man to take Isabel's sleeveless coat of mocha-colored, rough buffalo suede. Cecil looked with approval at the Jean Muir silk jersey dress with its voluminous sleeves held tight at the wrists, its deep V-shaped neck which revealed nothing but suggested everything, and its slim skirt. The sash of the same material was held not by a buckle but by an antique Cartier brooch of diamonds.

Isabel looked around the room and received a few admiring looks in return. There were the usual English gentlemen on the company lunch, a few foreign men, but hardly any women in the dining room. The women that were there were purely decoration for their escorts—an Englishman always likes "a bird in the hand."

Over champagne and oysters Isabel told Cecil about the telephone call from Sir Alexis Hyatt, omitting that she thought he desired her. Actually, Ava had done her work well the night before. What Isabel had interpreted as a personal interest in her, she now no longer thought even a remote possibility. Isabel saw herself through Ava's eyes: a woman alone, only to be used.

Cecil was a good friend and a shrewd businessman. He made it very clear that he was available to her for anything that she might need on her project with Sir Alexis.

As Isabel sipped her wine and dissected her moist and sweet roast pheasant, Cecil told her what he felt she should know about her new client.

Before the pheasant carcass was removed from the table Isabel had learned that Sir Alexis Hyatt was one of the richest men in Egypt. His father was Coptic, and the family could be traced back to 250 A.D. Historically the family had always been involved in both church and state, serving under kings and presidents. The name Hyatt had never been tarnished by scandal.

Sir Alexis's mother was a Moslem whose ancestors had come to Egypt in 645 A.D. and had ruled that country under the Ottoman Empire. Saladin, Muhammed Ali and a most unusual slave who became queen around 1245 A.D. were only a few of her famous family.

The Hyatt estate included vast tracts of rich land, some agricultural and some prime property in many capital cities around the world. There were corporate holdings, art collections, a fleet of ships. The scale was such that no one had ever thought to estimate the family's worth. For all their wealth the Hyatts always kept as low a profile as possible.

There were two younger brothers who handled most of the business side of things, along with their advisers. The eldest always went into the service of his country, which was what Sir Alexis had done so admirably. But he was the head of the family, make no mistake of that.

As Isabel listened, she realized why sweet old Cecil was springing for vintage champagne and wine. He was so happy to see her get a really top client. Cecil was a snob, perhaps, but Isabel knew that he was just enough of a softy to want this all to work out well, not to mention that he would be happy to deal with Sir Alexis Hyatt any-time through her. She knew, however, that personal gain was not Cecil's reason for taking her to lunch, so she de-cided to repay the favor by having a jolly time listening to him. As she did, she scooped up spoonfuls of *fraises de bois*, tiny wild strawberries whose taste was so pure and fresh that it sparked memories of a beautiful day made of laughter, sunshine and love in a wood somewhere in the heart of Provence long ago.

Over coffee Cecil wound up his biography with what, for a man, were usually the least important details, but for a woman, were usually the ones that added the spice of life. Sir Alexis Hyatt was married once when very young to an extremely rich, beautiful Persian girl. About fifteen years ago they divorced when she ran off with a famous architect. The marriage left him with two sons— one a doctor and one a farmer on a grand scale. Around fifty-five years old, Sir Alexis usually traveled with one or the other of the two women who had been in his life since his wife left him.

"Well, my dear, that is just about all I know of your Sir Alexis Hyatt, except that he is a gentleman." Cecil smiled. "Don't let him go."

"But, what does he look like?" Isabel asked impatiently.

On this point all that Isabel could get out of Cecil was that Sir Alexis was very tall and slim, with dark coloring. Her luncheon companion shrugged off her queries with an irritable, "I have no idea what you mean by 'handsome'; let's just say that he is pleasant to look at and leave it at that."

Considering the slight touch of annoyance in Cecil's voice, and knowing his vanity, Isabel realized that Sir Alexis Hyatt must be at least as good-looking as Cecil, and most likely better-looking. She was inwardly amused and thought, *How dark, Cecil? Tan, the color of milk chocolate, or perhaps Cadbury's dark bitter kind? Are his eyes tiny as pinpoints and does he wear thick lenses, or are his eyes big, dark and liquidly sexy? What do you mean by "tall"? Do you mean he is tall for an Arab, or taller than you? Never mind slim; that's always good, es-pecially when it's how one man describes another.*

Isabel leaned towards Cecil and, turning his head, gave

him a very gentle kiss on the cheek. He smiled, reached out and stroked her hair, then launched into an anecdote concerning the Louis XV chairs that he had just bought. She went with Cecil to see them after lunch and they were indeed marvelous, without question the best chairs for sale anywhere in the world.

Rubinstein and the Chopin ballades, Joy's sweet singing and the rhythmic click of the loom as she threw the shuttle, changed treadles and pulled forward and back on the batten, these were the sounds that set the atmosphere in the studio. Isabel was at the very opposite end of the room, sitting at her drafting table, selecting various things to take with her to Egypt. Drafting pencils, tracing paper, templates, tape measure, slide rule, quarter-inch scale, small triangle and T-square were all standard equipment for an assignment abroad. Other things she would take included a color chart in small book form, a lighting catalog, her smallest recorder for dictation, and a small, blank-paged book covered in fabric. In it she would write down everything of importance on the Hyatt job; her way of keeping a record.

After putting all the things in a wicker basket, where they would stay until packed, she covered her drafting table and walked through the potted trees and sculpture that were scattered the length of the large room, to see Joy. Isabel gave her a list of the things to be done during the week she was away. As usual, all the animals converged on them wanting to take part in the conversation. The dogs had to be held, and Arthur the cat had to find his way to Joy. There seemed no other way to silence them except to send them downstairs, which neither woman would ever think of doing.

The hum of the elevator told them someone was coming. The dogs began barking and Arthur went into a Nijinsky jump. The two women laughed as the pets squirmed this way and that until all three animals were lined up, waiting for the elevator door to open. Out came Joanna and the din started all over again. No-nonsense Joanna shooed them down the first few stairs of the staircase that wound down around the elevator shaft, and the three women spoke and then went down to the library where Isabel paid them for the week's work and the following week as well. Joy wished Isabel a good trip and went off for the weekend. Joanna went over her work with Isabel, and Endo came in to ask if they wanted tea. Isabel ordered tea for Joanna, but passed it up for herself, since she was invited to tea with the Hayakawas.

The phone rang, and Endo announced that a man who introduced himself as Alexander Gordon-Spencer was calling on behalf of Sir Alexis Hyatt.

It turned out that Mr. Gordon-Spencer was responsible for the travel arrangements concerning Isabel's journey. The Hyatt jet was ready to take off from Heathrow on Sunday evening at five, which meant that they would arrive at Cairo airport at midnight Cairo time, or the plane could take off at midnight from Heathrow, arriving at Cairo at seven, Monday morning, Cairo time. Isabel told Mr. Gordon-Spencer that she did not mind a night flight and thought that it would be better to arrive early Monday morning rather than at midnight on Sunday.

"The night flight would be best," the caller agreed. "I have some information you might want to have, such as the address where you will be staying and the telephone number where you can be reached," he continued. "I have the address where you are to send your invoice. When would it be convenient for me to come round with the information and at the same time pick up your passport? I will need it for passport control and security clearance, to avoid unnecessary delays."

They agreed that 7:00 P.M. would be the best time for both of them. Isabel had a delightful hour with the Hayakawas and then a catnap before Endo announced her visitor.

Alexander Gordon-Spencer turned out to be far from an errand boy. He was, in fact, the managing director of one of the Hyatt companies, whose offices were the handsome seventeenth-century house on South Audley Street, just a few doors away from the Egyptian Embassy.

While Endo served drinks Mr. Gordon-Spencer gave Isabel a few more slivers of information: A car would pick her up at eleven on Sunday evening; there would be two other people on the plane; on arrival in Cairo there would be someone to take her from the plane to Sir Alexis's villa. She sent Endo for her passport, asked when she could have it back and was told on her arrival back in London.

Isabel was not happy. She had lived in Arab countries

on and off for years and had made many a scene in order
not to let that passport out of her sight for longer than ten
minutes. Once in Ethiopia they had held it for four
hours, and she almost had apoplexy, for how could she
call for the Marines to get her out if she did not have her
precious American passport, an instant exit visa from any
and all trouble? Never mind that the slim little book con-
tained a photograph of her looking more like a resident
of a prison than an honest citizen, and that the official
stamp of approval from the State Department had
managed to land the eagle on her face, so that she not
only looked like a prisoner but a Mongoloid as well. With
her passport Isabel felt protected; without it, utterly
alone. Except, of course, in England, where one *never*
feels the need to be protected.

Isabel and Mr. Gordon-Spencer had been talking about
Egypt when Endo returned with the passport and gave it
to Isabel. She hesitated, and was about to demand that
she have her passport returned to her as soon as she
landed in Cairo, when Mr. Gordon-Spencer went over to
Isabel, took her hand, raised it to his lips and said, "Miss
Wells, you must not worry. Your passport will be safe. I
am to see that you are *both* well cared for. You are, after
all, under the protection of Sir Alexis."

Isabel still wanted to say something about the return of
the passport, but somehow did not feel anxious once Mr.
Gordon-Spencer had put it in his inside jacket pocket.

It was only after Endo had seen Mr. Gordon-Spencer
out that Isabel began to wonder if there had not been a
twinkle in his eye, and a knowing twinkle at that, when he
said that Isabel was under the protection of Sir Alexis.
Again it crossed her mind that Sir Alexis wanted an affair.
Then she checked herself, remembering Ava's words, and
Sir Alexis's very businesslike manner on the telephone.
God, how she hated Ava for being so realistic.

II

WHEN ISABEL drew the draperies open in her bedroom on Saturday morning it was raining. A nasty cold October wind drove the rain down, sometimes in heavy sheets that in their turn were dashed away by more gusts of wind. There was no letup in the rain all day, and by late afternoon a thick wet fog had settled in as well. It was the same on Sunday, and one could feel the gray, cold wetness of it right through to one's bones.

Isabel loved it. It was the perfect excuse to stay tucked in the house with the animals, and the fires going. She worked a bit on *Ashanti Sun*, packed her cases and played with Rita, Winston and Arthur. She read the Sunday papers and did some cooking for Sunday lunch: roast beef (sublime), Yorkshire pudding (a flop and into the rubbish), baked apples filled with nuts and cinnamon (sheer ambrosia). Endo arrived on the scene and, horrified by the mess of his kitchen, took over and made the salad. Isabel sat in a rocking chair watching him and waiting for the phone to ring telling her the plane had been canceled and the job was off.

She was completely relaxed and ready to go, but for some reason she had a feeling that something would happen, and it was not going to come off. She had heard nothing more from Sir Alexis. The only call she'd had was from Cecil, wishing her a good trip. She'd broken down and asked Cecil if he was sure Sir Alexis was reliable—he had her passport. Cecil's annoyance cut through, followed by a brief lecture on the "chance of a lifetime."

By nine that evening the rain was still pelting down, but it did seem that the fog had lifted, for she could see through the tops of the trees in Berkeley Square. No one had called to cancel the flight, so she went up to her room, bathed and changed into her traveling clothes.

She went into the kitchen to tell Endo that he could

28

close the cases and bring them down, then into the drawing room where she stood close to the window looking at the rain. The garden seemed to be absolutely waterlogged. Her dress, in a white thin wool, with its rare white jade discs that buttoned down the front, dolman sleeves and a built-in elastic waist, fell smoothly across her hips, but was full in the skirt; it was an easy dress for traveling. She wore no stockings and high-heeled white sandals. She had planned to look perfect when she stepped off the plane in Cairo, but there was all this water to get through first. . . .

Well, never mind, she knew that an umbrella would cover her as she was whisked into a car and then into the plane, but all she could do was hope for the best about her lovely shoes. What was most important was to be dressed as well and as lightly as possible, in preparation for when she stepped out of the plane and the heat of Egypt hit her. She had learned long ago to dress for her destination when traveling from a cold climate to a hot one. Now at least she would not wilt away in London clothes as she tried to get through the landing, customs, and getting unpacked syndrome.

She went over to the fireplace and put another log on the fire. Standing there watching the flames she became sad. How she hated having to leave her animals and "Meredith Montague" behind, not to mention Max. She was more than a little upset because she had heard nothing from Max since Friday, and he *knew* that she was going away on a job. There was something wrong there, but she put the thought from her mind out of fear of losing what she did have with Max by wanting something more. Sometimes free love does backfire; she wistfully sighed.

Isabel had picked up the poker and was rearranging the logs in order to gain more heat when the doorbell rang. The dogs raised their heads just a little to see who came into the room. When they saw it was Endo, they went back to their dozing. He told Isabel that the car had arrived and someone was on his way up. She picked up her white alligator shoulder bag and made no fuss whatsoever about saying good-bye to the dogs, because she could not bear to. Quickly she left the drawing room, closing the door as gently as possible. It was too late: Just as the door was about to shut she could see them bounding towards her. Endo told them to be quiet in a firm voice, and much to Isabel's surprise they were. Then, going to the chair in the hall, she picked up her raincoat, which she threw around her shoulders. She would take it off once she was settled in the car, and give it to Endo to return to the house. She turned around, and much to her surprise, standing in the hall was Alexander Gordon-Spencer.

"I had no idea you were coming to take me to the airport—or are you?" Isabel smiled.

Kissing her hand, he said, "No, I'm *not* going to take you to the plane. I'm going to take you to Cairo." With that he turned to a Sudanese servant who had come in with him and gave instructions for Isabel's cases to be put in the car.

"I did not realize that you were coming to Cairo when you were here on Friday evening."

"The truth is," he said, "I did not know that I was going when I was here on Friday."

"But surely you are not making this trip just to accompany me? I assure you, I am quite capable of getting there on my own."

"Now, Miss Wells, I have no doubt that you are most capable in all that you do, but as it happens Sir Alexis has two other guests going on the same flight, and when I spoke to him this afternoon, he thought it might be more hospitable for me to accompany the three of you. I do think we should go now."

He took Isabel—who was feeling quite foolish—by the elbow, and they went down to the car. Isabel had a few words with Endo as the three of them went down the winding staircase.

The rain had not let up, and although it was only a few steps to the car, Isabel looked with dismay at the water she would have to prance through in her nearly bare feet. She braved it with Endo holding a large umbrella over her head, and dashed into the waiting dark blue Mercedes 600. Settling in, she removed the raincoat and handed it to Endo, who had been waiting by the open car door under the umbrella.

Endo said good-bye and gave Isabel a small bow, something he never did unless he was trying to impress someone. Isabel picked up his cue and said, in perfect Japanese, "Good-bye. Take care of the house, and most of all, the animals." He closed the door with his head slightly bowed and stood waiting in the rain until the car was out of sight before he went into the house.

There was only the chauffeur in the front and Mr. Gordon-Spencer in the back seat, next to Isabel. She wondered what had happened to the Sudanese servant, and where the other guests were; why did this Gordon-Spencer call *her* a guest—she was, after all, an employee—and where was her passport? Her feet were cold, and as she fought off the impulse to rub them, she wondered why she was not more anxious, which was usually the case with Isabel.

As the extra-long, dark Mercedes shot through the shiny wet streets of Mayfair, she and Alexander, on first-name terms at last, spoke about London, her ability to speak Japanese (so he *was* impressed; clever Endo) and his knowledge of Arabic. In spite of their trivial conversation, there was something nice about Alexander. She felt he was holding something back, but then so was she. Why were they both so cautious? He was kindness itself and certainly doing all he could to make her comfortable, but of course he was under instructions from Sir Alexis to do just that. She wondered if he knew that she was going there as an employee. If he did, he never mentioned the matter. All she knew was that she was feeling well cared for and she settled even deeper into the royal blue velvet cushions as the car sped on.

Isabel noticed that the rain had let up considerably, and by the time they drove around to the back of Terminal 3 at Heathrow Airport, the rain had stopped. The car pulled up at a pair of high, open, wire-mesh gates set into a fence that ran to the left and right as far as Isabel could see. The chauffeur sounded the horn. Two guards came forward, flashed a light at the license plate and opened the gate. Then one of the guards spoke to the driver, took a pass from him and came to the rear of the car. Alexander pushed a button and the rear window went down. He spoke to the guard, and it was quite evident that they knew one another. The guard tipped his hat and wished Alexander and Isabel a good flight. He went back to his partner and they pushed the two large gates wide open. The car sped through, passing a few cars parked in a vast empty space, headed onto the tarmac of the airfield and pulled up at a flight of stairs leading up to the open entrance door of Sir Alexis Hyatt's jetliner.

Isabel looked up at the huge aircraft. All the lights in
the plane were on. It looked like some great prehistoric
bird that had been grounded. It was painted white and
glistened with rain, looking altogether mysterious and
beautiful as it stood on the slick, wet tarmac against the
black of the night.

Alexander turned to Isabel and asked her to wait in
the car for a few minutes. He opened the door and went
up the stairs to the airplane. Isabel noticed that there was
still a fairly heavy wind, but no rain. She could see into
Terminal 3, all ablaze with light, and thought of the many
times she had been stuck in that dismal place. So why did
it look so inviting from where she was sitting?

After a few minutes Alexander appeared on the platform at the top of the stairs, while the same Sudanese
servant who had taken Isabel's cases descended with a
thin cashmere shawl over his arm. The chauffeur opened
the door for Isabel, and the Sudanese servant smiled and
said, "Welcome, madam," draping the shawl around her
shoulders. It was as soft and as light as feathers, and she
drew it around her body against the cold wind as she hurried up the stairs. Alexander took her hand and helped
her off the platform and into the plane, the servant following behind. As she turned from the entrance to enter the
main cabin she saw two men running across the tarmac.
When they reached the stairway one went on each side to
pull it away. A young man came out of the cockpit,
looked Isabel over, closed the door and double-checked
the lock.

The main cabin of the plane had large, comfortable
easy chairs, upholstered in navy blue glove leather and
mounted on swivel bases. The chairs were arranged in
groups, around coffee tables piled with periodicals. All the
walls of the plane were paneled in American cherrywood.
It looked very elegant, simple and comfortable; what one
imagined the ambience to be in the most luxurious club
car on the old Twentieth Century Ltd.

The main cabin took up about one third of the plane.
There were a pair of doors that opened up to the next
section, which had a closed-off kitchen to the left of the
entrance, and to the right a small room equipped with
desk and typewriter. Straight ahead was the dining room,
dominated by a long, oval table with ten chairs on each
side. At the end of this room was another pair of doors

that led to a hall with bathrooms to the left and right. Straight ahead was the last pair of doors. Alexander stepped aside as the servant unlocked the doors and then threw them open.

Sir Alexis's private room had the atmosphere of a study in a French country house. There was a large Provincial desk, and two chairs covered in camel-hair cloth and trimmed in chocolate-brown-colored braid. The sofa was a country bed of polished steel with curved ends. The mattress and cushions were plump with down and made up for sleeping, with deep peach linen sheets and pillow cases trimmed in cream-colored lace. Folded at the end of the bed was a lightweight blanket of fine cashmere in a small checkered pattern of peach and white; all four sides of the blanket were scalloped and the edging on the scallops was of thick, white silk thread, so tightly stocking-stitched together it looked like piping. There was a Provincial commode with heavy brass mountings and on the yolk-yellow marble top there were decanters of whiskey, one of water, and glasses on a heavy baroque silver tray. In front of the sofa bed was a long slim table whose top was no more than six inches off the floor. Isabel recognized it as an Arab tailor's table, one of the finest she had ever seen. She guessed its age to be about 150 years. On the inlaid wooden top of the table was a low bowl filled with jasmine which trailed aimlessly, almost covering the table's surface in some places. She saw a white card in an envelope among the blossoms, but chose to ignore it for a moment.

"Isabel, Sir Alexis hopes that you will make yourself comfortable. You are welcome to sleep in this room if you like. Your luggage is in the dressing room beyond, and the bathroom is beyond that." Alexander pointed to a door at the end of the room as he continued. "This is Gamal, and he is to be your servant until you return to London. If there is anything that you need, he will help you. His English is quite good." He then turned to Gamal and said, "This is Miss Wells, Gamal. Sir Alexis wants you to help her in anything she needs."

Gamal said he understood and smiled at Isabel approvingly. He showed her where the button was to call for him if he was needed. Then he turned to her and asked if there was something she wanted now. She thanked him and told him there was nothing for the moment.

Alexander asked Isabel if she would join him for a drink in the main cabin. The other two guests were in the cockpit and would be joining them presently. He went to the desk and picked up the telephone receiver, buzzed through to the cockpit and asked when they were to take off. Turning to Isabel, he told her that the plane would be ready to leave in ten minutes. The only rule that Sir Alexis had on this aircraft was that when the captain announced takeoff, everyone on board had to be in the main cabin, buckled into a seat, which they could not leave until the captain announced that the plane was safely airborne.

Isabel asked for five minutes to comb her hair. Gamal opened the doors and Alexander and the servant left the room.

The moment the doors clicked shut, Isabel went directly to the table and reached down to the jasmine blossoms, whose heady scent had filled every inch of the room. She plucked out the little white envelope: It was sealed.

Isabel felt a flutter of excitement as she tore the envelope open and quickly pulled out the little white vellum card. Written in black ink with a wide nib fountain pen was "Alexis Hyatt." Nothing else, simply "Alexis Hyatt." Isabel took the card and her profound disappointment over to the mirror hanging above the commode. She opened her handbag, slipped the card and its torn envelope inside, took the small hairbrush out of her bag and ran it through her hair briskly.

My God, what did you expect? she lectured herself. *Disappointed over a man you don't know and can barely remember meeting! Behaving like a schoolgirl or a desperate old spinster. Pathetic. Must Ava always be right?*

Her five minutes almost up, she went swiftly to the dressing room, where she opened the smallest case and took out the latest Iris Murdoch. She was looking forward to reading it, and she hurried along to the main cabin.

Alexander greeted her and ushered her to a section of the cabin where four chairs had been swiveled around to make a circular setting with a coffee table in the center. The tabletop, of soft beige Travertine marble, had two circular wells cut into it. One of the wells held a silver ice bucket filled with crushed ice and two bottles of Taittinger Conte de Contes. The other well held another silver container overflowing with a sumptuous arrangement of fruit: peaches and pears, apples and plums, bananas, tiny sweet green and huge voluptuous purple Colma grapes, mangoes, ishta and fresh lychee nuts. There were magazines and newspapers, an ashtray of heavy silver and a few ecru-colored linen napkins edged in an inch of heavy Ghent lace. Rounding off the array was a silver salver filled with handmade Belgian white chocolates.

Isabel sank into one of the chairs and swiveled it slightly to look out of the window. Alexander sat in the chair next to her and was pointing out a Concorde slowly traveling up the tarmac to its berth, when two stewards appeared and said good evening to Isabel and Alexander; one bent down and buckled Isabel into her seat, then Alexander into his. The young men were very smart in their slate gray uniforms as they announced that as soon as they had an all clear from the captain they would serve caviar, scrambled eggs, toast and coffee. Assorted sandwiches and other hot drinks were available on request. At that time the champagne would be opened and glasses and plates brought. They smiled and went to the rear of the plane towards the dining room, where they fastened themselves into seats. Isabel noticed two more stewards come out of the kitchen and take seats as well. Gamal was already in a seat near the cockpit.

The captain announced the usual over the intercom, and two minutes later the Boeing taxied across the shiny wet surface to the runway, where it revved its motors until Isabel could feel the surge of power right through her body. Suddenly the brakes were released, and the plane pushed forward down the runway and soared into the air.

Isabel always found takeoff thrilling. This night, in these privileged circumstances, she found it more than thrilling—she felt it was positively sexual. She swiveled round, faced Alexander and was about to say something to him when she saw it again—that hidden meaning in his eye.

Not for the first time did she feel a fool. Was it in her mind? No, damn it, it was *not,* and so instead of telling Alexander what a thrill she always felt on takeoff, she said most aggressively, "Alexander, I have the distinct feeling . . ."

He held up his index finger. "Shhush, please, Isabel, don't say anything." He bent forward as much as his seat belt would allow and gently turned Isabel's chair slightly away from him, towards the window again. "Not now. Let's just look out at the lights of London."

He had done it again—silenced her questions and foolish feelings with just a gesture. They watched the city light disappear as the plane climbed into the night, and soon Isabel felt calm again.

Alexander asked her if she was a game player—cards, backgammon, roulette? He was not very impressed when she said she was a bad gambler, a poor gin rummy player and mad about Scrabble. Isabel learned that he was a keen backgammon player and that one of the men in the cockpit at the moment was a world champion at the game.

Just then the captain told them over the intercom that they could remove their seat belts and smoke. The same steward that had fastened them into their seats helped Isabel remove the belt. Alexander did his own, stood up, stretched and asked the steward to open the champagne. Isabel stood up as well and wandered aimlessly around the large main cabin of the plane, picking up a book and reading the title, putting it down and going to another table to look through the papers. She heard the cork pop and turned to see the wine being poured into huge tulip-shaped Lalique glasses. Alexander called her back to their table and handed her a glass.

While the four stewards busied themselves with various chores in the main cabin, Alexander touched his glass to Isabel's and said, "To you, beautiful Isabel. Egypt will love you."

"I hope so, Alexander, because I'm ready to love Egypt." Isabel raised her glass in a toast to Alexander and said, "And to you, Alexander, the best nanny I've ever had and, I have no doubt, Sir Alexis's best emissary."

"You're a very lucky girl, Isabel." Alexander grinned as he gave her a warm kiss on her cheek while he caressed her shoulder. The steward put down a large bowl of Beluga caviar set in a silver bucket of crushed ice and refilled Alexander's glass. When the steward went to top up Isabel's glass she put a hand over it. Isabel told Alexander just how lucky she really was. Why Alexander thought she was lucky was unimportant and she did not venture to ask.

During their conversation Alexander noticed her half-empty glass, and asked her why she did not have more of such a splendid wine. Isabel explained that she did not like alcohol, or what it did to her, although she appreciated and drank fine wines, but never more than a glass or two at the most.

Alexander teased her about not having many weaknesses. No gambling, not a drinker—what were her vices?

"I suppose that my biggest vices are sex, hashish, writing books and wanting enough money to practice my vices," Isabel said, not in the mood to play coquette and deciding to play along with Alexander by telling him the truth.

"And pursuing whatever I do to the ultimate." She smiled at him, clinked her glass to his and sipped a little more of her champagne.

Alexander was amused. "Now, Isabel, since I am your 'nanny' at the moment, and do have instructions to give you anything you so desire, should you care to practice any of these vices, you have but to ask me and I will arrange things for you."

Now, this was more like it, a fun game of cat and mouse. No, Isabel told him, she did not need him to handle her sexual life; the writing had been put away until after this business trip and as for the hashish, since it was not addictive, she had no problem and could easily do without it. She had left it at home since she would have had to take it through customs and she would not want to cause Sir Alexis any problems.

"My, my, Isabel, you are an interesting girl."

"Oh, dear, Alexander, have I revealed too much? That was far from my intention."

"No, not really. Any man who knows women and looks at you would know that you are sexual. As to the hashish, it is always a possibility because of our day and age. Something about your presence, I think my son might call it your 'creative awareness,' makes your writing a book not at all extraordinary. I certainly did not know that you were going to Egypt on a business trip. Sir Alexis never mentioned why you were going. Now, summing all that up, I would say that no, you did not reveal too much, but I do know more about you and would like to learn even more."

"I'm a fool! Ever since we met I wanted to know what

you knew about me, and for you to tell me about Sir Alexis and my trip to Cairo and what happens: I tell all and you tell nothing. I would make a rotten CIA agent." With that Isabel pouted effectively.

Alexander put his empty glass down and went to Isabel. He put his arms around her, giving her a great cuddle, and touched her lower lip with his finger. "Now, my pretty, since I am your best nanny and I am to give you everything to make you happy until I turn you over to Sir Alexis, I will tell you that in Sir Alexis's study on the commode there is a lapis lazuli box with gold mounts. If you open that box you will find inside cigarettes rolled with the best Lebanese hashish. They are there for the guests of Sir Alexis and you are welcome to smoke them, except in front of one of the other guests, who will soon come out of the cockpit. He is the older man, André Beshawi, a business associate and friend of Sir Alexis, and would not approve. As for the other man who will join us, he is an American painter, and it will not matter in front of him."

Alexander was about to say something more when the steward appeared to pop open the second bottle of champagne and fill his glass. Alexander accepted it with one hand, and with the other around Isabel's shoulder, he bent and whispered in her ear, "Isabel, I am a person who gets a great deal of enjoyment out of arranging things for people. If ever you should have need of my talents, I am at your service." He gave her a peck on the cheek and drank down his glass of Taittinger.

Isabel realized that Alexander was well on the way to getting drunk and wondered what kind of a Mayfair millionaire's pimp he was. Well, she had learned nothing about Sir Alexis, except that he obviously told this man nothing.

He was bending down and filling his glass again when Isabel asked Alexander, "Why did you think I was going to Egypt?"

"Now, Isabel, that is what's called a leading question. Being an American, you will understand very well if I plead your Fifth Amendment. I believe it goes something like 'I refuse to answer that question on the grounds that it might incriminate me.'" Both were laughing when they were distracted by the entrance of the two other guests.

Alexander introduced André Beshawi, a Syrian who had lived for fifty years in Beirut. Isabel remembered him the moment that she saw him. They had met fifteen years before when Isabel had been in that part of the world.

André Beshawi had the most beautiful and famous of the old Arab houses in Beirut, as well as one of the finest collections of art and artifacts in the Middle East. Isabel remembered she had been brought there to tea by a mutual friend. The only other time they had met was the day she was leaving Beirut. He presented himself at the St. George Hotel, where she was staying, and asked if she would have tea so that he could congratulate her on having bought the finest piece of Syrian sculpture that he had ever seen. It was a most gentlemanly thing for him to have done since there had been a running battle for more than a week between the dealer handling the piece, Mr. Beshawi, and Isabel over who would get it. Isabel had held her ground, and with the backing of the museum, she'd had the courage to outbid him. Seeing him in this plane was a great surprise. He greeted her warmly with a smile, called her his most beautiful opponent, kissed her hand, turned to Alexander and said, "Alexander, be careful of this woman. She knows what she wants." Then he told them the story of how she had defeated him.

It was all very flattering to Isabel, who during the telling of it had a great deal of trouble keeping her eyes off the American painter who, in turn, had much the same problem. Finally Alexander introduced them.

"Anthony, you have not met Isabel Wells. Isabel, this is a compatriot of yours, Anthony Moressey."

They exchanged greetings and Anthony turned to Alexander and said, "Alexander, you're wrong. I *have* met Miss Wells, many, many years ago. How are you Isabel? Time has done well by you."

"And you, Anthony."

"I say, Isabel, you seem to know everyone. That is jolly," Alexander interrupted. "Come, do sit down and have some drinks and a snack."

The stewards filled the glasses, and fortunately, the three men started to talk. All Isabel had to do was listen. It gave her a chance to pull herself together. For years she wondered how she would behave seeing Anthony again. The years went by and she stopped worrying about it, then more years went by and she rarely even thought about him, and now here he was. He had been her great love, the man who ultimately changed her life long after she had left him. It was over long, long ago, but seeing him now she realized that she still loved him.

The stewards brought plates, knives, forks and antique Russian caviar spoons. The long straight handles were of ivory, and the bowls and tips of the handles were made of an ancient and rare wood that was as hard as stone; the color and pattern of the wood was not unlike bird's-eye maple. The Russians always preferred wooden spoons for caviar, never metal, no matter how valuable that metal might be.

All the trimmings were brought for the caviar, along with a platter of hot, fluffy scrambled eggs. There were also tiny sandwiches—smoked salmon and *pâté de foie gras*—on thin brown bread.

A great deal of champagne was consumed along with the delicious food, and over the small cups of hot sweet Arab coffee, fruit and chocolate, it was decided that André and Alexander would have a six-game tournament of backgammon, the prize a case of Mouton Rothschild '66. The backgammon table was set up at the end of the cabin near the cockpit.

Isabel and Anthony, meanwhile, huddled over a selection of movies that had been recorded on video tapes. Isabel suggested that he select the movie he wanted, for she would watch only for a short time, and then go on to the study and have a sleep before the aircraft landed in Cairo.

Anthony chose an old Bogart/Bacall film, *To Have and Have Not*. He had never seen it and had always wanted to. The steward asked if it was convenient for them to take the pair of chairs set together at the end of the cabin nearest the dining room, since the cassette recorder and TV set were already in place there. He pointed out that it was the best place because the chairs had their high backs to the rest of the room and they would not be disturbed by the players or the light at the other end. They agreed it would be fine and the steward said whenever they were ready, just to let him know.

The three men and Isabel sat a while longer over their wine and coffee, and eventually the two players went off to their end of the cabin to start their tournament.

All through supper Anthony had said nothing meaningful to Isabel. He was utterly charming, and on the one or two occasions when his eyes met with hers, her heart turned over while her mind drifted back to the years when they loved one another. Then, she had wanted nothing more than to make him happy. Those were the years in New York together during the late fifties and early sixties, when he had painted better than he ever had, or ever would again.

Isabel thought about those years. Were they the happiest? No, in retrospect she had to admit they were not, but they were exciting.

New York at the time of the nation's great transition: America's moment of external Fascism was over; the American dream was having yet another revival. The so-called second-class citizens of America—artists, writers, movie people, anyone creative and with a bit of courage —were becoming America's new first-class citizens.

The time when they could form such obscenities as the Un-American Activities Committee to investigate Hollywood writers, painters or anyone that might influence another human being against the American way of life had just ended. Political discussions began to reappear on the college campuses. University professors, who were afraid to speak for fear that they might be misinterpreted, lose their jobs and be hauled up before Joe McCarthy and his despicable Mr. Schine, could now speak their minds. Julius and Ethel Rosenberg had been burned not in the electric chair, but at the stake. When they pulled that switch, the shock reverberated through the States. The reality was that Americans, discontented with their country and life, had been executed. "The Land of the Free" had been in grave danger.

All this had been dragged out, fought and was now behind America. It was another victory for democracy, or a victory of sorts at least.

The painters who, during the Depression, painted murals in post offices all over the United States in order to survive in their own medium, banded together in groups so that they could afford the price of a studio. Only some were Communists, but all were considered Bohemian or to lead a Bohemian life. They were no longer young except in heart, and their struggle to survive led them everywhere, even to the Manhattan art galleries. Then the dealers discovered them, dragging them up from the Village to the East Sixties in force. The dealers created a great American art market. A de Kooning painting that could be bought for $500 in the mid-fifties would be sold now for $50,000, if you could get a dealer to release one. Mr. America himself—he might be a shoe manufacturer from Boston, an insurance man from Connecticut, a toilet manufacturer from Wisconsin—now embraced the artist, the new first-class citizen.

And there I was, thought Isabel, right in the middle of all this with a handsome, blond, elegant man who was a painter, and a Bohemian. Who suffered for Art's sake, but left America to live like a prince in the art world. He had returned because America was now ready to recognize his talent. This beautiful man who walked like a prince through the galleries, and charmed the dealers with his looks, his elegance, and his house and studio near Picasso in the south of France, hawked his paintings and himself not to the highest bidder, but to the most influential buyer, his eyes ever on the future.

How I used to close my eyes to his whoring is easy to understand. I was in love, and so very young. He chose to live with me, he made love to me, but he never exploited me. He did not have to because I gave him everything. . . . Was he not a prince?

While I dined with friends at the Café Nicholson, Romeo Salta or Le Pavillon, he stayed in his studio to paint. I would go alone to stay out of his way, then would come home to make him dinner. I had nothing but admiration for him. When he went out and socialized without me, all in the name of Art, I stayed at home and waited. When we entertained the pundits of the art world, I had nothing but admiration for him.

He thought about his exhibitions, and his paintings, and how many were sold, and how many were reserved, and who had bought them, and what the reviews said, and who had to be charmed for the next step up the rung of success. He thought about the paint, canvas and new brushes he needed, about how his house in the south of France needed a new roof and how the garden needed so much more done to it. He thought only about what he needed, would paint all in the name of Art. I believed in him and loved him, and so we lived together in secret (again for Art's sake; it was better for his career).

He once told me, "All the flowers in the world are for me." I remember asking, "What about me, don't I get any flowers?" He answered, "No, you have my paintings."

Then I was touched and in love. Now I have fresh flowers and no paintings. Strange that now when I think of it, the only time we really were together was when we had sex. All the rest was not love, or happiness. It was the excitement of those years in New York.

Here he sits, this American from the Midwest who has lived in Europe for most of his adult life. This man who thinks of himself as a prince of France, and of the art world. I never knew how he really saw me all those years ago. . . .

Isabel reached for her coffee and drank the very dregs of it, then swished the remainder of the coffee around in the bottom of the cup. It made little designs on the white inside, and she concentrated on them. She thought of the way it had all ended. She had become pregnant, and he had said that she must do what she wanted, but for his part he could not cope with the problem. He said he would go away for a while and when it was all over and she had solved her problem, he would be back. She solved her problem. The baby was gone, but when he returned, she'd found that her love had gone as well. Isabel remembered the last thing that he said to her: "You'll never forget me. I changed your life, gave you the world of art, and I loved you and fucked you better than any man ever will."

Well, he was partially right. They met once after that, in the south of France. He took her to his villa, undressed her and fucked her intermittently all through the night. It was wonderful, but more like rape than lovemaking. In the morning she bathed and dressed. Over breakfast he said he found her sexually as wonderful as ever and was happy that she was back. She said she wasn't, she had just come for the night; and then she had left him. That was ten years ago, and this was the first time they had met since that night.

A steward came with another small pot of hot coffee; he filled their cups and left. Anthony bent forward and put a peeled lychee nut on the side of the little cup and saucer. "You always did find them sexy to eat," he said.

He was as handsome as he had ever been. She'd once thought him the most handsome and charming man she had ever known, and so did many other women. And here he was, all these years later, still laying on the charm. Well, she could say one thing for him: If you have been had by Anthony Moressey, you have been had by the best. He did bring one gift to the women he had: He ruined it for any other charmer. After Anthony the last thing one wanted was to be charmed ever again.

As they sat there sipping the last of the coffee, she watched him covertly. She looked everywhere but in his eyes. He was a big man, six feet two inches tall, wide in the shoulders, but not too narrow in the hips. He had a big handsome head with blond, straight, silky hair worn on the longish side, now mixed with streaks of white, that always fell over one eye and which he constantly pushed back by running his fingers through it. His eyes were of the deepest blue and his large exquisite nose was straight. The dimple on one side of his face, and his mouth and lips, still made Isabel melt. She'd always wanted to kiss that mouth, to hold and suck his lips with her own lips, to run her tongue over them. That is what she always wanted when she looked at his mouth, and that is what she wanted now.

She knew that he had been discreetly watching her all through the supper. Maybe discreetly was not quite the word. It was more like watching her with indifference.

Isabel had decided that she would like to smoke a joint of hashish before the movie. She excused herself and said she would be back in a few minutes, and not to start the movie without her. She went to Sir Alexis's room and found the lapis lazuli box, took out a joint and lit it. There was a light tap at the door and it made her jump. She asked who it was. It was Gamal wanting to know if Isabel wanted anything. She opened the door and said she would want nothing before morning, and for him to find a chair and go to sleep. He thanked her and said goodnight, and to ring the bell if she wanted anything during the night.

Closing the door, she turned around so her back was against it and drew deeply on her cigarette. For a moment she had thought it might have been Anthony. Oh, how she wanted to get close to him! But obviously he was having none of it. It took only a few puffs on the cigarette before she felt that lovely buzz. She put it out, ran a brush through her hair, added a touch of lipstick and started back to Anthony. As she stepped through her doorway she saw him go into one of the bathrooms. There was no one in sight, and so she went to the bathroom door and knocked gently. Anthony opened it and Isabel went in. Not knowing what to say to him, she said nothing, but simply slipped her arms around his waist, pressed against him and kissed him: on the lips, next on one cheek and then the other; she kissed one eye, the tip of his nose, then the other eye and back to his lips again. This time his lips parted and she kissed him deeply. He never touched her. She stood back and looked at him. He pulled her towards him and held her and they kissed deeply again. Then he looked at her and said, "It's too late now, Isabel, years too late. I like boys now."

Isabel was not surprised. There had been talk about it for as long as she had known him. Some said that he was exclusively homosexual, but, of course, she knew better, and had guessed that he was simply bisexual, but had never known the truth until years after they parted.

"Isabel, you are as lovely as ever," he said. "There are a hundred things I would like to say to you, but it is all too late. Let's go watch the movie before we are missed. I don't think it would be a good idea to be caught together in here."

Isabel knew that he was right; she also knew that everything was over except a silent bond that would never be broken, talked about or used.

"I will go first," she said.

He touched her hair, smoothing some strands that had been out of place. "Yes, go. I will wait a few minutes." He smiled. "I never thought you could do this to me again. You go ahead."

Isabel made her way through the dining room and into the main cabin of the plane. She was relatively composed concerning Anthony, and was far more disturbed about her memory of the past and the role that she played in their love affair. If she was upset now about what had just happened between them, it was not with him, but with herself. Isabel did not take failure very well at the best of times. She saw this as another mistake, an act of aggression, not of love, hence a failure. Although Isabel no longer tormented herself over circumstances that she could not change, she wondered about real love for and with a man.

It had taken Isabel a long time to throw out of her life all that she had been taught about men. All the experiences that she had been through as a result of that teaching boiled down to the reality that she was capable of real love for a man. What she'd felt at the moment she saw

Anthony was not love but desire. Their sexual feelings for one another were so highly charged that it created an instinctive bond between them. Because Isabel would not recognize that this sexual attraction was a matter of surfaces, she was dishonest. Because of her own vanity she'd been completely wrong about Anthony and love.

How horrid and unjust to both of them that she should have lied to herself all those years ago and labeled that highly charged sexual feeling between them something more than passion. How much damage and hurt had been done by her, out of her desperation to find love? No longer desperate, she could wait, and if genuine love were to come to her she would recognize it, just as she could now recognize its pale imitation.

She went to the far end of the cabin, where the tournament was in progress. The stewards were standing around the backgammon table watching. Gamal was fast asleep in a chair. One of them came forward and asked Isabel if she was ready for the movie. She said as soon as Mr. Moressey returned. Just then they saw him enter the main cabin and so they went forward to meet him. The steward settled them into their chair, which was more of a love seat, actually. There were ottomans to put their feet on, and when they were both settled in, it was like a large chaise longue for two. At each side there was a table: one held a pitcher of orange juice and a siphon of soda water, the other a bucket of champagne. A cashmere blanket rested on each of the ottomans in case their feet got cold. The steward put the movie on and adjusted it, gave the remote control panel to Anthony and showed him how to work it. He then said that he would be at the other end of the cabin with the other stewards. The main lights were put out and the cabin settled down for the night. The only light came from the television screen at their end of the long cabin, and the recessed pin light which lit up the backgammon board to their rear at the other end. The sound of the powerful airplane motors droned on, as did Bogart and Bacall in *To Have and Have Not*.

The movie credits were streaming across the screen when Anthony discovered a button that released the back of the love seat they were sitting on. He adjusted it to an angle that put them in a half-reclining position; with tiny pillows for their heads and their feet stretched out before them on the ottomans they gave their attention to the film.

An experienced traveler, Isabel had chosen a dress that buttoned down the front. Now she unbuttoned the first few at the neck and the last few at the bottom, so that she could move around easily without wrinkling her dress. She wore nothing underneath it and was completely comfortable. Reaching down she took the lap robe and draped it over her legs. She was still busy making herself comfortable when she looked up and met Anthony's eyes. Obviously, he had been watching her.

She offered him the other lap robe. He refused it, but reached over and squeezed her hand in a friendly, if indifferent way, and became engrossed in the film.

It was a film that she had seen half a dozen times, and tonight it did not hold her interest. After fifteen minutes she became restless, turned on her side with her back towards Anthony, reached over and poured herself a glass of half orange juice and half soda water. After taking a few sips she put it down and remained in that position, looking out of the window into endless black space. She patted her pillow, tucked it into a cosy position between her head and her cheek and pulled her knees up until she was in a semifetal position. In this half-lying, half-sitting position she drifted off into that black space with her thoughts.

Oh, if Kate were here now, to see her snuggled into her corner of this plane with Anthony next to her, happily watching the film. Kate hated Anthony, but then, was there ever a man that she liked?

Isabel closed her eyes and thought about Kate and what she had done to Isabel, to Ava and to herself. Usually, if she had any thoughts about Kate, it was about Kate's funeral, but there was something about seeing Anthony again that triggered the past and her relationship with Kate.

She slipped into a half sleep, and into daydreams and flashbacks. Kate in her youth, wife of Sam, mother of Isabel and Ava. A tiny woman, just five feet tall, pretty, stylish and with a zest for life. She ran her home, her husband and her children with kid gloves on iron fists. Good to her neighbors, respectful to her relations, obedient to her husband and indulgent to her children. In addition to these things, she was not in love with her husband, but dependent on him financially. She thought him socially and intellectually beneath her, and to be avoided sexually whenever possible.

His family were of peasant stock from Middle Europe and to be forgotten and never discussed. After all, *her* family were of upper-class aristocracy: Hungarian and Austrian. While she was born in Massachusetts, he was an immigrant and *that* immediately put him beneath her. They were both Jewish, but with a difference: She came from a family born into Jewry but so reformed that they could not speak one word of Yiddish. On the other hand, he could barely speak one word of English. When he did it was with a heavy mid-European accent that he never lost until the day he died.

Kate's dream was to reform him, change him, and then leave him. Isabel, her firstborn, was to grow up and become rich and famous so that they could run away together. Kate was a hard worker, and once she had her dream and her plan clear in her mind, she worked at it hard.

Her first breakthrough came when Isabel was born. She loved and pampered Isabel, who was a happy, lazy, good-natured baby, one that responded to all the love and adoration by being an obedient mummy's little girl. Then mummy's little girl was turned into a little Jewish Shirley Temple that could not dance, had no voice and was downright rotten at the piano. *Oh, Shirley Temple, have you any idea what your genius and success have wrought upon so many plain, fat, little dull children?* To this day Isabel could remember the whack of the cane on the bare boards and the screams of "Pick those feet up, up, up; pick those feet up," as an uneven chorus line of fat five-year-olds tried to keep time to "Take Me Out to the Ball Game." The tears of exasperation in the eyes of the teacher, a poor man's Fred Astaire, whose great claim to fame was that he had taught Eleanor Powell to dance. *Thank God Shirley Temple got old and became a lousy actress.* Isabel smiled to herself.

By then, Ava was two years old. A funny-looking little baby . . . well, not so much funny as ugly. She cried most of the night and screamed a good part of the day. She was an unhappy baby and difficult beyond belief, and she never changed as the years went on, never stopped in her bid for attention and care. What was so amazing about nasty little Ava was that she got it. As a baby she thought it her due and was never happy even when she had everything she cried for.

Out of sheer meanness Ava gradually began to dominate the household. It would be safe to say that Sam, Kate and Isabel were terrified of the child. Mary, the maid-cum-nanny, was more amazed than terrified.

But Kate still had her dream, and although she found it more difficult to do her household chores in the morning and tear out of the house for the day with little Isabel, she carried on.

The years rolled by and the three women grew into their patterns. Ava finally stopped crying, went into sulking and whining and then to a moody silence. Sam kept working and paying the bills. Kate kept loving and adoring and praising Isabel, kept *trying* to praise and love little Ava, kept providing the wifely duties to Sam and had lots of nervous breakdowns that manifested themselves in hypochondria and several operations. Isabel loved Kate, this wonder-woman and martyr who suffered marriage and a difficult child like Ava, and whose whole world was wrapped up in Isabel, her only reward for her trying life.

By the time Isabel was ten, Kate started to shift some of her responsibilities onto her firstborn. When she was in the hospital the maid would do the cleaning, but Isabel would try to keep Sam and Ava happy. The meals were heated, and some even prepared, by Isabel, with the help of Kate on the telephone. She tried to please Sam but never found the way. As for Ava, she mostly took care of herself and only spoke to Isabel when she needed something.

The milestones of childhood: from happy, smiling, gurgling baby to fifth-rate Shirley Temple, to mama's little *balebosta* (that's Yiddish for an overachieving Jewish housekeeper), to the Kissinger of the Wells family. By this time the family did need a Kissinger for Kate and her depressions and frustrations. Hypochondria and illness came periodically and what little Isabel did was everything Mummy asked, willingly and lovingly, in the hope of a little peace in the family.

If there was not Mummy to be pacified, there was Ava; if little Ava was not happy everyone suffered. If little Ava could not sleep, no one else was allowed to sleep. If little Ava would not eat, she was bribed. If little Ava had a tummyache, she whined and carried on until every-one else had a headache. So the undertone and overtone chant of the household became "Pacify, pacify, pacify."

Where was Sam in all this? He worked, made money, ate, slept and pacified.

Isabel broke out of her daydream for the moment. She shifted and pulled her knees up a bit more, then snuggled deeper into her chair. She had not opened her eyes and was deeply drowsy, although not asleep.

There she was in the first year of her teens, a young beauty whose mother told her that she would never be more beautiful. She was a young Jewish princess who could go out into the world and have anything she wanted. The other thing that Mummy told her darling daughter was that she had youth and beauty, and must not *ruin* her life as Mummy had. What she must do is go out into the world, become rich and famous, and when Isabel had enough money then Mummy would get a housekeeper for Daddy; Ava would go away to school; and Mummy and Isabel would run off together. This con-fused Isabel. Was she a Jewish princess or a Jewish prince?

There were other things, but nothing really *serious* . . . Isabel grew up with not one problem to dominate her life, but a series of conflicts that would take her a lifetime to peel away.

When Kate talked to Isabel about Daddy, it was in the form of ridicule when he was trying to talk to them. She put down his work (he was a traveling salesman for the Del Monte tinned food company), made disparaging re-marks about his lack of ambition and did everything she could to destroy his relationship with his two daughters. Her mimicking of his Yiddish accent and imitation of him playing cards were superb as comic relief, but mon-strous if trying to learn to respect your father. But some-thing went wrong with Kate's plan, for Isabel did respect her father. Years later, when her mother kept harping on how she would one day leave Sam, Isabel shattered her when she said that if Kate did leave Sam, *she* would stay with her father.

Kate taught Isabel that marriage to anything less than a millionaire was ridiculous, and love was never men-tioned. In all this it never crossed Isabel's mind to ques-tion Kate. All that Isabel knew was that Kate loved her, was good for her, gave her everything and suffered her life of unhappiness for Isabel. So there grew a bond of love between them. There was no bond between Isabel and her father, and, as for Ava, how could a bond of love grow there?

Ava by this time had a life of her own. When at home she stayed away from whatever family life they had together. Ava did not like the way they lived, and most of all, she could not bear Isabel's kindness, her beauty or the attention she received.

Kate made sure that the two little Wells girls were always the best dressed in their group. By the time they were in their midteens, they had been to more theater, concerts, opera, than any of the other children in the community. They had also traveled more around the country. They were, after all, Kate's playmates.

Then Isabel developed tits, big tits at that, and along came boys and dating. Those were the days of bobby socks and brown-and-white saddle shoes, the last days of the big bands, the first screaming years of a skinny singer with a bow tie: Frank Sinatra. The boys went for Isabel and she liked it. Suddenly there was a life outside of the one Kate had planned, but how could Isabel take her mother along with her?

Kate figured it out. She told Isabel not to worry. While she was out having a wonderful time, Kate would stay home and do some work around the house and wait for her to come home. Kate would have all the fun dressing her for the date and helping her to decide where to pin the camelia the young man sent that afternoon, and Isabel was to remember every detail of the evening. When she came home, Isabel could tell her everything and it would be just as if they had been together. A hundred times during the evening Isabel would think about Kate and how unfair it was that she was not out having a good time like Isabel. Poor Kate, poor mother, poor martyr.

Isabel liked being away from home, in school, having girlfriends, dating boys, even being alone. The last caused the problems between Kate and Isabel. School was a necessity, as was dating, but schoolmates, homework, sitting alone in the house and reading were attacked by Kate. She used her headaches, nerves, illnesses, like a sword to cut away all that separated Isabel's life from her own.

Suddenly Isabel decided it was important to get a job

on Saturdays so that she could learn to earn money. Suddenly the Jewish princess with the wardrobe of a queen became for the first time a traveling salesman's daughter. The money was not for household expenses, to be put aside from an education or to be given to charity—it was for Isabel to buy more of what all little princesses need. Kate, of course, promised to bring her to work and back again in their white convertible Oldsmobile. It seemed that the more Isabel tried to get away, the more Kate would rope her in. The first thing that Isabel did with her paycheck on Saturday night was to buy a red rose for Kate and the house. That made Ava hate Isabel just a little more.

The years rolled on and so did the pressures. When Isabel was ready to leave high school for college, the urge to escape from Kate and home was almost intolerable. The only thing that made it possible for Isabel to control herself over the joy of leaving home was her pity for Kate's unhappiness and the desire to not hurt her any more than life had.

When she was seventeen years old Isabel was told that there was no money for her education, that there never had been. Sam at last opened his mouth, and with Kate prodding him along, declared that he did not mind working hard and supporting his family, but he did not believe in educating girls. The sacrifice to the family would be too great.

Isabel realized she had to support herself with no means whatsoever to do so. She had been brought up extravagantly and thought herself a well-to-do girl, the Jewish princess her mother told her she was. The truth was that she was spoiled, poor and hardly a princess.

Now Isabel started to fight for her freedom, for what she felt was due to her. She started to fight in order to leave Kate. With much stubbornness, determination and manipulative bargaining she finally wangled out of them the promise of a year of support in a fashion-design school in New York City. They had it worked out: She would then come home, work in a dress shop for a while, and if she was good, she and Kate could open a small shop of their own. She could become rich and famous in time, and they would support her and be partners with her as long as she lived at home. She said yes verbally while she screamed to herself: *No, never, impossible*. To her their plan was a living death. She felt guilty for her duplicity and was determined to cram all that she could learn into that one year, once she got away. She need not have felt so guilty. After three months she went home for a weekend to be told she was too costly a burden, and that her precious year had been cut down to six months.

And so Isabel was out in the world with a total lack of understanding about love, relationships, truth, and a massive dose of guilt for the overwhelming desire she had to leave her drab family behind.

The daydreams were now slipping into nightmares. The fight for survival had only begun when Kate started tugging hard on the guilt strings. Isabel no longer wanted to go home to Kate and tell her about the men in her life, or her work. Kate was spending as much time as possible on New York surprise visits. Sometimes she sat in on Isabel's classes, other times she waited in the car in front of the building Isabel lived in. When she was not in New York, there were the phone calls.

"Have you found a man?" Kate would ask. "Is he Jewish?" and "What does he do?" or "What do you mean, you haven't got a date? You look for the wrong men. A girl like you, why can't you find some guy to bring home one weekend?" Then, if she found one: "What a jerk! Is that all you could find? Why do you bother with these men? We didn't send you away just to have a good time, you know. I hope you're working. Have you any idea how hard it is for us to support you?"

"Yes, I know," Isabel would sigh, thinking, *But, Kate, what you don't know is how happy I am not to tell you about my life, my work, my men. When you ask, "What did you do last night?" I am thrilled not to tell you how I loved a young man, how terrific it was when he sucked on my nipples, what a relief it was to get rid of the burden of my virginity. . . .*

After three years of being dragged back and forth from New York to open the tiny shop of exclusive fashions called *Isabel & Kate*, financed by Sam, Isabel's dream was that Kate would become famous and rich and leave her alone. But no, she tugged even harder on the strings of guilt and used even softer kid gloves over her steel fists.

During all this little Ava grew up to be a tiny, pretty, young lady. She had been cleverer than Isabel, and had saved over the years the bits and pieces of money that were given to her, or that she had earned working on Saturdays. Others said that she had her first nickel, and that was true. She borrowed some money from Sam and she had her one year at college; time enough to find herself a young husband not approved of by Kate, but by then it was painstakingly clear that there never could be such a man. As for Sam, well, he listened to Kate. The young couple went to live in Mexico. When Isabel said good-bye to Ava, she saw that smug smile on her sister's little face when she said, "Well, Isabel, this is one thing I beat you at."

Ava turned her back on the three of them yet again. She never wrote or spoke to them until she needed them, and that took ten years. There were Christmas cards once a year from Mexico. There were letters from Kate to Mexico once every two weeks, like clockwork. Ava may have been finished with the family, but Kate kept up a front for the postman. The entire town was told that Ava was so rich that she called instead of writing.

Now Kate had another weapon against Isabel. Since Ava was gone, there was only Isabel to help out in their business venture and happy home. But at last Isabel had a possibility of getting away—she was now twenty-one. Of age, so to speak, according to the law, an adult, and Sam and Kate had no legal hold on her.

There followed the years of running away to make a life in New York, and having to leave it periodically because of gall bladder, kidney, or appendicitis trouble, of heart palpitations and the need for someone to take care of Sam, Kate's last weapon.

Finally Isabel confronted her. Isabel had just completed a three-month stay at home with Kate and Sam while Kate was recovering from an operation. Isabel had announced that she was returning to New York in a few days. The two women decided to have lunch together. They left the shop in the hands of a most competent assistant and off they went to a country restaurant on the banks of the Connecticut river. Kate was clever about Isabel and knew that she would not change her mind for the moment and so was very jolly and amusing, maybe a bit too amusing. They had a delightful lunch, and after, when they were walking through the restaurant gardens to the car, Kate slipped her arm through Isabel's and told her how wonderful she was, what a lucky woman she was to have Isabel, etc., etc., etc. Isabel looked down at Kate, who was all but pawing her by this time, and made up her mind.

They settled themselves in the car. Isabel was at the wheel and before she started the car she said, "Kate, please let me go." Isabel broke down and wept, begging for her freedom. It was a horrifying experience for both of them.

Kate, although very upset, controlled herself. She told Isabel to wipe away her tears. The only thing that she said was, "Go, but don't come back. When we get home, pack your bags and leave today. There is a six o'clock train, you can make it. I will tell Sam that you had a call from New York and that you had to go. He need not know about this."

Isabel left that night and Kate never let her enter her house again. Nor did she ever allow her to come to her hometown again. They spoke on the phone once a week, in short, cold, clipped sentences, and met in restaurants fifty miles outside of the city limits about once a year. Birthday calls and gifts were always exchanged, and once every few years they met in New York.

Isabel had her freedom and a great deal of guilt, a legacy from her mother. Kate suddenly became completely wrapped up in her shop and Sam. As for Ava, she was blind to everything, as always.

Isabel slowly opened her eyes, her mind and body still half-asleep. She heard the sound of the heavy airplane motors and focused her eyes out the window—nothing but blackness out there.

She remained in her half-reclining position on her side, too lazy even to shift herself, and turned her head over her shoulder to see if Anthony was asleep. He was gone —was he a dream? No, he was real enough. She returned to staring out into the night.

Slowly closing her eyes again, she had but one thought before dozing off: *The past is with us, like it or not.*

She was in a deep sleep, dreaming that she heard Anthony calling her in a faraway voice.

"Isabel, Isabel."

It was Anthony, only he was not far away, and it was not a dream; he was whispering something to her. She started to move, but he stopped her by putting his hand on her shoulder. "Isabel, don't!" he hissed.

She was wide awake now. "What is it, Anthony?"

"Listen, Isabel, everyone is asleep in the cabin except the backgammon players, and they are not going to come down this way. I was just up forward with them and have told them you are fast asleep. I told them I would read for a while and then finish the movie. That we did not need anything and if we did, we would ring for a steward. We are safe for hours. Don't move."

He very slowly and gently pulled the cashmere lap robe off the lower half of her body, saying, "Isabel, I want you. You would like that, I know. That is what you wanted when you came to me."

Isabel's heart began to beat quite fast. She whispered, "What if someone does come? It is far too dangerous."

"I told you that no one will; I've seen to it. All you have to do is lie very still. Make no noise," he warned.

How wonderful it will be to have him inside me again, Isabel thought. *To have him touch me and fill me.* But she said nothing.

He began unbuttoning her dress from the waist down. She started to move her leg, and he said, "No, no. Don't move anything. I want to take you the way you are." Isabel became very excited. She wanted him very much. He folded her dress back, exposing her bottom to the cool air of the cabin.

She lay there on her side in a semifetal position, the top half of her body at a reclining angle, staring at the window. He moved his hand over her hip and down her haunches, easing himself along beside her as he did so. He ran the edge of his hand along the deep crack of her buttocks and followed the line to the soft inside of her thigh, barely touching her pubic hair. He lifted her thigh to push her knee even higher towards her chest, and she felt the outer lips of her vagina separate ever so slightly as he did so. He continued to pull on her knee, which in turn pulled on her thigh, and exposed her slit just a little bit more. Now she could feel the cool air on her exposed genitals. She was enjoying the position and waited excitedly to be taken.

Anthony moved his erect penis down the crack of her ass. He pushed at her anus lightly with its head, and moved on to the soft lips of her partially open cunt, encircled by curly, dark hair. His penis was very hard now as he laid it along the length of her and pressed gently, then rubbed it back and forth once again before he took it away.

Isabel was madly thrilled. The drone of the motors and the occasional voices of the two players in the distance were hardly audible and seemed to add to the excitement.

She waited for Anthony to reach in and fondle the pink inner lips and her clitoris, but he did not. Instead he piled into her, ramming his way up with such force that she felt him touch her uterus with the tip of his cock. It was so thick that he filled her completely.

She grabbed on her knee to hold back and not scream out in shock at the split-second of excruciating pain. She opened herself even more, and before she could catch her breath and say something, he pulled out and rammed into her even deeper. This time she started to speak, but he quickly put his hand over her mouth as he pulled out slowly, and said, "Shussh. Remember, this is my favorite position. I feel you more this way than any other way. Don't you remember?"

It was true. She did remember. She moved her head and watched him slowly coming out of her. She looked around, wanting him to see in her face that she remembered.

He bent forward and kissed her on the ear, then said, "This is what you wanted, and this is what I am going to give you. Don't move."

And he banged her again and again. Something was wrong, for she was not having the orgasms she once had when they had sex. She thought, *It is over for me,* and decided just to relax and let him bang away. She may not have been having an orgasm, but she felt sexy, and with every thrust he touched her everywhere inside, and she loved that feeling. The more she relaxed, the more sensuous she felt, and suddenly she realized she was no longer dry inside. He was moving just as hard and as deep, but it was in luscious wet and warmth. She could not stop coming—he knew it, and had her again and again.

Isabel was somewhere high and exquisite, and she floated along with her feeling. She wanted to scream out with the joy of it, but bit the pillow instead and kept floating. He held off as long as he could. After he came he lifted her leg away from her chest and draped it over his thigh. They lay there, jackknifed together. He rested his head on her shoulder and dozed off for a very few minutes. When he opened his eyes and pulled out of Isabel, he took a handkerchief and gently put it between the outer lips of her vagina, then draped the lower half of her dress to cover her nakedness. He stood up and slipped into his trousers, put his shorts into his pocket and fell back onto the seat next to her. Isabel started buttoning the lower half of her dress. He reached over and squeezed her hand, then patted her hair and handed her the lap robe. She turned away from the window and rested square against the back of the seat. She had slowly come back to earth.

Isabel touched his arm. He turned and smiled at her in the dark, picking up the remote control to the TV cassette machine. He punched a button, the light from the TV screen lit them up, and for the first time she saw some of the old Anthony in his eyes. She ran her fingers through the hair that had fallen onto his forehead. He gently took her by the wrist and removed her hand. He turned up the sound and watched what was left of *To Have and Have Not*.

Isabel's eyes were on the set, but she saw and heard nothing. She was not into the film. The daydreaming had started again. She knew she was wrong in wanting to reach out and touch Anthony: There was simply nothing to get emotional about. So she decided to distract herself.

She thought about Sir Alexis Hyatt and the job that she was going to. How lucky she was to have arrived . . . to be in a position to get such fine and rare jobs.

She remembered that there was a time, years ago in New York, before the good jobs had come along. Those were the years of night school, and apprenticeship at the Museum of Modern Art. Those were also the years of selling flatirons at Macy's while waiting for a job as a design consultant with Walter Gropius. Then there was Partridge's, where she learned about fine French furniture, and Charles Eames, where she learned about contemporary furniture, and the years she was an assistant in the best gallery for modern art in New York. There were the endless lectures and seminars on literature and the history of art—on and on it went. About the only thing that she did not work at was fashion. That was Kate's idea, and she would never work at that again. Slowly she picked up her education, and slowly people began to recognize her and her work and search her out. At first the jobs that came were small, and then they grew, as did her reputation as the years went by.

Now she was in a position to pick and choose any job that was offered to her, but if the truth were to be known, winging her way to Egypt for a job was only second best to Meredith Montague. She wondered why she did accept a job that she really did not want and decided it was because when he first called she thought he fancied her.

Well, it was certainly turning out to be an adventure one way or another. She had never made love on an airplane, nor with an old lover who claimed to be a faggot.

Wide-awake now and not at all interested in the film, Isabel found her book on the floor, then reached under the lap robe and, lifting her dress, removed the handkerchief that Anthony had placed between her legs. She rolled it into a little ball and kept it in her left hand. She folded the robe neatly and bent over to place it on her empty seat. Anthony ran his hand over her bottom, but kept his eyes on the film. She turned to him saying, "I am going to my room."

"Isabel, don't lock the door," he said, switching off the TV and standing up. "If it is very quiet and safe, I may come and visit you. Whether I do or I don't, we must promise each other that this is a one-night thing between us, and when we step off this plane, we will be just two old friends. I meant what I told you before. You are now a dormant part of my life and always will be. That is the way I want it."

"I understand, Anthony. I'll leave the door open. You do as you think best for both of us."

Isabel had control of herself again, and before she started for the room she went to see the backgammon players. Passing the stewards and Gamal, who were fast asleep in their chairs, she made her way quietly and saw the two men were deep in their game. She watched for a few minutes and then it was all over. The fourth game was Alexander's and he was triumphant, for it was his first win and he was still in the mini-tournament. Before they began again, he poured out some champagne and offered Isabel a glass, which she declined. Did she enjoy her film? Yes, she did, she replied. But she fell asleep.

By the way both men behaved, she was reassured that no one had guessed anything about what had been going on. *Oh, Alexander,* she thought. *How you would have enjoyed watching it all.* She wished both men goodnight, asking Alexander to please have Gamal wake her one hour before landing.

Making her way to the rear of the plane and Sir Alexis's private room, she passed by Anthony, who was watching the last five minutes of the film. She squeezed his shoulder as she went by.

She bathed, took her book with her to the French bed and slipped between the sheets all clean and naked. Isabel wondered how she would ever be able to face going on a commercial flight again after such luxury. Before she even opened her book she was fast asleep.

It was morning and the room was filled with sunlight. Isabel had bathed for the second time, dressed and made up her face carefully.

She had left the bed straightened out but unmade, and was sitting in the Bergère close to the desk reading her Iris Murdoch. She felt fresh, bright, very happy to be alive and was looking forward to landing, although she could have done with a good night's sleep. There was a knock on the door. It was Gamal with a silver salver and a cup of black coffee on it. He announced that they would land in one hour and that breakfast and the gentlemen were in the dining room.

She noticed when he left that he no longer had on his trousers and jacket. He was now in his galabia of cream-colored shiny cotton with a fine stripe of dark olive green in it. There was a dark olive sash around his waist, and he had a turban of simple white cotton covering his hair. The three deep scars slashed in his cheek seemed more regal and less sinister than they had looked in London. Isabel knew those slashes to be a tribal ritual. The Sudanese were proud to wear them.

Once Gamal had left the room, Isabel sat back with her cup of coffee and sipped the thick, sweet liquid slowly. She reminded herself to tell Gamal no sugar and read a few more pages of her book before placing it in her nightcase and shutting it.

She then went to the commode and checked her looks in the mirror. Isabel knew that she was a beauty, but she never took her appearance for granted. Her long dark chestnut hair was shiny and falling in just the right way, and the elegance and simplicity of her white dress were perfect for the impression she was out to make.

Slinging her handbag over her shoulder, she turned around and checked the room to see that all was in order. For one fleeting moment she thought of Anthony and the night before. She was not looking forward to meeting him in the presence of the two other men. The fact was that she would never again experience the Anthony that she knew last night. She sighed, not out of unhappiness so much as resignation. The one thing Isabel had learned, and the hard way, was to accept as graciously as she could what life had to offer her.

She turned around and left Sir Alexis's cabin. In the dining room the three men rose from their seats as Isabel approached the table. André Beshawi kissed her hand and wished her a good morning, Alexander reached across the table, took her hand and gave it a firm, friendly pat, saying how lovely and radiant she looked this morning and how did she manage it? Anthony came around, pulled a chair out for her and said he hoped that she had slept well.

The table was a wonder. The night before when she had seen it, it appeared to be nothing more than a conference table, stark and very businesslike with its twenty chairs around it. This morning, the center was filled with lilacs and tulips in white and pink and with peach-colored zenias; there were heavy, ornate silver pitchers of mango, orange, pineapple, and coconut juices, heavy crystal goblets and an enormous silver bowl of tiny white peaches. There were placemats of pink-and-peach silk organza with hand-painted white polka dots and napkins to match. The plates were of silver. The cups and saucers were white Belleek.

The same stewards were attending the table, and one came over to Isabel to explain that they would only serve juice, fruit and coffee. Breakfast would be served at the house later.

Everyone was a bit subdued. Alexander seemed more like the Alexander she had first met. André Beshawi and Anthony were discussing the latter's visit to Sir Alexis. Isabel listened, wanting to hear why Anthony was in Egypt and his connection with Alexis Hyatt. She could have guessed it.

Anthony had sold Sir Alexis two paintings a few years before. Recently, by chance, they met in Paris, and Sir Alexis said that he thought that one of the paintings was in need of some restoration. The pigment was cracking and some had even flaked off. Would it be possible for Sir Alexis to send it to Anthony for the work that had to be done? He would have it put on his plane and delivered directly to Anthony. Anthony, of course, suggested that he fly out to do the repair whenever it was convenient for Sir Alexis; in that way he could see the painting and where it was hung, which would be a great pleasure. He would repair it on site, much better than moving such a large painting about, and so Sir Alexis had arranged for him to fly in for a few days.

Anthony—as smooth a hustler as ever. Isabel was sure that he would get to see and do everything that he wanted to, and most likely sell a few paintings to a few charmed ladies just for good measure.

The end of the plane journey seemed to come upon Isabel rather quickly. Not that she was rushed. It was more like a rapid succession of movements, all perfectly organized and played out in slow motion.

From dining table to being buckled in one's seat for landing, to the descent from the clouds, to flying up the Nile, to passing over Cairo, to landing and the cut of the motors, to being released from her seat, to seeing two Mercedes pull up to the plane, to the stairs being rolled across the tarmac and up to the plane, to the door being opened and the hot rush of air and sunshine that invaded the interior. Isabel was in Cairo.

Alexander told her that they would go in two cars: Anthony and André in one and she and Alexander in the other. Would she please wait? He took the two men down to the first car after they said their farewells. When they were halfway down the stairs a man emerged from the car and went to meet André Beshawi. For a moment Isabel thought that the man was Sir Alexis, but he never greeted Anthony, and barely acknowledged Alexander, so it was obviously just a friend of Mr. Beshawi's. They disappeared into the car and Alexander returned to Isabel.

That is why we are going in two cars, Isabel thought. *No room.* Alexander reported that it was lovely and not too hot out, just about eighty degrees with a nice breeze. He asked Isabel if she would wait for a minute while he went forward to check something out with the captain. Isabel sat down again and looked out of the window; while she had been talking to Alexander another car had pulled up in front of the Mercedes that was left on the tarmac. It was a maroon Rolls Royce, a very large and not very new one. The driver was standing next to the rear door, closest to the stairs. She could see no one was in the car, then realized it must have been sent for her and Alexander. The Mercedes was probably for the luggage.

She stood up and was starting forward, towards the entrance of the plane, thinking she would wait outside in the fresh air. Gamal, who had been standing close by her, just waiting for them all to leave, asked her to please wait for Mr. Gordon-Spencer. While they were standing there having their little conversation, Isabel saw a shadow at the entrance door of the plane cut through the light and spill across the floor. Someone had come up the stairs of the plane. Isabel had missed seeing who it was get out of the Rolls.

Gamal respectfully retreated back to the dining room. Alexis Hyatt had entered his plane.

There were just the two of them there in the main cabin as he went forward to greet Isabel. She knew at once who he was, for he looked like a handsome prince. She automatically went towards him. They stopped a few feet apart. He smiled and said, "I have thought about our meeting for a very long time. Welcome to Egypt. I am happy that you are here."

He picked up her hand, looked at it and kissed it lightly. "Did you have a comfortable flight?"

"Yes, most comfortable, thank you."

"What am I thinking of? Why am I keeping you standing here? Come, we will go home."

Isabel smiled at him, and he took her by the elbow and led her to the top of the stairs. Just before they started down he took both her hands in his and stepped back a few paces.

"Let me just look at you for a moment. You are really more beautiful than I remembered."

"Please, Sir Alexis, you are embarrassing me."

And he was too, because he was looking at her from top to bottom, making her feel quite naked.

"No, not Sir Alexis, Isabel. Alexis, I beg you. And I would never for the world want to embarrass you. The next time I tell you that, I am sure you will not be embarrassed. Now, come along."

As they were about to start down the stairs they were stopped by Alexander, who greeted Alexis. The two men shook hands. In Arabic, they said a few things to one another.

Alexander said good-bye to Isabel and that he hoped that she would be very happy in Egypt. He kissed her hand and when he looked into her eyes there was that same hidden meaning that she had seen in London.

Isabel was not at all mad, she realized. Alexander Gordon-Spencer knew more about her and her trip to Cairo than he wanted her to think he did.

At last they were down the stairs and in the car, but just before they pulled away Gamal appeared. Sir Alexis rolled down the window, and he and Gamal greeted one another. Gamal spoke with him for a minute, Sir Alexis laughed and smiled, gave a few instructions, dismissed Gamal and turned to Isabel. With a broad smile he said, "You have conquered Gamal." Then he told the driver something in Arabic, and they were on their way.

"You do not remember me, do you?"

Isabel did remember him, but not from that night at the Chicago Art Institute. "Yes, I do, Alexis. But I will confess that you are not the man I thought you were when I spoke to you on the telephone."

"And who did you think I was?"

Isabel looked straight into Alexis's wonderful face, his piercing dark eyes, hawklike nose and thick black hair flecked with gray. She found herself smiling, and that led to roars of laughter. He sensed that she was not laughing at him, and her laughter was infectious. Laughing madly, the two of them sat in the back seat of the Rolls that sped towards Cairo.

He finally said, "Isabel, what are we laughing about?" She brought herself under control and told him.

"The night you called me in London and told me where we met, I racked my brains trying to remember the men that I met that night. Then it came to me: I remembered meeting very briefly a man who was from either Cairo or Jeddah. He was about five feet tall, wore a banana-colored suit, had eyes that were the size of pinheads, and when he focused them on me I knew that he was having a momentary fantasy. He was one of the most singularly unattractive men I have ever come across."

Her smile played at the corners of her mouth, as she continued. "So you see, when you called me and were so charming on the telephone, I had only the image of that man to fall back on. And that was even a blurred image inasmuch as the moment I saw the look in the man's eyes, I said, 'How do you do,' and left as quickly as possible, not to get involved and not to be rude to him since I am sure he was a nice enough person." She stopped to catch her breath. "Actually, as you spoke to me all I really saw clearly was the banana-colored suit. But there was something about the way you spoke, something about your voice that made me unsure if you were that suit. Now, you will understand that when you greeted me a short time ago on the plane, I was quite bowled over to see you were more than five feet tall and that, when you looked at me, I realized you had the largest, most beautiful eyes I have ever seen. Don't be embarrassed, I have calmed down now."

They both started laughing again.

"But you said that you did remember me. From where?"

Isabel touched his arm. "Oh, look, Alexis! They are marvelous! I love camels!" She pointed out of the window at a herd of camels racing along next to the road. They were being herded—all fifty or more of them—by half a dozen drivers. The camels, their hooves beating with dull echoes from the density of the sand, their strange bleating sounds, and the Arabic curses coming from the drivers, high up in their saddles, bouncing along in the clouds of dust, raised quite a contrast to the shiny, sleek Rolls racing along beside them.

"Where are they going? They are so wonderful looking! I adore watching them race along," Isabel cried.

"They will be driven through the heart of Cairo to the camel market." He did not want to tell her that most of them would be sold to the slaughterhouse and be on someone's table before dark.

"Have you ever been to a camel market?"

"Oh, yes, many times. I know a few Arab countries quite well, but this is my first time in Egypt."

She was then distracted by a bicycle they were passing.

Two sheeps' heads stared at her from a pole that had been lashed to the back of the bicycle seat. Blood still dripped from their severed necks. With their curly hair still on them she could hardly believe they were dead, except for the bright red blood dripping on either side of the rear wheel, leaving a spotted wavy trail along the black tar road as the bicycle zigzagged along. Pedaling the bicycle was a young man in a filthy galabia and brown cotton turban, wound sloppily around his head. Sitting along the crossbar was a younger boy in a wide, blue-and-white-striped, rough cotton galabia that was torn and mud-spattered. In front of the handlebars was another pole with two more heads hanging down. These heads had not been severed with clean cuts, and the jagged flesh moved back and forth all red and wet. Occasionally the boy on the crossbar would slap the mutilated flesh with his dirty, scabby bare foot.

Isabel felt quite queasy as they left the bicycle behind them. She turned towards Alexis.

"You look quite pale, Isabel. Come now, this is Egypt." He touched her cheek. "They are coming in from the country to deliver to the butcher."

"I know, but it is such a macabre sight, and I am a bit on the soppy side about animals, alive as well as dead. I live in England and you know how mad the English are about animals? Well, we Americans are even worse!"

"Oh, dear, you *are* upset." He picked up her hand with the palm up, brought it up to his mouth and kissed it.

Isabel felt a tremor of excitement go through her and was slightly taken aback. As soon as it was possible without being too abrupt, she removed her hand from his with the pretence of having to find something in her handbag.

"You are very kind indeed to rise so early in the morning and meet me," she stuttered. "I hope that my choosing this hour to arrive has not been inconvenient."

The moment that Isabel said it she knew that it was a mistake. His expression changed from one of warmth to a cold look, and an air of reserve was immediately apparent. He was obviously interested in her and they both knew it. She could only hope that he would understand that it was her own insecurity that had taken over. She made up her mind to still her fear and take anything that came along for what it was and live it. She could only hope that she had not spoiled something for them.

"Alexis."

"Yes?"

Isabel turned and, tucking one leg underneath her, faced him. "Alexis, that was a foolish thing for me to say. What I wanted to say is, you are a lovely surprise, and I am happy to be here with you, but I did not know how to say it. I think I was trying to say thank you."

The iciness went out of his face. He brushed aside a long heavy lock of her hair, and took her face in both his hands, lightly kissing her on the mouth.

Breathless, Isabel sank back in the seat and faced forward. Alexis was holding her hand. They were each looking out of opposite car windows, watching the traffic begin to pile up as they came closer to the center of Cairo.

"Isabel."

"Yes, Alexis?" she replied softly.

"Remember, I have been trying to find you for six months. I have thought about you for six months. I have held you in those thoughts for a very long time. I have never let you go since I met you. You must not be frightened. It is sudden for you, but for me it is not sudden, only a reality."

Smiling, he squeezed her hand as the Rolls was slowly swallowed up by the sounds, the sea of traffic, the sun of Cairo.

Alexis pointed out things while en route past the Semiramis Hotel and the Nile. The varied modes of transport were astonishing. Bicycles and motorcycles pulling makeshift wooden carts on rubber wheels; wooden carts pulled by worn-down, almost hairless, abused donkeys; Cadillacs with Chevrolet fenders; Minis; big old Buicks kept shiny; and sad old horses pulling flat carts loaded with scrap metal, piled so high as to look like moving pyramids of rubbish ready to topple at any time. There were elegant Mercedes and Rollses of all ages and sizes, and red Ferraris which could go no more than a foot a minute in the traffic jam while their constantly revved motors screamed to take off.

The tramcars and pedestrians mingled with the traffic brought on more to see and marvel at, and then came the vendors weaving through the traffic selling cold drinks, scarves, stockings, fruit, coffee, prophylactics, flowers, kebabs, feather dusters and falafels.

One of the vendors rapped repeatedly on Alexis's window to offer white honeysuckle and jasmine blossoms, all strung together on a four-inch-wide bracelet. Another attacked the windscreen with a filthy cloth as the car inched along. The chauffeur screamed at the man to go away, but Alexis silenced the chauffeur and bought two of the bracelets for Isabel. He tied them both on the same wrist. She loved them and the mad traffic of the city.

They were through the center of Cairo now, and Alexis explained that he had several residences in Cairo, among them one of the finest old Arab houses, dating back to the early seventeenth century. Another was a lovely house built in the middle of an amazing love garden on an island in the Nile near old Cairo. There were several small but perfect early-eighteenth-century houses in the Muski area, on a small street about halfway between the mosques of Barkuk and al Hakim. They were all fine and open to the public when he was not in residence, except for the one on Sharia el Nil, which was his official residence. His home.

"Isabel, I want you to see them all. I want you to see everything you can while you are here. We will stay today and tonight in the house on Roda Island. Tomorrow we will stay at Sharia el Nil. They are only a half-hour apart from one another but are indeed worlds apart. You will see."

Slowly they edged their way out of the traffic and away from the excitement of the people, the cars, the slender minarets and the stately architecture that vie with the modern buildings and wide avenues, the shady parks spotted along the Nile, with its feluccas slowly moving up and down, their sails billowing lazily in the hot wind. The city seemed as if thick honey had been poured over everything; everything slowed down by sweet, slow motion.

Isabel adored what she saw, and was more than a little captivated by Alexis. There was excitement, but a comfortable excitement. It was strange, but she almost felt as if she had been there before. It was as if she were returning home. She half expected to find her pets—Rita, Winston and Arthur—waiting for her at Alexis's house.

The Rolls was driving through lush green trees and flowering bushes. They were on Roda Island. It was quiet, with just a few cars on the road, and there were birds to be heard. The bright sun filtered through the trees and made patterns everywhere.

They made a turn and went through a pair of huge, magnificently ornate, cast-iron gates. There were guards on either side of the gates dressed in the same type of galabia and headdress as Gamal. They bowed very low as the car went through and was swallowed up by the loveliest, most exotic garden Isabel had ever seen. She turned around and looked out the back window and could see the guards closing the gates as the car went slowly up the winding drive to the house.

The house was actually a small palace. The driver opened the door to the car and bowed low as Isabel got out. Alexis was directly behind her. She turned away from the house and faced him.

"Alexis, I am overwhelmed."

"No, no, not yet. Wait until you are inside; then you may be overwhelmed." He smiled broadly.

Two servants opened the door as they mounted the steps. Alexis had her by the elbow and was leading her. The servants bowed very low in welcome.

The massive oak doors were framed in brass and inlaid in gold and silver. The palace was a mixture of Ottoman, Moorish, Persian and Arab styles. Everywhere one looked it was covered with mosaics, mushrabiya or some intricate work of art. Taken all together it was a *tour de force* of beauty. Alexis was right; Isabel was now completely overwhelmed.

"Come, I wish to show you the room I have chosen for you. I think you will be happy with it. Gamal will be your servant. Anything you want, merely ask him. Do you want to rest, or do you think you will wait for a siesta after lunch?"

"I will wait for the siesta."

"Good girl."

They approached a door and a servant who had been a few feet down the corridor stepped forward and opened it for them. They stepped inside the magnificent room, and there was Gamal with most of her cases unpacked. Even her makeup had been laid out on the dressing table. Alexis said a few words to Gamal and the servant disappeared. Alexis removed the alligator handbag from her shoulder, took both her hands and led her to the French doors, whose shutters had been closed. He opened them and led her out onto the balcony, which overlooked a tropical garden with fountains and rare birds of all colors walking about; there were pools of lotus flowers and gold-fish with great fantails; flowers and songbirds were every-where.

Isabel gasped. "Alexis, I don't think I can take any more."

"Oh, that would be a pity because the best is yet to come. And I am sure you will be up to it. Isabel, come inside."

He took her hand and she followed him dutifully. Once inside he unbuttoned the first four of the white jade but-tons of her dress and slipped his hand inside, fondling her gently for a moment, then gliding his hand over her breasts to her neck. He bent and kissed her tenderly on the mouth. Isabel unconsciously opened her lips and he ran his tongue over the inside of them, kissed her on the lips and then the neck.

"Why not freshen up and come down to breakfast? The others are here and waiting for us at table. Don't be too long." He started for the door and halfway there, re-turned. "Isabel, I almost forgot. There is a package for you on the dressing table. Just a token. Something to please you, I hope, and to say welcome. Oh, and the other thing is that there is an open line for calls, if you want to make any. The telephone system is notoriously bad in Cairo and I have secured a line for us here at the house that will be good for the next hour. Just tell the operator the country and the number."

He started out of the room again, but stopped after a few steps and returned to Isabel. He bent down and whis-pered in her ear, "You have lovely tits," gave her a quick kiss on the mouth and a pat on the ass before she could say anything; then smiled and left the room.

Isabel stood in the center of this amazing room, with its antique Turkish paneling and decorated ceiling, over-whelmed, and not only by the decoration. Alexis Hyatt was gorgeous and obviously desired her.

What was so extraordinary was that Isabel did remem-ber meeting Alexis Hyatt. It was a little over a year ago. She had been in Regine's in Paris with a group of friends —smart, chic, French intellectual types. It had been an evening of excellent food, wine and conversation. They had all gone to Regine's for a dance and a nightcap. But once there something went very wrong. The party seemed to break up into a lot of superficial chatter and table-hopping. Isabel had suddenly felt quite out of it; she did not belong there at all, and wished more than anything that she were home in bed with a good book.

Out of sheer boredom she became interested in the table just next to theirs. A beautiful young girl, a true English beauty with her long, blonde hair and milk white skin, was with a man who was tall and slim with a great deal of thick, black, slightly wavy hair with silver gray in it. His skin was fair for an Arab gentleman, but clearly he was from the Middle East. His face was dominated by a pair of large, black, sultry eyes and a very sensuous mouth. He exuded a kind of smooth sexiness kept under control by good behavior, and there was something princely in his bearing. All these things put together made Isabel think. *There is a deliciously, slightly decadent man, one who is more than a little bit of a debaucher.*

Isabel was fascinated by him and the way he handled the young girl. When he laughed at her, he revealed a pair of deep dimples and a smile that would captivate any woman. The tiny little wrinkles at the corner of his eyes had a tinge of the wicked: a look that made him even more fascinating to Isabel.

The girl was obviously upset over something that amused him. Isabel could not help but listen to the conversation. The girl was attacking him, saying, "You are going to fuck her, aren't you? Well, answer me. *Aren't you?* Well, if not, then get rid of her. Are you going to fuck her or are you going to fuck me?"

"Why are you so upset, Anne? Calm yourself. I am going to fuck her and I am going to fuck you. You will fuck each other. We three are going to bed and we are all going to have one another. I will watch you while you both have each other, and then I am going to take you both in turn, any way and every way that pleases us. Now, why are you making such a fuss? It seemed to me that you were very happy this afternoon, when we were all in bed. You kept telling us how wonderful it was when she made love to you. Why are you so upset now? If you are unhappy and do not want us, I will take you home right now. There is no problem."

"I want you to myself."

"No, I do not think that is true. I think what you want is to have Yasmine all to yourself and you are jealous because she is making up to that beautiful young man she is dancing with. You are besotted with that woman and too jealous, my dear."

With that the young beauty became very pink in the face and pounded her fist on the table.

"Now, now, no scenes, not at my table, little Anne. If you want her, you must go and take her away from the boy, or wait for her to come back to the table. You wanted to come to this place. You know I do not care for this kind of night life, but I am here. You should have prepared for this sort of thing with Yasmine. I suggest you find the ladies' room and calm yourself, or have another glass of champagne. When she comes back, we will all three go home."

The young girl, enraged, jumped up from the table, went to the dance floor, cut in on the young gigolo and started to gyrate with a lady who must have been six feet four inches tall. She was as slim as a boy and coal black; the chignon of black hair at the nape of her neck only accentuated the animal beauty of her face and body. She looked and moved like a panther dressed in Yves St. Laurent from head to toe, a magnificent animal. The two women danced and one could see the blonde girl grow more calm. The man watched them, never taking his eyes off the scene.

They returned to the table, the young girl quite happy now. The magnificent Negress sat between the man and the blonde girl. They were quite jolly, and Isabel saw the Negress fondle the man under the table. He removed her hand and said "No."

"But Anne would not mind, would you, Anne?" the Negress taunted. "You will not become jealous?"

"No." The blonde girl pouted.

Then Yasmine turned to Anne and lifted her breast out of her dress and sucked on it for all to see. Anne became so turned on she kissed the black beauty full on the lips and begged to be taken home.

The man called for the bill and paid for it while the two women fondled one another. He spoke in Arabic to the black girl, who started for the cloakroom with Anne. As he was passing the table, he jolted Isabel's chair. He touched her shoulder and apologized in French. Their eyes met. He started to say something, but before he could get it out the black goddess pulled him away.

Isabel thought he was fabulously attractive. When their eyes met, she felt for a split-second that their two souls had become one. As he was dragged away from her, Isabel realized how much she wanted to be closer to this man.

That man was Alexis Hyatt.

Isabel stood for a long time in the center of the room just where Alexis had left her. She gave a deep sigh, a sigh of excitement that comes from joy. Moving very slowly to the dressing table she realized that she was attracted to Alexis in more than a carnal way. Not wanting to think about it, she immediately went about brushing her hair and repairing her face. While looking in the mirror she was aware of the fact that she looked different. Perhaps it was because of some kind of inner feeling of bliss.

The mirror also reflected a box covered in silver paper and tied with a string of gold. Inside, lying on a bed of natural shredded silk, was an exquisite Pharaonic scarab of pure gold about the size of her thumb. Isabel lifted it out of its bed of shredded silk and as she did, she gasped with surprise and admiration at what she saw. Attached to the scarab and hidden in the silk threads were ancient gold beads that had been strung together with occasional large freshwater pearls. It did, in fact, turn out to be a four-strand choker, the clasp being under the scarab.

There was a card in the bottom of the box. It said: "Isabel, this is a token gift simply to say thank-you for coming. Alexis."

She put the choker on immediately and opened the top two buttons of her dress. Where should she wear the scarab? Front? Back? Side? Should she wear it to breakfast, or should she be cool and not wear it? She would wear it. No, she changed her mind; she would not.

How should she thank him in front of other people? Or should she not? Perhaps a note? Or should she ring him on the phone? She did not know quite what to do.

In the end she wrote a note and gave it to Gamal to deliver to his master. It read: "Thank you. You are spoiling me with so much beauty and attention. Please do not hold breakfast up for me. I will make a phone call and be with you shortly."

Five minutes later a note was delivered to Isabel by Gamal. "Get used to it. I have only just begun. Alexis."

III

Monday/Athens

Dear Isabel,

Either you call from exotic places like Cairo on a line where I can barely hear you, or nothing. Ava said you called her a few days ago from London. I don't know what you said to her but she was annoyed about something. I know what is really bothering her but I can't say. She would like to tell you off but won't. You didn't tell her you were going to Cairo. What is the secret, why so mysterious? It would have been more sensible to call me before you left your home, what if there had been a plane crash, how would I know where you were? I bet you don't even carry an identification tag on your body. Darling, I know you only mean well, but you do not think things out in a practical way. We are not getting any younger. Try and be more responsible.

It was so nice to talk to you a few minutes ago, bad line and all. I wish you had let me know that you were going to Egypt. I have always wanted to go and see the pyramids. Do be careful, remember that they hate all Jews. I recently met some people who went on a cruise and they said that Egypt was filthy, such poverty and flies. When they went on that famous Nile the captain told them not to fall overboard, that they would be dead before they hit the bottom, that is how many diseases there are in it.

How disgusting.

You always look for trouble.

I still don't understand what you are doing there, you said you were not on holiday. What kind of job could there be for you there? Well, never mind, what you do is your business. I never know what to say to people when they ask how you are and what you are doing. I tell them you are well and busy working, what else can I say?

What a busy week this has been for me. I would have told you on the telephone what the doctor said but you cut me short when I told you that he said I would live. Would live, darling, does not mean I am in the best of health, so next time, don't cut me short.

We are having such beautiful days here, I am very happy with the climate. There are other things that I am not happy about but I don't want to complain. If there is anything I am not, it is a nagging complaining mother. You must admit that I have done very well on my own since Daddy died. I have been no burden on anyone and have taken nothing from you. Think of the mother that I might have been, then there would be none of these little flings in Cairo, would there, kid?

Don't try and fool me, I know you are there on a little holiday and that you just kept it from us because you probably did not want to hurt our feelings, having decided not to visit your mother and sister. Ava and I understand you better than you think, you can't fool your old mother. Good luck to you. You know what I always say, you better laugh and go when you are able to because when you get older, you have had it. I am a good example of what happens. Your children and friends hardly have time for you and rightly so, and if they do, your health gets in the way from being with them.

I have a very good life here and it was very lucky that Ava and Alfred inherited their house and built their pool when they did, all those years ago. The life here is social and easy and the climate is wonderful. Of course, I suffer too much in the heat of the summer, even with my air-conditioner.

My dear, listen to your old mother, it is hell to be old and alone. I moved here because it is closer to you girls than Massachusetts. I bought this flat and there is no return for me but it is a compromise. I am so tired of making compromises, but what can I do? Where was I to go? At least I am near Ava, who is wonderful to me. Of course, I would rather live in London, such a wonderful city, but I cannot afford a London life, I am not a famous whatever-you-are in the art world, and in Athens I can live well. Ideally, I would prefer six months in each

*place. I do not go to London for the simple reason that I
do not want to be a burden on you. Not that I am on Ava,
I have all my own life going here. Too bad you don't come
and live near us. Oh, if I had my life to live over.*

*I am sending this letter to your house in London since
you say that you will be back there in a week's time. For
the same money that you paid to go to Cairo, you could
have stopped off to see us. We are your family, you know.*

*On the phone you could not give me a hotel where you
were staying. What were you afraid of, that I might appear? I do resent having to ask that Chink where to reach
my own daughter.*

*Ava and I went shopping. She is looking as beautiful as
ever and still gets the eye from the men. I bought a new
pair of shoes and they are really lovely, not the expensive
Charles Jourdan that you wear. I hate their styles. They
are too extreme. Actually, I honestly think they only look
good on girls in their twenties, not older ladies like us,
but, darling, don't let me stop you, as long as you can
walk in them I suppose you will be stubborn and wear
them.*

*Believe me, Isabel, you have the right attitude. Being
selfish is a much better bet. I hope you had a nice holiday
in Egypt, write soon, love you.*

Mother

The October sunshine lit up Kolonaki Square. The traffic
was in abundance, and the outdoor cafés were filling up
with people on their way home for lunch and a siesta.
There was a freshness in the air, but it was warm.

At the Café Byzantium most of the tables outside were
filled, and the waiters were doing their rush-around with
ouzos, Camparis, whiskey sodas, tiny saucers of rich,
black olives, salted peanuts and potato chips. Now and
again a waiter would appear, and with a flourish of white
cotton a table would be set for lunch.

The Byzantium had the most comfortable chairs, the
oldest waiters, the best food, and the drinks seemed a bit
larger than those in all the other cafés in the square. It
had something else: the oldest and the most interesting
clientele. The younger people that favored the Byzantium
were writers, painters, movie directors, poets and a sprin-
kling of pretty young girls who were brought along for

decoration. It was more serious than fashionable, more solid than flash and always amusing to watch.

Sitting at one of the tables with his back to the plate-glass window of the café was a man with a shock of white hair. He was a big man with a rough, craggy handsome-ness and kind blue eyes. A retired admiral of the Greek Navy, this man of seventy had an impeccable reputation and was admired by young and old alike for his courage and service to his country. There was always a stream of people passing his table to say hello or shake his hand. Constantine Dendropoulos usually arrived at his table every day at 12:15. Friends and acquaintances would sit and chat with him through drinks, lunch and coffee until four o'clock. Then he would leave, to walk diagonally across the square to his penthouse flat, where he lived with a cook, maid and a famous maritime library.

The admiral had been widowed for eight years, and every matron in Athens was after him for marriage, but to no avail. Three times a week he paid a visit to a mar-ried woman in Glyfada who was separated from her husband. She was his lover and friend and had been for fifteen years. He found her when she was eighteen years old. Everyone in Athens knew about it, but since he never took her out in public, no one ever gave it much thought.

The admiral's money and pension, as well as the aura of respect he had around him, were only a few of the things that made this man so attractive to women. He was a gentleman in every sense of the word and, although re-tired, worked five hours a day for the Navy on all sorts of interesting projects. The Naval Department had given him a young officer named Dimitri Ionou who assisted him and traveled with him everywhere, including the vis-its to Glyfada. At those times he remained in the car with the driver.

During the midday outings at the Byzantium, Dimitri, who also acted as a bodyguard, took a table close by and spent the time reading his paper and receiving a few friends of his own. On his days off he was replaced by a seaman who acted as bodyguard only.

On this day, the seaman, named Petros, was sitting at the table close to Constantine, watching the girls go by. A few old cronies of the admiral were also sitting at his table, and they were having a heavy political discussion, about a country other than Greece, for a change. It was

broken up by a young man who came by to collect one of
the men and take him home for lunch. The other man left
when Constantine called a waiter and ordered his own
lunch.

The admiral had waited for over an hour for the American lady who sometimes lunched with him. They had met
here at the Byzantium when she tried to order lunch one
day, in vain. She spoke no Greek, and since she was sitting at the table next to his, there was nothing to do but
help her out. They met many times after that, always sitting at their own tables and now, after several months,
she always ate with him when she came to the café.

Constantine was close to being a chain-smoker. He
reached into his pocket for a cigarette and remembered
that he had smoked his last one. At that moment one of
the endless line of unattractive Athenian widows, dressed
in the traditional widow's weeds—black, black, black
and dull, approached his table. Always the gentleman,
Constantine stood up and greeted her with as much politeness as possible. The inevitable invitation to dinner
was extended by the lady, and his inevitable refusal was
accepted, if not too graciously, by the lady. They
said good-bye and he went into the café for a packet of
Papastratos. Petros, the seaman bodyguard, started to follow him but Constantine waved him to sit down. Returning to his table, he was delighted to see Kate Wells
waiting for him.

She looked flustered, upset, angry. Something surely
was wrong. He sat down, picked up her hand and kissed
it, telling her how delighted he was to see her, and surprising himself with the realization that he truly meant it.
There was something about this tiny, plump American
lady that warmed him. She was so soft, sweet and considerate—something he rarely saw in the Greek widows,
something rare even in the young Greek girls. She was always dressed with taste and quality, and more than once
he had seen and heard Greek ladies remark on her
clothes as she went by.

"Kate, you are very late today. I had almost given up
the idea of seeing you."

"Oh, I had to go to the post office to mail a letter to my
daughter. She just called me from Cairo and invited me
to join her there for a few days. She hates to travel with-

out me. She always says that she has a much better time with her mother than most other people."

"Are you going?"

"No, I told her she must learn to do without me. I will not always be here, and frankly, Constantine, I am too happy with my life here in Athens to bother traveling. Oh, it is something with these children. You would think that once they grow up, they would leave you with some peace and quiet, but they don't."

The elderly couple parted after lunch, Kate to her daughter Ava's house for a visit, and Constantine across the square to his flat, with his seaman, Petros, trailing a few paces behind. Petros was carrying a package of chocolate-chip cookies that Kate had made for Constantine. She was always doing nice little things for him. There was the time that she knew his cook was ill and had sent over a roast for his dinner; once she had brought him a carton of cigarettes that someone had given her—on and on the gestures went, finally adding up to a kindliness offered with no strings attached, something unusual and very pleasing to the old admiral.

Often, when they parted the admiral immediately sensed a loss of something comfortable. She was the only American woman that he had ever met for more than a brief introduction, and he liked her, thinking her brave to have given up her own country in order to live her last years out near her daughter in Greece. He had a large circle of friends with as full a social life as he cared to have. They were all Greeks, but most of them spoke English as well as French, and had traveled extensively. He had brought Kate Wells to meet them several times, and they all seemed to find her a pleasant addition to their group. The old admiral was beginning to think she would be quite nice to take to bed.

They had been out to dinner a few times with the daughter, Ava, and son-in-law, Alfred, a charming couple. The daughter was an attractive flirt, and had all but made a pass at him. Obviously, the girl had a great frustration in her life. There was something both aggressive and childish about her, a kind of hardness that the mother did not have. He wondered if the daughter had a lover. Probably not. She would be too difficult for a casual affair and seemed too conservative and moral for a steady, longtime lover. He knew the daughter to be very good to

Kate, but found her too authoritarian towards her when they were together. He also realized that Kate needed someone to take care of her.

It came as a surprise to Constantine that he was thinking of taking care of Kate Wells himself. He thought she might be happier to have a husband, and a home to run again, and he saw her as a pleasant companion to that end. They both loved the Kolonaki life and his country, so their last years certainly would be comfortable. As for his lady in Glyfada, he would always visit her for sex, unless Kate's life with him made Glyfada unnecessary.

Constantine knew that Kate was attracted to him physically by the way she subtly managed to bump against him, touch his arm or take his elbow when they walked together. Often she would brush a crumb off his lapel or remove a white hair from his jacket. There were so many signs of affection that she showed, and yet never once did she push or press him for attention. There were other things that fascinated Constantine about Kate. For instance, her background.

There had never been anything but Greek marrying Greek in Constantine Dendropoulos's family for as far back as the family archives and property deeds could prove. They were Greeks on his mother's side who were sea captains and landowners from the islands of Naxos and Siphnos. On his father's side were shipbuilders and shipping merchants from the island of Andros. They were all simple island people who made their fortune through hard work and shrewd dealings, and they were proud Greeks. The family had been in the service of their country for hundreds of years. In all the family, there had only been one Dendropoulos who emigrated from his country to America, and he was only spoken of when absolutely necessary. About the only good thing in that emigrant's favor was that he returned home to find a wife, married a girl from the Mani and shortly afterwards dropped dead from a heart attack before he could return to America. That was fifty-six years ago. Constantine's family's story was one of deep roots, security and contentment, and it was no wonder that he was fascinated by Kate's background.

Kate Wells was born in a small town in the mountains of Massachusetts, the youngest of ten children. Their mother and father, Yarina and Sigmund Tannenbaum, were a legend among the New Englanders within the fifty-mile radius of Stockbridge, where the Tannenbaums originally settled. There was not a small town or a village where they were not respected, admired and looked up to as the first foreign couple to make a home among these staid New Englanders.

The Tannenbaums settled in Massachusetts in 1896, strangers in a strange new world. Theirs was a true love story, one that never ended, even after their deaths. Not one of the ten children ever truly forgave them their love for one another. Least of all Kate.

Sigmund Tannenbaum was a six-foot-three-inch, devastatingly handsome man. It was his looks, charm and amazing sense of humor combined with his upper-middle-class family that gave him the privilege of being an officer in Emperor Franz Joseph's private cavalry. He was the token Jew of the regiment.

The same qualities helped the dashing officer to resign his commission (not an easy task) a few years later. It was made quite clear to him that once that was done, he would have to leave Austria. He emigrated to America and a new life immediately after his resignation was accepted.

He landed in New York City along with hundreds of thousands of other immigrants. Being a token Jew in Franz Joseph's private cavalry was a far cry from being an immigrant Jew, and he resented it. However, the small amount of money, the magnificently tailored wardrobe, his elegant manners and his ability to ride a horse did one thing for him: It distinguished him from all the other struggling immigrants, which pleased him.

He decided to learn a gentleman's trade and leave the city as soon as possible. Since the only thing that he did know was how to wear a well-cut suit, he decided to become a master tailor. Every day in the city was a torture for him, but he struggled to learn his trade as quickly as possible. A chance meeting with an officer from the Hungarian Army who was in New York for a month made him his only friend.

Eight months after Sigmund's arrival in America he went with his Hungarian-officer friend to a kaffeklatsch. The house-gathering took place on what was then upper Fifth Avenue. For the first time since Sigmund had been in America, he felt at home. The house, the people, the

atmosphere, were high with elegance, warmth, beauty
and laughter. The host and hostess were the Hungarian
ambassador and his wife. The tables were laden with coffee and bowls of heavy whipped cream; the cakes were a
wonder to see and to taste. Every spoon, cup, saucer and
napkin was of great charm and beauty. There were tinkles
of laughter and chatter as the ladies rustled around the
room in their silk taffeta. Sigmund almost wept with joy
at finding the life he had lost.

Then, in the midst of all this, walking across the room
towards him with his Hungarian hostess and his friend,
was the most beautiful young girl he had ever seen. He
fell in love at once. As for the young girl, from the moment he kissed her hand, she would never love anyone
more than him until the day she died.

Yarina Gabor was sixteen years old when she fell passionately in love with Sigmund Tannenbaum. She had
been in New York, staying with her aunt, for only five
days when they met. She had not liked the city, it was too
busy and crowded, and there were no great, green fields
and trees. Her aunt, whom she had never met before her
arrival, was kindness itself, but Yarina was very close to
her father and missed him terribly.

Anton Gabor, her father, was a very great landowner
in Hungary. An extraordinarily kind and sensitive man
who fought for freedom among the people of his country,
he was loved and respected by all. Their estate began
about 150 miles outside Budapest and included the finest
woodlands and sheep farms. A great advocate of the dem-
ocratic system, he admired America from afar all his life.
He had two sons. One died in a riding accident, the other
entered the political life in Budapest with modest success.
But it was Anton Gabor and the way he ran his estate
and people who was an example for all the Hungarians.
He was wealthy—very wealthy—but when there was un-
rest in the country it was never around him. His people
supported him always.

Anton Gabor was half-Jewish. If he had not been, he
might have been a minister of the country. He and his
wife were not particularly religious and the family had a
history of intermarriage with Catholics. His sister in New
York had been converted to Catholicism but still was
considered a Jewess. All the intermarriage in the family

only affected Yarina in one way—she knew that she was a Jewess but not what it meant to be Jewish.

Then Yarina met Sigmund and her passion for the former Austrian officer could not be held in check. The aunt was aghast when they announced they would marry as soon as possible. She forbade it, and so one afternoon they ran away and were married, returning only to announce their good news. They hated New York and the coarse life they would have to live, but felt they could wait until Yarina's dowry arrived from her beloved father. Then they would decide what to do with their lives and where they would go. Finally word came: Her brother had been sent to take her back to her father, and the marriage would be annulled, otherwise her father would disown her completely. He never relented, and died leaving everything to Yarina's brother, but that was years after Yarina and Sigmund left New York, never to return.

They had heard of the green hills of Massachusetts. After purchasing a horse and wagon and loading it with all their worldly possessions, the young couple, with $540 in cash and a young Irish immigrant hired for his food and lodgings, struck out to make a life for themselves.

Yarina made the transition from a child into a beautiful young mother. She remained all of her life a great beauty who ran her home, no matter how humble, with great elegance and total love for Sigmund. Giving birth to ten children, she saw each of them, one more handsome than the last, leave home and make their way in the world.

Good-looking, amusing, intelligent Sigmund, adored by his wife and every friend and stranger who ever crossed his path, was unloved by his children. He ruled his home and his wife as if he were still an officer in Franz Joseph's cavalry—demanding complete obedience from everyone. Not one of his children was spared the cruelty of his outrageous temper.

He supported his family by becoming not a gentleman's tailor, but an extraordinarily fine ladies' tailor. His little shop would bring people from miles around. The Tannenbaums were never rich, but they were always comfortable.

Kate Tannenbaum was no different from any of her brothers or sisters. When the first opportunity to leave home came her way she was off, even if it meant marrying a man for whom she had no love. She did as millions of other women did—made the best she could of a life with a stranger.

When she went into her marriage she brought with her all the beauty, gentility, polish, refinement, taste and gracefulness that were bred in her at home.

This is what Constantine knew of Kate's background. What he could not know about his friend Kate was that the years with Sam Wells and the children were spent creating, living, teaching—the same beautiful traits that Yarina had taught her. But what went wrong was that Yarina happily let her children go; she had her passionate love for Sigmund. Kate could not release her children, for she had no passionate love for Sam, only for her first child, Isabel, whom she saw as an extension of herself.

When Isabel finally escaped, there was nothing left for Kate but her husband. Slowly this elegant woman and mother—who as a young matron had tried to force Yarina's way of life on Sam—finally buckled under the effort. Kate needed more than giving lovelessly, she needed a response from Sam, and there was none.

She became coarse, almost common. She no longer read books, went to the theater, saw those friends who were intelligent, amusing, refined. She looked for lower-class friends. Suddenly, inexplicably, she was very Jewish; there was not a sentence now that did not have a Yiddish word in it, an impossible thing when she first married Sam. Even her clothes became dowdy. Kate had given up. Sam, who now wore Brooks Brothers suits and button-down shirts, had at last taken over Kate's life.

Kate now had a kind of bitterness, though sugar-coated on the outside, towards everyone and everything. It would never be possible for Constantine to know this bitterness, for Kate was a master at hiding it from everyone, including herself.

It would take some odd little incident to set her off. Any sort of disapproval and something would snap. After her tirade, she would stop, usually with, "Why am I getting myself upset?" Seconds later all would be sugar sweet as she pulled herself back into control.

Sam had been dead for five years now. Kate had sold the house that he had bought so many years ago, but kept on with her little dress shop in order to make an independent life for herself. She became more aggressive as the years went on and more bitter. Certainly more bitchy.

But she was not happy. She decided to travel and then set up her home in Greece, where she had a daughter and son-in-law. Everything was sold or given away; she would show them all and begin again.

That had been years ago. The Kate that Constantine knew was far better now. The coarseness and bitterness had slowly begun to disappear. She dressed well again and forgot many Yiddish words. Kate was better, even on the verge of happiness, and certainly putting on a good show for the neighbors. But Kate was erratic. She was just as much on the verge of being unhappy as well.

Today, for instance, she was unhappy.

Kate had given up long ago trying to work out the whys and wherefores of her moods. She merely looked upon her unhappiness with anger born of a simple view. She was a senior citizen, over sixty-five years old, and had worked enough, suffered enough and been courageous enough. The world owed her happiness. It was that simple. The United States owed and should support her for all the income tax her husband had paid. Medicare owed her and must now pay. Every young person alive owed her because she had lived and cared for the young. Her sisters and brothers owed her because they had not cared enough for her all through the years. Her children owed her because she had given them birth. Her friends owed her because she was a better friend than any of them had ever been. And, most of all, she owed herself a life of comfort, security and admiration. And she was determined to get it before she left this world.

There was only one debt that she would never collect on! Isabel. Isabel owed her more than any of them and both she and Isabel knew that the debt was so high it would never be paid off. Kate was making sure that there would never be the possibility of it. Kate, in fact, worked constantly in building that debt. All three women—Kate, Isabel and Ava—knew that Isabel had long ago given up trying to pay off her obligation for being born and leaving her mother. Kate thrived on it, Isabel was guilt-ridden about it, and Ava resented it.

If Kate tortured herself with what various people must do to *pay* their debt to her, she tortured herself even more on how to *keep* Isabel in debt to her. Kate had become extremely clever about this and was able to use Ava and Isabel admirably by keeping them divided.

Yet today Kate was very unhappy.

The day had started with the call from Cairo. The line was filled with crackles and static. Isabel sounded very happy and told her that she was looking over the possibility of a job, giving vague answers to Kate's questions. She would not allow Kate to join her, and wiggled out of it by saying that even if Kate did arrive and did find a hotel room, which was almost completely impossible in Cairo, Isabel would not even have the time to see her. Some feeble excuse about a client.

Isabel's lack of interest in Kate's health problems was what really rankled. Kate knew how angry Isabel became when she went on about her health and wanted to upset Isabel, so she kept at it until finally Isabel said she was sorry for poor Kate, but please, write it all down and drop it for the moment.

Kate was her mother, and she could put Isabel in her place. She did so by telling her she would pay for the phone call. No expensive gestures were welcome from Isabel, and Isabel better know it.

Kate was enraged by the telephone call. She wanted to be with Isabel, to travel, to have a holiday, to meet new people. Why was Isabel such a bitch? Had not Kate proved to her through the years that she was not a burden, that she was sought out by people because she was amusing and interesting? Well, she would see Egypt without Isabel. Who needs her? Kate drove herself and her rage on until she sat down and wrote the letter to Isabel. That seemed to calm her a little.

She dressed and went to the post office. It was a lovely day, the weather was perfect, just the way she liked it. The sky sparkled a vibrant blue, and billowy white clouds raced high over Athens.

The post office was filled with loud-mouthed locals who used their elbows like machetes to cut their way through the tourists sending postcards of Delphi, the Acropolis, the Forum, or their letters about the wonders of Ancient Greece and the beauty and magic of the country. Kate was bruised and bumped, just like all the other foreigners who had closed their eyes to the fact that the Greece of their fantasies had been dead for two thousand years.

Another elbow, another push, another queue-jumper

and that did it. Kate used her senior citizen routine: a touch of the vapors along with her own elbow and she finally mailed her letter.

Her little act of aggression and scar-winning performance gave her a small pick-me-up. She was energized and ready for Act Two: lunch at the Byzantium with Constantine, and then Act Three: coffee with Ava and Alfred.

Ava, so secretive. Ava, with all her little hobbies and projects. Pretty little Ava, so hard and tough with herself and everyone around her. Ava the flirt, who made up to anything, from the barrow boy to Constantine. She had that superior attitude that looked down on everyone and everything unless created, produced and executed by Ava or Alfred. Ava was stubborn and determined to do only what she or Alfred wanted to do. Ava was generous and good to Kate with money and attention, to inflate her own importance. Kate understood this about Ava, and even respected, accepted and was proud of it. There was only one thing that Kate asked of Ava—that she and Isabel never be united.

She told them all about talking to Isabel in Cairo. Only after she had finished her tale, adding a few of her own interpretations to the facts, did Ava say she had spoken to Isabel as well. She said nothing else. When Kate asked questions about their conversation, she was cut short and given not one word of what the two sisters had spoken about.

Now, walking home, she wondered why Isabel had called Ava. Something was happening, or was going to happen; she felt it in her bones but did not know what it was. Isabel was going to spring something on her in the next few weeks. If only she knew where Isabel was in Cairo, then she could surprise her with a visit and find everything out. Ava either knew and was keeping it secret, or she knew nothing and did not care because it did not affect her. In either event, Ava would tell nothing.

And what was all that teasing about Constantine? Telling her she should think about him as a suitor, and how lucky she was that he paid her so much attention. Well, they had another thing coming if they thought she would end up married again. Once was enough, thank you. There was not a man alive with whom Kate would make a life now, as she told them. No more taking care of a man, picking up his cigarette ashes, listening to him cough and taking care of him when he was sick. And, as for sleeping with him, never. Just the thought of it made her angry. No, not even with a room of her own and if he never touched her; not even if he gave her a fleet of servants, would she marry. She would rather be lonely. Anyway, she had her children.

She did not like the way Ava pushed Alfred about. He was an intelligent, quiet, self-centered man, who was nothing but the perfect gentleman to everyone. He was indeed a model husband, never rude, unkind, or crude in manner or taste. Maybe he was not as thrilling or interesting as some other men, but he gave Ava the security that she always sought, and if the truth be known, her three former husbands were all cut of the same cloth. Ava was clever—she never left one man until she had a commitment from another, and she always moved up to more money, more security, a bigger, better home, and a better life-style.

Ava's strategy was to flirt, coax, tease, but only fuck when a proposal was ninety percent in the bag. Once the man committed himself to marrying Ava, then fuck to her heart's content for a week, announce to the cast-off husband it's over, and leave. Presto, a divorce and a new husband. One had to give Ava credit. She worked hard at whatever she did and got whatever she wanted.

That night Kate slept badly. She woke up constantly to scheme, making little plans on how to get to Egypt and find Isabel, or get her to come to Athens at once. But Kate was getting old, and although her head and heart were still running and scheming she no longer had the energy. Knowing this, she thought she must make sure of any plan she had, and, in fact, of what it was she really wanted.

In the early hours of the morning Kate was sitting in her little garden. She was almost catatonic, having driven herself to that state by her desperate mind games. By the time the sounds of the city were heard in the garden and the rattle of the shutters going up reached her, the sun was high.

By noon she was sure of what she wanted and what she would do. She would make a plan, but not today. Today she was going to take it easy. There was no rush now that she knew where she was going.

No more than an hour after she realized what she

wanted and what she would do, Kate was dressed and looking marvelous. She was going to move to London and live with Isabel for the rest of her life. Isabel and she would take care of one another. Kate would start the ball rolling tomorrow. But today was going to be lovely; she would hurry not to keep dear Constantine waiting. She really did enjoy being with him so much.

She left her house and walked out into one of those magic days filled with sun, warmth, and a fresh breeze coming up from the sea. Well, I can always come back for visits, Kate thought. She thought of what Ava would say about her leaving and then put it out of her mind. The last thing she wanted to do today was to think of her two children. She just hoped they would be happy and leave her in peace.

That evening Kate and Constantine were dining together at his home. Kate had accepted his dinner invitation at lunch the day before. She had not realized that there was to be just the two of them. Kate was at ease about it, now that she had her plan. There had been no word from Isabel, and Kate had started sowing the seeds of discontent with Ava. It would take time, but before long she would be living in Mayfair, London, with Isabel.

Constantine found Kate more lovely and sweet than ever, for she was leading him on, flirting a little. He found it enchanting and all through dinner was delighted with the prospect of bedding Kate Wells after the servants had left the house.

During dinner they spoke about their lives and the future. It was a natural progression that led the two elderly people to discussing their relationship. Constantine took his drink and went over to sit next to Kate. The servants had long since gone.

During the evening Kate had been very flattering about Constantine and how much he meant to her. After putting his drink down and putting out his cigarette, Constantine picked up both her hands, and stroking them tenderly, he told her how much her friendship had meant to him.

There was mutual agreement as to how lucky they were to have found each other. Constantine stroked her arm and touched her cheek, again with tenderness. It was at this point that suddenly, but not abruptly, Kate started to get up from the sofa, saying that it was very late and she must go home.

Constantine stopped her by putting his hand on her shoulder and saying how silly of her, she must not go home. Turning her head to face him, he gave her a kiss full on the mouth as he fondled her breasts. Kate was more surprised than upset as he opened the top of her dress and buried his face in her tits, his fingers seeking her nipples. She asked him in as gentle a manner as she could muster if he did not think he was acting stupidly for a man of his age.

He raised his face away from her and told her that, no, he did not think it was stupid. If anything was stupid, it might be that he had waited so long to take her. Still touching her everywhere as they spoke, her breasts, her stomach, her hips, he then raised her skirt and slipped his hands between her legs.

Kate removed his hands, telling him how surprised and disappointed she was to see a man behave in such a low manner.

Constantine could not believe that Kate was serious. He stood up and pulled her to him, telling her he wanted to take her to the bedroom and remove all those clothes she had on. He wanted her naked so he could touch her everywhere. She pulled away, saying she was going home, and started for the front door. He went after her and pulled her to him, kissing her passionately on the mouth.

She struggled away from him and, standing back, admonished him for being so sexy for a man his age.

"Kate, are you so foolish that you will not let me give you this pleasure? What do you mean 'I am too old'? I have a very active and happy sex life, and I want to share it with you. Surely you know how I feel about you now, and I want you to be my wife. That is what this is all about. I want us to go to bed now and be naked and explore each other. I want to do everything to you to give you pleasure, and I want you to do the same for me. Is that such a surprise to you?"

Kate was furious and saw Constantine as being loathsome, repulsive, sickening. She pulled her hand away. "Don't touch me again, don't come near me. I would rather die than have intercourse with you. I don't want to have you wet all over me," she said, her eyes filled with tears of anger. "I am happy enough to see you in the

Byzantium or any public place, but I don't want you to get close to me and, more to the point, I would find it disgusting to be intimate with you. You are a dirty old man. Do you understand? I think this attempt of sex with me is disgusting. I don't care if you *are* a retired Greek admiral, rich and secure. I don't want your home or your house or you as a reward for accepting your filthy sexual needs. I don't want you to buy me lunch anymore, and I don't mind telling you, if you do go around fucking old women and having those animal passions, you are not the man I thought you were, and I don't like you very much."

Kate was in an advanced state of hysteria by this time, with tears running down her face. All she could babble on about was that she wanted to go home and where was the front door?

Constantine Dendropoulos was indeed a fine gentleman, and not a Greek admiral for nothing. He was quite capable of handling situations. He became very firm and said, "Kate, go over there. Compose yourself at once." He told her that he would not harm her or go near her again, but she would not leave his house unless she was calm and collected. They were, after all, still friends.

And that, in essence, is what finally did happen. When she was calm, had had a drink and been under control for about twenty minutes, the old Greek admiral got up, brought her coat to her, helped her on with it and rang downstairs for his driver to bring the car round. He took her out onto his terrace for a few minutes of fresh air and asked if she was feeling well enough to go home.

He insisted on seeing her home. At her door he said, "Kate, I am sorry that you did not understand my deep affection for you and the fact that I wanted to take care of you. If you did understand it and did not want it, that is something else. I will be at the Byzantium tomorrow, as usual, and if you should decide to stop sometime and have a drink with me, you will be welcome; you must also know that I will never ask you to join me. That is the last thing I would ever do. I am sorry for your unhappiness, Kate. I hope you have some happier plans than living alone here." He reached for her hand, but she pulled back slightly, and he saw nothing but ice in her eyes. He kissed her hand and left.

When undressed and in his bed, the admiral thought how unfortunate it was that this lovely Kate Wells had a sexual problem so great that it destroyed something very special between them. Looking at his watch, he saw that it was 12:15. Not very late by Greek standards. He picked up the telephone and called Glyfada. That night, for the first time since he had known the lady, she was brought to his home in Kolonaki Square. She made passionate love to him, and then told him when they were lying in each other's arms that she was a little nervous being in his home for the first time in all their years together. He kissed her and then made love to her with great tenderness. Before she left the house in the early hours of the morning, she took the active role again with the old admiral, moving him to such a peak of passion that he took her with a wildness he had not known for years.

Kate closed the door and leaned against it with the relief of being in her own home. She heard Constantine's footsteps clicking away from her down the marble hall. When she could hear them no more she switched on the lights in the room, poured herself a glass of water, swallowed two sleeping pills, undressed and fell into bed.

Dozens of gaily colored glossy travel brochures sat on Kate's desk. In the four days since she had received her proposal of marriage, she had calmed down and was organizing herself for her holiday in Egypt and her move to London. Her plan was quite simple. She was waiting for Isabel's return. As soon as she knew that Isabel was there she would write and tell her of her trip to Egypt and give her the date of her arrival in London. She would arrive for a short holiday with Isabel. That is all that Kate would write.

In fact, the plan was to get the least expensive holiday for the shortest period of time in Egypt. Just long enough to have her picture taken at the Pyramids and send postcards, for she really hated the Arabs. Back to Athens to have a few days' rest and close up the flat, and then she would pack as many of her clothes and personal belongings as she could get into two large suitcases and go to London and Isabel's home for her visit.

Isabel would never refuse her a visit, and once there, Kate would never leave. She knew that Isabel would not throw her out, just as she knew that Isabel would never invite her. So it was very simple: Kate would make the first move, and in time Isabel would understand they would live happily ever after. Had they not always had a good time and been happy together?

Kate went about her flat whistling a happy tune, fired by her new scheme. She started sorting out things that she would take with her, thinking about how wonderful a time she and Isabel would have in London. Kate would not push Isabel, but slowly she would make her understand that she did not need that slimy Jap houseboy to run things. He could easily be replaced by a nice English charlady. God knows how much he had taken from Isabel! Well, she would fix his wagon.

It would be made obvious that she was a great asset to have around. There would be no problem about a nice comfortable room for Kate. It would take just a little adjusting on Isabel's part. Her bedroom was much too large for one person: All she would have to do would be to add another bed. The room, after all, was just for sleeping and the two women could be most comfortable sharing a room. The worst thing that could happen would be that Isabel would have to change that ridiculously large bed for a smaller one. As for money, well, naturally Kate would insist on paying for her own bed.

Then the little guest room could be turned into a private room for Kate so she could have a small sitting room of her own. In that way Isabel would have her privacy. Yes, all that she would do in time, but for now, she would be the perfect houseguest for as long as it took Isabel to realize that she was there forever. Kate knew her girls; with all their so-called independence they really needed their mother, and, who knows, maybe in time Kate could become Isabel's assistant? Isabel was not a very good manager and they both knew it.

There had not been another word from Isabel since that one phone call, and that was almost a week ago. She said then that she would return to London in a week's time. Kate thought she should wait till the end of the day before calling London, just to make sure Isabel's flight had arrived.

It was Sunday. Today she would go and meet Alfred and Ava for a coffee at the Piccolo Café in the square. A thought came to Kate. She hoped that Ava and Alfred would not bump into Constantine and invite him to coffee. She had not told them that she had rejected his pro-

posal of marriage. This was the first time she had thought
of Constantine since that night. She had seen him many
times in the square, and although she had greeted him
most cordially, it was no more than that and with no feelings whatsoever. She greeted the butcher, the newspaper-
man and the street cleaner in the same way.

She no longer saw him as the white-haired gentleman
admiral. He was another man who spoke English with a
rotten accent and who wanted to use her to relieve himself. The filthy fool! Well, she told him off. He would not
get hard again for a long time, if ever. She would bet on
that.

The telephone rang—it was Ava. Coffee in the square
was off. She would come to Kate's place in half an hour
and they would have coffee there, just the two of them.

Kate dashed around putting things away. She did not
want Ava to see what was going on. There was much to
tell Ava, but Kate wanted to do it her way and not
through a million questions from her daughter. She
wished that Ava would not always be changing plans. Did
it never occur to her to ask if her mother wanted to have
coffee in or out? *My God,* Kate thought, *what selfish children.*

IV

ISABEL WAS sitting propped up among half a dozen ruby-
red-and-gold silk-embroidered cushions on the large antique bed that was covered in an ancient boukhara,
patterned with pomegranates. High above her head was
a wonderful crown of carved wood, finely gilt and suspended from the ceiling. From the crown canopy of the
bed hung billowy folds of the finest white mosquito netting, draped back and tied with very large gold-and-white
tassels.

She looked around the room, down at the floor, up at
the ceiling and was yet again overwhelmed by the sweet-

ness and sheer beauty of the antique *boiserie* with its painted panels of flowers, birds and little vases. The paint had faded with time, only making the scenes more romantic looking.

Every detail of the room was perfection, and obviously created with great care. The room reflected an atmosphere of sumptuous erotic feminity. Every flower, every scent in the room pricked the senses. The heat, the sunlight, the shadows, only added to its voluptuousness. The mirrors were placed to reflect only more of what was there. It was a room of which dreams are made. Surely it must have been created for a queen, at least a princess and, if not, certainly someone's favorite concubine. Isabel had been floating along with the room, and what had dragged her back into reality was talking to Kate.

It never failed; whenever there was something good happening in Isabel's life, she was never allowed to share it with Kate. How sad that at this time, when Isabel felt something really special, something that had not happened in years—a kind of happiness, a strange feeling of security within herself and with this stranger who had sought her out—Kate would not let her share that feeling with her. Even if this were to last only a day, why would Kate not accept some of Isabel's joy?

Isabel took a mother-of-pearl hand mirror from the side table and looked at her necklace. It was quite incredible that it fit perfectly, high up on her long, slender neck. She put her hand around her necklace, and there was a good feeling coming off it. She thought of Alexis and felt more calm thinking how lovely it would be to get to know this man.

She was waiting for a phone call to go through to Ava. Having placed the call, she now had no idea why. Leaving the bed and going to the dressing table, she picked up the note that Alexis had sent a few minutes before with Gamal: "Get used to it. I have only just begun. Alexis." Oh, but that made her feel good.

Just then the phone rang. It was her call to Ava.

"Hello?"

"Hi, Ava, how are you?"

"I am very well. Why are you calling again? I only spoke to you a few days ago. Why are you wasting the money? You really should write, you know."

"I called because I wanted to talk to you and . . ."

"My God, Isabel, you are extravagant. I mean, it is nice to hear from you, but you are extravagant. You know it is different when I want to call you. After all, I am married to a rich man, but can you afford all these extravagant phone calls?"

"As a matter of fact, I am not paying for this call, Ava. I am calling from Cairo."

"I thought the line was particularly bad. What are you doing in Cairo?"

"I'm here on business, for a week. I will be back in London Monday or Tuesday, if all goes as planned."

"Business, what kind of business could you have there? Will it pay?"

"Well, I really can't answer that at the moment, Ava, since I only arrived an hour or so ago and have not even looked the job over to see if I can do it."

"Oh, no. You mean that you had to pay out all that money just on the possibility of a job? Really, Isabel."

"No, I did not. All expenses are paid. Ava, I did not call you about how I work and money. I simply called to let you know where I am and that it is for that client, the one I told you about when I called you from London."

"What client?"

"Sir Alexis Hyatt."

"*Sir!* You didn't tell me he was a Sir. Well, you know what these titles are, never have any money, and if they do, they hardly part with it easily. I certainly hope he pays you."

"Well, of course he will. As a matter of fact, he asked for my bill before I even made the journey. That is far from the point. . . ."

"Far from the point, really, Isabel, get it in proportion. That is the *only* point."

"If we are going to talk about him, what you should know is that he is turning out to be quite a terrific man."

"Look, Isabel, I don't want you to waste any money telling me all about that. If anything comes out of the job you can write me all about it. Is there anything else you want to tell me?"

"Yes, listen, Ava, I called mother to tell her I was here. She seemed extremely peculiar about it and wanted to come. That is hardly possible since I am here with a client."

"Don't be ridiculous, of course she is not going to go.

She is perfectly happy here. I see to it that she has everything that her heart desires. You never come here and
see what a good life we have arranged for her. I can't
say that I am very fond of the friends that she has taken
up with, except for the Greek admiral, whom I find utterly fascinating; and so why would she want to be with
you? I never seem to have trouble with her and I think
you make much more of what she says than is necessary.
You only look for trouble. Why did you call her in the
first place? You should have just called me."

"I don't know, I simply thought that one of you should
know where I am and honestly, it has been such a good
beginning, I just felt like calling. Who knows why I called.
I suppose . . . oh, I don't know what I suppose. At this
point I don't know why I called at all."

"Well, that's what I mean about extravagant. You
could have sent a letter."

"Yes, Ava, I suppose I could have. But as long as I
didn't and I am on the telephone, how are you? All right?"

"I am fine, just fine. I am going away myself on
Wednesday for three days. We do seem to be busy with
our careers. I wrote to the *Reader's Digest* and gave
them an idea for an article. I received a letter telling me
that if I write it up and send it to them, they may use it. I
am going to do the research for it."

"Ava, that really is very good news for you. What is the
article about?"

"The title tells it. It is called 'A Massachusetts Lady in
a Greek Island Village.' The subtitle is 'Her Effect on
the Village and the People.' "

Isabel thought how extraordinary Ava's vanity was,
but she said, "Well, that sounds interesting. Look, what I
think I'm really calling about is that I am quite overwhelmed by Alexis Hyatt, this job and what has happened since I arrived here. He is quite a remarkable man,
very special. I am feeling really flattered that he asked
me here."

"Now listen, Isabel, I am really not interested in all that.
All those phony rich men that hire you do not interest me.
Nor does the fact that they have to hire you because they
cannot do it for themselves make me respect them. I can
only think it unfortunate that money has to be wasted the
way they do. I certainly can see why you have to accept
them and am happy for you because it gives you a way

to make money, but I truly wish you were more realistic about it all. But we have been through this before, I simply have no enthusiasm for your projects. I find them boring. I have my own work, which is very important. In *my* profession I at least make a contribution."

"What profession?"

"Why, my *writing* profession. I mean for this to be a successful career. After all, this is going to be the second article I will have contributed to the *Reader's Digest*. I know that you look down on it, but you know not everyone is interested in the avant-garde the way you are. At least I reach the bulk of the public, not just a selected few, fawning, arty-farty types. Of course I am happy for you and I wish you the best. Good luck to you. But I can't get that interested and I have to go now anyway.

"As for mother, don't worry about her. I will straighten her out, that is, if there really is a problem, which I doubt. There is no problem here. She is happy, as happy as she will ever be. Everything is just fine. Will you be stopping here on your way back to London?"

"No, Ava, I can't. I came by private jet."

"What do you mean, you went by private jet?"

"I mean that Sir Alexis Hyatt sent his plane for me, and I imagine that he will send me back the same way."

"Well, I never. I mean, if he has that much money I hope that you charge him enough. Everyone knows how vulgar those rich Arabs are. I suppose they want you to do something for them because you know how to handle flashy things with more taste than they do. Yes, I can see where they would like your kind of thing.

"Look, the best of luck to you and write to me when you get back to London. I will be only three days on the island and back here long before you return to London. Listen, I must go now, my telephone bill has been astronomical this last month."

"Ava, I am the one who called. It's not costing you anything."

"Oh, well, I have to go now anyway. Bye."

Isabel took the receiver from her ear and looked at it in wonderment. Ava was impossible, not to mention insensitive. There was no way of getting away from it—Ava had a sickness, a pathological love for nothing but herself.

Isabel was furious with herself yet again for not accepting Ava the way she was. Would she never learn about calling Ava and Kate and trying to share the good things that came into her life with them? This had to be the last time. They wished her well but they deeply resented the good things in her life. Now, at this time when there was something she felt might be the happiness she had been seeking all her life, where were they with their support?

Ava, as always, had kept both eyes on the mirror during the conversation with Isabel. Never moving her eyes from her own reflection, she'd put down the receiver, cutting the call from Cairo. She tilted her head in order to see herself in a better light, and with her forefinger went over her eyebrow a few times, opening her eyes wide.

She had listened to nothing Isabel had been telling her, only what she had been telling Isabel. Therefore she simply had no idea why Isabel had called her, and was feeling pleased with herself in making sure Isabel understood how frivolous she and the people she worked for were.

As Ava played with the tiny wrinkles at the sides of her eyes, she thought about her problem. She could not find any pink pearl buttons in all of Athens, and she needed them for the blouse that she was having made.

Ava had always lived a conventional life and loved it. Convention and security made her feel in control of herself and her destiny. That is why the pink pearl buttons were important. The blouse, its pattern, the pink silk material from Rome, and the pink pearl buttons had all been planned and organized. Any change, such as the buttons, was unthinkable.

Ava did not like Isabel because she was essentially unconventional. Since Ava loved herself and her own lifestyle, she looked upon everything else with a sense of pity. And threat.

For years and years Ava had kept a good cover on her true feelings about Isabel. The fact that she was able to look down on Isabel as some kind of second-rate citizen compared to herself made it easier for her to conceal her true feelings. In her heart, however, Ava carried resentment, jealousy and the desire for complete success of every kind over Isabel.

Ava was humming away as she jogged around the house, doing her chores. She changed her clothes and went shopping for the buttons.

She found them in the eighth shop that she went to in Monastiraki. It was the twenty-fifth that she'd tried since she'd started looking for the buttons.

Ava hurried herself along up Kanaris Street to Kolonaki and then through the side streets home, with a high sense of accomplishment. She was looking forward to the village on Siphnos, where she would go in a few days. She loved the island people and they loved her. They called her a *koukla*, a little doll, and were thrilled because she could speak their language perfectly. Greece was good to Ava; she was always better, happier there than in most places.

Once home, Ava poured herself a drink, sat down in the garden near the pool and waited for her husband to come home for lunch. He was working on a project of some kind with an old school friend. Ava thought to herself that nothing would come of it, of course. It would end as all projects with old school friends always ended. Lots of expensive luncheons and gay dinners filled with reminiscences, but no business.

Alfred was *so* dependent on her. They did everything together and now that she would be gone for three days, she wondered how he would occupy himself. The old school friend, she supposed.

Ava knew that they had a good marriage because they were so much alike in so many ways. Their self-interest and conservatism held them together.

Ava and Alfred's sex life went more or less like the rest of their life: smooth, uninspired, conventional. She treated him more or less like a baby in their everyday life, and he treated her more or less like a brother. It was no different in bed, but it wasn't bad, not bad at all. It was just that it was not great, either.

Ava's vanity told her that he had never had a woman on the side; in fact, however, Alfred liked whores. When separated from Ava he always hired them. Ava never knew it.

Three times in her marriage with Alfred, Ava had tried to step up and out. She managed to reduce the men to devoted slavedom, but when too much time had passed and the question was not popped, they were dropped. And when Ava dropped, she dropped for good.

That was years ago. In the last few years Ava had decided to concentrate on Alfred, her career and those few flirtations that went nowhere and would produce no problems. This plan—and Alfred—seemed to keep her more or less happy and satified.

It was the third try not coming off that cooled her down. Number three was Professor William Warfield, a lecturer at Harvard University. His subject was physics.

Ava and Alfred met Professor Warfield and his wife, Louise, on a transatlantic crossing. Ava did her usual flirtatious routine, and William Warfield fell. While Louise, Alfred and another couple were playing a tournament of bridge across the Atlantic, Ava and William crossed the Atlantic, growing closer together. Their affair lasted for eighteen months. William Warfield was completely enchanted by Ava. His children were married, and his wife and he had drifted apart because his first love was his work. A very rich Bostonian whose ancestors came over on the *Mayflower,* he was certainly able to handle financially a divorce with no trouble whatsoever. His position in the social and academic worlds was certainly so well established that there would be no problem there.

There was the promise of talking to his wife in time, and once Ava had him ninety percent in the bag she and William started a sexual life together. He fucked her as no other man had ever done in her life, giving her orgasm after orgasm, and Ava reveled in it.

They made plans for what they would do when they were married. Dreams of a new future together were their life and their hope. Ava wanted him, and she believed that it would happen. For the first time in her life it was because of sex that she wanted a man. The rest was, of course, important, but it was the sex that was the great new thing for Ava.

She became more sweet, more gentle, more compassionate. She was able to get closer to people. All who saw the change prayed that it would stay that way. How could they know that Ava was merely sexually satisfied for the first time in her life?

There was only one thing wrong: He was not moving fast enough for her to leave Alfred. After all, Ava was not an adulteress; it was to be a new marriage. But things were not moving; something was going wrong.

Finally he told her that he could not bring himself to leave his wife. He was working on something big, and uprooting the family at this time was more than he could handle. Could not they go on the way they were?

No, they could not. A promise broken to Ava was a promise never mended. She left him and this time it was more difficult than ever before because it meant leaving her sexual happiness as well. It was not going to work out, and she would not take the chance of losing the security she had with Alfred for a lifetime of good sex on the side.

The years passed by, and that was the stage that Ava was in now: sexually frustrated, but never acknowledging that any more than the other frustrations in her life.

On Sunday Ava prepared to visit her mother. It had been a lovely week. As usual Ava and Alfred's life had run smoothly, organized and on schedule. She had been to Siphnos, explored the island, stayed in a dismal concrete hotel in Hora. She'd talked to the islanders and visited their private chapels and whitewashed churches, with their domed roofs and dark interiors smelling of beeswax, candles and incense. The churches were sparsely fitted with mediocre icons and an occasional tall, heavy brass candle holder. The gold icons, silver church fittings and best little domed churches were all locked up and waiting for the owners and their families to return to the island for Easter, Christmas and the summer holidays. She talked with the potters who had been born on Siphnos and worked there all their lives, as did their fathers and their fathers before them.

The weather had been bad; the sort of rainy, windy cold that eats into the bones and never lets one get warm, no matter how many sweaters one puts on. The boat never even docked, but merely anchored just outside the small harbor, dumping the ten islanders and Ava into a small caïque, amidst a great deal of shouting, pushing and endless instructions on how to jump from the last step of the rickety ladder hanging on the side of the large ship, into the bobbing wooden boat, with its "putt-putt" motor, belching smoke.

Except for a young boy, eighteen years old, with whom she flirted outrageously and who followed her around like a puppy dog, and an old man of eighty who spoke to her of the days of old, the people turned out to be rather dull.

Ava looked at her watch—it was time to go to Mother's. Alfred was taking his afternoon siesta after their Sunday lunch at a friend's house. Ava, very pleased with her article, had a copy to take to Kate. Come Monday, she would send another copy to London for Isabel. The copy to the *Reader's Digest* was sent out from the main post office, registered, that very morning.

Along with the five pages of the article in the post to New York were two photographs. One of Ava between two young men from the village on Siphnos. They were dancing an old Greek dance, with arms over her shoulders. The men looked dark, swarthy and deeply into their dancing, Ava was staring straight into the camera, head tilted, mouth all smiles. The other photograph was of her in a black leotard standing in the village square with half a dozen children in assorted scruffy clothes, teaching them push-ups in an exercise class. The two photographs were representative of the article: embarrassing and boring.

Anyone who has ever lived in Greece, especially on a Greek island such as Siphnos, should know that there is little that a foreigner can contribute to the community. Still, Ava had gone in like a bulldozer and in three days was sure that she had won them over and made a great contribution to their life-style by organizing gym classes and donating a bicycle to the school, for thirty-six children to fight over.

Ava's article was boring, embarrassing, untrue, dishonest and well written. She was on a lovely high, thinking her new profession was working out just fine.

When Kate's doorbell rang she ran so as not to keep Ava waiting. They greeted one another warmly and were obviously happy to be together, but did not kiss.

Ava handed Kate a shopping bag with two oranges, an apple, two pieces of roast chicken and lettuce. Kate smiled, thanked her and wished she had the courage to tell her not to clean out her refrigerator before she came for a visit. Kate hated having to smile over Ava's garbage.

Kate gave Ava some flowers that she had bought when she went out early in the morning. Ava refused them flatly, saying, "You keep them, Mother. I have flowers from the garden." Kate took them and put them in a vase, setting it on the table in the dining room.

They had a really good time. Ava told her all about her three days on the island, and gave Kate a copy of the article, making her read it while Ava was there so that she could get Kate's reaction. Of course Kate loved it. Why, it almost made Kate want to go to the island, only to be told, "Don't bother. It's not worth it, and anyway, the article covers everything."

Kate's turn came, and she told her daughter about her week. She could not resist telling that she had turned down a proposal of marriage from the Greek admiral. Ava was furious, but then both women had a good laugh when Kate described his sexual ardor.

Ava's good mood was infectious and it put Kate in good form. She thought that maybe it was a good time to put out feelers concerning her plans. She asked if Ava had heard from Isabel. No. Neither had Kate.

Somehow, as was usual, the story of her plans got twisted as she told them. The new version was that Isabel had sent a letter from Egypt inviting Kate to London for a long visit, and before she was to travel to England, Isabel would arrange a cruise up the Nile for her. Ava had no objections. She thought it was about time that Isabel did something nice for Kate and the timing was very good because Ava would be very busy with planning more articles for the *Reader's Digest*.

"When will you go?" Ava asked.

"I don't know, I suppose as soon as I can get things together here, and Isabel is in London," Kate mused.

And so the afternoon went on with the two women talking about their different plans and projects, oblivious to what Isabel was doing or might be doing in the future. Before they parted, one thought of herself as the female Lawrence Durrell, and the other was split between the Queen of the Nile and the Queen Mother of Berkeley Square.

They kissed each other good-bye on the cheek and went their happy ways, waiting for tomorrow and to hear from Isabel.

V

ISABEL FOLLOWED Gamal from the house down some stone steps into the garden, and along a narrow path between giant papyrus plants. The tops were in blossom and looked like great white puffballs two feet in diameter. There were other flowering water plants of strong yellow and white, and as the path wound on, they came to streams on either side, filled with lotus flowers and huge red-and-pink water lilies. There were large, fantail goldfish from China that swam amidst the flowers.

Slowly the path widened and led up to a grass verge. There, sitting in the sunshine among bright red flowers, were André Beshawi, Anthony Moressey, Alexander Spencer-Gordon, Alexis Hyatt and an extremely beautiful woman called, as Isabel soon discovered, Anoushka Malek.

They were sitting around a table laden with flowers and food; a proper English breakfast in a love garden in the middle of Cairo.

Approaching the table, Isabel saw Alexis watching her. He did not smile or make a sign of welcome to her, and she was glad she'd decided against wearing her new necklace in front of all these people. When the other men rose to greet her, Alexis raised himself from his chair, went forward and took her by the hand, seating her on his right. He introduced her to Anoushka, who was completely at ease, charming and sweet. The two women exchanged greetings, taking an instant liking to one another.

There was an atmosphere of camaraderie in the lighthearted conversation between the group at breakfast. Isabel had no sooner sat down than she too was drawn into the party and was swept along with the fun of it all.

When everyone was busy eating or in animated conversation and laughter, Alexis slipped his hand under the table to take Isabel's hand in his. He did not once look at

her but went on talking and laughing with his guests.
Playing with her long, slim fingers, he finally slipped his
fingers between hers and their hands were locked together
in a firm grip.

The warmth and flow that passed between them gave
so much pleasure that without a word the two turned and
looked at one another at the same moment. Their eyes
met and so did their hearts. It lasted only for a short
time before André Beshawi drew Alexis's attention away
with a question. The answer made everyone laugh and
tease André.

No one at the table was aware of what was going on
between Alexis and Isabel. Only Gamal, who was standing behind Alexis's chair, could see them holding hands.
There had not been a personal word between the two
since she had sat down, and Isabel was aware that she
was being treated with great discretion by Alexis in front
of the guests. She was also aware that she and Alexis
Hyatt were together. She could not remember ever having
felt such bliss, such ease, such peace.

It was Anthony Moressey who posed the question of
when he could leave to go and look at the paintings he
was going to work on. It was finally decided among the
group that Anoushka would go with Anthony to the house
on Sharia el Nil, where the paintings were hung. She
would help him to settle in since he would be sleeping
there, and see that he had everything necessary to get
on with his work.

In an hour's time André would take Isabel to the
Muski while Alexander and Alexis had a meeting. They
would all meet at Sharia el Nil for lunch at 2:00 P.M.,
and after that Alexander would fly back to London.

Alexis slowly released his hand from Isabel's, looked at
her and said, "Isabel, that will give me an hour to show
you some of the rooms in the house."

Everyone rose from the table and started wandering
through the gardens. Anoushka went to Isabel, kissed her
on the cheek and told her how much she had enjoyed
meeting her. She hoped they would see a great deal of
each other while Isabel was there. Turning to Alexis she
said, "Alexis, I would like to take Isabel around to meet
some of my friends and show her Cairo. Please, will you
call me when she is free?"

It was a charming gesture. Isabel knew that it was an invitation given with sincerity.

Anoushka and Anthony entered the car that was waiting for them, and smiling, they waved good-bye. André quickly went up the stairs and disappeared somewhere in the palace to make phone calls, promising to meet Isabel in an hour's time in the palace mosque. He told her that he considered it one of the loveliest of the palace buildings and he wanted to see her face when she saw it for the first time. "Oh, Isabel, by the way, you cannot outbid me for it. It is not for sale, so you can not have it."

As he went on, Alexis whispered in her ear, "Yes, you can. I give it to you."

Alexander excused himself, saying he would meet Alexis in an hour's time in the office in Garden City, said good-bye to Isabel and hopped into another waiting car and sped off towards central Cairo.

Isabel and Alexis walked up the stairs together. When they were in the house, Alexis explained that the house was so marvelous that there would be little that he could show her in an hour, that she would have to spend months seeing it all. He had no doubt that she would return many times.

"Since time is short, I will show you only one thing," he began. "I think I will take you to the reception quarters of the women, in the east wing. It is Syrian in design. Its walls and ceiling are covered with wood taken from El Azm Palace in Syria and fitted by Syrian artisans brought to Egypt for the purpose."

They traveled through room after room of such beauty, sensitivity, opulence and purity that Isabel was overwhelmed by the time they arrived at their final destination.

It was indeed a wonder of craftsmanship. The muted colors of red, gold, mauve and rose marvelously set off the walls and ceiling of ancient wood paneling. A square fountain, recessed in the marble-inlaid floor, bubbled slowly. The sound in the stillness of the room was sheer music. Great bronze birds from Persia stood near the fountain as if ready to drink. Bright shafts of sunlight were filtered by the windows to a sweet soft glow the color of amber.

Huge cushions and bolsters covered in exquisitely embroidered material were piled on the floor. Isabel, so sensitive to surroundings, could not help but feel the aura of warmth and sensuality.

She was aware of Alexis watching her and her reaction to it all. Flushed with excitement, she went up to him and kissed him gently. "Oh, Alexis, it is so very beautiful. Thank you."

He touched her cheek and put his arm around her, then walked her to the fountain in the center of the room. There were some very large, two-foot-thick cushions lying at their feet. A shaft of amber light seemed to fall over them like a theater spotlight. They stood there for a few minutes in silence, arms around one another, listening to the music of the fountain.

"Thank you for my wonderful necklace," Isabel whispered. "I love it and wish I had it on for you now." She kissed him again, only this time, when their lips met, their kiss was more passionate than gentle.

They parted a few inches. Alexis began to unbutton her dress, while she, in turn, started to unbutton his shirt and remove his jacket. He knew that she had nothing on under the dress except a pair of bikini panties. He could tell by the way she walked and moved; after all, he had been searching for her from that first moment in Chicago. He knew even then that she was a sensual, passionate woman who had been made for love.

Her dress was completely unbuttoned now and he held it open and wide away from her body. He gazed at her wonderfully large breasts with their pointed nipples, hard now from the passion and excitement aroused between them. He slipped the dress off her shoulders, letting it drop to the floor. With sensitivity and gentleness he caressed her neck, her shoulders, her breasts.

He took her nipples between his fingers and pinched them, then bent his head to take one in his mouth, biting and sucking on it as his tongue went round and round. Only when Isabel let out a whimper of pain, mixed with pleasure, did he withdraw his mouth to the other breast.

He could feel her tremble with excitement as he moved his mouth between her breasts and down over her stomach. When he straightened to kiss her hard and deep her mouth opened wide. He kissed her more deeply and ran his hands down her back and around her narrow waist, then over her hips.

His hands found the two little hooks on the sides of the

bikini pants. He undid them and from the back he slowly
drew the tiny triangle of beige silk away from her crotch,
letting it fall on the floor on top of her dress. His hands
now wandered over the wonderfully full and rounded
cheeks of her ass as he pulled her even closer to him.

He held her like that for a time and then released her,
moving back a few paces to look at her standing in nothing but her high-heeled, open white sandals, with her long
slender toes tipped in bright red nail varnish peeping out.

Isabel's whole body was voluptuous and aroused with
such passion that he almost felt it oozing from her. Her
face was flushed pink, and her eyes seemed larger and
sparkled brightly.

He placed his hands on her pubic hair and ran his fingers through it and then down between her legs. She
moved her legs apart as wide as she could, and now his
fingers were underneath her, playing with her labia.

Isabel took his trousers down, then his shorts. She bent
forward and lifted his foot, removing one leg of the trousers and shorts and then the other. She unlaced his shoes,
took off his socks. She stood back and looked at him. In
the amber light they found each other wonderful.

He had a marvelous body for a man his age, and his
handsome face, with its sensitive and sensuous look, was
not unlike the rest of him. He had a fair amount of hair
on his broad chest, and it was far more gray than that on
his head. He had a great deal of dark brown pubic hair,
and his penis was long and thick. She held it in her
hands, caressed it. It was hard and seemed to throb with
a life of its own.

He was so big that she could not reach her fingers all
around him, and so she moved one hand up along one
side of his penis and followed along at once with the
other hand; that way she encompassed him completely
and continually with her hands.

He was lovely, like the life-size bronze statue of Posei-
don in the museum in Athens. Sometimes, as she moved
her hands over him, she would squeeze, and feel him almost burst out between her fingers as he expanded that
little bit more. She reached underneath him to his testicles. They were large, and she played with them, touching every part of their roundness, stretching and plying
the sack that they lived in with her fingers.

He spread his legs as far apart as he could while standing, and she reached around behind his testicles to his ass. They stood like that, the two of them, and played with each other.

He had brought her to orgasm a few times just by playing with her, and the thrill of touching him brought her close again. It was when she thought of having that large cock inside her while he manipulated her clitoris that she shuddered with a huge wave of orgasm.

At that moment they both fell on top of the large embroidered cushions near the water fountain, and lay in each other's arms. She was everything that he thought she would be and more. He fondled her breasts, spread her legs wide and played with her pubic hair and the outer lips of her vagina. He found the clitoris again and teased it into a series of orgasms. He rubbed her everywhere with the tip of his huge cock until he was at the very edge of pushing into her and then he removed it, turned her over onto her stomach, and worked his fingers and his cock on her anus. Afterwards he turned her over and spread open her cunt to see the wetness covering those inner pink layers.

All the time this was going on she was touching him wherever she could reach. Now that he had her wide open and wet, he knew that all she wanted was him to take her. As much as he desired her, he could wait. He wanted to have her in bed all night when he took her, so that he could go deep inside and linger there, to fill every bit of her slowly and with a pleasure neither one of them had ever known. No, he did not want to take her quickly in this room.

He cradled her in his arm, and with her clitoris between his fingers, he told her that. She begged him to fuck her, and he kissed her deeply and slipped one finger high up inside, then another and then a third. He felt the strong contraction of her cunt around his fingers and then the release of a huge warm rush of wetness as she came again, calling out. He put her gently down on the cushions and lay on his back next to her, watching the water in the fountain as it bubbled up and ran down into the pool.

Isabel rolled over and kissed him. She turned him over and drove him almost to the point of orgasm by playing with his anus and testicles until he begged her to stop. He reminded her that he wanted her in a special way, not just in an erotic wonderful hour while André waited for her down at the mosque. Isabel knew that he was right, and so she pulled herself away from him, got up and bent over to pick up her bikini pants. Her legs were wide apart and when Alexis saw her in that position, naturally erotic and open, he moved his shoulders and head along the floor to look up between her legs. She laughed because now all she could see was his wonderful erection and balls as he lay on the cushions with his legs splayed.

Still straddling him, she dropped to her knees and kissed him on the face, ears, lips, one nipple, biting hard into it, then the other; down on his belly she bit him and then, taking him in both her hands at the very base of his hard throbbing penis, she slipped her mouth over him.

"I could not stand that, Isabel," he moaned, stopping her. "I would never be able to hold back. Please, let us wait."

With that he started to get up, but she pushed him down again and started to dress him. He finished dressing himself as Isabel finished doing up the last button on her dress.

Alexis put his arm around her tenderly and told her that he was in no condition to take her down to André, that he would ring for Gamal to come and show her to her room. He was sure that she wanted to go and have a wash. When she was ready, Gamal would take her to the mosque.

He went to the wall and rang for his servant. Then he returned to take Isabel in his arms until Gamal knocked at the door. He had managed to cover his erection, which had not gone down, but could not do up his trousers. Gamal entered the room but stayed a good distance from his master while Alexis gave him instructions on what to do. He told Isabel that if she became bored or wanted to leave André and go somewhere else, she only had to tell Gamal. With that he picked up her hand and kissed it and they parted.

He remained in the room and looked out of the window into the inner courtyard, waiting to see Isabel cross it and go into another part of the palace. He watched her, all white and shimmering in the hot sunshine, as she moved across the marble paving and up the stairs with Gamal following faithfully a few footsteps behind. Only when the place below was empty and silent did he move from the window and ring the bell again.

A servant arrived and Alexis gave him instructions; after he had left, Alexis made his way slowly to his own rooms, where he undressed and lay on the bed. He lay there for about ten minutes with his eyes closed, resting. He had at last emotionally composed himself about Isabel; he was in love with her and that was that. He had not composed himself sexually and was as hard as when Isabel had slipped her mouth over him. He closed his eyes again and waited.

There was a light tap at the door and it swung open. He did not have to raise himself from the bed to see who it was, for he knew. He had summoned the three beautiful women who entered the room.

They were Doreya, Maryka and Juju, his sexual servants. Doreya had been with him for twelve years, and was the most accomplished masseuse he had ever had. She also was the more interesting sexually. She was brought to him when she was fourteen by a madam in Alexandria who ran the best bordello in Egypt.

She had been a virgin, which was what he wanted, and together Alexis and the madam trained Doreya in erotic love. He hired her for himself and for his sons who were then growing up. He wanted them taught the art of love as his father had taught him. She was used by them and their friends only, and had the right at any time to leave their employ with a week's notice.

The same madam furnished him with Maryka and Juju a few years later, but these girls were less erotic and more pornographic. They were at their best in bizarre sex and extraordinary when on exhibition or in orgies. Maryka and Juju were lesbians.

They were all completely devoted to Alexis and his household, and in all the years that they had lived under his roof, not one of the three women had caused a problem. They and Gamal were his personal servants and cared for his every desire. At all times at least two of the women were ready to service him, and most of the time, all three.

He opened his eyes and thought them very pretty in their pale, flower-printed dresses. The only rule that he had about their garb was that they should look and be clean and pretty at all times, and be naked under their dresses. He wanted to be able to take them when and where he pleased and liked knowing they were always

open and ready for him. He would tell them when he
wanted them to dress in a special way.

He had them take their dresses off and arrange themselves one on each side of him, with the third across the
foot of the bed. He did not care who went where, and no
one was to take an active role. He would fuck each of
them in turn. While Juju was sent to arrange a few lines
of cocaine for Alexis, he had Maryka call Alexander
where he was sure he would still be. The madam answered the telephone and Maryka gave the message to
tell Monsieur Alexander not to hurry. Mr. Alexis would
be an hour late. The madam said she would give the message.

Now all Alexis wanted was to be inside a woman.
Nothing gave him more pleasure than fucking women, in
every way. He had all three of them, going from one to
the other in every position imaginable. Juju begged to be
sodomized and the two women prepared her, for Alexis's
sheer size would have ripped her apart had she not been
helped.

Before he left the bed he had filled each of them with
his sperm. While he had Doreya bathe him he relaxed
and thought of Isabel. From his bath, through the double
doors to his bedroom, he watched Maryka and Juju making love, on the bed. He always liked watching women;
he had Doreya fondle him in the hot soapy water as he
gazed at the girls. Finally he told her that he must dress,
and she became his valet. He kissed the three girls good-
bye and told them to return to their quarters.

Alexis walked very quickly through the palace to his
waiting car. By God, he felt good. He realized as the car
pulled away that all the time he had been inside the three
women, he had fantasized that it was Isabel's cunt. He
thought about Isabel all the way to his office. He did not
take her because he wanted to know her better; he was
clever enough to know that she was a sensitive, passionate
creature and he was taking no chances of losing her.

Alexis meant to be with Isabel spiritually, as well as
sexually. They were together in love, but the reality of life
is something else, and so he intended to work on that.

Alexander was already in the office, waiting for him.
The two men shook hands and sat down.

"Alexis, is nothing sacred in Cairo? However did you
know where I was?" Alexander laughed.

"Well, my friend, it was not difficult to guess." Alexis smiled. "Where else would an English gentleman go in Cairo for a few hours of amusement? I hope that you enjoyed yourself."

"Almost as well as you did, old boy. An hour late, eh? I'm sure *you spent it well*. That is a very good pun, Alexis!"

The two men laughed. Alexis called for two coffees and then said, "Alexander, we have known each other for many years and have helped each other many a time, but never have I been more indebted to you than I am today. I will never be able to thank you enough for the way you handled bringing Isabel to Cairo. I do not think I have to tell you how much this means to me. Is there any way that I can repay you?"

"No, Alexis. This is the first time in many years that I have been able to repay all your kindness to me. I have never known you to want something so much, and I only hope that you are happy. How is it going?"

"Well enough, I think. I am looking forward to knowing her. After all, I know nothing about her and her life except what the museum man told me and that was precious little. Except that she is very good at her job."

"Alexis, I know a great deal more than that, but I think it best if you find it all out your own way. Unless, of course, you want me to tell you what I do know of her."

"But, of course, you must tell me all that you know."

Alexander did, and what Alexis learned only made Isabel more interesting to him. The two men had no business whatsoever to discuss—that had all been contrived to cover up the fact that Alexander was merely to get Isabel Wells to Cairo the fastest way possible and deliver her into Alexis's hands, relaxed and happy. He had done his job admirably, as Alexis had been sure he would. As a gesture of thanks, along with Alexander's first-class Swissair ticket back to London, were the deeds to a large stretch of the most beautiful untouched beach property at Mersa Matruh. There was an old Arab beach house already on it where the two men had spent many a happy time. The sand was like white talcum powder, and the sea the color of the finest aquamarines in the world. Nothing but a few old donkeys and fellahin in tumbled-down houses lived nearby. Alexis owned two miles of the beachfront on either side of Alexander's gift, and three miles of land from the sea back to the main road.

The only condition of the deed was that if Alexander were to sell it, Alexis would buy it back at any price he asked.

How surprised the two men would have been had they known that Isabel had guessed that she was the main object of the exercise. Now, while the two men sat in Alexis's office, pleased with themselves about it all going so well, she was still uncertain about Alexis and what he wanted from her, for he had not said anything about his feelings. She knew, but like all women, she wanted to hear it. Until she did, she would never be sure.

From the first shop the heavy scent of jasmine and tuberose carnation and lily of the valley hung in the air, as Alexis's car carried André and Isabel to the Kan-el-Kalili. Soon they were swallowed up by the Bazaar.

They moved forward between the hawkers, beggars, salesmen and endless mob of craftsmen all working in the street. A mixture of garlic, roast lamb, and spices from all over the East hung in the air. The streets were filled with the fellahin, tourists, shopkeepers, collectors, dealers and vendors of Kan-el-Kalili.

They tried to walk as quickly as possible, so as not to be dragged by the arm, pulled by the dress or tapped on the shoulder by the young runners telling in any number of languages that they knew the best shop for copper, heavily and intricately engraved; inlaid ivory boxes; camel saddles; special erotic ointments; antiques; silver; gold; jewelry; carpets; silks; brocades; of great variety and rarity; elixirs; and fabrics of all kinds.

The Kan-el-Kalili was no different from other bazaars in any of the other Arab countries, Isabel thought. The good things were hidden in back rooms. Those rooms were guarded by heavyset Arab dealers who made their legal money selling the secondhand rubbish to the tourists. But everything changes the moment a real collector such as André Beshawi is spotted. The tourists are all shooed to another end of the small, cluttered shop and the honored visitor is slipped into the back room to view the real treasures. Before people such as André and Isabel are in the Kan-el-Kalili five minutes, word has been passed along to all the dealers.

André told Isabel about the not-so-secret places that you hear about only if you are a Cairene or a friend of one. There is the famous old soothsayer in his eighties who holds an object of the client's in his hand and can tell you all. This old man was born in the Kan-el-Kalili and has never lived or been anywhere else. Perhaps, André thought, that is the source of his power.

Another secret place, not far away, has men standing day and night to protect their establishment and its clients. It is the house called Qalawoon, and is a male bordello. Famous the world over for its twelve- and fourteen-year-old boys made up as women and dressed to tantalize. Dressed in ancient Arab diaphanous dresses and antique jewels, they dance, make love and torture their clients with their charms. Almost beyond imagination. Qalawoon produces everything for its clients short of death . . . but not too far short of it.

The other Qalawoon speciality was the heavy coal-black brutes, famous for their sexual stamina. Oiled and naked, their exhibitions and acts of sexuality drew the most sophisticated, elegant, intellectual, and often depraved, homosexuals of Europe.

Many a famous English baronet, French diplomat, Swedish ambassador, countless princes and even an almost-king have spent days in sexual madness in Qalawoon. But ask anyone in Cairo if they have ever heard of such a place and they will tell you no.

André and Isabel had returned to Alexis's car, but the vehicle was forced to roll along far slower than the mass of people encircling it. For the last five minutes the chauffeur had done nothing but hang his head out of the window and lean on the horn.

They inched along at a snail's pace through the masses of people, pushcarts, wagons, horses, three-wheeled vehicles, bicycles and men bent in half with huge loads on their shoulders. In the time they were there, Isabel saw a man carrying thirty bags of charcoal; a coffin floated through the air until she looked down and saw the pair of bare legs running along under it; half a cow with its carcass towards the sun and a swarm of flies all around it was carried on yet another back.

They were but a few hundred feet from their destination: the entrance to the Muski. André suggested that they get out and walk.

They were the last of the guests to arrive at the Sharia el Nil house. It was a thirty-room stone building, designed by a French architect who had been responsible for many similar to it in the *huitième arrondissement* and on Avenue Foch in Paris.

The iron gates were open to the cobblestoned courtyard. Several cars and their chauffeurs were standing around. The house porter greeted them and spoke to Gamal, who had been with them all the morning, acting as bodyguard to Isabel. Gamal led them through the vast ground-floor hall and up the magnificent winding staircase. André called to her not to be too long, he was starved. He was also in a bad mood because he could not purchase a piece of Pharaonic sculpture for the price he wanted to pay. He went directly to the paneled study where he knew everyone always met before lunch. Isabel went to the powder room to freshen up.

Knowing that they were late, she quickly tended to her makeup, washed her hands and put a brush through her hair. Out of her bag that she had hung on to for dear life all the time she was in the Muski, she took the silver box and removed the necklace that Alexis had given her. She put it on, with the scarab dead center in the front.

Earlier that day, after she had left Alexis and returned to her room, she had bathed quickly and changed into a lemon-yellow raw silk suit. All the time in the Kan-el-Kalili she had kept it buttoned up, but now she opened the jacket, revealing a patterned blouse of pretty pansies in yellow against a brown-and-beige background printed on sheer silk chiffon. The wide oval neckline of the blouse showed a great expanse of neck and chest, almost to her cleavage. She was very pleased with what she saw and only hoped that Alexis would be.

Bending down she adjusted the strap on her high-heeled, open, yellow calfskin sandals, straightened up, took her jacket off and put it around her shoulders. Another check in the mirror and she quickly left the room.

Gamal led her down the stairs and into the study, where she was taken slightly aback by so many people. No one had warned her that lunch at Sharia el Nil was almost always open house for anyone who wanted to come and dine. The greatest surprise of all was the hostess, Alexis's mother. The woman must have once been an extraordinary beauty, for even now the eighty-two-year-old Sama Genaina Hyatt was exquisite.

Sama was gracious and hospitable to everyone, and

when all went into the dining room, she sat Isabel across from her with Alexis on her right and an old friend of Alexis's, Magdi Biwa, on her left. Sama had on her right a Saudi Arabian price who had been an admirer of hers for forty years and on her left the Italian ambassador.

The round table when fully laid sat twenty people. To-day, in addition to those who had been at Alexis's break-fast party, there were two of Sama's grandchildren, the Italian ambassador's wife and three Cairene beauties. Later Isabel would find out that two of those women had been Alexis's mistresses on and off for years.

Isabel was thinking about the luncheon as she rode in one of Alexis's Rollses back to Roda Island and the palace. Alone for the first time since she and Alexis had been to-gether, there was time to collect her thoughts about all that was happening to her in Cairo. Alexis had told her that he would meet her at six o'clock, and they would have a few hours to talk before the guests invited for din-ner arrived.

During lunch he had been charming and attentive, but no more so than to any of the other women at the table. In any event she had been kept busy by Magdi, Sama and the Saudi admirer, Abduhl. Still, when she had sat down in the car, Alexis had slipped in next to her, kissed her hand and said, "It was kind of you to wear the neck-lace. It is the scarab of Tutankhamen, part of the richest treasure ever found in Egypt—that is, until I found you. It gives me so much pleasure to see you wearing it. Go and sleep. I will stay here with my mother and have a small siesta, a meeting with the prime minister and then be with you as soon as possible."

He touched her cheek and then left the car. He waved as her Rolls left the courtyard.

The traffic was down to a trickle since it was the middle of the siesta hour. Isabel kept thinking about the people at lunch. She was happy that at last someone had asked her what she was doing in Egypt. She explained that she was there consulting with Sir Alexis about the possibility of doing some work with him. That seemed to take some pressure off.

If anyone suspected that there was anything between her and Alexis, she now thought that their suspicions were diverted.

The ringing telephone pulled Isabel out of a deep sleep. It was Alexis.

"Hello. Did you have a good sleep?"

"Oh, yes, lovely."

"Were you sleeping when the telephone rang?"

"Yes."

"Were you having sweet dreams?"

"No, I was not having any kind of dream. It seems to me that my dreams are when I am awake since I met you."

"Oh, that is nice, very nice." He chuckled.

"Where are you?" Isabel asked.

"I am just going to leave the prime minister's office. Why don't you bathe and dress, and we will walk in the garden and have tea together, just the two of us."

"Oh, I would like that, Alexis. Will I have time later to change for dinner?"

"Yes, just put something on for the two of us. We will not be bothered with other people until half past eight or nine at the earliest."

"That will be lovely."

"You know, Isabel, when I hear you so soft and warm and know that you are lying in that bed, I can hardly believe it is true."

"Alexis, you are not the only one!" They both laughed.

"Now listen, Isabel. You are not to do anything. Ring for Gamal and tell him that you want to bathe. He knows what to do, and when it is prepared for you, he will call you."

"I can manage a bath by myself, Alexis."

"I know that, but I want you not to have to manage. All right, my dear?"

"Yes, Alexis," Isabel said obediently, smiling to herself.

"I will be home in forty-five minutes, and he will bring you to me in my sitting room when you are ready. Goodbye, my dear."

Isabel did as she was told and a few minutes later two young girls entered the room. They introduced themselves as Maryka and Juju, and Isabel thought them very sweet and pretty. One went to the window and drew the shutters open and the draperies back, while the other turned the covers down and helped Isabel out of bed.

One went to the bathroom and started to run the bath;

the other sat Isabel at her dressing table to clean her face.
Isabel giggled at the luxury of it all. So this is what Eliza-
beth Arden tried to achieve with her lacquered red doors
around the Western world. Juju pinned her hair up and
tied a scarf around it very tightly, then cleansed and massaged her face perfectly. Isabel almost dozed off again,
she was so relaxed, but just at that moment Juju bent forward and said softly, "Madam, come, your bath," squeezing Isabel gently by the shoulders.

She left the dressing table and went into the bath,
thanking the young girls and dismissing them. They
laughed and said that she did not understand: They were
there to bathe her. Isabel was delighted. She had had two
bath ladies in Morocco when she stayed there and had
never felt cleaner and more toned-up in her whole life.

Maryka opened Isabel's kimono and took it away. Isabel felt embarrassed in front of the two girls and quickly
got into the bath. As it was a marble tub in the middle of
the grand bathroom, the girls were able to get on either
side of her.

The two washed Isabel with loofahs and pumice stones,
scented oils and foaming hot water. She lay there in the
tub, her head resting on a pillow as Maryka worked on
the left side of her body and Juju on the right. They massaged and washed her arms, armpits, the back of her
neck and her breasts, releasing every fraction of tension.
She was so relaxed that she felt as if she were floating in
the bathtub. Finally Juju said it was getting late and they
must dry her, for she must be ready for Alexis when he
arrived.

Isabel stood up, and when she did, Maryka sponged off
the oils and foam from the bath with fresh, clear, lukewarm water. Then, with the flat of her hand, in strong
swift movements, she wiped away the water. As she
worked her way down the front of Isabel's body, Juju did
the same down the back. After Maryka squeezed the water from Isabel's pubic hair, she slipped her hands between Isabel's legs, and with a very soft flannel washed
high up into her vagina. For an instant Isabel panicked,
but the girl used such tact and subtlety that a fuss could
hardly be made. As Maryka worked on the front of Isabel's thighs, Juju performed the same act on Isabel's anus.

Finally the two women had finished working between
her toes and asked Isabel to step out of the tub so that

they could towel-dry her. She was then dusted with powder and was as clean as she would ever be in her life. The
girls helped her into her dressing gown after they had
rubbed oils of tuberose, jasmine and gardenia into her
body. Isabel thanked them both and told them that she
would prefer to dress herself. They understood and were
very sweet, touching her tenderly, as they took down her
hair and brushed it out. While Maryka followed Isabel
into the bedroom, Juju disappeared, to return with an
enormous white dress box. In very bad English, she said,
"Sir Alexis makes you one gift. One surprise, please to
put on."

Isabel ran to the bed where Juju had placed the box.
She was terribly excited over Alexis's gift. She had been
with him for only a few hours, but there was no question
that whatever he chose would be sublime.

She ploughed through the tissue paper as the two girls
stood there giggling. She gasped as she pulled out a very
pale, blue-gray, silk velvet galabia completely embroidered
with tiny bumblebees in pure gold thread. The collar and
the opening, which went down as far as the waist, were
thick with gold embroidery and small buttons the size of a
pea, each in the shape of a bumblebee.

Isabel thought it exquisite, and the girls helped her into
it, arranging it as they thought it should hang. The collar
and plunging neckline stood away from her body ever so
slightly, framing her face and breasts. It had long, wide
sleeves that were just the right length, and when she was
looking at herself in the long mirror, she saw pinned between her left elbow and cuff a diamond bumblebee set
on a spring attached to the pin—when she walked it
moved as if it were buzzing or flying.

The girls watched her, and when she turned around to
show it to them, Juju reached into the plunging neckline
of the galabia and touched Isabel's breasts, and kissed
one.

Isabel was nonplussed to say the least. It was all too
heady. They smiled and said good-bye, indicating to her
that if they were wanted all she had to do was tell Gamal.
She thanked them and they left. It was only after she was
settled at her dressing table applying her makeup that she
realized the girls must have been lesbians. Alexis had obviously told them what to do with her.

She put her makeup on perfectly. Very excited, she de-

cided to stretch out on the bed again for a few minutes before she would tell Gamal she was ready to be taken to
Alexis.

She had always been a passionate sexual creature, and
when she had first seen Alexis in that nightclub she had
recognized that he was too. Now that she knew that he
was a very erotic man who intended to lift her to the most
sublime heights, she was overpowered with happiness and
only waited to be taken.

Oh, God, the girls had aroused her again. When she
thought of the bath and how they had treated her body,
and how Alexis had arranged it all, her senses melted with
desire.

There was a knock at the door and Gamal came in. Isabel stood up, and a broad smile spread across his face.
She smiled back and followed him.

Isabel stood in the courtyard of the palace and waved
good-bye to Alexis as his car pulled away. She watched it
disappear down the drive and then turned to go into the
house.

Contentment, joy, admiration and respect all seemed to
be mixed within her. She could hardly believe that at this
time in her life she was lucky enough to find someone like
Alexis Hyatt.

Gamal, who had been discreetly standing in the shadows of the garden, stepped forward and opened the door
for her. He started to lead her back to her quarters, but
she stopped him and told him she could find her own way.
Would he bring her another cup of coffee?

She went through her room and out onto the balcony
that overlooked the love garden. She sat down and went
over in her mind what had been one of the most wonderful nights of her life.

The day before, when Gamal had taken Isabel to Alexis's rooms, she'd met another side of Alexis. He was
dressed in a fine camel hair galabia, and he looked far
more Egyptian than she had realized before. He was very
flattering about how she looked in the magnificent dress
that he had given her. They kissed, and arm in arm, wandered through the palace to the gardens.

She'd tried as best she could to express how overwhelmed she was by his generosity.

He'd kissed her and replied, "Oh, I like it! It gives me

such pleasure to spoil you, give you things, to surprise you, overwhelm you. Yes. I certainly do like that. I hope I *do* spoil you so that you will never be satisfied by any other than me!" He went on to tell her about the dress and the piece of jewelry pinned on its sleeve. How, when he heard she was coming, he was so overjoyed that he went out on a shopping spree.

He was such a romantic, sensitive man that at one point as they were walking through the garden, he'd made her stand still and then, walking a few yards away, asked her to come forward so he could look at her and how she moved. He watched her and when she was up close to him, she kissed him again with thanks.

She gazed out over the balcony, slowly sipping her coffee, and saw the very top of the love pavilion, off in the middle of the garden. She closed her eyes and tried to conjure back what had happened when they'd gone into the pavilion.

She saw again the octagon-shaped building with its veranda all around. All the mushrabiya doors opened out, making it look like a great ceremonial umbrella standing in the most luscious of tropical gardens. The floor was covered in layers of Oriental carpets, and on top of them were great mattresses covered in antique embroideries from Afghanistan. Dozens and dozens of small cushions in jewellike colors were scattered everywhere. The seating was arranged in the same octagonal shape of the pavilion, with places to walk through to the center. There were small ivory tables in front of each of the seating sections. From the center of the ceiling hung an enormous birdcage filled with white and yellow doves whose murmuring filled the air. Off a small section of wall between the open doors were fountains of marble in the shape of flowers that spilled forth water into small basins with lotus blossoms floating in them. Everywhere were old copper containers holding masses of tulips and hyacinths that were out of season everywhere in the world but here. They were grown in the hothouses continually, were always in the pavilion, and had been for as long as anyone could remember.

One of the small tables was filled with fruit, little plates and silver forks, tiny cups and saucers and a pyramid of glazed cakes. A narghile, or water pipe, stood close by, and there was the scent of Egyptian jasmine, like no other in the world.

The two of them had lain down on a mattress against a big fat bolster, arranging a mass of cushions behind them so that they were in a comfortable half-lying, half-sitting position. Gamal appeared to pour coffee for them, adjust the charcoal in the narghile and place it at their feet. He passed the pipe to Alexis first, who drew deeply on it and passed it to Isabel. Hashish—and smoked through the narghile, it was marvelous, lifting them high with a feeling of breathing it instead of smoking it.

The two of them had puffed away, talking their heads and hearts out to one another. Never had Isabel felt so close to a man or, for that matter, that a man was so close to her.

They'd talked about their personal lives, their politics, their souls; her insecurities, his diplomatic career, her work, why she had never married, his divorce. They spoke about travel, about literature and poetry; he told her about how much he loved his sons, she told him about her mother and sister.

They'd told one another about their hopes, what they thought life meant to them. Occasionally they touched each other and kissed, making love with their heads and their hearts as they fondled each other's bodies.

She remembered being terribly high, floating somewhere between the earth and heaven. They'd watched the sun go down. First everything seemed to go pink, then mauve, and suddenly the sun went out. There is no sunset in Egypt as there is in the West. One minute it is there and the next it has gone.

Gamal had continually gone back and forth with fresh coals and hashish, and just before the room had gone dark with night, he'd arrived with candles lit in antique copper lanterns of the sort used in the Bedouin tents in the desert. The lanterns were drum-shaped and made with sections of wavy glass. They had flat bottoms, domed tops and gave off a soft pink glow.

They'd held each other close, and talked on and on, forgetting about time and the world. Gamal arrived and whispered something to Alexis, then took away the narghile. Isabel saw him disappear out onto the veranda to be swallowed up by the night.

Alexis had run his hand over her hair, then kissed her

on the lips, then raised her bumblebee dress to kiss her on the stomach. He drew her dress down with a reluctant sigh, and said, "Isabel, it is time to go. We must change for dinner; our guests will be here very soon. You take your time, it does not take me long to dress."

She remembered him pulling her up off the cushions and holding her close, and she remembered kissing him with childish pecks all over his face and neck.

Holding hands they had followed Gamal, who had led the way with a lantern through the dark garden to a side entrance of the house. Alexis himself took Isabel to her room, where he removed her dress, took her in his arms, kissed her deeply and with a great deal of passion and then left.

Isabel opened her eyes now and looked out again at the top of the little pavilion. She thought about him, so bright and soulful, so intelligent and sure.

She remembered what he had said about Egypt, the Egyptian people, and about himself. They were a good-natured people, friendly and accommodating. The softest of the Arab peoples, he'd told her. Egyptians were "body" people; they loved to slap, hug, kiss, push, shove and touch each other a great deal. They were openly warm and affectionate and indulgent.

Alexis had said that she must understand that he was half-Coptic and had lived a good part of his life in the Western world. Having been educated in France and later in England, he had taken up a great many English ways. He restrained the Egyptian ways he felt when dealing with the outside world, but he was still that "body" person, and when alone together, he wanted always to be able to touch her in every way imaginable. The ultimate for him was coming inside a woman.

She wondered if she had been foolish in telling him that she wanted to make love to him too, in the same way. That there was nothing that she did not want to do with or to him sexually. She'd confessed that she was drawn to him like a magnet and had an enormous desire to give him pleasure and make him happy. Of course she had not been foolish to tell him that, because she remembered how he'd held her in his arms, almost sobbing, and said yes, that is how it should be . . . that was what he'd wanted from her since he first saw her in Chicago.

Isabel rang for Gamal and asked him to bring more

coffee. Then she went to the cupboard in the bedroom and took out the bumblebee dress. She held it up to herself and looked in the long mother-of-pearl mirror set in the wall. Although it was of silk, velvet and gold, there was something ethereal about it. She was sure that it was in the color, cut, and the placement of the golden bees.

She returned it to the cupboard, went to the dressing table and picked up the diamond bumblebee. She had a cream-colored fine wool dress on with balloon sleeves that were tight at the wrist. Over it she wore a beige suede gilet. She pinned the bumblebee on the collar of the dress, but took it off again. She knew that it was not just a little diamond bumblebee to be worn on a tour of Cairo, for the diamonds that made up the body of the bee were much larger than she had first realized.

Any time now Anoushka would come and fetch her. The two women were going on a tour of Cairo. Plans had been made the night before for Alexis to meet up with them at the mosque of Ahmed Ibn Tulun at noon. His mother had invited them both to lunch at her house, and after that they would spend the rest of the day together going through some of his collection and museums.

There was to be a large dinner party at Sharia el Nil that evening. Alexis hoped that she would enjoy it. It had been planned weeks ago. The prime minister would be there, and the president. He would see that she was taken care of and introduced to people who would amuse her. They would reside at Sharia for the rest of her stay in Cairo. There was no need to pack anything, Gamal would take care of all that. Isabel could hardly believe that she would leave this house and most probably never return.

She went to the dressing table and placed the bumblebee in her jewel case in exchange for a pair of large, pure gold loops with lion's heads. They rested on the ear lobes, dated from 200 B.C. and were Phoenician. On her wrists she slipped a pair of Cartier bangles and around her neck half a dozen handmade pure gold chains. She checked herself in the mirror and knew that she looked just right for lunch, and Alexis.

As much as she wanted to see Cairo with Anoushka, she could only think of being with Alexis. She took the coffee cup from Gamal and went back out onto the balcony to try and pull together the pieces that had made up the rest of the previous evening. She did not ever want to forget it.

She remembered how after Alexis had left her standing naked in the room, she'd tried to think of getting dressed but was too stoned. She managed to get into her kimono and rang for Gamal, telling him she needed help. He saw that she was terribly high and returned shortly with Doreya, and a large glass goblet on a silver tray. It was coconut milk, the juice of the ishta and mango, and honey. He told Isabel to drink it down and she would be fine.

After the delicious drink, she stretched out on the bed for a few minutes while Doreya went to the wardrobe to select the dress that she would wear.

Soon the drink had taken effect, and she'd been able to coordinate her clothes and makeup. With the help of Doreya she dressed for dinner: a black silk jersey Jean Muir dress with nothing underneath it. Isabel decided that as long as she would be in Egypt she would not even wear her bikini underpants. She wanted to be open and ready for Alexis always.

The dress could not have been more elegant, or more sensual. She slipped her feet into black-satin, high-heeled sandals. The dress had a plunging V-shaped neckline that showed a small amount of the swell of her breasts—just enough to be chic, but not vulgar. She picked up the bumblebee and pinned it on the soft material as close to her nipple as possible. It sparkled against the black dress. She shook herself, and as her breasts moved, the little bumblebee shivered. Both she and Doreya laughed, and then the final touches went on her face. By the time she arrived at the party she was miraculously straight.

It had been a small dinner party and she'd been grateful for that. A man named Michael, a UNESCO archaeologist, was on her right, Alexis on her left. Most of her evening at the dinner table was spent talking to Michael, who was half-French and half-American, and charming. He acted as a part-time curator of the palace museum for Alexis and advised on some of the Hyatt traveling exhibitions of Egyptian, Islamic and contemporary art and artifacts.

From Michael, Isabel learned a great deal about the vast amount of work Alexis was involved in for the Arab world. She was fascinated to hear about it all, as well as Michael's work, which in itself was something special.

At one point during the dinner, Michael was talking to a woman in Arabic, and Alexis was busy with a guest on the other side of him. Isabel sat there watching them all and suddenly realized that the woman at the end of the table, whose name was Hamida, was acting as hostess. Hamida had been at lunch that day as well. For a fleeting moment she wondered just how much Hamida meant in Alexis's life but forced herself to let the thought drop.

Ruefully, Isabel reminded herself about her proclivity for finding an excuse to mess up something going well for her. She thought of Ava, who would say, "Face the reality, you are just a week's diversion"; Kate, who would have said, "Forget him, what do you want with a man, to fetch and carry for him? Get what you can from him and get back to reality. By the way, if you tried to ring me the other day and did not find me, it was because I was in the hospital. Thought I was having a heart attack, but it was indigestion." Instantly Isabel felt depressed.

Her thoughts were interrupted by Alexis, who took her hand under the table and put it between his legs. He flattened her hand out and pressed it against his erection, making her rub it from its base to its tip.

Even through the cloth of his trousers Isabel could feel him grow larger and longer at her touch. Her face went pink with embarrassment, and afraid that someone was watching, she tried gently to pull her hand away without making a fuss. It was impossible. He held her wrist tightly, and continued to move her hand up and down slowly while continuing his discussion with Sama on his left. He never once looked at Isabel during the time he kept her hand moving.

It seemed an interminable time before the servants came around to pick up the first-course dishes. Even then he was so naughty that he held her hand until the servant actually came between them to pick up her dish. Only then did he release her, but not until he had forced her to caress the head of his penis. She quickly took both her hands and folded them together on the table. He looked at her at last and smiled.

"Isabel, you look a bit flushed. Are you all right?"

She remembered that he was still very, very high and

did not know that she was down by now, or did he? He seemed to know everything.

"You are a cad," Isabel answered and then softly continued. "If you do that to me again, I will bend down into your lap in front of all these people and take you in my mouth, I promise it."

Alexis roared with laughter. Someone asked what the joke was and he said, "You have all heard it at some time or other." He then went into roars of laughter again.

Infuriated, Isabel addressed the guest, "I don't mind telling you."

"No, we must keep them in suspense," Alexis broke in.

"Oh, please, Alexis, let me tell them," she teased mercilessly, but when she saw a strange look on his face, she knew it was time to stop and did, changing the subject by telling a very funny joke. Everyone laughed.

Alexis kissed her hand, loudly saying, "Well done, Isabel." Then, in a whisper, "You are wonderful. I am so happy you are here."

Isabel looked deep into his eyes. She knew he meant it.

The evening went on pleasantly, but the people seemed to stay forever. Finally Isabel excused herself, saying that yes, she would be ready for Anoushka at nine in the morning, but would have to go to bed now. She went to her room hoping everyone would get the hint and go home. She wanted Alexis to take her. Oh, how she wanted him to take her. It worried her because she was sure that he knew it.

She lay waiting now in bed in her nightgown. An hour and a half passed and he had not appeared. More time passed and at last the phone rang. She grabbed for it at once. It was Alexis. Could he come up? Oh, yes, please, she answered, adding a request that he bring a joint.

He entered the room dressed in a galabia. Again she was surprised at how Egyptian he looked. He had an ivory box with him. Gamal followed behind with an ice bucket, holding a silver tray with a bottle of wine and two ruby-colored crystal glasses on it.

Isabel quickly pulled the covers up when she saw Gamal enter the room. Alexis folded the covers down as far as her waist and told her, "Do not be foolish. Gamal sees only the right things." To Gamal he said something in Arabic and the two men laughed lightly.

She sat there in her French, handmade, peach-colored

silk nightgown. She was covered well enough she knew, but she still felt exposed, and a little annoyed with Alexis.

Gamal was busy with his back to them, opening the bottle of wine. Alexis pulled the galabia off over his head and dropped it to the floor. He slipped into the bed and pulled Isabel close to him, tucking the covers tight all around. Gamal went to the bed, adjusted the pillows behind their backs and brought them the wine. They touched glasses and he said, *"Bukra fil mishmish."* Isabel asked him what it meant.

"Bukra means tomorrow," Alexis said. "It is the tomorrow of the future. It has no time limit. *Bukra fil mishmish* —tomorrow when the apricots bloom—is a special Egyptian tomorrow stretching to infinity."

Isabel relaxed, thinking, *I can adjust to all this. I will not fight it. I am happy and am going to stay this way.* She touched her glass to Alexis's and said, *"Bukra fil mishmish."*

They both drained their glasses. The wine was ambrosia, like no wine she had ever tasted in her life. Alexis said he had selected it himself. It was a bottle given to his father by King Farouk. He called Gamal and they passed their glasses to him.

Alexis turned to Isabel and said, "Do you know that is the first thing I have heard you say in Arabic, and you said it perfectly."

Alexis put his arms around her, and she snuggled up tight next to his naked body. He kissed her on the hair, and with his finger went over the shape of each of her eyebrows, then drew it down the straight of her nose, to follow the outline of her lips. He was very serious as he kissed her lightly, showing such tenderness that Isabel melted. Still looking at her, he reached to the table next to him for the ivory box.

Alexis called Gamal over. He took two cigarettes out of the box, giving one to Isabel, and keeping one for himself. Gamal bent forward and lit them. Then Alexis said something in Arabic to Gamal, who picked up the bucket with the wine in it and started to leave the room.

Alexis looked at Isabel and said, "I have given instructions to Gamal to take the bottle with the remainder of the wine up to the fountain, in the room where we were together for the first time. He will pour it in the fountain, then break the bottle and bury the pieces in the garden near the pavilion. I hope you do not think it too romantic or strange, but that glass of wine was for us for once and always, and would never taste the same again. I have ordered the bottle broken because I never want anyone to drink from it again."

Isabel was overcome with emotion and said nothing. She simply bent forward and kissed him deeply. She then kissed his nipples lightly, resting her head on his chest.

They were lying there quietly smoking joints when Gamal came in. He went to one of the cupboards hidden behind the paneling, pushed a button, and there was soft music. Returning to Isabel and Alexis, he put down a cigarette lighter, said goodnight and left the room.

The sounds of Stan Getz and Charlie "Bird" Parker filled the room and their heads. They smoked a great deal. At one point he selected more music, and when he returned to her, he turned the covers down all the way to the end of the bed. He gazed at her in her sensuous nightdress and got onto the bed next to her. On his knees, with his legs tucked under him, he bent forward and kissed her hair, her lips, her breasts. Then, with both his hands, and in one stroke, he ripped her nightdress apart.

When she protested he told her to be quiet. He sat there looking at her, and ran his hands all over her body. He slipped what was left of her nightdress off her, and threw it on the floor. He held her close in his arms again while they listened to the music and lit up two more joints.

They spent the rest of the night that way, listening to music, and using their hands and mouths over each other's bodies, more tenderly and lovingly than passionately. Some time during the early hours of the morning they fell asleep together, like two young innocents. They still had not fucked. It did not seem to be so important because they were making love to each other with their heads and hearts. Now it was the next morning, at nine, and Gamal appeared to say Madame Malek had arrived and was waiting downstairs for her. Dressed and ready, Isabel picked up her handbag, slung it on her shoulder and followed him down to the car.

Anoushka was delightful. She gossiped continually about everyone and explained to Isabel that it was not just the women in Egypt who gossiped. The men were marvelous at it too. It was a great part of the social life of

Cairo, but not as great a part as love affairs. Everyone had them, no one was faithful, but the men and women alike were very clever in their sex lives and rarely was there a tragedy.

Whatever that means, Isabel thought.

Anoushka told her a little bit about herself. She was thirty-five years old, and Saudi Arabian. Her mother was the third wife of a high-ranking royal Saudi prince. She was his favorite wife and he denied her hardly anything. When Anoushka was born, she was named after a Russian princess who was a friend of her mother's and the concubine of her uncle.

Anoushka herself was married to a minister in the Saudi government who was a royal Saudi prince as well. She had five sons, all in boarding schools all over the world. Her husband was at the moment in Saudi, and arriving today for the party. She would return with him in a few days.

"Isabel, you must promise to come and visit. Of course, there, if one were found an adulteress, one would be beheaded, or actually stoned to death," she giggled. "But, darling, I am my husband's favorite and am very discreet in all that I do. Rules, my dear—even in gossip and affairs there are rules."

On and on she went as they were driven by her chauffeur and protected by her bodyguard, who never left her side. Anoushka was an excellent tour guide, obviously well educated. It was one wonderful experience after another. There was a quick visit to the Pharaonic Museum, but only to see the Tutankhamen rooms, because Alexis had told Anoushka that he would take Isabel there himself. "You know, Alexis is building a new wing now for them?" Next was the Coptic church and museum. Isabel fell in love with Coptic art yet again. As they walked through the City of the Dead she felt strange things: She knew some of the dead were walking with her. The sun was high now, and it was nearly noon as they walked through the streets and miniature buildings and palaces, through the fine sand everywhere and the dust that it raised. She looked up and saw a white moon as well as the sun, in a pale, yellow sky. Half a dozen little children followed them through the huge burial ground. They were from the poorest of the families who had nowhere else to live, and so made makeshift dwellings among the tombs of the caliphs, their mosques and mausoleums.

Isabel would have liked to stay longer, but Anoushka said, "Enough, Isabel, Alexis will be angry if we are too late."

The two women waited in the car, close to the entrance of the mosque, for Alexis to arrive. When the plum-colored Rolls pulled up, Isabel started to get out to go and meet him, but was held back by Anoushka. She sweetly adjusted a few of Isabel's hairs that were out of place, and arranged her collar as well, saying, "Isabel, don't be too Western. Wait for him to come for you. You know it is always better that way. I am your friend and I want you to come here to Egypt many times."

Isabel understood. Gratefully, she smiled at Anoushka and thanked her for everything. That was the closest the two women ever came to talking about Alexis and Isabel.

As Alexis reached the car door the driver jumped out and opened it. Alexis helped Isabel out, asking the two women if they had had a good morning and inviting Anoushka to lunch with them. She declined, saying that she had to go to the hairdresser because she wanted to look ravishing for her husband and the party that evening.

They went into the mosque of Ahmed Ibn Tulun. The keeper of the mosque came forward and greeted Alexis, calling him Hyatt Bey. They spoke in Arabic; two more assistants of the keeper came along and bowed low to Alexis.

For a long time Isabel had heard about Ibn Tulun, and she had seen many fine photographs of it. Its simplicity and perfect symmetry made it one of the most beautiful buildings in the world. The mosque represented the purest of Islamic architecture, and it was this purity that Isabel loved so much in design. At some point she forgot about herself and Alexis, and was transposed and as high as if she were on hashish.

Alexis noticed her fascination and smiled. "Ah, my dear, what a woman you are. You understand everything."

Isabel heard him, but then did not: She was only half there, so grateful was she to be alive and able to experience everything. Alexis wandered away from her, wanting to give her the privilege of experiencing it all on her own.

They met again at the far end of the mosque and walked through it once more together to the entrance where they had come in.

After that they drove to the Citadel and the Muhammad Ali mosque. They spoke about where she had been, what she had seen. She asked about his morning and all he said was that the best part had only started when they met.

The Citadel was on the slope of the Muqatta Hills and offered a breathtaking view of Cairo, the Nile, and in the far distance, her first sight of the Pyramids of Giza. The mosque, with its domed cupola and graceful minarets, was an extraordinary example of Islamic architecture. Its walls, both inside and out, were covered with alabaster.

They saw the tomb of Muhammad Ali, which was a mausoleum set in one corner of the mosque. Alexis told her that the Ayubites, the family founded by Saladin, who held Egypt for eighty years, had embellished Cairo with outstanding architecture.

"You see, working for my country is a big part of my life," Alexis explained. "My mother was an Ayubite, with Muhammad Ali a close relation. You must talk to my mother about her family. They were magnificent and have passed down to us a great responsibility."

Later Isabel wondered how she could tell him her father was a Jew from Bialystok, and decided not to.

After the Citadel they went to his mother's for lunch. Sama Hyatt's house was a two-story miniature *chateau* at the far end of the huge garden of the Sharia el Nil estate where Alexis had his home. Made of the same stone as the main house, it was a little jewel. It reminded Isabel of a small Malmaison. But once inside it was a Turkish sultan's palace. There were photographs, *objets d'art*, paintings, and carpets of extraordinary quality and beauty, each with its own history. The two women had a wonderful time talking about it all.

Isabel was enchanted by Madame Hyatt and could not wait for the time when she might be invited again. She told her she hoped she would see her that evening.

Madame Hyatt explained that she was in semiretirement. She went out rarely, but received people, and Isabel was welcome to come again. Alexis would arrange it. They said good-bye, and Alexis and Isabel walked back to the main house. They had chatted and stayed through the siesta hour and Alexis made it very clear that he was concerned that Isabel should not be too tired to enjoy the evening.

He took her up and showed her the rooms that she would stay in at the Sharia el Nil house. They were on the first floor and magnificent, but very different from the house on Roda Island. The house and garden reminded Isabel of the Rothschild house on the rue du Circe in Paris.

The bedroom that Alexis brought her to was painted pure white. The Aubusson carpet was in subtle shades of apricot, peach, beige, mauve and the palest of yellows. There were bergères French commodes and huge gilded mirrors that would have made poor old Cecil Davenport envious.

In the center of the room was a large, round, marble-top table on which rested a magnificent ancient Persian ceramic bowl, vibrant in pattern as well as color, filled with yellow lilies. There were a pair of matching chaise longues in the provincial style: walnut with simple carving, and caning. The cushions on them, big and feather-soft, were covered in silk Bokhara embroidery in a deep pomegranate color. Draperies of heavy, buttercup-yellow silk were tied back, revealing the sheerest of white silk undercurtains. The bed—a large four-poster with canopy—had its original hangings and bedcover of embroidered birds on the background material of the same yellow silk.

She saw that the dressing table already had her things on it, and her kimono was draped prettily across the bed. Alexis took her by the hand to show her the yellow-marble bathroom with its sunken bath. Then, leading her back across the bedroom, he opened a large pair of doors that led into a sitting room decorated in seventeenth-century French *boiserie*.

"Isabel, we will share this sitting room while you are here," he said, as he walked her quickly through the room.

They came to another pair of doors, which led to his bedroom. Alexis threw them open, and she saw at once that it was yet another magnificently paneled room, but before she could look in detail, he put his hands over her eyes. Isabel had been telling him how wonderful the paintings were as he led her through their quarters. Between the three rooms she had had fleeting glimpses of

Renoirs, Cezannes, Matisses, Braques, Pissaros, Picassos, Rousseaus. Now, with her eyes very tightly closed, Alexis marched her to the bed. He put her in a sitting position, and when she started to open her eyes, he admonished her not to cheat. Then he kissed her lightly and said, "Now you may open your eyes and see the painting you will look at when we are in this bed."

She opened her eyes and gasped. The enormous wall held only one painting. It was a Monet. The water lilies. It was the one that the Jeu de Paume in Paris did not get. She estimated that it was about twelve feet wide and eight feet high. She had only seen it once in a traveling exhibition at the Louvre, and at that time she knew that it was privately owned, but not who the owner was.

The day before, when they had been very stoned in the pavilion, they'd discussed art, and she had told him about this very painting, and how if she owned it, she would never need to see another. He had kept the secret that it was his, and now all she could do was sit there and gaze at it. Alexis laughed and kissed her again. "Stay there, darling. I will call down for some tea and we will have it here. While you are looking, I will have to rush around doing some things."

When the tea came, he returned from the sitting room, where he had been talking with his secretary, and closed the doors. He lay down on the bed next to her and said, "Well, what do you think?" They spoke about the painting for a few minutes and then he asked her to pour him another cup of tea. She rolled on her side with her back to him and picked up the teapot from its silver tray.

She felt him slowly raise her dress, exposing her. He moved his hands across it, and she melted from his very touch. By the way his stroking became more aggressive she could tell that he was getting excited as well. It felt wonderful. She replaced the teapot on the tray and just lay there letting him do what he wanted with her.

With one hand he kept playing with her ass. Sometimes just massaging her round and round, at other times kissing her. Once he bit her hard, and she called out. He told her to be quiet, his secretary was in the next room. She could tell by his voice that he was very excited. He gave her a very hard spank, first across one cheek, then pushing her flat on her stomach, hard across the other.

"Oh, Isabel, I like you like this. You are divine." He

lifted her to her knees and she lay there with her bottom raised high, her face in the pillows, all dressed except where she was exposed. She heard him take his trousers down and get back on the bed behind her. He moved her legs apart until he had a full view of her from the rear, and continued to stroke and bite her. With one hand he wet the crack between her cheeks with saliva and used his finger around her opening. With the other hand he played with her vagina, slipping two fingers deep as he could inside her, and one on her clitoris. She started to come, first slowly and then, as the orgasms grew stronger, she moaned with pleasure.

Alexis was delighted that he could do this to Isabel and kept telling her that. He kept talking to her, telling her all the other wild things that he wanted to do to her. Isabel said yes, yes, oh yes, to everything, unable to help herself. That seemed to excite him more. He told her to stay just the way she was and left the bed for a minute. When he returned it was with his alligator belt. He whipped her lightly across both cheeks a few times, until she begged him to stop. Then he bent down and kissed the pale pink marks across her ass.

Alexis was erect, and Isabel was exposed and wet. He spread her lips wide open and drove deep into her. She let out a whimper of pain mixed with pleasure. He told her not to move a muscle, he could wait no longer, he had to get inside her; but he refused to give her a quick, cheap fuck. He asked her to please let him stay inside her and told her that when he withdrew, they would stop until they could be together all the night. She tried to understand. She wanted him now. She was mad with desire to have his sperm inside her, but she said nothing.

He was very big; the thickest she'd ever had. He filled her completely, but somehow or other he managed to move around inside her and she came again. When he felt the warm wet on him, he moaned with pleasure himself but pulled out, first slowly and then very fast in order not to come himself.

He pulled himself up next to her and collapsed. Turning on her side, she faced him. He looked at her and she could see his passion and desire. His enormous member, very pink from the blood pumping in it, was all wet and glistening. Isabel licked and kissed herself off of him, while Alexis watched. When he could bear holding back no longer, he pulled her off him and held her in his arms.

They lay there like that until he went limp. He told her she was the most erotic woman he had ever had, adding, "We will be very happy together." He went on, "Listen, darling, I want you to sleep now. Please, it is a big evening, and I am afraid you have not had much rest since you arrived."

He got up and tidied himself. Isabel left the bed and joined him near the Monet. She said. "Alexis, can I come back? I really did not get much of a chance to see Monsieur Monet's lilies from the bed." They both laughed, he kissed her and they walked to the sitting room, where she was introduced very formally to his male secretary.

Isabel was amused to hear Alexis tell the assistant that he had been giving her a tour of the paintings, and that she might be doing some work for them. It was the first time Alexis had mentioned such work since she had arrived.

Taking her through to her room, where the bed had been turned down, he told her he would have her awakened at eight, giving her an hour to dress. Before he left, she asked him about the evening. Should she be at her grandest, or wear something simple?

"I have just seen and felt you at your grandest," Alexis taunted. "I don't want you down there like that." He smacked her ass.

"Oh, please, Alexis, what shall I wear?"

"Surprise me," he said. As he was about to close the doors he added, "Isabel, it is black tie, if that helps you."

Isabel was sitting at the desk in her room. She had slept well and was feeling very relaxed thanks to Juju and Maryka, who had again helped her bathe and dress for the evening. She had on her Yves St. Laurent evening dress, a garment of ultimate elegance and chic.

The skirt, in a paper-thin silk taffeta, was the color of a pale opalescent gray pearl, with just a hint of pink in it. It fell smoothly over the hips, and then billowed out lightly at the hem, like a harem skirt rather than pants. The skirt bottom came to just about her shoes, which were silver high-heeled sandals. The top of the dress was made in accordion-pleated silk organza, hand-painted in iced pink and the palest shades of mauve, beige and white. It had bell-shaped sleeves and a round neck in the front that came to below the collarbone. As it fell over her breasts, it stood away from the skirt, hanging four to five inches below the waistband. It had one silver button in the back, high up on the neck, and was cut in such a way that it fell open whenever she moved her arms, revealing her bare back from the waist up. She wore nothing underneath it.

The diamond bumblebee was pinned high up on her shoulder, and her antique Cartier diamond brooch was worn close to it. Her makeup was perfection.

She had been writing for about ten minutes in the covered notebook she had brought from London. Inspired, she had sat down to work on her latest Meredith Montague. Isabel could have stayed there happily for the rest of the evening.

Alexis quietly entered and watched her for a minute or two before he went up and kissed her on the top of her head. He asked her what she was writing. Going a bit pink, she said, "It is one of my secrets that I have to tell you. It is a detective novel. I am Meredith Montague."

He started to laugh. "I simply do not believe it. It is true?"

"Yes."

"I adore Montague. I have read them all. Once I pick her up, I can never put her down. She is my great escape in literature."

"Alexis, you are too kind, but we both know the novels are not literature."

"Isabel, is it true? You are not teasing me?"

"No, I am not teasing you. Yes, it is true, and you must promise to keep it a secret, Alexis, it is important."

"My dear child, you are the most amazing of women. Now I have another reason to admire you. Will you tell me about it? Your secret will be safe with me."

"Yes, but not now."

She stood up and he looked at her, saying, "Oh, Isabel, you are perfect. Just perfection. All Cairo will be here tonight and the gossips will have much to say about that dress. Come, let me see you."

She turned around for him and the skirt swirled out. He made her turn around slowly, and when he saw her back as she lifted her arms over her head, he said in Arabic, "You are a devil."

"In English, please."

He repeated it, first in French and then in English. She laughed and turned around and faced him.

"That is the most sexy dress. You will have much trouble with the men tonight, my dear," Alexis warned. He walked around behind her and lifted the two corners that hung loose in the middle of her back, exposing her from the waist up. He slipped his hands under the front of her blouse, to her breasts.

Isabel pleaded with him to stop, saying, "No, Alexis, you must not. I will get turned on, and if I do, my nipples will go hard and more pointed, and they'll show through the pleated organza. Please, don't excite me."

He laughed again and rolled her nipples between his fingers, pinching them hard. He held up her blouse and said, "Now, let me see."

Of course Isabel's nipples were hard, very protruded and very dark. He arranged her blouse over them and the accordion pleats separated. You could see them easily through the dress. Alexis laughed at her and said, "You are quite right, I cannot take you down now. The men will die like flies from heart attacks."

"I don't think that is one bit funny, Alexis," Isabel pouted. "Now what shall I do? I can't just say, 'Hey presto,' and make them go down."

"Never mind, darling. I will go down and send Gamal for you in ten minutes. Come now, let me see how you look again," Alexis coaxed.

She waltzed around the room, constantly trying to repleat the silk that was separated by her breasts. Laughing, he started for the door, promising to keep his hands off her body for the rest of the evening.

She went back to being Meredith Montague, forgetting immediately about her nipples.

Some time later there was a knock at the door. It was Gamal, to take her downstairs. Isabel stood up and went to the mirror to adjust her dress. She was relieved that all that could be seen through the top of the dress was the faint outline of her bosom. Gamal looked at her and went down on one knee to adjust the back of her skirt. He then stood back, looking faintly pleased, and opened the door.

Just before she stepped out into the hall a sudden feeling of insecurity came over her. Was she being foolish about Alexis? Was this all just a wonderful erotic escapade to make her comfortable and happy so she would come and work for him? Insidiously, Ava and her mother flashed into mind—their disapproval of her life-style and their pleasure at her aloneness. She knew that she was being foolishly negative because of her guilt feelings. Oh, how stupid!

Isabel disliked parties. Large groups of people always made her feel even more isolated, which was why she rarely went to such affairs. Poor Gamal felt concerned when he saw her standing there, staring out into the hall.

"Please, miss, come. Sir Alexis, he waits you." Gamal said "please" and "come" in a normal voice, but when he said, "he waits you," it was almost in a soft whisper.

She smiled at the servant, and he led her towards the main staircase. She looked over the balcony down into the main hall. To her horror it was filled with men in black tie, women in magnificent evening dress and jewels, and dozens upon dozens of servants in white, shiny cotton galabias with olive-green sashes, wearing white turbans. They were tall, impressive-looking Nubians and carried silver trays filled with crystal glasses of champagne.

She took a deep breath, let it out slowly and started down the stairs. Halfway down she was able to pick out Alexis standing close to the drawing room doors, which were open to reveal yet more people. He was standing and talking to half a dozen guests, and on his right was Hamida. She was all smiles and it came to Isabel that she definitely was acting as his hostess.

Everyone who came in greeted Alexis and kissed Hamida. Isabel kept going down the stairs, trying not to be jealous, and then saw Alexis look up at her. He excused himself from the group and, saying something to Hamida, went to greet her.

He looked handsome and happy as he welcomed her by kissing her hand and saying, "You are ravishing, and I certainly hope they will stay down, darling." She went pink in the face and he began to laugh.

As Isabel realized how much he enjoyed teasing her, Alexis led her by the elbow into the crowd of people and began the endless introductions.

Hamida came forward and addressed her warmly, pecking a kiss on Isabel's cheek. A few words were exchanged and Hamida left them to greet other guests. Alexis told Isabel to stay more or less near him for a while, because the president would arrive within the next five minutes. The prime minister was already standing with them. Then Michael, the archaeologist she had previously met, joined them and introduced her to a very handsome, quiet, scholarly-looking man called Mahmud Wassif.

It was obvious that Alexis and Mahmud liked and respected one another very much. Alexis said, "Isabel, I hope you two will have a chance to talk. Mahmud is one of Egypt's most respected writers. I am flattered that he came this evening. Usually he declines all large social functions. I am afraid I see too little of him. He is almost as pure and inaccessible as a monk."

Ah, Isabel thought, a kindred spirit. Mahmud kissed her hand and said a few words, but before they could get into conversation a large group of plainclothesmen streamed in through the front door, followed by the president and his wife.

Alexis presented Isabel to him and the First Lady. She found them both extremely pleasant and most unpretentious. There was a great deal of warmth and charm about them. After talking only a few minutes with the president, she realized he was a far more vital human being than she had imagined.

It was a dazzling party, filled with fascinating, sometimes handsome men, with a twinkle in their eyes. Isabel was taken up by one man only to be passed to another. There were diplomats, writers, painters, museum people, doctors, lawyers and even a Nubian chieftain. The women sparkled like their jewels and gossiped like fishwives as they powdered their noses in between bouts of coy flirting.

Isabel even had a chance to talk to Anthony, who was having a wonderful time chatting up the rich ladies. He was very complimentary about her and whispered in her ear, "Is he a good fuck, Isabel?"

When she gave him a look of annoyance, he said, "Listen, Isabel, he is one terrific man. The more I see him and talk to him, the more I like him. You deserve something good. I only hope he fucks you as well as I did."

Before she had a chance to answer, she was swept away by yet another person. Later she looked back towards Anthony and caught him cruising a beautiful young Arab boy of eighteen or so. During the evening she would see them together and she knew that soon they would be lovers.

The party continued. Anoushka finally appeared with her husband: a tiny, quiet man, obviously besotted by his wife. She thought Isabel's dress admirable. When she saw the back, she said, "Youssef, come, come look at this," and lifted a corner of the back of the blouse. "Oh, please, Isabel, would you be angry if I had one?"

"No," Isabel said, laughing. "I would not be angry at all. Just call Yves St. Laurent."

Twenty tables had been set up with flowers and candles, the place settings exquisite with silver and crystal goblets. A sumptuous buffet was laid in the dining room. Everyone helped themselves and sat where and with whom they liked. It was Michael who claimed Isabel for dinner and escorted her to the buffet. They sat at the same table as Mahmud Wassif, Anoushka and her husband, Youssef, Anthony and his young Arab, and half a dozen other people whom Isabel had not yet met.

There was a great deal of laughter as their wine glasses were constantly topped up by the four Nubians serving the table. At one point Anoushka said, "Mahmud, you must take Isabel up to the roof garden; in a few minutes the *son et lumière* will begin. She can see the Pyramids lit up and maybe, Isabel, you will be clever enough to get him to recite some of his work while you watch."

He agreed that it was a good idea and borrowed a shawl from one of the ladies at the table so that Isabel would not be cold.

The small elevator took them to the roof garden, which was lit up by old Arab tent lanterns. Chairs, sofas, chaises and hammocks, all covered in old kilims, were scattered about, and there were trees ten and fifteen feet high. The space was broken now and again with screens of mushrabiya.

There were twenty or so people scattered about in small groups. Mahmud took her to a quiet corner and said, "Those foolish people, this is the best view."

From where they stood, they saw only a few lights from the city and these soon petered out into the dark desert. Then, not too far off in the distance, there was a bright, strong light. The Pyramids of Giza appeared, illuminated.

Mahmud told her about it. The lights changed to a hot red and then they went off, only lighting up one of the Pyramids. It was a spectacular show designed by the French, and if you were in the audience, you would hear told their history. Intermittently there was dramatic music. Mahmud argued that it was better from this vantage point.

Isabel leaned on the railings with her elbows and watched it. Mahmud stood behind her telling her their history in almost rhyming poetry. His voice was beautiful and hypnotic.

In that position her blouse fell open and forward, exposing her bare back. Mahmud bent over her body, touching her behind; he draped the shawl over her shoulders. She was about to thank him as she felt his hands under the shawl move over her back and around to her breasts. "Mahmud, please," she said, straightening up.

"Do not move or make a fuss. It would be foolish," he admonished. "Not ten feet away there are people, and we would not want a scandal."

Isabel felt mildly indignant at this last remark, but relaxed. With his hand he gently pushed her forward to her original position. He removed his hands and she started to move, but he held her down by the waist. "Stay exactly as you are. Just keep looking ahead at the Pyramids."

Isabel pleaded that he had her at a most unfair disadvantage. "Someone will come over; someone will see us."

She felt his erect cock against her as he warned, "Don't do anything to attract attention. That would be foolish and cause us a terrible scandal. No one need ever know."

Isabel was outraged. She was about to push backward and away from him when one of the ladies in a group very close called out, "Isabel, *il est merveilleux, non?*"

In the dark she could not see who it was, but said, "Yes, wonderful, let's enjoy the view together." At last she was able to straighten up and turn around.

"Before you say anything," Mahmud began, "I want to ask you please not to be angry."

Mahmud took her by the elbow and introduced her to the other people who had been so close to them all the time. They watched a few more minutes of the *son et lumière* on the Pyramids and then they all started down to the party. The incident was over.

The party was still in full swing. It was some time later that Alexis finally found Isabel and asked if she had enjoyed the *son et lumière*. "Yes," she told him, "I don't think I will ever forget it as long as I live."

The party went on for hours. Isabel saw Alexis only at

fleeting moments, but it hardly mattered since they could hardly have made any kind of intimate connection. She saw Anthony and the beautiful young boy leave together and Hamida kiss Alexis on the cheek. The affectionate couples among the crowd made her feel painfully alone.

Anoushka appeared. "What a wonderful party it is," she trilled. "The women, Isabel, they want to know who you are. Where you bought your dress. Do you have a lover here?" Anoushka never told Isabel what she had told them, but what she did say was, "Please not to worry, Isabel. I told them you are a very good friend of mine and I know you bought your dress at Balmain."

It was impossible not to laugh with her.

Finally Anoushka got around to Hamida, who at the moment was giving Alexis yet another kiss on the cheek. Isabel noticed that he was not too quick to pull away.

"Eh, poor Hamida. She has been trying to be Lady Hamida Hyatt for seven years now. He is too clever, you know; he has always made her share him with another mistress. Poor Hamida, I think she knows he will never marry her."

At a few minutes to four in the morning there were still a few dozen guests left in the house. Hamida and Michael finally went off with half a dozen others to the houseboat—a nightclub on the Nile. They had asked Isabel to join them, but she saw Alexis give her a look that she was sure was asking her to say no. She begged off saying that she was exhausted and going to bed.

She was saying good-bye to a few people and making her way towards the stairs when Alexis came up to her and said, "You were an unqualified success, Isabel. At least a dozen men asked me if you were available. Two dozen have asked me if I have had you. How many have tried to seduce you tonight?"

"I plead the Fifth Amendment."

"Very American, my dear, very American. The telephone will be ringing constantly. It will be very amusing." He smiled, obviously very proud of her.

"Alexis, what did you tell them when they asked if you had had me?"

"I thought it best to tell them that you were a famous design consultant and that you had just arrived, that I found you a wonderful surprise but have not had time to know you. I do not think they believed me. The prince from OPEC was the worst problem."

"Why?"

"Well, because unfortunately he is very direct and almost impossible about taking no for an answer. He saw you and simply said, 'Alexis, I must take her now. Will you be a good fellow and lend me a bedroom?'"

"Ah, now tell me, how did you get out of that?"

"Well, I did not; you cannot thank me, my dear. You must thank Anoushka. She came up to us at that moment and, wanting to make a joke out of it, I told her. She patted old Hakim on the cheek and said, 'How unfortunate for you. She is a friend of mine and it is not the right time. You must wait for four days.' So, my dear, you have a four-day reprieve."

She looked at him, then asked, "Alexis, why aren't you laughing?"

"Because, my dear, it is not so funny. He means it. He will only wait until he thinks you are clean, and then he will do everything to take you. But do not worry; I will find a discreet way to have him forget you. You see, even if I did not want you for myself, I would never deliver a woman to him. He is a dog with women. He does terrible things to them. He likes all the pleasure for himself and to give the woman pain. He bit one of his wife's nipples completely off, and once had a lover's clitoris removed because she had orgasms. No, no, never would I give you to him."

Isabel went pale at the mere thought of such a beast. A little pain sometimes brings a great deal of pleasure, but pure pain for pain's sake was horrifying. She wanted to say, 'You sly devil, Alexis. All you had to do was tell him that I am yours,' but she thought to herself: *He would not say that because that would be a commitment. Well, you learn from everything. Now I know where I stand.*

Alexis put his arm around her shoulder and played with her diamond bumblebee. "Isabel, it was a joy to see you at this party. I do not do this kind of thing very often and find it a great chore when I do. Tonight your being here made it easier for me."

He was so happy with her, himself and the evening that it gave Isabel great pleasure. Wiped away were her insecurities and the humiliation of the Mahmud incident. Alexis saw something of it in her face but of course had no idea what it was. To him, it was simply Isabel looking at him with overwhelming tenderness. He asked her if she were very tired and she replied that she wasn't.

Alexis smiled. "Wonderful. Be very clever and discreet and wander up those stairs alone to your room. Take your dress off and slip into something. Trousers and a warm sweater, if you have them. In twenty minutes Gamal will come for you. I will go and change and we will meet outside."

"What about all these people still here?"

"Never mind them. They will never know we have gone. If we are missed, they will think we have gone off with lovers somewhere."

Isabel made her way upstairs as she was told and quickly washed. She climbed into a pair of fine wool, camel-colored trousers, wide in the leg but snug across her bottom. Over her head she pulled a cashmere turtleneck sweater of the same color, then slipped on a sleeveless, chocolate-brown calfskin leather jacket. She was pulling on a pair of flat, shiny brown shoes when Gamal knocked at the door. He waited while she repaired her makeup, and then she followed him.

When they were in the upstairs hall he indicated that she was to stay close to the wall. She realized it was so that the people below would not see her. They went through a door that she had not been through before, and down the servants' staircase, through the kitchen and into the service courtyard.

The plum-colored Rolls was waiting at the kitchen door. Gamal opened the door to the front seat and there was Alexis at the wheel. Gamal got into the back seat and they drove away.

The streets were completely empty and silent. They took the road alongside the Nile and headed for the Pyramids, flying along at a reckless speed through the night. He called back something to Gamal, and a few minutes later two joints were passed over to Isabel. She lit them with the lighter from the dashboard and passed one to Alexis. It was Indonesian grass this time, her favorite.

The sky was just changing from black to that dark blue that softens the night before daylight comes. They passed the Sphinx, which looked like a magnificent, dark animal about to pounce out at them. When Isabel asked to stop, Alexis said there was no time. They picked up yet more speed. She turned quickly to look through the rear window of the car and saw it again. Framed by the window, it sat there like a great, grand shadow.

They passed the Mena House and she felt yet another surge of speed. Finally, in a cloud of dust, Alexis swung the car off in a slightly different direction, to cut across the desert. It was still too dark to turn off the car's headlights. It was weird and thrilling, like driving through a void.

After fifteen minutes the lights struck a small site. There were four camels and several men in front of a rambling, dark tent. When the lights shone on them, the men scrambled off the ground to light lanterns.

The sky was getting light now. Alexis told Isabel to get out of the car, and they went over to the camels. The men were all smiles, very pleased to see Alexis. The camels were magnificent, hung with kilims and saddlebags of old worn Bokharas. Dozens of wool tassels in faded colors hung everywhere, and Bedouin silver camel jewelry and bells were draped over the animals' heads.

Isabel nearly clapped with joy, the animals were such a show. Alexis put his arm around her, loving the excitement and enthusiasm that he saw in her eyes. He wanted to take her in his arms and hug and kiss her for it, but of course would never think of doing such a thing in front of all these simple desert men. Instead he asked, "Do you like them?"

"Yes, yes, I love them, I adore them, they are divine," Isabel laughed.

"Well, this one is mine. He is called Liban because he is white," Alexis explained. "And this one, do you like this one?" He pointed at a great tan beast.

"Oh, he is marvelous," Isabel exclaimed. "He is wearing so much jewelry. What a beauty!"

"Well, you must name that one. He is a she, and because I have not given you a gift today, she is all yours: camel, jewelry, trimmings and Hosni, her keeper. My surprise for you."

"Oh, Alexis, is it true? Are you teasing me? Mine? My God, you mean it! It *is* mine!"

"Yes, it is yours. I bought it for you ten minutes after we arrived from the airport. She is all yours and you must name her. We will look at her later, but now we must get up and ride if we are going to see the sun rise over the Pyramids and leave before the tourists get there."

She was speechless—simply could not believe it. It was like the Arabian Nights—all the romantic stories and dreams she had ever known.

"Of course you have been on a camel?" Alexis asked.

Fortunately, she had, many times. She was helped into the saddle, and the reins were given to her. The camel was sitting calmly. When all were finally satisfied that she was seated well, the Arabs called, "Hep, hep," pulled and pushed a little and with a few jerks forward and back, the camel rose, Isabel with her.

Alexis was saddled and ready, shouting instructions, and in a few seconds the other two riders were mounted and ready to go. They rode slowly away from the tent, leaving four men and Gamal. Alexis rode on one side of her, one of the men on the other, and one in front of her, towards Giza and the Pyramids. After about five minutes, Alexis said, "Isabel, Hosni thinks you are all right and that we should trot as fast as possible, for the light is coming up rapidly now. Is that all right for you? Do you think you can manage?"

"Yes," Isabel said, "but not for long because the movement sometimes makes me quite sick."

He laughed and told Hosni, who also laughed and let out a bloodcurdling scream and several commands. They were off at a fast trot.

Suddenly Isabel saw the shadow of the Pyramids looming up through the pale gray morning. It was becoming light now as quickly as if someone had pulled up a window blind.

Stoned and bewitched by the whole adventure, she called out loudly to her camel, "Ayah, hup, hup, hup, hup." She took the switch from where it was tucked in the saddle and whacked the animal lightly into a fast canter.

Hosni fell in love with his new mistress and followed suit. Alexis was thrilled with her and did the same. The leader called out as they caught up with him and raced ahead.

They were a sight, all the camels and their decorations tinkling and waving in the warm wind, clouds of sand flying. There it was, a hot red sun coming up over the horizon just to the side of the three pyramids. The sky went pink and then turned bright blue; they raced for the red disc of the sun.

Once at the Pyramids they slowed down. Isabel had

some difficulty, which Hosni saw and closed in on her. So did Alexis, and Isabel's camel was brought to a halt. They moved slowly around the Pyramids in the daylight, but as soon as people started arriving, they rode off for the tent. Alexis was adamant that Isabel's first visit to this wonder of the world would not be ruined by tourists.

When they arrived at the tent, Isabel's camel gave her a great deal of trouble. The men were all off their animals, but Isabel still could not get hers to sit down. Alexis thought it amusing at first, but things quickly grew out of hand. It took the four camel drivers and Alexis finally to get her down. Isabel almost did a somersault over the camel's head. It was Alexis who grabbed her and, lifting her to him, held her tight.

For the first time she saw him anxious and angry. He shouted at the drivers. It was obvious that he was furious because the camel was not trained as it should have been.

Isabel, who was quite shaken from it all, quickly recovered and said, "Alexis, please, it's all right, Alexis."

"No, it is not all right," he said firmly. "You will never ride that camel, never without Hosni. In one week's time that camel will be trained perfectly, but I do not want you riding ever without Hosni. He is responsible."

Isabel tried to calm him, telling him how much she loved her camel, and said, "I will never ride without Hosni, I promise. Alexis, it was the most glorious present and I am so happy. Please stop overreacting."

He looked at her and started to laugh. "There it is, another Americanism *par excellence*. Overreacting. Sometimes I forget you are an American until you come out with something like 'overreacting.' I wasn't really overreacting, was I?" He winked. "No, don't answer that. You will probably plead your Fifth Amendment."

"Alexis?"

"Yes?"

Isabel grinned. "What am I going to do with a camel in London?"

"Don't be silly, you will ride her in Hyde Park and house her in Berkeley Square." His good mood had come back. "She is for you when you are here. I promise no one else will ride her but you and her keeper. What will you call her?"

"Oh, I have to think about it."

They went into the tent. It was a black, huge nomad's

shelter, from Saudi Arabia. It was a gift from Anoushka and Youssef and was complete to the last detail. It stood there permanently, along with two other smaller tents which were for the keepers, the kitchen and supplies.

Alexis told her he owned about thirty miles of desert around the Pyramids, and that he used this tent and the camels fairly often. He liked the idea that there was always some life out there in the desert. "Do you like it?"

What a question! Isabel adored it. Gamal came with two fresh joints. They smoked them while lying among the cushions. The servant draped a lightweight blanket of rough white wool over them because there was still a night chill in the air. As they dozed off, Gamal quietly lit an old brass brazier.

They were awakened by Gamal asking Alexis if he could come in with breakfast. Alexis looked at his watch, shook Isabel; the couple kissed each other good morning.

Alexis lay back, and while telling Gamal to come in he unzipped his morning erection free under the covers. Isabel saw the blanket rise and said, "Oh, my Lord, it looks like a miniature teepee."

He said, "I beg your pardon, there is nothing miniature about this teepee," as he took her hand and happily ran it over him. She was turned on at once and reached in to fondle his balls.

Gamal and two assistants arranged a sumptuous breakfast in front of them. Isabel took her hands away, and Alexis adjusted himself and handed the blanket to Gamal.

Suddenly the room seemed to be filled with people: Gamal and his two assistants, two of the camel drivers and Hosni, all squatted down on the magnificent antique carpets around the floor.

Alexis turned to her and said, "I forgot to tell you, I have breakfast with them when I come out here. We talk about their work. While all this is going on, why don't you select a name for that beast I have bought you?"

While the men talked about Alexis's camel herds and the hunting planned and the hawks, Isabel racked her brains for what to call her lady camel. She started to leave the tent.

"Where are you going?" Alexis called after her.

"I am going to go and look at her again. Study her to give her the correct name."

He smiled at her enthusiasm. "All right, but don't be too long. Come back and have breakfast with me."

Isabel walked slowly around her magnificently dressed camel, talking to her as if she were a pampered pet poodle from Park Avenue. The more sweetly she spoke, the more bored and annoyed the camel looked as she chomped away, grinding her teeth in a circular motion.

Isabel was standing directly in front of her seated beast, thinking she had eyes like a doe, when the lady of the desert came forth with a horrible sound and a yawn that showed every yellow tooth in her halitosis-ridden mouth. Knowing a little of camels, Isabel jumped back, thinking the camel was going to spit at her. The drivers stood around and laughed as discreetly as they could. Isabel did not care. She was now looking over the camel's decorations and her jewels.

In the tent again, she sat down close to Alexis. When he looked away from his men to her, Isabel was filled with happiness and went to touch him. He stopped her by saying sharply, "No, not ever in front of anyone but Gamal." She was hurt and embarrassed at having made the mistake, but she understood.

Eventually, after the traditional three cups of coffee and breakfast (eaten with their hands), they all left except Isabel's camel keeper, who was waiting for instructions and the name of her camel.

A pencil and paper had been found for her, and she now had a short list of names. When Alexis asked her what her decision was, she asked, "What do you think of Ahmar Qamar—red moon?"

"Isabel, for a camel?"

"Well, let me give you the others and then you can help me decide. There is Asal Kharoof—honey lamb, Helwa Ald—sweetheart, Helwa 'ain—sweet spring, Sahara Hosan—desert horse."

Alexis and Hosni were speechless with laughter, and when they were quite through talking back and forth about the names, Alexis said, "Isabel, my darling, you have not been given a great Arabian stallion that is going to run at Ascot; it is a poor desert camel. Do make it a bit less embarrassing for Hosni. He cannot just take Arab words and link them together. They do not have the same meanings as you think."

Then there was Hosni, who was against every name she

suggested. Desert Horse was an insult. Red Moon would assure the camel a bad disposition, Honey Lamb would make Hosni the laughingstock of the camel drivers. Sweet Spring would make her too weak-willed, and as for Sweetheart, it was simply out of the question. Especially with the camel's already bad disposition.

By this time the men all had smiles on their faces, and as for Alexis, he was so amused that he said, "This is one of the funniest conversations I have ever had. Hosni is very serious."

"So am I." Isabel pouted.

"I know, darling. That is what is so funny."

"Well, what does he think I should call her?"

Hosni by this time was really annoyed. He said, "The best name would be Abdullah, or no name at all would be even better."

"Oh, Alexis, that is impossible. One is a man's name for a girl camel and no name would make her just another camel in the desert."

"Isabel, I think you are getting Hosni's point."

"Alexis, help me."

"Oh, no, you leave me out of this. She is yours, you name her."

Isabel decided it had gone on long enough, and so she stood up, and when she did, Hosni followed suit. She looked the trainer in the eye, and then said to Alexis, "You tell him the camel's name is Ishta. That is it. And I want not one word against that name."

It was obvious when she turned to Alexis and saw his face that he was having trouble controlling himself to keep from laughing. He told Hosni, and there was a miraculous nod of approval. Then Hosni said something back again.

"All right, Alexis, what did he say? And it better be good."

Alexis smiled. "He said, darling, 'Sir, it took her long enough to understand how embarrassing her name would have been for a noble camel, but thanks be to God, she saw the light. Ishta is a very respectable name. I compliment her, and will care and train Ishta for the lady. I hope soon to be able to take her into the desert on real rides. I think she has the feeling for our desert.'"

Isabel, who was ready for a fight, was delighted. She

reached forward and shook Hosni's hand, leaving him smiling.

The trainer left to care for his new charge. Alexis and Isabel sat down and took their breakfast alone together.

"Alexis, it is the most wonderful present." Isabel beamed. "Will you take good care of her while I am away? I promise I will come back as often as I can to see her, but when I am not here, will you sometimes ride her for me?" Isabel was silent for a moment, then said, "Oh, Alexis, I am so happy you saw me in Chicago and liked me, even happier that you went to the trouble to find me."

"So am I." He put his arm around her and gave her a hug; then they kissed. He moved his hands over her breasts. The cashmere sweater was so soft in his hands. He kissed her a second time and said, "It is wonderful for me to know you, have you here, to feel you. That you are no longer that elusive woman that I might never have found."

He loosened her trousers and exposed her soft belly as far down as her pubic hair. He felt her squirm slightly with pleasure.

Alexis frowned. "Isabel, we must go back to the house. I have some meetings at Sharia el Nil, and there may be some bad news. It is possible I may have to leave you for a few days. If I do, I will arrange things for you to go to Upper Egypt. We will not talk about that now. You must be exhausted. When we get home you will sleep. I will wake you at lunchtime and there will be the rest of the day for us."

She lay in his arms and he knew from her eyes that his hands over her belly and through her pubic hair were making her very passionate. He kissed her deeply and Isabel squirmed and spread her legs wide. Alexis slipped his fingers along the moist outer lips of her vagina, and when she arched her back, he slipped two fingers inside her. She whimpered softly as she came.

Alexis gave a deep sigh. He zipped up her trousers and they lay together on the cushions in the tent, just looking at one another.

Finally Alexis said, "This evening we will have an early dinner with Anoushka and Youssef. Afterwards we will go home and you will spend the night in my bed. I am going to fill you with my seed. I want you to love it, enjoy it, the way I love your orgasms. I could drown in you. I want you to love the taste of me the way I love the taste of your wetness. Tonight I am going to all but drown you inside and out with my cum."

Sir Alexis Hyatt's plane had flown him to a deserted airstrip somewhere deep in the desert of Oman close to the troubled area of the Yemen. He was whisked away in a cavalcade, the black, bulletproof Cadillacs kicking up clouds of dust. Their destination was a sheikh's mud palace where a secret conference was being held. There was always deep trouble between Arab brothers when it came to politics: Alexis held a position of rare respect among these men. He was an excellent mediator and a brilliant diplomat.

After a day of exhaustive sessions to try and solve this latest crisis before it flared up, Alexis and his party were entertained nobly by the sheikh.

Alexis, unknown to Isabel, had brought Hamida with him as well as Juju, Maryka and Doreya. The four women were of course relegated to separate quarters. He generously sent Maryka and Juju to amuse the host.

Alexis wanted to go directly to bed and called for Hamida to join him. He would fuck her when he wanted to sometime during the night and again in the morning. Alexis knew himself well. He had a woman or some sort of sexual satisfaction at least once a day every day of the week and, more often, twice a day. He enjoyed his virility and his love for women.

However, his quiet night was not to be. His host sent him a couple, two very black beautiful Nubians. A man and a woman, they performed an amazing exhibition for Alexis, Hamida and Doreya.

The man was of gigantic proportions and magnificent looking; the woman was quite small with beautiful breasts and an amazingly lovely, big and high ass. The man performed extraordinary acts on the woman; some Alexis had never seen before. It fired Alexis and the two women. To watch that huge cock disappear into that little woman and see him standing up with her feet wrapped around his waist as he moved her back, then ramming her forward on it as he walked around the room, drove them all into an orgy. He gave the man to Hamida and watched them, at one point joining the Nubian; then he took the black woman and Doreya in turn. Alexis climbed into bed with

Doreya next to him, who had lit him a joint. Together they watched the two Nubians work on Hamida.

Alexis found himself thinking of Isabel and the night before. Of all the women that he had ever had, he had never loved or enjoyed a cunt more than Isabel's. There was some wonderful chemical attraction between them, he knew. He had held off from consummating the act for those two days after her arrival because he wanted to see how sensual she was. He kept her tuned up and on the verge of coming as much as was possible without spilling into her.

Alexis knew how much she wanted him when he finally took her. And he had been right: She was magnificent. He had fantasized for so long about how he would fuck her that he did it just the way he had dreamed. He came inside her, but not until she was in such a frenzy of orgasm that every muscle was working with him. Alexis never really knew what happened, but as he came in her he heard himself scream, something he had never before done. It was a primeval scream that broke something wonderfully deep down within, allowing him at last to let go.

It was in the early hours of the morning when he had his third orgasm. There was not much sperm left, but there was enough to have her feel it trickle down her throat into her body. Alexis sighed with satisfaction: He *had* filled her with himself as he had always wanted.

They had slept, and when he woke later in the morning, he took her again. She was half-asleep and with her eyes still closed. He ran his hands and mouth all over her. She stretched, moving through her drowsiness to his every caress, and sighed as she felt new passion. He lifted her legs and rested them, wide apart, on his shoulders, still caressing her everywhere. His penis was large and full again, and as he drove into her she caught her breath from the impact. She kept her eyes closed as he fucked her slowly. They came together, all the time speaking tenderly to each other. Then she opened her eyes. It was like having a dream come true.

Alexis was amazed at how much he felt for her, how much he had loved her again as he had the night before. She was the woman for him—he was sure of that. That was why he sent her to Upper Egypt instead of taking her with him to the meeting. He knew that they both needed time and space.

In the next two days away from her, Alexis would re-evaluate his love for Isabel and what a life with her might mean. He had found the one woman as close sexually to him as was possible, and he liked the way she thought. He would find out about her work and what it meant to her. Yes, he would find out everything that made Isabel happy, just as he had found out how to keep her sexually. He wanted to make her happier than she had ever been in her life. It gave him infinite pleasure to think of spending a lifetime with her. Yes, he could be very happy spending what was left of his life with this amusing, intelligent, beautiful woman. Keeping her sexually tuned at all times, always ready to receive him. She seemed to want it and he adored her for it.

Alexis thought of Isabel: of all the lovely pleasure that would pass between them. Of all the women in his life, he had never felt the rightness or release that he did with Isabel, this woman whom he had only known for three days. He could give his soul to her, and he knew that she would give her soul to him.

VI

ISABEL HAD been in a deep sleep. Suddenly she sat bolt upright in her bed, grabbing for her heart. The fright passed and she was calm. She remembered where she was and reached out through the mosquito netting all around the bed to turn on the light.

The room was very large with a ceiling that must have been twenty-five feet high. It was sparsely furnished in what must have been the grand style in the twenties. Now it was still grand, but on the verge of being seedy. There was something shabby and worn about it that made her feel all the more a hotel guest. Just another of the hundreds of thousands who pass through the Winter Palace at Luxor. They had come, as she had come, to see Karnak, the Temple of Amun, the sacred lake, and the Temple of Amenophis III. They would have crossed the Nile as she did and been pulled upstream in an old felucca by fellahin in their white galabias tucked up into the tops of their baggy, white, rough cotton shorts. The fellahins' bare feet squished along in the mud of the high bank as they kept up their rhythmic tugging on the heavy rope over their shoulders, their large white headdresses bouncing with them.

A mile upstream their boat would have been released by the men as hers was, and they too would have sailed back down the Nile while the felucca crossed over to the west bank, just opposite where they first started out. Today there is a motor launch that will take you straight across, but then, that is really not crossing the Nile at Luxor.

If they had made the pilgrimage as she had to the Valley of the Kings, to the Tombs of the Queens, the Temple of Ramses II and the smaller Temple of Merneptah, then they would be, as she had been, swept away by the thought of time. The short time we live and the long time we stay dead.

Isabel went to the oversized doors of the bedroom that led out onto the balcony. She pulled up the noisy old wooden shutter just enough to bend underneath it and stepped out into the night air.

The middle of the night was heavy with quiet. There was a warm breeze moving the tops of the palm trees, the only sound breaking that silence. She stood leaning against the stone balustrade, looking out over the Nile. The water was there, but the night was so black she could barely see where it was. In fact, she had to imagine where it was. At one moment a carriage went by with its small lanterns on either side of the driver, and its tinkling bells on the horses made romantic music as they trotted along the road next to the river. It was quiet again after the carriage had gone by. Off in the distance she heard the hollow bark of some poor dog. Isabel was feeling chilly but was rooted where she stood, overlooking the Nile towards the Valley of the Kings.

The soft breeze suddenly stopped. Everything became totally still. Not a leaf moved, there was not one sound. And then, there before her, she saw very clearly the

Nile. It appeared, looking an almost translucent blue. Isabel looked to the left and then to the right. As far as she could see there was the river. It seemed larger, wider and to have come closer to her than it really was. Then she saw the river rise. The Nile, looking like a heavy white mist, just wafted itself up and floated away into the black sky. There was nothing there now. Just the dark night, no river to be seen at all.

A chill went through Isabel, and she started shaking violently. She wrapped her arms around herself, hoping to hold down the near convulsions. The tops of the palm trees were moving again and another carriage went by with its high-stepping horses and their tuneful bells. Two people were laughing in the rear of the carriage.

Something had happened, some extraordinary phenomenon. Isabel had had a vision. There was a calmness at the realization that she had seen something extraordinary. Her only reaction was that her life would never be the same again.

A part of Isabel had disappeared upwards and away with the vision of the Nile vanishing. From across the river on the west bank the moon appeared. Its beams fell across the Nile, lighting a portion of it directly in front of her. Now she did see it; muddy, blue-brown, with a fairly swift current.

She returned inside, lifted the mosquito netting and crawled into bed. Isabel lay back against the pillows and turned off the lamp next to her. As she lay there in the quiet of her room, she remembered a dream that she once had when she lived in New York. It was about another river—the Hudson River. Now, after all these years, that dream came back to her vividly.

It was of the Hudson River near the piers where the luxury liners docked. Somewhere near Fifty-second, Fifty-third and Fifty-fourth streets. There they were, the three great, beautiful, transatlantic luxury liners always looking streamlined and impeccable with their black and white bows and their simply printed, elegant names: the *Queen Mary*, the *Normandie*, the *Ile de France*. Those three glorious ladies of the deep waves were lined up in her dreams. She was standing on the overpass at Fifty-fifth Street looking at them as the traffic raced by her. Then, suddenly one bow rose up out of the water, high into the air. When it was almost perpendicular, it slipped slowly backwards and sank into the river. The water made circles as if a large stone had been thrown in to make the waves.

She saw the second one, the *Ile de France,* proudly raise her bow and in the same way, slip into the river. Then the *Normandie* did the very same thing.

Isabel had been haunted by that dream for years. Once she asked a psychiatrist at a dinner party about it. He told her that it was what they call a "complete dream." It had a beginning, a middle and an end. She was the ship and would rise out of her present life, which was the river, proudly to reach out and up and die back in the river. Then she would be born again in the next ship. It would happen twice more in her life and in essence what it meant, was rebirth. She would have a total and complete rebirth three times in her life.

She had often wondered if he had been right. Until this very night she had forgotten what he said, but had never forgotten the dream of those three magnificent ships on the Hudson River. She always had the feeling that one day she would understand what that dream really meant. The doctor only had part of it right, and she never really believed him.

Isabel knew just one thing for sure. The river was death but the water was life, and it had something to do with her. Now this, another river, not a dream but a vision. What did it mean?

She lay there and was aware of something. She could not exactly put her finger on it, could not rationalize or explain it. It was not in any way a strong clap of thunder, a streak of lightning: There was not a crash of cymbals or five hundred trumpets in fanfare. There was no shock at all to warn her that something had changed. She simply felt different.

At first she thought it felt like a new kind of calmness, but no, it was not as simple as that. It was more like a feeling of being. An inner voice told her that she had just passed through a great mystical experience. Sleepiness came over her, and before she drifted off, she thought of the Temple of Hatshepsut and had a feeling of being blessed.

At the foot of the Theban Hills, the Temple of Hatshepsut, built by the queen, is one of the most spectacular monuments in all of Egypt. Its vastness—with its terraces and colonnades—is unique in ancient Egyptian architecture. Its location at the foot of the towering cliffs enhances its majesty and leaves one enraptured at the sheer presence of it.

One drives through small hills of sand and rubble for a considerable distance when approaching it. The broken, bashed-in, old Chevrolets travel over bumpy tarmac at breakneck speed, and then the rusted chariots of today approach a great open space to veer off the road in a cloud of sand and dust. There it is, framed by the hills with a great wide ramp leading up to it.

Isabel stopped the driver a good distance away, wanting to approach the temple on foot. Gamal was never too far behind, and the museum guide walked close to Isabel, setting the scene in history for her. The driver of the car drove just behind them at about two miles an hour. Finally she made it clear to them that she wanted to approach the temple alone and quietly; the entourage dropped back. She walked along, feeling divine. With every step she took towards Hatshepsut's temple, she fantasized that she moved around with some of the sperm left in her by Alexis.

When she had bathed that morning, she had been so careful not to wash away any of the moisture inside her. She loved being full of him and, more than anything else, hoped that she was still carrying some of him in her now.

Isabel was back in the Sharia el Nil house. The journey to Upper Egypt had been marvelous. The two days and a night that they had spent there were hardly enough to constitute a real visit, but she knew that one day she would go back and see it all. Anthony, Isabel, a curator from the Cairo Museum and Gamal had flown up in a small plane. They were as thrilled with the trip as she had been and probably just as exhausted.

Now, back in Alexis's sitting room, waiting for him to come home, she realized that she had not had a chance to think about him, let alone think about their relationship and what it meant. Those two days and a night had been wrapped up in the antiquity of Upper Egypt, and then there was her experience with the Nile. The amazing contrast between Cairo and Upper Egypt astonished and awed her.

From the moment Alexis had first seen her, he had

done nothing but prime her and tune her like a fine Strad-
ivarius, and she knew it. With all her senses taut and
quivering, she had little choice but to fulfill to the utmost
their passion.

Isabel had spent a lifetime of doing just that in her
work, but had never successfully achieved it in her emotional life. Without his manipulation of those senses, she
was sure that she would never have experienced the Nile
vision. She was open and receptive to everything. All her
barriers were down. As a result, she had become spiritually richer, and that very spirituality had made her far
more secure emotionally.

Isabel sat pondering all those Western rationalities that
clog the mind and heart. Suddenly all her old London and
American values seemed silly and irrelevant. Isabel was
in love at last with herself and Alexis. She knew from experience that passion burns out; the love she felt was
timeless.

Alexis had shown her that to be fulfilled by your senses
was not a crime—a feeling that had been bred in her—but
love. She had always been a sensualist but had tried to
hide that fact. Now she had been set free. All those years
of fucking with Max were wonderful, but there was no
substance. If there was any love or affection between her
and Max, then it was out of gratitude. Or was there something else between them? She did not know, but she
would have to find out when she returned.

She thought about Ava, and the Avas of this world, and
suddenly it came to her that she would never be anxious
again. Then she thought of Kate, and suddenly there was
nothing to think about. All those years of anxiety and guilt
were gone, washed away. And Isabel started to laugh. Isabel Wells had at last been released from these two women
—her sister and her mother. Fate and the river. Isabel
and Alexis—their union, their oneness—had helped her
around the last boulder. There was a clear path ahead for
her now, and she knew it.

Gamal was standing by her, waiting, when she came out
of her thoughts. He wanted to know when she would have
dinner; and Mr. Moressey would like to see her. Would
she receive him? Dinner at ten, in an hour's time; and yes,
please tell him to come.

Gamal drew a box from a pocket of his galabia and offered Isabel a joint. She smiled to herself, thinking that

Alexis had this arranged as well. He lit her cigarette, handed her a cable, and left.

The cable read: "Isabel Darling stop Arriving Cairo 3:00 A.M. stop Look under your pillow before you go to sleep stop I will be with you in the morning stop Love, Alexis."

Isabel thought with amusement how well organized Alexis was and what a brilliant diplomat he must be. His knack for getting Isabel to do as she was told and love it was an example. The normal thing for her to do would be to run at once to the bedroom and look under the pillow, but she would wait happily just as she had been told.

Halfway through the joint, Anthony came in. She found him beautiful to look at as always. They spoke about the wonders that they had seen in Upper Egypt. There was not a trace of the intimate relationship that had been theirs for so many years, not even a spark, yet, when they were ready to go to the dining room, just the two of them, Isabel recognized something that had never been there before. Anthony and Isabel were deeply attached to one another. They walked side by side down the stairs, behind Gamal, two old friends who were very close.

Their dinner conversation was easygoing, even rewarding. She asked him why it had taken them so many years to be as they were that evening.

"Until you met Alexis Hyatt, you closed it all out," Anthony said. "If at any time I was able to reach you, you would turn it into something other than what it was. Now, I see the Isabel that I once fell in love with the very first time that I saw her. It is over for us, Isabel, and I see that I was not the man that Alexis Hyatt is. He is stronger than I and will not let you down when you need him the most. I could not stand the torture you put yourself through. I am not a guilt-ridden soul, and had we stayed together, you would have made me one. I had no idea when I fell in love with you that your family, your background, your fight to free yourself from them, would tear us apart. I never left you for good, I only left you, if you remember, to get your mess straightened out. I did come back, but you threw me out. I have no doubt now that you were right. I would never have been strong enough to stand by you. The Isabel I left is dead and you, my beloved friend" —he smiled, taking her hand—"are born again."

Isabel listened to everything that Anthony had to say,

and was overcome with joy and relief. Their conflict had been resolved, and they would be together as friends all the days of their lives.

She could not help but think of Ava and Kate. Whatever path she decided to take, she knew she could never resolve her relationship with them.

Anthony asked Isabel when she expected to go back to London.

"I don't know, but I must wait for Alexis to arrive. He is coming in the early hours of this morning. I would like to be in London by eleven A.M. on Monday. That is what I will tell him when he returns. What about you, Anthony?"

"Well, let us see what the man has to say. I would, of course, happily travel back with you. The sooner that I get to my studio, the better. You see, Isabel, I am going to return here to Egypt as quickly as I can get my things in order. I have met a rich young man who was kind enough to offer me an extended stay and I want very much to live here for a while. I think it would do me a great deal of good."

They kissed each other goodnight at the top of the stairs. Anthony went off in one direction and Isabel in the other.

Isabel was now extremely tired and could think of nothing but sleep. All those passion-filled nights were catching up with her. She slipped in between the soft sheets and then remembered Alexis's cable.

There under the pillow was an antique green velvet case. She picked it up and opened it. Inside was a Cameron box of ivory inlaid with gold and black onyx. It was exquisite, a lady's powder box, the most perfect compact.

It was five inches long, three inches wide and only half an inch high. The clasp was a crown in platinum with small diamonds, and inside was a beveled mirror and a powder puff of pure down feathers. The craftsmanship was Cameron at its best.

Lying on the sheet where the box had been was a note: "My darling, this box was made for Catherine the Great. Need I say more than I love you. Now, get out of bed and go to sleep in front of the water lilies. There is something under the pillow there waiting for you. I will be next to you as soon as I can. Love, Alexis."

Isabel was ecstatic. She wanted to pinch herself to make sure that it was true. She did. It was. What was it about that man? Was it the way that he did things, the way that he made love to her, the gifts, the romance of it all, the man himself? What was it that made her love him? He thought she was as good as Catherine the Great, and he could not wait to be with her! She flew around the room, picking up her bumblebee dress, which she would wear for breakfast. Wrapping herself in her dressing gown, her slippers in her hand, she took her ivory box and dashed through the sitting room into Alexis's bedroom.

Faithful, dependable Gamal was becoming more a part of her life every day. He was standing there with a broad smile on his face. She could not help showing him the box. They both beamed. The bed had been turned down; there was a hot drink next to it. She thanked him and he left.

Isabel dashed for the bed and under the pillows there was a large flat package, wrapped in egg-yolk-yellow tissue paper. The wrappings were held together by an ancient Arab necklace of heavy silver and chunks of amber. Very barbaric, heavy, majestic. It was, as usual, splendid.

The necklace was finally removed, and she tore the paper away, gasping with pleasure. There, under the paper, was something unexpected and dazzling. A twelve-by-fourteen-inch color photograph of Alexis and Isabel in full gallop on their camels. The camels' heads were pushed forward, their necks stretched high and pulled back by the reins. All their silver trimmings and tassels of a variety of colors were caught flapping in the wind. Behind them was Hosni and another rider. Alexis was looking directly into the camera so that it caught him full face. He looked glorious. He had one arm raised with his whip in his hand. And there was Isabel, sitting straight as a poker, riding hard and fast on Ishta. She was either screaming with laughter, or it must have been the moment when she let out a yell for Ishta to run for her life. All the excitement of that morning had been caught in the photograph.

Who in the world had taken it? There was just a corner of the Pyramid showing, and the sun was still hot red. She tried to recapture the very moment but could not. She looked at her face in the picture. Her facial expression was filled with excitement, joy, youth and passion. Isabel looked at it and knew it was the photograph of a lifetime. She would never ever look like that again.

It was the most wonderful photograph of the pair of them that she could ever hope to have. It was under glass and framed in Fabergé ivory with a fine gold inlay of flowers all around it. In the center of each flower was a rose-cut diamond.

She slipped out of her dressing gown and under the covers with her gifts. Eventually she put the photograph next to her on the bedside table. The box sat next to it. She wanted to wait for Alexis. She put on her heavy silver necklace and sat up in bed waiting. A short time after she finished her hot drink, her eyes would simply not stay open. She slipped down on the pillows and fell sound asleep, not waking until morning.

The first thing that she saw when she opened her eyes was the Monet water lilies. The room was only in half-light because the draperies were still drawn. But the water lilies were there; she could feel them, not just see them. Isabel grasped why it was that she could see the water lilies so clearly in the dim light. Of course! It was because they were painted that way. Not in a dim light, but through the dim eyes of Claude Monet. He painted the great series of the water lilies in the very last years of his life, when he was almost totally blind. He constructed the lily garden over a period of years in his beloved garden. Monet rarely left his garden. He had no need, for he had created heaven in the earth of Giverny.

In the quiet of the room the lilies shimmered forth at her. They had been painted with energy that came from Monet's soul and went out through his fingertips. It was a masterpiece painted through the depths of his being, out of love for the lilies he could no longer see.

Isabel, with her eyes still wrapped around the painting, and the painting wrapped around Isabel, softly caressed Alexis, fast asleep, beside her in the bed. Another time she could have cried out with gratitude for the privilege of being able to appreciate such a painting, but she did not have to now.

All her life she would be free to cultivate her senses, to appreciate without guilt and gratitude. Some dreadful wound in her was miraculously healed. The miracle of the disappearing Nile perhaps? She would not question; she would merely accept.

Now she remembered something of Dostoevski's she had once read: "He has no more pressing need than the one to find somebody to whom he can surrender, as quickly as possible, that gift of freedom which he, the unfortunate creature, was born with."

She lay there for a long time looking at the painting; then, turning on her side, she leaned on her elbow and looked at Alexis. He continued to sleep deeply. Almost soundlessly Gamal opened the door and slipped into the room. He went to the window and opened the draperies. The light spilled forth. Alexis still didn't move. Isabel, still in her same position, leaning on her elbow watching him, merely drew the covers over her to hide her nakedness. Gamal went to the window on Isabel's side of the bed and more sunlight flooded the room. He padded out of the room leaving Isabel to look at Monet's water lilies in the light of day. They would never be anyone else's water lilies.

Gamal returned to put a cup of tea on the table next to Alexis and another next to Isabel. He pointed to his watch and left the room. She understood. She was to wake Alexis.

Very quietly she moved across the large bed to him. Their bodies nearly touching, she ever so gently kissed him on his lips. He did not move. She kissed him again a little harder, and still he did not move. She opened her mouth ever so slightly because the very touch of his skin thrilled her. She pressed her lips to his now with a light, passionate kiss, and he opened his mouth and kissed her deeply.

There were two hours before he had to be dressed and in his study with his secretary. In those two hours they made passionate love, talked about their two days apart, what they had done, her gifts, and then they made love again.

Their sex the second time was less gentle and loving. It was filled with wilder passion. His desire for her the second time was more overwhelming, and he fucked her long and hard, bit her and licked her.

Again when he came, he let out that same primeval scream. Although he was on top of her, he pulled her up and crushed her tight to him and rocked her back and forth. They stayed locked that way, all spent but together.

Then they lay in each other's arms, saying nothing. There was, after all, nothing to say. They stroked each other's hair and occasionally kissed and nibbled at one another with a touch almost as light as air. Eventually there was a light tap at the bathroom door. It was Juju. Their bath was ready. Alexis told her that they would be in shortly.

Turning on his side he faced Isabel. He turned down the covers of the bed and ran his hand and mouth over her body. Her nipples were no longer tender, but sore. Just his wet tongue over them made her squirm with pleasure. He buried his face in her moist pubic hair, reached in between her legs and spread their wetness all over her body; then he said, "Come, darling, we will bathe together."

They went to the bathroom, where he dismissed Juju and Maryka. He washed Isabel inside and out. Then, when it was her turn, she bathed him. They were two radiantly happy people as they dried and powdered one another. He stepped into his galabia, she put on her bumblebee dress and they went into the sitting room between the two bedrooms.

Breakfast had been laid for them. They were both ravenous and ate greedily. It was over breakfast, after he put his paper down, that Isabel said, "Alexis, I want to speak to you seriously."

"Yes, darling?"

"Alexis, you really did not bring me here to work, did you?"

"No. I wanted to be with you. I wanted to know you. I used the work as an excuse when I sensed over the telephone that you mistrusted me. It was unfair, I admit. Just an excuse to get you here. I am not sorry. That is why I insisted that you be paid in advance before you arrived. I knew that you would not accept money, and not come. Are you angry?"

"No, Alexis, but I do want to tell you that I never did accept the job or the money you offered. My man, Endo, had an envelope with the check and a letter of regret that I had written in London before I left. He had instructions that if I did not call him by Tuesday morning, he was to deliver it to Alexander to hold for your arrival."

"How extraordinary. Why?"

"Well, there was something in that phone call you made to me in London. I wanted to believe what you told me, that you really wanted me. Out of fear, anxiety and conflict, I had to turn it into a job to believe that you could want me. By Tuesday I thought I would know the truth and by Tuesday, I did."

"You are wonderful and amazing, Isabel. How nice that we do not have a problem. I was a bit concerned because I knew that I was causing you confusion. You see, darling, I am a beast at times. I do what I have to do to get what I want, especially when I know it to be right. If a job had been offered, would you have taken it?"

"No."

"Why?"

"Because I would have taken it out of greed and to inflate my ego as well. I no longer get the pleasure that I once did out of being an art consultant. To work for money and one's ego only is too humiliating. I only thought that way before I went to Upper Egypt. Now, of course, since my trip, it would be impossible to do. I need not even think about it."

"Isabel, I respect what has happened to you as I know you do. A very long time ago I had a different experience, but no less effective on me than yours has been on you. For many years now I have been standing outside the affairs of the world. Although I am here, involved in the day-to-day living, I too became liberated from my ego. I have contemplated the laws of life and so realize that knowing how to become free of blame is the highest good. Having learned that, living it has brought me more joy, pleasure and the freedom to help others without bias. If other people involved with me do not understand this, it can be painful for them. It is, in fact, painful for anyone who does not live it, but so few know that." Suddenly his face darkened. "Isabel, have you been happy? I wanted very much to make you happy . . ."

"Happy?" Isabel exclaimed. "I think I have waited all my life just for these few days!"

Alexis reached across the table and took both her hands in his. She saw that his eyes were filled with emotion, almost on the verge of tears. Her eyes did fill with tears. "What a sentimental pair we are!" Alexis said in a hoarse voice and gave her a light smack on the hand.

"Now listen, my darling, I do not know how much this week has meant for you, but having you here has meant a great deal to me. I am not going to let you go, but I am going to have to be away from you for a while. I have some important work to do, and I need some time because you have affected me very deeply. I won't lose you, will I, Isabel?"

"I don't know, Alexis, but I can't imagine a life without you now."

"Well, that is something anyway." Alexis paused. "Darling, I am going to send you home tomorrow."

Isabel went visibly pale but said nothing. Alexis saw it but thought it best not to draw attention to it and so went on, "We will have lunch with my mother today. She will want to say good-bye. You know she is very impressed with you. Tonight will be our last night together here in Cairo on this trip. Tomorrow we will fly to Damascus, and then, in the evening, the plane will fly you on to London. There will be many people on the plane. You will go directly to my cabin and I will join you as soon as possible. When the plane flies you to London, you will, of course, have the run of the plane. Anthony, who, by the way, I have grown to like very much, will travel with you and Gamal. Alexander will be in Damascus and see you home as well. Now, darling, what do you want to do about tonight?"

"Oh, Alexis, I simply can't believe it is our last night together."

"No, darling, it is not our last night together. It is our last night together for now. Now, what would you like?"

"Well, let's begin at the beginning. I want Gamal and a car and driver and the day off. I want to make a surprise for you."

He looked delighted. "Done," he said.

"Then, I want the most sumptuous, sensuous supper prepared."

He looked even more delighted.

"And I want to have it on an exquisitely set table in front of the Monet in your bedroom. Can we?"

"Brilliant idea."

"Then, I want to make love to you and then I want to give myself to you and I want you to make love to me wildly and with total abandon."

"I think I like that program very much."

"Oh, and there is one thing more."

"Yes?"

"I don't want either one of us to get sentimental about this trip that we have had together."

"Done."

"And, I . . . oh, nothing. Just thank you."

They left the breakfast table and he kissed her. She

knew, although he said nothing, that he was feeling sentimental about her.

Together they walked to her room. He closed the doors,
took her over to the chaise longue and lifted the bumblebee dress over her head. He put it neatly on the bed and
came back to where she was standing. He touched her
hair and then pulled her close to him. He ran his hands
down her back and over her round, beautiful ass, then he
turned her around and looked at her back view. Throwing off his galabia, he held her close up against him. Then
he slipped his arms around her waist and rested his hands
on her soft belly. He moved his hands to her breasts. His
penis was erect again, and he slipped it between her legs.

During the time he held her that way he had his eyes
closed. She felt him sigh deeply. When he opened his
eyes, he moved his hands over her belly, around to her
hips and back up to her breasts again. He kissed her on
the ear, on the back of the neck, and then he gave her a
very hard slap on the rear and told her to get dressed.

He sat on the bed and made phone calls, watching her.
His first calls were to arrange things that she wanted for
the day. All the time he was on the telephone he kept his
eyes on her. He saw her arrange her things. She laid her
dress out on the chaise and went to her dressing table and
made up her face.

He thought again how lovely she was as she walked
around the room, quite naked. When Isabel went over to
the chaise and bent over to pick up her shoes, he hung up
the telephone. He walked up to her, told her not to move
and, rubbing his hand over her buttocks, spread her legs
wide, and he, none too gently, drove into her.

They said nothing as he moved in and out of her a
dozen times, at the same time playing with her clitoris.
He drove into her, and she contracted every muscle to
hold him tight. When she released him, he slipped in and
out of her with ease a few more times and then withdrew.

Isabel, completely turned on by him, sat down on the
chaise, pulled him towards her, and took him in her
mouth. He stopped her and said, "I want you to remember
when you are in London how beautiful it is: you, all
naked but for your necklace and your makeup, eating me.
Get on your knees and look in the mirror; now you will
see me disappear into you."

She did and slowly he moved in and out of her,

amazed yet again as to how wet he could make her. He
withdrew, lifted her up and held her close to him. After a
moment he said, "Now, go finish getting dressed."

He was on the bed making phone calls again, but he
was still erect and wet from her. She had recombed her
hair and was about to slip into her sandals when she
walked over to him and climbed onto his lap. He tucked
the telephone between his head and shoulder so as to hold
her by the waist.

She lifted herself up and slipped onto him, riding him
ever so slowly, saying, "Alexis, you are the sexiest beast I
have ever met," and then climbed off.

She turned around to finish dressing, but not before he
caught her and spanked her ass, shaking a finger at her as
if to say, "Bad girl." Not once through it all did he stop
talking to the man on the telephone in Arabic.

She put on the dress that she had worn when they first
met. She went back to her dressing table and put some
rings on her fingers. He was at last off the phone and told
her to come near him. She stood a few feet away and
pirouetted, as he had asked.

Alexis looked at her with a very critical eye and in a
very serious voice said, "Could it be possible that I find
you even more sexy dressed like that? I do like that dress;
it was the dress you had on the first time we met, and the
necklace is perfect. Why do I feel such pride when I see
you? Hand me my galabia, please."

He put it on and said, "The only thing that I ask you is
to be here at two for lunch with my mother. I have made
appointments, so you are free after that, but come home
by nine. The rest of the time is just for us. Now, come
with me while I get dressed."

He took her by the hand, and they went through the
sitting room to his bedroom. He rang for Gamal and told
Isabel to pick a suit for him. She watched him dress, and
at one point he asked her what she was thinking.

"Just how happy I am you have not got a banana-
colored suit." Isabel smiled, and they both laughed.

"Go and pick me a serious-looking tie," he said. "We
must have a serious tie for serious business today. Other
than you, there is very little light in my day. Now, run
along while I become a very important man for the next
few hours."

She handed him a tie and they kissed, this time without

passion but with a great deal of affection. He asked her to leave by the hall door because he was sure his secretary was in the sitting room next to them.

Isabel left him, going through the hall to her room, where she picked up her handbag. When she opened the door, she almost bumped into Gamal.

Before she left the house she asked for a telephone and called Anoushka. After the call, she was starting for the front door when she heard Alexis, from the first-floor balcony just above her. "Oh, Isabel, I was afraid that I had missed you," he said. "How stupid of me. Are you going to spend any money?"

"What an extraordinary question," Isabel replied. "I am not going to tell you."

"Please, darling, don't be ridiculous. If you are going to spend any money, you must tell Gamal. He will bargain for you, for whatever it is. You are not to pay, do you hear me?"

"Alexis, I do not want your money. I want to use mine."

"Now, listen, if you are going to be foolish and Women's Lib, and all that, then you can pay me later. But you must let him handle it."

"Oh, all right, Alexis."

"Good-bye, darling," he called down to her.

Isabel had a glorious day. She went back to the Kan-el-Kalili with Gamal, and they visited the same shops she had been to before with André Beshawi.

In the third shop they found what Isabel was looking for. The owner recognized her immediately. She asked about a netsuke, carved out of a chunk of amber and signed by one of the most famous makers, who died in 1548 A.D., in Kyoto, Japan.

The netsuke was about the size of a large walnut but slightly more flat than round. It was carved so that the light that shone through the amber revealed every detail. It was like a large glob of dark, rich honey in the shape of a curled-up, sleeping dog. It was warm and sensual to the touch. She chose it partly because it was something that Alexis could carry with him on his travels, even small enough to slip into his pocket. It was made to hold and to touch, a soothing stone.

She did as she was told, allowing Gamal to bargain for the piece. Thrilled with her purchase, she then went to meet Anoushka, whom she had invited to tea at Groppi's.

Groppi's was a landmark in Cairo. Its location and ambience have always made it a great rendezvous spot and one of the most famous patisseries in the world. If it was in London, it would have been Richoux; in New York, it would have been Rumpelmayer's; but neither of those comes near to what Groppi's really is.

Divine sweets and excellent coffee aside, the real treat is the gossip. No day was complete without dropping into Groppi's for at least a look, if not a meeting. When Isabel arrived, all the chatterboxes were in full swing. It was a delight. She was the first there and so waited at the table for Anoushka. Half a dozen people stopped to say hello. She had only been in Cairo a few days and yet felt quite at home. She chuckled as she thought to herself how she had lived in England seven years before anyone stopped her to say "Hello."

Anoushka arrived and was sweet and amusing. Isabel had thought this would be good-bye, but was delighted to learn that she would be at Madame Hyatt's for lunch.

They went from there to the Hilton hairdressers, and by the time they left, both were well coiffured; Isabel had learned that Alexis would be amused when he found out she had been to Groppi's.

"He will think I am a bad influence on you. You must tell him it was your suggestion," Anoushka said, and laughed. "You know, he is a very serious man, Alexis. He would not be caught dead in a place like that, but you will see, he is a Cairene, and, important man or not, he will ask you all the news."

When Isabel asked Anoushka just how important Alexis was, she was amazed. She said, "You really don't know, Isabel? He has declined the position of secretary of state twice. He is the third most important man in Egypt, but prefers to remain unofficial. He told Youssef that in that way he could be of more service to Egypt and the Arab world. He is brilliant."

Isabel left her there chattering to a friend and next went to the best flower shop she could find. She bought three dozen white arum lilies and sent them to Madame Hyatt. On the card she wrote: "How kind of you to ask me to lunch. Isabel Wells."

Then Isabel made Gamal stop at a cart near the old city and bought a dozen ishta. It was getting late, but on an impulse, she made one last dash back to the Kan-el-Kalili, where she decided to buy an antique Yemenite silver disc on a very long, heavy, handmade silver chain. The disc was carved around the edges in deep relief. From its bottom hung heavy silver chains, all close together like a fringe. Each end of the chains had a silver bell. It was a handsome piece and Gamal struck a hard bargain with the seller. She would pay the dealer, she told Gamal, only when he delivered it to her at four o'clock at Sharia el Nil with the inscription on the disc: "Ishta." There was a great deal of screaming for more money, but she knew her Arab bazaar men and she was sure it would be done and would be there. He wanted the money.

Into the car they went, and home. There were fifteen people for lunch. Madame Hyatt thanked her for the flowers, which were placed next to the Bergère the matron sat in when they had coffee. Amusing, gay, charming, Madame Hyatt was at her best, and it was a delight to be there.

Alexis never gave Isabel one intimate word or show of affection during lunch. She had been late, and when, on her arrival, she had apologized to Madame Hyatt, Alexis had merely smiled and said, "You see, Mama, Isabel has been here only a short time and she has picked up our ways."

At last everyone was gone. She said good-bye to Madame Hyatt, who left her with the impression that she very much approved of her. Nothing was said; it was just a feeling. Isabel and Alexis walked through the garden to the main house. It was nearly five by then. When they entered the door, Gamal came forward and told them that there was a man waiting to see Isabel.

Alexis took over. Who was he? What did he want? Did she know he was there? Was she expecting him? The man was brought in to the downstairs' study and Alexis watched Isabel finish her transaction for the "Ishta" necklace. The man was ushered out, and Alexis laughed uproariously. "What a sweet thing to do, buy your camel a good-bye present. You are wonderful, my dear. Sometimes you do things a young girl would do. Come over here to me."

He had been sitting more than a little pompously at his desk. Isabel went around to him and the two looked at the disc lying there before him. He put his arm around her waist. He said it was an excellent piece and that Ishta would love it.

"Alexis, I simply had to buy her something."

"And what else did you do today?"

He was himself again with her, now that they were alone. Because he seemed so happy, she told him about her day. He did just as Anoushka said he would and asked what gossip she had heard at Groppi's and said what a waste of time all that was. He said he knew she had had her hair done, touched it and said that it looked lovely. Then she told him that she had bought a dozen ishta for Hosni and that she was driving out to give them to him and to give Ishta her gift.

He turned his chair around so that he faced her and said, "You are the most . . . the most . . ." and buried his face in the material of her dress, feeling under it the softness of her belly. He stayed there for a minute very quietly as she ran her fingers through his hair. Then he sat back in his chair and said, "Is there anything else you did, beside the uncalled-for but generous gesture of lilies for my mother?"

"Yes, there is, as a matter of fact." She sat down on his lap. "I bought you a gift. I was going to wait and give it to you tonight, but somehow I think you should have it now."

She reached in her bag, which was lying on the desk near her, and took out the badly wrapped little parcel.

"Alexis, it is a small token of great love from me. Something small that I hope you will keep in your pocket or at least with you, when you travel."

He unwrapped the parcel and fondled the netsuke. He placed it on the palm of his hand and looked at it. Then he told her an extraordinary story.

"This belonged to a friend of mine," he began, telling her the date and everything about the netsuke. When his friend left Egypt, everything was sold. Alexis, who would have bought many things, felt it wrong because it was all too personal. He especially wanted the amber netsuke because he found something very spiritual in the tiny carving. The man who made it only carved one piece in amber throughout his entire life. And now here it was in his hand. A gift to him by someone he loved.

He thanked her and said of course he felt he could have

it now because it was a gift and that he would carry it with him always. "I love it, my darling." He held it in his hand, held it up to the light and then slipped it into his pocket.

Isabel put her head on his shoulder, and he rocked her gently as he kissed her, while caressing her hair. He moved his hands over her and slipped one under her dress. He kept rocking her and kissing her tenderly. When he felt her trembling with excitement, he opened his mouth and put his tongue deep into her mouth. She sucked on it and he slipped two fingers inside her to massage the wet walls of her vagina. A few minutes later he slowly removed his hand and gently lifted her off him. "Run along and have a lovely afternoon. Tell me everything tonight when we are together."

Off she went as if on a cloud. She simply was in love with him. She was not even sad about leaving. She was just happy.

She went to the car. Gamal sat in the front, and off the plum-colored Rolls went towards the Pyramids.

After Isabel had gone, Alexis took out the netsuke and thought how really special a lady Isabel was. He liked everything about that woman. Even how she handled her day and the things that she was doing. How lovely it would be to see her in her own environment in London. To spend some time with her there.

He had arranged some special things for their last night together. Juju, Maryka and Doreya would be available, along with the best cocaine, grass and hashish, and a dinner of pure erotic food made into superb dishes. That night Isabel would have three men fucking her all at the same time. They were very accomplished, these two other men, and along with himself, the trio would do the most delectable things to her sexually.

Juju and Maryka would help her on the bed and raise her up to just the right angle by adjusting cushions underneath her. Then they would take her legs and stretch them as wide apart as possible. With silk ropes they would tie her by the ankles to keep her legs apart. The ropes would be secured on hooks high up on the posts at the foot of her four-poster bed. She would then be propped up with pillows under her shoulders and her head, so that she could watch what was being done to her.

Juju and Maryka would suck on her nipples and take

turns stimulating her clitoris so that all her juices flowed continually. Doreya would sit at the foot of the bed and wait.

Alexis would then get on the bed between her stretched and open legs. She would be open wide for him because of her position; he would see the juices running out of her. The very thought of it made him hard. The two men would be dismissed, and Isabel would be bathed clean of the two strangers, but not Alexis. She would sleep in his arms and awake to him alone.

He knew that she had never had three men before, but that like most women, she must have fantasized such an experience. Oh, yes, he would do the most delicious things to her tonight. She would look so lovely stretched out like that, and, of course, he would have the added joy of being able to watch her face enjoying it all.

He touched the netsuke again and thought of her. How remarkable it was that although he wanted no other man to have her except himself, for this one night, he wanted her to have three men. He wanted to see her filled up with as much sperm as she could handle.

The telephone rang a few times and finally he picked it up. The meeting was about to begin upstairs in his study.

Isabel woke up alone in Alexis's bed. The curtains were open and the room was filled with sunshine. She shifted to sit herself up and realized that she was quite stiff, a bit sore in her bottom and very tender in her vagina. Then the events of the night before came back to her.

She had been in her first orgy. She heard the water running in the bathroom; then Alexis came in with a towel wrapped around his waist. He went directly over to her, dropping his towel, and climbed into bed. "Good morning," he said, taking her in his arms. "I have drawn your bath, and your toothbrush is in my bathroom. Hurry and come back to bed."

She kissed him back and fled into the bathroom. Not knowing what to say about the night before, Isabel hoped that he would say nothing. She brushed her teeth and bathed, then slipped into a great terrycloth robe that he had left there for her. It had her name embroidered on it. Alexis was a most extraordinary man, she thought to herself.

She went back to bed, making her way close to him. He held her in his arms and kissed her many times.

She thought to herself, he still loves me. She slipped on top of him, straddled, and then lay flat across him. Their nipples touching, she lay her head on his shoulder, and he patted her down the back and over her ass very gently. Then she rolled off him and tucked herself under his arm and laid her head on his chest.

Stroking her hair, he said, "Listen, darling, I want to tell you about today. First, select what you want to wear today. Just lay the things out on the bed. Then you are going to come back to me, and we are going to have breakfast together while Gamal packs your cases. After that, you will go and get dressed and we will meet in the downstairs drawing room.

"You and I will drive out to the plane together. When we board, you will go directly to my cabin. There are four important men traveling with me, two Saudi Arabians and two sheikhs. A woman among us would be out of the question. You do understand?"

"Yes, of course."

"We will fly directly to Damascus, where we are having a meeting. There is a luncheon for us given by the president, but I have arranged not to be there. The president understood and insisted on giving us his car and an escort. I have had a picnic lunch prepared for us. You, I, Anthony and Alexander, who is already in Damascus waiting for us, will have lunch in a grassed-over moat of the finest Crusader castle left in the Eastern world. Then we will drive back to Damascus and I will take you to the plane. I could have sent you a faster way, but then we would not have had those extra few hours together. I know you will be as happy as I am to have them."

And of course Isabel was. She kissed him, telling him that he was wonderful to think of everything.

"Now, go and choose your clothes," Alexis said. "Come back here and we will have a big breakfast."

As she scrambled off the bed she said, "Ouch."

Alexis reached across and pulled her back to him, kissing her on the back of the neck. "Darling, are you still sore?"

"No, I'm OK." Isabel smiled and grabbed for her robe. He stopped her and said, "No, don't put that on; it is for the bathroom. Here, put *this* on."

He reached down and pulled a large white dress-box from under his side of the bed. He opened it up and drew out a galabia made of the finest cream-colored heavy *crêpe de chine*. It was trimmed around the cuffs, the collar and down the front in white silk braiding.

Alexis slipped it over her head and Isabel went to the mirror to adjust it. It was sensationally feminine and beautiful.

She went over to him and he said, "You are beautiful in it, just as I knew you would be. I do like buying things for you. It gives me a great deal of pleasure. I think I like you in white more than any other color."

Isabel sat down next to him and said, "Thank you. You know that you have spoiled me for any other man."

He touched her hair and said, "That is my intention. Isabel, last night I gave you two extra men because I wanted to give you the ultimate in pleasure. I don't know if I will be able to share you again with another. If I truly have spoiled you for any other man, I think I am happy. But we will not talk about that any more. Now go and get your clothes out."

She squeezed his hand, then went quickly from the room.

Gamal and two servants were setting up the breakfast table in the study. As she went around them she passed his desk and was thrilled to see that he had the same picture that he had given her of them on the camels. It was also framed exactly like hers. She could not remember ever having known such happiness.

Isabel had been in the plane for over an hour, working on the Meredith Montague manuscript. During that time she occasionally looked out of the window to see dark automobiles pull up to the stairs that led to the plane. It all looked very official, very important, very impressive, and she was happy to be alone in Alexis's cabin, apart from it all.

Shortly after becoming airborne, Alexis managed to extricate himself from his guests and went to his cabin. He saw Isabel at his desk and sat down opposite her in the Bergère. He always liked this cabin very much and seeing Isabel there was an additional relaxing and pleasing sight. They looked at each other across the desk.

"Hello." Isabel smiled. "Are all your guests settled and happy?"

"Yes."

"Are you happy?"

"Yes."

When they spoke it was in calm, simple, uncomplicated terms, but there was now an attraction between them that was so strong and electric it made them tremble. They were like two strong magnets keeping a certain distance between them.

Here they were with a mutual desire to be locked into each other so strong, that the nights and days of their sexual pleasure, which were to have sated them, were forgotten. Instead of two mature people, they sat there as two young lovers wanting each other all fresh and new as if they had never made love at all.

If Isabel, simply by looking at him in his chair, felt her knees go weak and her nipples go hard, it was no different for Alexis, whose heart was beating fast with the desire to make her wet with orgasm, to fill her with himself.

He unbuttoned his jacket and heaved a deep sigh. They said nothing. The silence in the cabin became so oppressive that Isabel could stand it no longer. She left her seat and went to the commode where she took out a joint from the lapis lazuli box and lit it.

After two puffs, it was a little easier. After two more, a great deal easier. She bent forward over the back of Alexis's chair, slipped her arms around to the front of him, kissed him on the top of the head and handed him the joint. He drew on it four or five times and then stood up, crushing the cigarette in an ashtray on the desk.

He went to the cabin door and locked it. Then he went to Isabel and took her in his arms. When they kissed, they were both trembling. Without a word, they undressed each other, leaving their clothes in a heap on the floor where they stood. They lay down on the little French day bed.

He made love to her almost in the same way as that first morning they had met in the upper room, by the fountain in the Roda Palace. She made love to him with an equal amount of passion and tenderness. She licked him and sucked him and took him deep in her mouth as she had many times before. Only many times did not exist for them at that moment.

With every movement of her mouth on him, he moaned softly and trembled with the thrill of her. As he did, Isabel realized that she had conquered this man and felt the power of domination. She had by now come so many times that all she wanted was for him to come inside her. She became wild with ardor at the very thought of that first spray of sperm as he pumped her full. The thought of walking around with him inside her, of carrying him back to London, spurred her eagerness on. Although they did not speak to each other, he knew it, he could feel it coming off her, her desire was that great.

He put her on her back with pillows underneath her and he made love to her slowly, for a long time. He rejoiced in her. All he kept repeating was, "You are divine, divine, divine."

To Isabel, he seemed longer, thicker, the head of his penis bigger. Every thrust seemed to hit her deeper, harder. When he came, he opened his mouth wide and gave that same primeval scream, calling out all his passion and love for her. She could not hold back and seconds after him had a powerful orgasm that made her call out from the very depths of her soul.

Still inside her and still coming, he clasped his hand over her mouth to silence her because of the men in the other room. She sucked in every drop of him. He stayed in her and lay on top of her, holding her in his arms, both of them shattered, completely spent.

In time, he withdrew and lay on his back next to her. She rubbed her face in his pubic hair and on his now-limp penis. He was wet from both of them. She licked him clean and snuggled up to his face, asking him to open his mouth. He did and she ran her tongue over his and he tasted both of them, just as she had.

"That's us," she said. "That is how we taste together." She kissed him, resting her head on his chest.

Silently he left the bed, went to the bathroom, returned and dressed. Isabel did the same. She straightened up the bed and sat down on it. He came and sat next to her. That last love was their good-bye, their real good-bye, and they both knew it.

He rang for Gamal and coffee. Fifteen minutes later, at the Damascus airport she watched more large, black, shiny limousines pull away with the guests that had been on the plane. She watched Alexis see them off and run back upstairs to the plane. He took her from the cabin and she, Alexis, Alexander and Anthony met together in the main cabin.

They left the plane and went down to the cars waiting for them. Gamal and two stewards went with the picnic lunch in one car, their party of four in another. There was a lead car of plainclothes detectives and a motorcycle escort whose sirens were silenced by Alexis's instructions before they left the airfield.

The car tore at a mad speed to the Krak des Chevaliers through what would have been wonderful countryside if they had traveled slowly enough to see it.

There was an extraordinary picnic lunch, with both Anthony and Alexander being terribly discreet and leaving the two of them alone for long periods. They held hands and kissed tenderly as they toured the Crusader castle.

It was all easy between them and they were happy; but then it was over, and they returned to the plane. Alexis gave a few instructions to the crew, Gamal and the captain. He spoke for a few minutes to Alexander in Arabic and then started to say his good-byes; first to Anthony, then Alexander.

When he started to say good-bye to Isabel, both men asked to be excused, saying they wanted to be in the cockpit at takeoff. The stewards miraculously vanished, and they were alone.

Alexis had control of the situation. "Have you had a lovely day?"

"Yes," Isabel said quietly.

"I am happy for that. That is all that I wanted." He smiled at her. "You will take care of yourself, won't you?"

"Yes, of course I will."

"Isabel, I do not want you to forget me," he said simply. "I have something for you." He reached up and removed the gold loops from her ears, and from his pocket he took an earring and clipped it on her left ear, then the other on her right ear. He pushed her silky, chestnut-brown hair back and looked at her.

"Well, they do not go with your Tutankhamen necklace, but they do go with my love for you."

She reached up to take one off her ear and look at it, but he stopped her, saying, "No, please, not now. Let them be a surprise after I am gone. I was very selfish. I

would have left them for you in their box so you would
have had a lovely surprise during the journey home, but I
could not. I wanted to see how beautiful you would look
in them, and you are."

"Oh, darling, no!" She kissed him and repeated, "No.
Never could I forget you."

He held her close for a few seconds and then released
her. "I am sending you home with Gamal. If you need
anything or want anything, get in touch with Alexander.
He will see that I am found. For the moment, I do not
know when I will be in London, but we will talk before I
arrive."

She nodded silently to all he had said.

"Isabel, thank you, darling." Alexis kissed her hand,
but it was almost with disinterest. In his mind he was already far away from her. He left the plane.

Isabel, no different from any other woman, watched her
man walk away from her and was horror-stricken. He was
gone. She went to the window. He stepped off the stairs,
one step on the ground, and into the car. He never looked
back. The stairs were quickly rolled away. The stewards
had reappeared and closed the airplane's door. She was
buckled into her seat and was on her way to London and
her life again.

Alexis, unknown to Isabel, had stopped on a side road
at the end of the runway to watch his love take off. He did
not leave the airport until he saw her disappear out of
sight into a very bright and beautiful, blue, cloudless sky.

That was Sunday at 6:15 P.M., right at the time Ava
and Kate were having coffee in Athens and making plans
for their future and Isabel's as well.

The two men, Alexander and Anthony, were buckled
in their seats at the time of takeoff, having decided not to
stay in the cockpit. The three of them chatted about their
day and the Crusader castle and Damascus. Then, while
drinking champagne, Alexander said, "Isabel, if I may say
so, those diamond earrings are the most beautiful things I
have ever seen on a lady's ears."

Isabel had forgotten about them; she had not even seen
them properly yet. She took a small hand mirror from her
alligator bag and looked at them, hardly believing her
own eyes. They were magnificent. Later, in London, if
she went to insure them, she would discover that they

were a pair of eleven-carat, perfectly matched, square-cut diamonds set in platinum and slightly raised above the rim of small, cushion-cut diamonds.

Completely overwhelmed, she made her way as casually as she could to Alexis's cabin, where she looked at them in the large French mirror. They were utterly magnificent. She found the box on the desk.

It was a Van Cleef & Arpels box and inside was a small card: "just remember I love you. Alexis."

She could hardly conceive as to what such a gift from a man meant.

She put the box and its precious contents in her handbag. Feeling a bit numb from it all and more than a little frightened, she returned to the main cabin and the two men.

VII

BOTH FIRES were built up in the drawing room, the curtains were drawn, there were fresh flowers, the dogs were barking and the telephone was ringing. Isabel was home.

She had thanked Alexander for all his kindnesses over a drink. Now he was gone. Gamal had helped carry the cases into the dressing room. Isabel found it more difficult saying good-bye to him, but now he was gone as well.

The last thing that Alexander did before he'd left was return Isabel's passport. Now she held it in her hand, her mind flashing back to only a week before, when she had so reluctantly given it to him. She had felt so safe and secure during the week that never once had she thought about the passport. She hadn't even thought to ask for it back!

She took it and her handbag, and went up into her bedroom. There was a lovely fire crackling in the fireplace, and there were two dozen white long-stem roses in the bowl on the low Japanese table that stood between the Damascus mirror and the end of the bed. They were half-open, and against the room's dark background their whiteness stood out brightly. How extravagant of Endo, thought Isabel.

On the bed were laid all the gifts she had received from Alexis. She stood there just looking at them, and then she knew that the roses were from Alexis as well. She turned around to look at them again and, sure enough, lying on a small silver tray near them was a small, white card. She tore it open, almost trembling with pleasure. It read: "All the flowers in the world are for you. Alexis."

Isabel felt her knees go weak. The tears welled up in her eyes, and slowly she sank to the floor. With the card in her hand, she sat there and wept from the depths of her soul as she looked at the white roses.

She thought of the people in her life who had professed to love her. There was Anthony, who seemed to sum up all her relationships with men, until now. Anthony, who had said, "All the flowers in the world are for me." There was Kate, who said, "I love you. All you have to do is take me along. You will be my mirror, and I will bathe in my own reflection, your life. You will be famous and rich, and therefore, I will be famous and rich. You must not fail, so that I may not fail. We will have success." Intense preoccupation with herself, was, in the end, what Isabel's mother offered.

Ava, who said, "I am of your blood and therefore I must love you and you must love me." Her pathological narcissism was what powered her aggressiveness. Such people, so in love with themselves, have no room for love for anyone else.

Isabel Wells, who had been running away all her life from one kind of love, while voraciously seeking another kind, had at last to run no more. She had found it.

She sat there in her tears and flowers, remembering something she had read by Mary Gordon: "Where men and women are romantically involved there is a history of signs and gestures, so that the extravagant act, the visible emblem occurs instinctively, quickly. There is a rush of blood that tells us that it is right."

The stream of tears was only a trickle now, but she sobbed from relief at the thought of never again having to run away from the pathologically narcissistic family and men who had attached themselves to her. How desperate she must have been to have accepted them, to have even become the least bit involved with them. She reminded herself that they alone were not to blame. She must have met them more than halfway.

She buried her face in the roses, drew in their scent and got up. She went to the dressing room where Endo was unpacking her cases and took from the cupboard a heavy, tobacco-colored, raw silk galabia and a pair of slippers. She went to the bathroom and changed.

Returning to her room, she picked up the great silver-and-amber necklace that Alexis had given her and put it on. She sat on the bed and propped up the pillows behind her. As she was moving about she caught sight of herself in the mirror and thought how Alexis would like her in this robe.

She sat on the bed cross-legged, looking at her gifts. Endo came in, asking where the things were to go. He said that he thought the bumblebee dress was the most beautiful thing that he had ever seen. She told him how she had received each of the gifts and what a wonderful week it had been. But that there was no job. She could not help herself and confided in Endo, telling him she was in love.

She told him to put the passport in the safe and opened the Van Cleef box to look at her earrings again. She showed her pieces to Endo. If Isabel had been overwhelmed, then Endo was astonished.

"Please, Miss Wells, will you put them on?"

She did and became all excited again. They were just so overpowering. Endo told her that they were the most wonderful things he had ever seen, and fit for an empress.

"They were all good-bye presents from Sir Alexis," Isabel sighed.

"No, Miss Wells. A gift like that is more a hello present."

"Oh, do you think so? You clever thing, Endo!" She jumped up and gave him a kiss, she was so overjoyed. Then she showed him the camel photograph. He looked at Alexis and said, "Miss Wells, I am sure that man does not have a banana-colored suit."

They both began to laugh. At last she was seeing the amusing side of it all. The American, middle-class, not-so-young lady from an immigrant background makes good. Hits the jackpot. Gets the jewels, captures Prince Charming. Good. Life was a gas! Isabel was in love.

She told Endo she was ravenous. He said he knew that she would be and where did she want to dine? She told him "in style," and removed the silver necklace, and the gold hoops from her ears. She put on her diamonds, then the diamond bumblebee, and said, "Come on, Endo, we will eat in the kitchen."

He laughed and said he had dined.

"Well, then I will have a tray here in my room."

"You know, Miss Wells, with things like that, you may never eat in *my* kitchen again." And off he went.

Isabel sat there smiling. In the mirror's reflection, she could see the crackling fire, the lynx-covered bed and herself among her souvenirs. She moved her hair and looked at herself and thought of Alexis's generosity and their love for each other.

He wasn't with her, but she did not feel the loss that she might have. He was not gone, he was just absent.

It was strange that everything that she touched on the bed did not conjure up, as most souvenirs do, the memory of something that happened and is gone. When she picked up the bumblebee dress, or the ivory compact, she did not think of the past. She only felt that she had a marvelous gift that was now.

The week that she and Alexis had just had together was over in one sense, but that was merely physical time. She realized that there would never be a past for her and Alexis. There would only be now.

The very first call of the morning was from Cecil Davenport.

"Well, my dear, I just know he has hired you to take over all his museum projects and be the exclusive buyer for his collection."

Isabel laughed and said, "No, Cecil, my dear, he has not hired me at all. I did not get the job."

There was a moment of silence and a disappointed voice said, "I do not believe it. It is not possible. Oh, I know! He offered you the job, and for some one of your mad, ridiculous reasons, you have turned him down. Isabel, you did not send him packing, did you?"

"No, Cecil, I did not send him packing."

"Well, what happened?"

"Well, actually . . ."

"Oh, I know, you just put him off for some reason. Do you want to discuss it with me? Is that it? Oh, Isabel, I know one thing: He is a clever, intelligent man, and once he met you and saw how you do things, he would never hire anyone else. Why not have lunch with me today, and we will talk the whole thing over?"

"Cecil, that would be lovely, but not today. I have so much to do. Tomorrow."

"Fine, The Connaught at one. My dear, you did give me a scare for a moment."

"Cecil, what a dear friend you are. You always give my ego a boost. Until tomorrow, when I will tell you all."

The second phone call came from a girlfriend. They had a long gossip, and Isabel told her what a fantastic time she had been given and how happy she was. Her friend was thrilled and said, "Well, you deserve it. It's about time you met a good man." They made a date for tea on Wednesday, and the girlfriend promised to keep it all very quiet for the moment.

The third call of the morning was from her publisher. That, so far, was the best call. The film rights to the second Meredith Montague had just been sold. They were both overjoyed.

And on it went. She was still in bed at 11:20, on and off the telephone, when what probably was the seventh or eighth call of the morning came.

"Good morning, Isabel, it is Alexander."

"Good morning."

"I have called to see that you are well and ask you to dinner this evening."

Isabel smiled. "You are kind, Alexander, I *am* fine, thank you. But honestly, I think I *must* stay in and get my thoughts and life back together."

"Isabel, may I give you a word of advice?"

"Yes."

"Do not think too much. The world and things move the way they will go. I would like to have you join a party of friends; if you change your mind, please call. You do have my number?"

"Yes, Alexander, you are kind."

They rang off.

Isabel bathed and dressed and knew that Alexander was telling her not to worry, all was well with her and Alexis. He was turning out to be more a Mayfair cupid than a Mayfair pimp, in her case anyway.

She went up to the studio and saw Joy. They checked

the weaving and went over some enquiries about orders and an exhibition.

Joanna came in with the animals in tow. They had, at last, forgiven Isabel for going away and now jumped and barked and allowed her to greet them. They always did this and were so clever because Isabel really did feel badly when they ignored her in retaliation for her leaving them.

Endo brought the three women lunch trays up in the studio and Isabel asked Endo to join them. She was going to tell them about all the things she had seen in Egypt.

The little working household had a lovely time hearing all about it. They were all such sweet people and so happy for the joy that she showed. That first day when she went to Kan-el-Kalili with André Beshawi, she had bought them each a little gift, which she distributed after lunch.

They were all pleased, and Endo, who had just stacked all the empty luncheon trays in the elevator, said before he went down the stairs, "Now I will leave and she will tell you the best part. She is in love." He smiled broadly and fled down the stairs.

Isabel could not help but laugh. Endo was always so careful, so discreet in everything, but occasionally he would be cheeky and tease her.

Joy and Joanna were a bundle of questions: When was he coming? Was he handsome? How did she meet him? Could they meet him when he came? What were her plans?

Laughing, Isabel told them she knew nothing except that she was very happy and that, of course, if he came, they would all meet him.

After lunch Joanna went to the library to type up the manuscript. Joy went back to the loom, and Isabel went into the drawing room to read the week's work that Joanna had typed.

It was there, in the drawing room, that she took the call. It came through from Athens.

"Isabel?"

"Hello, Mother."

"Isabel?"

"Yes, Mother."

"Isabel, this is your mother."

"Mother, I know it's you, how are you?"

"I have been trying to get you all morning. Your line has been busy. You must have some phone bill. Well, better you than me. I thought that you would call me last night. When did you get in?"

"I arrived last night."

"Well, why didn't you call me last night?"

"I just did not think about it."

"Oh, that's nice. You *do* know that I called. I suppose that Chink didn't even give you the message."

"Mother, you must not call him a Chink, he is Japanese."

"Well, did he give you the message?"

"He gave me a list of messages. I never looked at them."

"Oh, well, if that is the way you want to conduct your business, I just hope you did not miss out on anything. It is a good thing I wasn't dying and had to depend on that Chink, oh, excuse me, I mean *Japanese,* to get in touch with you. Well, I'll fix him one day, you'll see. Listen, I don't want to waste money talking about that dog. How was your job in Egypt?"

"I did not get the job in Cairo."

"Never mind, sweetheart, you should always listen to Mother. She knows best. I told you never to fool around with those Arabs and their money. I spit on them, they should all drop dead. Let them go through what the Jews went through. Never mind, darling, they'll get theirs. If you didn't get the job, then why did you stay the week and waste the money?"

Isabel sighed heavily and said, "Well, first of all, stop cursing them. If the job had come through, I would not have taken it. Then, secondly, I stayed because I had the most wonderful holiday I could ever have dreamed of as a guest."

"I knew it, I knew that you went there on a holiday. I don't know why you have to feel guilty. If you went there to have a holiday, and you did not want me to join you, I can understand. But, to pretend that you were going there on business! You know that I am the first one to tell you to have a wonderful time in your life when you are young. When you get too old, you have nothing. Wait, it won't be long, you will see. Lie, since when do you have to lie, *to me* of all people? I *knew* when you were so vague about the job and where you were staying. I do wish that you would stop trying to pull the wool over my eyes. Never mind, I knew anyway. So, you had a wonderful holiday. What was so wonderful about it?"

Isabel wanted to explain, but it was useless. "Oh, there were just so many wonderful things to see and do, and the people were charming. From beginning to end it was a dream of a trip. I am so lucky to have had it."

"Well, good for you. I don't suppose you met somebody? I hope you did not get involved with an Arab."

"Yes, I did meet someone."

"Well, the holiday is over now. This call is costing a great deal of money. I want to hear all about it, darling, but that can wait until I see you. Look, I am going to come for a visit to London. I need a little holiday."

"When do you think you would like to come?"

"Well, frankly, some dear friends have asked me to join them on a short trip, a holiday, as it so happens, to Egypt. Now that I hear all about it from you, I think I should go and take a look at what you think is a wonderful country. Then I will come directly up to London."

"When does all this happen?"

"Well, I am waiting to hear about reservations at the moment. I will have to let you know. You have nowhere to go now that you have taken your holiday anyway, have you?"

"I honestly do not know what my plans are at the moment. I have only just come back."

"Ava sends her love. I'll call you. Look, I really can't afford to call, so I will write to you."

"Never mind. Mother, why not call me collect when you know what is happening?"

Isabel put down the telephone and knew instinctively that there was going to be trouble. She could always tell in her mother's voice when she was plotting something that was doomed to fail. She put it out of her mind and went on reading. Half an hour went by and the telephone rang again.

"Hello?"

"Hello,"

Her heart stood still. It was Alexis.

"I miss you," he said.

"And I miss you, Alexis. Your roses are wonderful! So beautiful in my bedroom!"

"I think about you all the time. Was the journey home comfortable?"

"Yes, perfectly."

"Why did you not have supper on the plane? I had dinner prepared for you."

"Oh, I don't know, I think you have overwhelmed my appetite."

He laughed. "Did Alexander call?"

"Yes, he asked me out to dinner this evening."

"Are you going?"

"No, I am going to stay in. I need to get my thoughts together and catch up on some sleep. How are you, is the conference going well?"

"Very Arab, dear, very Arab. But I think it is going well enough."

"How long will you be there?"

"Oh, I have no idea, a few days, I think."

"Then what are your plans?"

"I have no idea at the moment, darling."

"When will I see you?"

"I do not know that either at this time. Was everything well at your house?"

"Yes. Oh, I have some nice news. I think you will be pleased since you are an admirer of mine. The cinema has just purchased my second Meredith Montague!"

"How wonderful for you, darling! Oh, I am so happy for you."

After that their conversation became strangely hesitant. Isabel could not bear it and asked, "Is there something wrong, Alexis? What's wrong?"

"Isabel, I never asked you if you have another man in your life. I am sure you do. A woman like you, you must have men. Darling, before I come to London, I want you to think about us. See all your men."

"I have no need to see them, Alexis. I am in love with you."

"And I am in love with you, darling. But, those are words, Isabel. I mean to show you that I love you, and I mean to know that you love me. So, I want you to see those men, go to bed with them, to find out exactly where we stand and where the other men stand in your life."

"Is that what you are going to do, Alexis? See and sleep with your women?"

"Yes, darling. I am sure about us, but other people must be let down gently."

"You mean like Hamida?"

"Oh, I thought you might know about Hamida," he chuckled. "Yes, Hamida is one."

"What will you tell her?"

"There is nothing to tell her yet, darling. We must see each other again first. Will you see your men?"

"Yes, Alexis."

"I want you to be very sure. We will know everything when we meet again. Until then I will not call you."

"Oh, please call, Alexis."

"No, dear, but we will be together before the week is out. Will that give you time?"

"Alexis, I do not have an *army* to see, you know." She giggled.

"Isabel, I do not want to know. We will never speak about the past; it will be over. I wanted you very much last night. You do know that I love you? And we will be together, if that is what you want. You do know that? You must have no doubts about it."

"Yes, I know, Alexis."

"*Bon*, then, *à tout à l'heure.*"

"*A tout à l'heure, Alexis.*"

After Alexis said good-bye, Isabel sat for a very long time with her manuscript on the table in front of her. Things were moving very fast for Isabel, maybe even too fast. Alexis was a very clever man and knew exactly how to handle Isabel. That was something they both knew.

It was there, an amazing new feeling, one that Isabel had been looking for all her life, of being complete with another person. It suddenly made all the years of searching and loneliness worth it all.

If there were any doubts in Isabel's mind, they were not about their happiness together; but only that she would carry into a life with this man the years and habits of being alone. She had known for a long time that her aloneness, her quest for survival, had led her to a kind of isolation, a separateness. It had also led her to face the reality that many people insulated themselves against seeing: that all are alone, no matter how complete the relationship.

The very thought of walking through the world with another human being, with Alexis, was glorious. Alexis and

Isabel for all the rest of their days could rejoice in their love.

Isabel felt born again. She thought of the river.

Endo arrived with her cup of tea and a plate of rice cakes. After her refreshment, she went back to her reading.

Later that evening, just before dinner, someone came to the street door. She waited to hear the sound of Max's footsteps bounding up the stairs to her bedroom, but there was no Max. There was instead a light tap at the door.

"Miss Wells," Endo called. "Sir Alexis Hyatt's serving man, Gamal, is down in the hall."

Isabel left her book and immediately went down to meet him. She was pleased to see him, and thought he looked quite a sight with Arthur prancing over his shoes, back and forth, his tail curling around Gamal's trouser leg; Winston was barking, and Rita was being held and spoken to in Arabic. She was mesmerized into silence by the voice and the strange language.

There was a box on the floor next to Gamal. He greeted Isabel, put Rita down and gave Isabel the box. It was for her, he said. From Sir Alexis.

The two servants went into Endo's kitchen, where Gamal was offered a cup of coffee. Isabel carried the package, which was about the size of a small hatbox, into the drawing room. She opened it. Moving the tissue paper around carefully, she found neatly packaged the ruby-colored glass goblets from which they had drunk champagne in the Roda Island palace. There was a card that read: *"Bukra fil mishmish—Alexis."*

She remembered well what that meant. The literal translation was, "Tomorrow when the apricots blossom," but its true meaning was, "The special tomorrow stretching to infinity."

Isabel thought of how much Alexis really did care for her. She was naturally touched and longed for him to be with her right then, to take her and fondle her. She wanted to come, to have him fill and grow hard with desire for her so that she could take him in her mouth and make love to him, give herself to him, show him that she too wanted him.

She squirmed slightly in her chair and suddenly felt very aroused. She contracted her vaginal muscles a few times, not deliberately, but as a natural reaction to the very thought of coming and making love to him. The contractions were so numerous and strong that she felt her clitoris move along with the action and before she knew it, she came very lightly all by herself.

Endo entered the room to tell her that dinner was ready. Was it permissible for him to ask Gamal to stay and have supper with him in the kitchen?

"Endo, that would be very nice indeed. Are you getting on well enough between his English and your English?"

"Yes, we understand each other very well, and, you know, we both speak as much French as we do English, so it is quite possible to have an interesting conversation. I think he is a nice man and we are talking about our countries and our cultures."

Isabel was delighted. "Please, Endo, he has been very good to me. You may certainly have him to dinner, and make it very clear to him that he is welcome here any time you would like to have him. Now listen, Endo, these glasses are very special. I want them taken from the box and put on my desk in the library. I will place them myself later."

Isabel had her dinner in the dining room quietly by herself. Endo had made two of her favorite things: tempura and sukiaki. For dessert he had peeled fresh lychee nuts.

Isabel, feeling exhausted, asked him to bring her tea to the bedroom. She would undress and go directly to bed and watch television. At the kitchen door she stopped to say goodnight to Gamal and was pleased to see that they had set the kitchen table for themselves and were going to have a leisurely supper together. He bowed and thanked her.

Endo followed her towards the bedroom and asked, "Miss Wells, would it be all right for me to show Gamal the studio and the house, since you are in the bedroom?"

Isabel thought it was terribly sweet and told him it was quite all right to make him comfortable and show him anything Endo liked. She was really pleased, not only for Gamal but for Endo as well. He had been with Isabel for over three years and she knew that he did not make friends easily. Obviously he liked Gamal.

In bed she relaxed and watched an old movie. She thought again of her newfound luck. After ten years of

Meredith Montagues, she was now able to sustain herself on them.

The last thing that she thought before she went to sleep was that she must do as Alexis asked. She would get in touch with Max tomorrow. Endo had taken several phone calls from him, and Max had been told that she would return on Sunday evening.

There were other men in Isabel's life. But Max was the only one that she really had to see. The others were not really that important.

She could not help but wonder how many women Alexis would have until the next time they met. She was not unrealistic; he was a superb lover and would have a woman every night, that was for sure.

The next day, for her luncheon with Cecil, Isabel wore a navy blue silk dress. It looked like an old-fashioned child's smock, all loose with lovely long sleeves tight at the cuff. The yoke of the dress was elegantly done in smocking, and from there it hung full to the middle of her calf. There was something almost naive about it even if it was by Balmain.

With it she wore beige silk stockings and very high Charles Jourdan shoes in beige calfskin. Over the smock dress she wore a sleeveless sable coat. No jewelry except for earrings and the bumblebee pinned between the elbow and the wrist on the sleeve of her right arm. Over her shoulder she slung her navy leather handbag.

It was only a few minutes from her house to The Connaught. The sky was clear, and there was a cold nip in the air. There was that wonderful smell of autumn. As she skirted Berkeley Square, she could hear the leaves rustling, looked and saw them skipping through the grass.

Just as she crossed the threshold, Cecil caught up with her. They kissed hello, and he told her how elegant she looked as they crossed the lobby and separated, he to the men's cloakroom, she to the ladies'.

Cecil seemed to be in a flap, but slowly calmed down. They exchanged light talk while the waiter drifted around the table taking orders for food and wine.

When they were alone, he looked across at Isabel and said, "Well, my dear, now tell me everything from the beginning and why you do not have that job, for the moment, that is. There is no . . ." Then he stopped. "Don't tell

me, I can see it in your face. You have made a mess of it.
You have fallen in love with him."

Isabel, who could not resist teasing him just a little,
smiled and gracefully flung back her long chestnut hair.

"Oh, I say!" Cecil exclaimed. "He is in love with you
as well! My dear! Oh, my dear. I am speechless. It is very
serious, isn't it?"

"Yes."

"You truly love him?"

"Cecil, I am terribly in love with him."

"Oh, my dear friend," he applauded. "I am very happy
for you. This is wonderful news."

That was the first highlight of the luncheon with Cecil.
They talked about Egypt and Alexis, and he asked if she
was going to marry him. She told him frankly that she had
no idea what he had in mind. He had asked her nothing,
and honestly, she did not even know if he were the marrying kind.

"Are you prepared to be his mistress? Of course you
would."

"I don't know anything, Cecil. This is all new to me,
almost as much as it is to you. I only know that I am in
love with him, and I think he loves me."

"And what of the job, Isabel? You must be sensible
about that?"

She laughed. "There never was a job, Cecil."

Cecil was not a man who could cope with this sort of
thing. He could cope with anything that had to do with his
work, but with a friend and especially a woman friend in
love, he was useless. He could only give down-to-earth
practical information. And there was nothing to advise.
The only thing he said to her was, "Do not let him go,"
and, "Be happy."

Over coffee came the second highlight of the meal. In
walked Max with a beautiful young girl on his arm and
another young man.

After they were seated at their table, he went over to
Isabel to say hello, and she introduced him to Cecil. Max
was very formal and polite, asked when she had returned
and said that he would be in touch. He was very attractive
but seemed young to her, and she was more than a little
annoyed at the fact that Max, who always pooh-poohed
The Connaught and expensive restaurants and taking her

out to lunch, seemed to have different opinions where other friends were concerned.

Clever Cecil picked it up and said, "Isabel, you are not going to get interested in young men like that when you have a man like Alexis Hyatt, are you?" That was practical, sensible Cecil at his best.

They parted after lunch. Cecil, still overwhelmed by Isabel and her new relationship, wished her all the best, at the same time making her promise not to let her heart rule her head.

Max arrived at six-thirty that very evening. Isabel told Endo to make something simple for supper and, if he wanted the evening off, he could have it.

Max was exactly the same with her as he had always been, and only a short time after they were together, he was making love to her, touching where he knew she would get turned on quickly. At first Isabel was uneasy with Max. Then she realized that Alexis was so clever—there *was* something to resolve here; to be finished or maybe not finished. He was right; she had to find out how she felt, and so she relaxed.

Endo rang through on the telephone and said there was a buffet in the dining room. They should try and eat no later than ten o'clock or the dinner would not be so nice. He was leaving now if there was nothing else. That was his discreet way of saying that the house was now empty but for them.

Max asked about the man with whom she had been lunching. She asked about his friends. He asked about Egypt but really was not very interested. He rolled a few joints, and after they smoked they both felt more relaxed.

They went to the bedroom because Isabel wanted to change into a galabia. He would not let her go once they were there, but threw off his clothes and climbed into the bed, pulling her down on top of him. They lit up another joint, and while they smoked she asked about the girl.

Suddenly everything that he had ever said to her took on a different light. His caution, his private ways, his excluding her from his life except for sex. All this that she had accepted before, but resented now. His lack of generosity towards her was astounding.

Max remarked about her jewelry. He said it was dazzling, and where did it all come from? She told him Alexis had given it all to her. He asked her how they made love; clearly *that* was all he was interested in. She told him and it kindled his passion. He now had her in his arms and he kissed her and fondled her. When he sucked hard on her tits she became very excited.

He rolled her onto her side and moved his hands over her. He put her on her back and kissed her breasts again, and then her stomach, nibbling at her through her pubic hair. He lay on her stomach with his face between her legs and searched with his tongue until he found her clitoris.

His legs too were spread wide apart, and she could see his small asshole and his beautiful balls. She bent her head forward and took them in her mouth and rolled them around. They both became crazy with excitement; they had been making love for a long time and knew each other's bodies perfectly. He made love to her in every imaginable position. Then they used dildoes on each other.

Max would come to the edge of an orgasm and stop, prolonging it so he could have more of her. Sometimes in the middle of it all, they would just stop and talk until he was calm and under control, and then they would start up again. Never would he allow her to calm down though. He always kept her coming.

This night though, for the first time in all their years together, Isabel refused him something. When he wanted to come in her mouth, she could not do it.

He sensed something was wrong, but that only made him want her more. Eventually they went down to the kitchen and had some supper, then to the drawing room and lit up more joints. He took her again there. He was very aggressive with her. He had a fantastic stroke and his balls slapped against her again and again. He had her bent over a chair and pressed hard on her hindquarters as he pumped deep into her. With every stroke, she could feel him pounding her uterus. He had her coming now in constant orgasms, and when he finally came, and she felt him wash over the inside of her, they both moaned with the joy of it.

Exhausted, they went to the bedroom and fell asleep.

When they awoke, Isabel murmured, "It's very late, but I don't want to leave you. I wish you could stay, Max."

"Well, you know that's impossible," he sighed. "As it is, I will have so much to explain when I get home."

"What will you say?"

"Oh, that I was out with the boys. I don't know, I'll fig-ure something out. I'm so warm and happy here, I hate to go out into the cold."

"Do you want me to run you a bath? Stop kissing me, Max, it only makes it harder for me to let you go. Now, do you want that bath?"

"Yes, if you take one with me."

"You know I will. You know very well how I adore washing you all over, getting you all soapy and slippery. Let me go. Come on, I'll go run the bath."

"I'll let you go if you let me do with you what I want in the tub," he laughed. As Isabel climbed out of bed he gave her a hard smack on the bottom.

"Oh! Max! That hurt!" Isabel yelped.

"Well, I can't help it. When I see your round, full ass it's hard to resist giving you a whack. Come here, and I will kiss away those red marks."

"Come on, Max. Let me fill the tub."

"Well, now that I think of it, you're like the man in *The Picnic* by Renoir, without clothes on," Isabel smiled. "Now that we have decided that we are both masterpieces, I will go and see what the time is. Do you want a cup of coffee before you leave?"

"Make it tea, honey."

"Max, it's four o'clock," Isabel called. "Well, ten min-utes to four anyway."

"Oh, shit. There's going to be hell to pay."

"Max, I don't understand. I just don't. You're not mar-ried to her, you tell me that you don't love her, but you don't want to hurt her. You tell me that you're going to leave her, and yet everything that you do with her governs how far this affair of ours can go. Oh, I know . . . I promised that I would never talk about it to you. I used to be afraid to; we had something very good together, and I never wanted to ruin it. No, don't say anything. Let's not talk about it." Isabel stared at him, and she knew her de-cision was firm.

"Now, stop it," Max ordered. "We said we would not worry about it. Time will fix everything."

"That's right, Max," she shrugged. "Time has fixed everything. I used to think that your lady friend was the problem between us, but she's not really. There is no love between us, *that* is the problem."

"Come on now, give me a kiss before I go," Max said, avoiding the issue. "A brotherly-sisterly kind of kiss. Although, whatever you did to me, I couldn't get up again."

"Bye, Max."

"I'll give you a call. Listen, you know it's very difficult. I will come as soon as I can. But, remember that if I don't call or I don't come, it isn't that I don't think about you or that I don't want you. It's just that, well, things are all complicated. You know the story. But I will come as soon as I can."

"No, don't bother, Max. It's over."

"It's what?"

"Over, finished."

"Is that really what you want, to give up this fantastic thing we have together?"

"I am not going to give it up. I am going to have it with a man who loves me and wants to make me happy, and that is not you."

"Oh, stop being silly. I made you happy tonight," he scoffed. "I will again one day soon. Listen, I must go now." He kissed her on the cheek and left.

Isabel was both emotionally and physically exhausted. She saw Max leave, and with him, years of tension and hidden anxiety.

The house was very still. The animals were sound asleep. She went back up to the bathroom, where she picked up towels, mopped up some water and generally tried to put it in order. She took two aspirins because, suddenly, she had a splitting headache.

Picking up some fresh sheets and pillowcases from the linen cupboard, she went to the bedroom, stripped the bed and remade it. She opened a window, and the gust of cold dawn air moved the draperies and freshened the room. She removed her robe and collapsed into the clean bed, snuggled down deep in the eiderdown in a fetal position. She tucked a pillow close to her cheek and closed her eyes. She was terribly unhappy over Max's insensitivity and lack of understanding.

Isabel had no idea what she had expected. At the beginning of their lovemaking tonight it was difficult for her, and he knew it. He was afraid that it was over, and so he worked on her, seducing her down to the raw bones of sexuality. They stayed steeped in it. He gave everything and took everything.

It was not until she had ridden him in the bath and had collapsed, exhausted, ready to be held and cared for, that she realized that it was over for him. He was going home to another woman. At last, because of Alexis, she had spoken up.

Alexis offered her love and companionship, or at least the possibility of them. Max offered her nothing. . . .

She woke at one in the afternoon, mercifully, without the headache. Her body was completely exhausted. Ringing through to Endo, she asked him to bring her morning drink and some tea.

When he came into the room with her tray, he asked if she was well. It seemed that some time during the morning the dogs had barked and scrambled to be let out of her room, and she had never even heard them. She told him he was not to worry, that she was fine, but very tired. She would not leave her bed that day. "Oh, and if Max Aspinal calls at the house here, you are never to let him in ever again. If he should call on the telephone, simply say I am unavailable."

Isabel went back to bed and called the friends that she was to have tea with and canceled. The two girls, Joy and Joanna, had enough to do without her, and so she had her quiet day alone in her room.

She did not sleep; she just lay there quietly, resting with her eyes open, not even thinking. At four in the afternoon there was a light tap at the door and Endo entered carrying a five-foot-high orchid plant. There must have been fifty or sixty pure white baby orchids on it.

Endo had no need to tell her, she knew at once that they were from Alexis. She had them placed on the chest behind her bed. Endo handed her the card. It was just signed, "Alexis."

The flowers were staggeringly impressive and luscious when you looked at the entire effect the plant made. But when you looked at one orchid at a time—the little white velvety blossom with its short throat and small round tip that made the center of the flower look like a clitoris—its beauty made you want to weep.

By seven in the evening she was hungry. Endo brought her a tray of scrambled eggs, green salad and a peach. After her tray was taken away, she fell asleep and slept all through the night.

Ava had been flirting for a long time with an industrialist who happened to be a friend of her husband's. He was very rich, stable and married; had grandchildren, was intelligent, interesting, very gregarious and generous. Ava saw him as a responsible man, still virile. She played the coquette with him in front of his wife and her own husband. She teased and toyed with him, and everyone thought her very amusing.

He, in turn, found her fascinating, because of her preoccupation with herself, her little projects and her vanity. Being middle-aged and Greek, he liked the attention and flattery that she paid him. Never once in the two years that they had known each other had he ever overstepped good manners by putting her in her place for her sometimes cruel teasing.

He knew his friend, Alfred, to be the kindest, most honorable of men. If Alfred had any fault at all it was that he might be a little boring. The man *did* often ponder how frustrated Ava was sexually. There was something about her, something unfulfilled, and he knew that his friend, though he might have a good sex life with her, was too kind in bed to this woman. He had picked up long ago the underlying aggression Ava had towards men.

On Wednesday, the same day that Isabel was spending in bed in London, Ava met this man, whose name was Takis, by accident. Alfred was away for the day on business of some sort, and Ava had decided to go shopping in the morning and spend the rest of the day at home working on one of her articles.

Walking along Basilies Sophias Street, near the Benaki Museum, she was stopped by the tooting horn of Takis's new light-blue Mercedes.

"Ava, come," he said. "I will give you a ride in my new car."

She popped into the car and gave him a kiss on the cheek, then proceeded to tease him about his expensive new car. He invited her for a ride to his house in Sounion and offered her lunch in a small tavern near the sea.

On an impulse and because she really wanted to be with him, she said yes, she would love to, and off they went.

Ava flirted with him outrageously. She teased and touched his arm, his thigh; patted his cheek as he sped along the sea road through Glyfada. She kept drawing attention to herself: "Do you like this color on me? Do you think that yellow suits me? Takis, tell me, do you think this dress is too tight? Alfred says it shows my figure up too much. What do you think, Takis? I can hardly believe it! You look so young to be a grandfather. You know how Athens gossips. They will say next you have bedded me."

She laughed and smiled through her entire monolog on herself and now sat provocatively next to him. He occasionally got a word in about the quality of the ride, or the color of the upholstery, but she distracted him from his preoccupation with his car by sitting close to him.

He bought her a delicious lunch of *barbounia* and salad of tomato and onion swimming in heavy olive oil. She declined the salad, ate the fish, and crumbled half a loaf of bread to bits as they finished two bottles of Domestica.

She took his hand after lunch and pretended that she could read his palm. She played with his fingers and toyed with his hand. She pinched his cheeks and told him he was pudgy and lovely, like an old teddy bear.

He helped her up to the car from the beach taverna where they had eaten. She leaned against him lightly, pretending she was quite weak from drink. He picked her up by the waist and set her on her feet a few steps above him. She turned around and pulled him up the few stairs. "How strong you are, was I very heavy? I am not very heavy, am I? I work at it you know, how much do you think I weigh? Here, lift me again and you will be able to tell. Well, maybe I am too much for an old grandfather like you."

Takis led her to the car while she was still talking about herself. He decided to take her to the house in Sounion, open it up, and give her the fuck of her life.

She was too busy flirting and telling him about her great success in all that she did, to even known that she was about to get laid.

The gates were locked; he opened them, drove the new car through, and they went to open the house as its shutters were all closed. They opened a few and then he offered to make her a coffee. Now she was more than the little coquette, she was the defenseless little lady, all pretty and purring.

How wonderful to be there with him. She now saw a different side to him, but it was getting late and she had things to do. After all, she might compromise him if they were there too long.

He poured the coffee and put his arm around her. She pretended to pull away, telling him what a naughty man he was, and he slapped her on the cheek, none too gently, to get her attention. She pouted and he kissed her. She put up a very small struggle as he continued to kiss her until she relaxed and opened her mouth ever so slightly and then he had her.

Between feeble reproaches—"Oh no, no, we can't, no" —she helped him take off her dress so as not to wrinkle it. He put her on the sofa, on her back, determined to give her a really good fuck, the one that she had been teasing for over the past two years.

She did not have very large breasts, but she did have large nipples. He put one of them in his mouth and sucked hard on it, and every time she protested he gave her a light slap on the cheek. At one point he took his mouth off the nipple and said, "You be quiet. This is what you want; you be quiet for once," and back to her nipple he went.

She began to squirm with pain and finally told him he was hurting her too much. He left off and went to the other nipple. By now he was completely aroused. He played with her body as he had with her nipples. He did not have to ask her, she threw her legs up and out, and when he touched her vulva, she saw him rampant and ready to drive into her. She escaped him for the moment by rolling over on her side and starting to protest. At the same time she tried to get away from him and off the sofa.

He gave her a very hard smack on the ass and pulled her to him, telling her she had teased him long enough. With some gentleness, he touched her and fondled her, telling her that he was going to make her happy, more satisfied than she had ever been, to trust him.

He had her down on the sofa again, and while talking to her, found his way. Before she knew what was happening, he rammed into her. Once inside he stayed there and told her exactly what to do; he was an accomplished lover and knew very well how to satisfy her.

Ava did not have an orgasm, but she liked the attention and the effort that he made over her. So she faked it. Before she dressed, she did some of her gymnastics to show him how limber she was and to show off her body to this puffing, middle-aged Greek lover.

He told her he was going to take her in some of those positions. He told her he had a *pied à terre* in Athens, and if they were very discreet, they could meet in the afternoons. He said that now that he had her, he found her wonderful, but she needed more working on because, although he knew she had enjoyed herself, he was not sure she had been satisfied.

Ava dressed herself and looked impeccable. Not a wrinkle in her dress, not a hair out of place. He took her home and tried to make arrangements for the next day. Ava was clever.

Now she knew she had him hooked with the desire to satisfy her, and now she had given him a taste, but in the future he would have to work a little harder to get her. No, tomorrow was not convenient. Yes, of course she would like to be with him, but as he had said, they must be discreet.

And so Ava began another affair, thinking to herself that he might be a better husband than the one she had because he had so much more money and she liked him quite well. As for the sex, he was right. She wanted it, and he could work on her, and maybe it would all work out well. She would not mind having a big old stud like him for a change. Yes, she would work on that. She would never do anything to hurt Alfred, but if it turned out that they were good together and he offered her a better marriage, she would be obliged to take it.

At six she arrived home and took a bath, very sure to wash all the lovemaking away. Before she dressed she examined herself in the mirror, not so much in admiration as in an unremitting search for flaws, signs of fatigue, decay, any imperfection. There were none, or at least she saw none.

She reached down and with her left hand grabbed her left ankle. She raised her leg high, level with her shoulder, and looked at herself in the mirror, with her vagina exposed. She saw herself as a beautiful painting, a portrait of a beautiful young American woman.

As she began to dress she could not help but laugh to herself at Takis. How foolish men are about sex. Ava hated fantasy, just as she hated sleep. She had the utmost difficulty in sleeping. Sleep and fantasy took her away from herself. She felt defenseless and without control.

She went to the bar and poured herself a large Scotch,

knocking it back in one swallow. She poured herself another drink and took it out to the balcony. She stood there, looking over the city, thinking of Isabel and her amazing lack of success in having relationships.

It was obvious to Ava that Isabel's preoccupation with being creative and successful was alienating her from the possibility of making a life with anyone. Isabel would have to suffer loneliness all the days of her life because she simply did not stick to the basic rules. She herself had always obeyed the rules dictated by society and good manners. If Isabel were to be punished by having to spend her life alone, she brought it on herself. Isabel experimented with life; she lived in dreams, fantasies, illusions.

Typical of Isabel to go to Egypt on a holiday with the hope of picking up a job. Had she not warned Isabel about money and payment beforehand? About the phoniness of the rich who had to hire people like her?

As she put her empty glass on the table, she felt rather pleased with herself and her new lover. Her anger against Isabel had subsided, but only after the thought of how secure she was and how Isabel was not. She had her man, Alfred; and now a lover, if she wanted him. Isabel was a failure. She had never had a husband, and Ava was sure she never would have. If Isabel had any men in her life, they could be nothing but one-night stands. She was bad marriage material.

With that, her last thought, she went into her study and decided that she would waste no more time on the trivial thoughts of her family. After all, she had the *Reader's Digest* to deal with.

Kate was thinking about her clothes. What she should wear in Egypt. What she should take to London. *Silly, what's to think about. For London you take everything; you will be there forever.*

One of the travel agencies was going to find out about a cruise boat that stopped in Athens, next stop Alexandria. The boat stayed two days, and all passengers were offered a morning in Alexandria and a boat trip up the Nile for one night; the ship, the *Aphrodite*, then sailed directly to Southampton.

Now, if she could find a cabin on that ship, she could take all her clothes and a few household things as well, if they were all packed cleverly. In fact, she could take all her possessions. But she would have to make sure that once in Southampton the shipping line would store the bulk of her luggage.

What she would not want was for Isabel to realize that she had come to move in with her. Not that in the end Isabel would not be happy. It was more that she should be led into it gradually. After all, Isabel had lived alone all her life since she had left home. Now, in middle age, there would never be anyone. It would be better if she had her mother with her. What a good time they would have.

The very thought of London and a new life on Hill Street made her think of Endo. *When he sees how capable I am of protecting Isabel, he will go of his own accord,* she decided. *I would not for the world tell Isabel to fire him because she will not. I know her. But I intend to pay my share and then it will be possible for me to have a say-so in the house.*

Kate checked her schedule. If the boat arrives in Athens on Monday, that means it would sail sometime Tuesday or Wednesday to Alexandria. Try as she would, she couldn't remember how many days the travel agent had said it was to Southampton. Well, she'd find out.

On Saturday she would call Isabel and tell her when the boat docks. Then she would close the flat but not rent it out until she was sure she was happy in London.

She sat down and made a list of the brothers and sisters she had envied, hated, or loved across the years. She would write to them all, telling them that she was needed in London by Isabel and would be living with her for a while. She would tell them she could be reached there. After her trip around the Middle East.

VIII

ISABEL HAD not spoken to Alexis since Monday afternoon. She had no idea where he was and what was happening to him, or, for that matter, how he felt about her.

There had been no word from Max, and that was just as

well. Ava seemed content, and Kate was relatively quiescent. As for Kate's trip to London, who knew what would happen about that? She was so changeable; Isabel could only wait and see. Her work was ticking over nicely and she had the time and inclination to work on the present Meredith Montague. And she was with Alexis.

Late in the afternoon she took the dogs out for a walk, and on her way home she saw Gamal, struggling up Hill Street with a huge box wrapped in white paper with red polka dots. On top of it was a huge, red silk bow.

She called to him and walked quickly to meet him. As soon as they entered the house she called Endo to help him. Up the stairs they all trotted—dogs, Gamal, Endo, Isabel and the box.

"One gift for you, Miss Wells," said Gamal with a wide smile.

She untied the ribbon, tore off the wrappings and lifted the lid off the box, noticing that it was perforated. Before she could reach in, out leapt a pair of tiny, pure white, Chinchilla cats.

Chaos broke loose. Winston and Rita started to bark at the two fluffy, white creatures with the most amazing green eyes. Arthur appeared from nowhere to hunch his back and hiss. Just as Isabel went to grab Arthur, she saw one black, fluffy paw reach over the side of the box, then the other, and then a pair of huge, twinkly blue eyes and a tiny, almost minute, black button of a nose. She had Arthur by this time, and Endo took the black kitten. Isabel was enchanted by them.

By now all three of them had animals in their arms. None of them could stop laughing. They were having a wonderful time.

Before long things began to calm down. Gamal, amazingly, was able to get Rita and Winston playing with one of the cats. The servant handed her an envelope. She opened it and read: "My darling. I wanted you to have a Honey Lamb, Red Moon and Desert Horse. I will take you to lunch tomorrow. Claridges 2:00 P.M. in the bar. Love, Alexis."

Isabel was overjoyed. All she wanted to do was get on the telephone and call him. She could not resist it, and in her enthusiasm she asked Gamal, "Where is he, Gamal? Where can I find him? I want to call him."

Gamal, always the faithful servant, said for her to call

Alexander. She thought about it and said, "No, never mind. I will wait and thank him tomorrow."

He saw her disappointment and was very sweet and said, "The box was sent from Paris. You understand, Paris?"

She understood but still decided not to call Alexander; she would wait. She thought Alexis was mad, almost as mad as she was. Whatever was she going to do with this menagerie? Kate would think her insane, and what was worse, she would be upset because she was allergic to cats. She hoped that they would be as good about all the birds up in the studio as Arthur was. Well, Endo would train them to leave the Hill Street singers alone.

By this time the three of them were on the drawing room floor, playing with the animals. Endo invited Gamal to stay and have dinner with him.

Isabel was too excited and happy to remain alone, and of all the people she knew, and could have called, it was strange that she called Alexander. She did not ask after Alexis, but invited him to come and have a drink with her that evening, and see her kittens.

When he arrived they sat in the drawing room, having drinks. Endo and Gamal were in the kitchen. The menagerie was more or less calmed down but parading everywhere.

Alexander said, "You know, I think both you and Alexis have gone mad. This is more a zoo than a house, Isabel. Camels, Chinchilla cats, who knows where it will end!" For all his amused disapproval he managed to keep the black cat on his lap, petting her as she hung on to his tie with her little teeth.

Sir Alexis Hyatt arrived at Claridges with two of the sheikhs who had been at the conference with him in Damascus. They stepped out of the dark blue Mercedes 600 and were shown immediately through the lobby to the elevator. By the time they entered the elevator two cars had arrived behind the Mercedes and had disgorged the entourage of the two sheikhs.

Alexis was the first of the men to say farewell. The hotel manager, who knew him well, escorted him to his suite. Alexis heaved a sigh of relief. He was so pleased to be there.

The suite was perfect. It was the one that he always

had. It had two bedrooms, two baths, a drawing room and a large entrance hall. Designed some time in the twenties, it was a magnificent example of Art Deco at its best.

The rooms had several bowls of flowers in them, including the arrangement of four dozen pale pink tulips, exactly as he had asked. Out of the bedroom came Gamal to greet Alexis. He had been in the bathroom running Alexis's bath, having heard him arrive at the door. The manager handed Alexis his briefcase, they shook hands and he left. Alexis then went to the desk in the drawing room, opened the drawer and emptied the contents of his case into it. He handed the empty case to Gamal and began peeling off his clothes as he made his way first into the bedroom and then into the bathroom.

Gamal poured him a Scotch and soda and brought it to him in the bath. After rolling up his sleeves, he picked up a large sponge and started to wash Alexis's back.

Alexis was now beginning to unwind. "How is she, Gamal?" he asked.

Gamal told him everything. She loved the kittens. He had made a friend of her servant, who was very nice, and seemed to take care of her very well. She was an unusual lady. The house was like an oasis in London. She already had many animals and birds, and she had a weaving machine at which she worked. She had a Japanese garden, . . . and on and on he went.

Alexis was impatient. "All that is wonderful, Gamal, and I am happy to hear all about it, but now tell me about *her*. Is she well? Is she happy? Does she seem pleased? Those are the things I must know."

Gamal told him he thought that she was very pleased, very happy.

Alexis relaxed a little more in the bathtub, looking forward to seeing Isabel. In an hour's time he would be with her. He wondered what the separation had meant for her and how they would be when they met again. The very thought of her, just a few blocks away, aroused him.

As Gamal massaged the back of his neck, Alexis closed his eyes and felt the electricity that he still had for her. He became excited just thinking of them together. He was behaving like a schoolboy and began laughing at himself. He picked up the sponge and rubbed his arms with it and threw it back in the tub, telling Gamal he wanted to get out.

Wrapping himself in his great terrycloth robe, he went to the bedroom to dress. His new suit from Huntsman was laid out on the bed; a Turnbull and Asser shirt and tie were laid out next to it. He was pleased with the suit; it was charcoal gray with a faint pinstripe in it. When he put it on, he was very pleased indeed. The cut and fit were perfect. He sat down on the bed while Gamal put on his dark socks and tied his fine, shiny, black calfskin shoes.

While buckling on his wristwatch, he realized that for the first time since he had left Isabel on the plane at Damascus Airport he was beginning to relax.

It had been an extraordinary week. The meetings in Damascus had gone very well. A great many people had to make a great many concessions, but there was no question in Alexis's mind that there was going to be a better peace and more advantages for everyone as a result. The diplomats were all greatly indebted to him and had showed him the greatest courtesy and respect.

He had Hamida fly out to him the very night that Isabel was on her way to London. They had sex and talked together, and during their second night he told her that it was over for them. He was as kind as a man can be under those circumstances, letting her down as gently as he could, saying that of course he would speak to her and see her occasionally at parties, and so they must part as friends. Who knows, they might one day even have a casual fling together, but their deep relationship—her position as a part-time mistress—was over.

He gave her a gift; a two-bedroom flat in Monte Carlo. She had asked him innumerable questions, including was it because of the American, Isabel? He said yes, it was. When asked if he was going to marry her, he said he had no plans for the moment. He was taking things one step at a time. All he knew was that for the moment she was the woman he wanted with him in his life.

Hamida did not take it very well, but she had been given little choice. Alexis was a very clever man and saw to it that Hamida's sister traveled with her to make it easier for her.

Wednesday and Thursday he had spent in Paris, in his house on the Avenue Foch. He saw two of his other women. The great black beauty who was with him the first night that Isabel saw him at Regine's in Paris. She was difficult. He had had her for sex for a few years now. A destructive, strange creature, a sometime lesbian, but always a demanding female sexually. She was great in bed with him and serviced him well. He knew her to have a vile temper and had seen she could be very vindictive.

That Wednesday night when they went out and afterwards to bed, she asked to bring along a young man she had met. It had been a sexually erotic night, and in the morning he told her that it was over. That he would not be seeing her again, maybe for a long time, maybe forever. He wanted her to understand how good it had been and wanted to give her something as a thank-you. Was there something special that she would like to have?

She was very calm and collected about it. She said what she most wanted was a discotheque in New York, but she told Alexis not to waste the money; she would just run such a club into the ground. Instead she asked for a memento instead of a payoff.

It was this very thing that Alexis liked the most about her, besides the sex. He told her she could have anything she liked for a gift, and she chose a mink coat, the longest, most expensive one she could find. On the way from the furriers they saw a poster advertising the International Cat Show, at Wembly Stadium in London. Later, Alexis called Alexander and arranged the gift for Isabel.

The black beauty asked him if he had found *the* woman. He said he was not sure, but he thought he had.

She wished him luck and said, "I won't bother you. You call me if you ever want me, Daddy."

She left him on a corner, near the Place Vendôme. She was on her way to see her young man and show him her new coat. As she folded herself into a taxi, she called to him, "Thank you for the coat. It's been great, Daddy," and waved good-bye.

On Thursday he saw the woman in his life to whom he knew it would be the most difficult to say good-bye.

Alexis had bought her a flat on the rue Clement Marot years before. She was French, very beautiful, intelligent, clever, amusing, independent, and had left her husband for him. In all the years that they had been together she had known that she was sharing him with Hamida, as well as others.

She was an editor of a chic fashion magazine in Paris and always kept their relationship very discreet, not wanting the gossip columns to get hold of it. He liked her the most of all the women, but there was that something missing in her, a touch of sensitivity perhaps, that kept him from falling wholly in love. She had everything except that little bit of soul.

Gabrielle and he dined *à deux*. They made love, and then, during the night when they were lying together talking, he told her that this was his good-bye. She was the only one who did not ask why or for whom he was leaving her.

She made love to him twice more that night. When he woke in the morning, she was gone. In lipstick she had written on the mirror over the wash basin, *"Bonne chance";* Gabrielle was the one that he came closest to loving.

He looked at his watch again. It was ten minutes to two. He went to the mirror and put a comb through his hair and went down to the bar. In the elevator he was surprised when he realized that he was feeling a little nervous.

When he entered the bar there were few people, as he knew there would be at that hour. The string quartet was playing as he walked through the large, open room with its comfortable chairs and small round tables. The waiter brought him a Scotch and soda, and he sat back and waited.

He chose his table because from there he could look straight through the room, past the quartet, into the lobby, and down the two marble steps to the revolving door at the entrance. He would see her the moment she came in. And there she was.

She walked, almost hurried, up the two stairs, through the lobby and into the room, looking around for him. Oh, she was beautiful. She had on a sleeveless sable coat over a white silk jersey dress, with sleeves long and loose. Her coat was open and he could see with every step she took towards him the simple V-neck and the sensuous material moving over her body. She had one hand tucked in her pocket as she casually swung into the room in her high-heeled, light brown, alligator shoes. She carried no handbag and her hair moved, all silky and clean, showing off her face and her diamond earrings. He had forgotten

about her legs. Suddenly, for the first time, he was
aroused by her legs.

She saw him and he stood up. Isabel walked right up
to him and into his arms. He automatically slipped his
hands under her sable coat, touching the sides of her
breasts, and gave her a hug. He did not kiss her.

They sat down and he said nothing. He just kept drinking in the look of her.

Finally she said, with a very happy smile, "Hello, you.
Where shall I begin? The pussycats, they're wonderful. I
cannot wait for you to see them."

He was smiling at her now. "I am pleased that you
liked them. What will you drink?"

"Campari and soda."

After he had ordered for her, she thanked him for the
rest of her gifts and asked him how his work went, but
avoided asking what she most wanted to know: about the
women. They went into the dining room and were ushered to their table. When she slipped off her coat, the
simplicity of the white dress complemented her radiance.

At one point during lunch, while she was talking to
him, he picked up her hand and kissed it. He said nothing, just picked it up and kissed it.

Isabel suddenly began to feel nervous because she was
becoming aroused. She kept talking a great deal, but it
was all a great cover-up. She found him more handsome
and more quiet than before, and was almost painfully attracted to him.

Alexis knew this as he sat there listening to her, interested in everything that she was telling him. But he was
more intrigued by his desire for her, not just sexually, but
for her herself. Every word that she said, everything that
she did was lovely to him; the way she touched her napkin, played with her fork, silly things that he had not noticed before.

She longed to say, "I love you, let's go to bed," because
that was the way she felt, but she was not sure enough of
him.

They were the last two people in the huge dining room,
with half a dozen waiters hovering. Over their second cup
of coffee, hardly touched by either one of them, she asked
how long he was going to be in London.

"I have told the plane to stand by for departure on Saturday night or Sunday morning, depending on what happens here," he replied.

Isabel's heart sank. He was here on some sort of business and would be leaving her again. She hoped that she covered up her disappointment well.

He offered her another cup of coffee because theirs were cold; she said yes, trying to prolong the lunch.

Alexis looked around the dining room and said, "They want to close the dining room. It is unfair to keep them. Come upstairs to the suite. We will have coffee there."

He helped her from the chair, and his hand brushed against her hip. His very touch thrilled her. In the elevator going up, he saw through the white silk jersey that her nipples had grown hard and pointed. The fact that she still reacted to him pleased him. As they walked from the elevator along the corridor, he watched her and saw that she had nothing on under the dress. She was naked for him. Oh, yes, he was pleased, and oh, yes, he wanted her and would have her. There would be no coffee.

He knocked at the door and Gamal let them in. Isabel was relieved that he was there. It gave her a chance to pull herself together—she had been trembling like a young girl—while he and Alexis spoke. Gamal disappeared through a door, and Alexis took the coat from over her arm and put it on a chair.

He pulled her to him and ran his hands over her as he kissed her. She opened her mouth and felt his tongue pierce her. Her nerves melted and she almost collapsed in his arms as his hands roamed over her. She could not help herself: She murmured with the pleasure of his kisses.

He stroked her hair. "Oh, I missed you," was all that he said.

Isabel was joyful. The way he said it told her all she wanted to know.

He unzipped the back of her dress and slowly drew it forward, down over her arms and breasts, her hips and stomach, and let it drop to the floor. She started to undress him, and he helped her. They stood there naked. He pulled the coat off the chair and threw it on the carpet and slowly pulled her down with him and laid her on her back over the sable.

Her breasts looked bigger to him, heavier, more round, more full. He kissed the under part of them, then sucked hard on her nipples. He rolled her on her side facing him.

She held his penis in her hands and it felt wonderful to her. She could not hold back, but kept telling him how wonderful he was, how marvelous he made her feel. She slipped one leg underneath him and the other over him and took him inside of her.

That was all that he needed. When he felt that wetness touch the head of his cock—with one stroke, very swiftly and with a great deal of strength—he pulled her forward and rammed her onto him.

He fucked her on the side like that. Oh, God, she was wet and warm; how he had missed her! As tight as she was around him, her juices kept him moving in and out of her with a silky wet ease. She cried out, and he could actually feel the rush of her come every time she cried, which excited him beyond measure. He moved fast and hard; called out her name loudly as he poured forth into her. Then he held her in his arms.

They were all limp and wet, but still he had desire for her. He helped her up off her coat and half carried her to the bed. They collapsed on it, and lying in the middle of the huge bed, wrapped in each other's arms, dozed off together.

Before she dropped off into a deep sleep, she whispered in his ear, "I love you." He lazily stroked her hair until he fell asleep.

Her last thoughts before sleep took over completely were of his tenderness towards her. He was filled as much with tenderness as he was with lust. He could do anything to her by way of lust, because of that very tenderness.

She was lying asleep on her side when she felt it. His tongue licking her anus and then his finger spreading his saliva along the crack of her ass. She raised a knee and tucked her foot behind her ankle, which raised part of her buttocks, and still in a half sleep, she felt him begin to penetrate her. Her heart was pounding from anticipation, for he was a big man, and she knew the pain would be sharp. He grabbed around for her breasts and kissed her on the back of her neck as he drove into her.

She called out as he penetrated deeply and then relaxed as he fucked her slowly. She quivered from the thrill of him.

"I love you like this," he told her. He had a steady,

deep, rhythmic stroke and never stopped playing with her clitoris. He kept it up until she was insane with orgasm. She begged him to do everything he wanted with her, she was his slave.

When he withdrew there was cum running out of everywhere. They smelled of pure unadulterated sex and they reveled in it. They lay like that and he went to sleep again.

Alexis was still fast asleep when Isabel woke up. She slipped out from under his arm and very quietly found her way to the bathroom through the now-dark bedroom. It must be night, she realized, as she quietly closed the bathroom door and turned on the light.

Isabel had slept and been full of him. She ran the bath as quietly as she could, then stepped into it. The water felt wonderful. She had tied a towel around her hair, and she lay back and dozed in the bath.

When she awoke, he was standing in the door. She had no idea how long he had been there.

From the cupboard he took a terrycloth robe and put it on, then held a bath sheet out to her. He dried her off, even between her toes. She asked him to please bring her clothes from the drawing room, so that she could dress.

While he was tying his tie, he saw her pull out from the pocket of her sable coat the Cameron compact that he had given her. He pulled her close and they kissed tenderly.

In the sitting room she sat down on the sofa, staring into the open fire. He rang through on the telephone to Gamal and told him something in Arabic. When he hung up, he told her he had ordered something for them to eat and drink.

Alexis called Isabel over to the desk where he was sitting. He stood up and put his arm around her. "Have you thought about me this week?" he quietly asked.

"Yes, I have."

"And have you seen all your men?"

"Yes, I have."

"And are you happier being with me?"

"I am more ecstatic with you than I have ever been in my life," Isabel said adamantly.

"Would you like to stay with me?" he asked.

"Yes, Alexis, very much. I cannot imagine what my life would be without you."

"I would like you to stay with me." He was close to tears now, and seeing that, Isabel was too.

Opening the desk drawer, he said, "Isabel, I have brought you a present from Paris. I hope you will accept it with all my love."

"Oh, Alexis," she exclaimed. "How can I? You are so generous to me."

He kissed her, smiled and said, "Darling, this is not the time to say no. If you take the present, you will give me everything."

There were two boxes. She opened one and could not believe it. He lifted the ring out of the box and slipped it on the fourth finger of her left hand. "Will you marry me as soon as possible?" he asked. "Make me happy and say yes. I would like to be able to spend the rest of my life with you."

"Yes, as soon as possible," Isabel whispered. "I love you very much, Alexis."

Overcome with emotion and their new love for one another, they clung together and kissed.

It was Alexis who came out of it first; he was wonderfully gay and happy and said, "Darling, you forgot this." He opened the box and this time slipped another ring on the fourth finger of her right hand. She was dazzled.

Isabel threw her arms around his waist and pulled him close to her, saying, "I want to make the rest of my life half of yours."

He could see the passion in her eyes when she said it, right down to her soul. That same old magnetic sexual attraction sprang up between them. She unzipped her dress herself this time and they both walked back into the bedroom. He undressed and took her to bed for the second time that day.

Later, when Isabel moved her hands over his face, he started to laugh. She asked him why.

"Well, darling, I have never made love to a lady with nothing on but a twenty-two-carat, cushion-cut diamond on one finger, and a wedding band of square-cut diamonds on the other," he managed.

Isabel raised both her hands close to her face, looked at the jewels and roared with laughter as well. She grabbed him by the neck and kissed him, saying, "Did I ever tell you that I have always liked big diamonds?"

"I see," he teased. "You are marrying me for your jewels!" They kissed and laughed.

There was a knock at the door. Alexis rolled off her, reached down and picked his shirt up off the floor, handing it to her. When she had a few buttons done up, he told Gamal that he could come in.

The servant entered the room, wheeling a table up to Alexis's side of the bed. There was an enormous bowl of Beluga caviar set in crushed ice, a chilled bottle of Dom Perignon and assorted plates of trimmings for the caviar and toast.

Gamal opened the champagne and poured out two glasses. Alexis sent Gamal for another glass. When he returned they told him they were to be married. Gamal was very happy for Alexis and Isabel. He had served Alexis since they were both small boys; he adored and only wanted joy for him. He said something in Arabic to Alexis, and Isabel could see at once that the master had been deeply touched by his servant.

They piled their plates up high with caviar and drank champagne, toasting to their life together. Dressed again, they ordered a sumptuous dinner to be served in the drawing room.

It was half past eleven when they finished dinner, and they were both now wide-awake and very excited about the reality rather than the prospect that in a few days they would be creating a life together.

They decided that Gamal, Alexander, Endo, Alexis's mother and Isabel's mother and sister were the only people that would be told about the wedding. Neither one of them wanted a drama made out of their happiness. It was much too personal. Because of Alexis's position, the wedding had to be either totally secret or a mammoth celebration; too many people would be offended otherwise. Rather than upset anyone, they decided to swear the few people who would be told to secrecy. Alexander would be the only witness at the wedding.

"Isabel, you know what the Cairenes are like," Alexis mused. "They will be killing us with kindness and good wishes if they get the least idea that we are being married, so the question is where? We can be married on the Nile somewhere between Memphis and Cairo, and then sail up the Nile to Abu Simbel, stopping along the way to see some of the Upper Egyptian villages. Would you like that?"

"Alexis, that would be wonderful," Isabel agreed. "I honestly must tell you that I feel our marriage should be ours alone. Let's not have any hoopla at all. That is a gorgeous plan. Oh, I would like that very much. It's wonderful!"

After dinner they went for a walk. As Isabel was putting on her coat, she said, "Alexis, you have never even been to my house."

"That's true. Well, why don't I come and spend the night there with you?"

"That would be wonderful."

He called Gamal and told him that he was going to spend the night at Isabel's, and to bring his things over in the morning, very early, as there was much to do. Turning to Isabel, he said, "Darling, I will give you Gamal to help Endo in getting your things together. Between the two of them I think they can get you packed, and we can fly off early Sunday morning."

"It's awfully rushed, Alexis, but I don't care." She laughed. "To tell the truth, I am so excited that the longer I have to get ready, the worse it will be."

"Never mind. I will take care of the details," he soothed. "You just sit back and be happy."

They left Claridges and walked up Brook Street, arm in arm. Along Bond Street they checked out all the windows and at one point they were standing in front of Wildenstein's looking at an early Braque painting. They stood, his arm around her shoulder and her arm around his waist. There was a streetlight behind them and they could see it and the reflection of Bond Street in the plate-glass window. They both saw themselves at the same time, turned and looked at each other, then back to the window again, looking at their happiness reflected back at them.

They walked on up towards Old Bond Street, and as they did, Alexis told her again how happy she had made him.

Once they arrived home at Hill Street, Alexis was wide-awake. He was enchanted by Isabel's home and life-style. He wanted to see and know everything. Isabel was delighted to offer him this little bit more of herself that he did not know.

Endo was awake and in the kitchen. He had been

called by Gamal and told that they were going to spend the night there. He remained where he was, but left the light on and the kitchen door open so that Isabel would know that he was available if needed.

After Alexis got over the initial greeting of Winston, Rita and Arthur, he was taken immediately into the kitchen to meet Endo and Desert Horse, Red Moon and Honey Lamb. The barking and jumping up and down of the dogs and the chasing around of the cats amused him very much, and when he at last was able to say a few words to Endo, he liked him immediately.

Isabel told Endo that they were to be married within the next few days. He behaved impeccably, congratulating Alexis in a formal, but friendly, way. He suggested champagne for a toast, but they declined, and Alexis asked for tea instead.

Isabel took him all through the house. He was interested in everything: the studio, the loom, the yarns, the weaving, her drawing table. He told her that he loved the studio, with its great sliding glass roof, and the night and stars shining down on them and the potted trees, with the now-sleepy, silent songbirds hanging in cages from them. In the library, he was impressed with her collection of books on Eastern as well as Western philosophies. He was almost sentimental when she showed him the first book off the presses of each of her Meredith Montagues. He was interested in what kind of typewriter she used, her dictating machines, her writing notebooks and the box files covered with beautiful decorative paper, where she kept the original manuscripts. When she told him that she wanted to get a computer one day so she could store in it any number of ideas and information, he was delighted with the idea and said he would give her one. He told her to be quiet and dragged her by the hand, saying, "Show me more."

He thought the drawing room exquisite. Endo had put the lights on in the garden, and they went out to look at that as well. Then he was shown the tiny guest room, the quarters where Endo lived, the dining room and, last, the bedroom, bathroom and dressing room. The white roses were beginning to drop their petals, but the orchids were perfect for the room. He was very pleased with himself for having sent them. It put his mark in her room.

He remarked to her that the bedroom was almost Zen

in feeling. He felt an atmosphere of great warmth and peace. They left it arm in arm, and he gave her a gentle, tender kiss as they went back down to the drawing room. Alexis felt as if he had come home.

They threw cushions down in front of the fireplace and stretched out together. Endo arrived with the tea, a plate of peeled russet pears and some small, white rice cakes. He put the things down on a tiny low table near the fire, excused himself and said goodnight. Before he left, Alexis asked him to stay for a moment and told him their plans.

"Endo, I know this is all very fast, but I want you to know that your job is secure with Miss Wells and with me. I hope that you will stay with us both always." Isabel was delighted.

Endo said that he would be pleased to stay because he had always been happy working for Miss Wells.

"Endo, we must keep the marriage a secret until a few weeks after the wedding," Alexis continued. "All I will ask you is that you will allow Gamal to come tomorrow to help you pack up everything that Miss Wells wants to take with her so we can fly out on Sunday morning. Isabel, what are your plans for this place while we are away?"

"I have not even thought about it, but I suppose the thing to do is to leave Endo in charge of the house." She paused. "Joy and Joanna have their work set out for them; it will tick over nicely."

"Then, you are in charge, Endo," Alexis said. "You do as you would normally when Miss Wells is away, and in a few weeks, when we know more of our plans, we will let you know."

"Alexis, what about the animals?" Isabel cried.

"Well, darling, we could take them all with us, but there is the quarantine factor to deal with. Why not leave them with Endo for the time being?"

"Alexis, I think I would like to take the dogs."

"Think about it," he cautioned. "Of course, you can take the dogs, but remember, we can never bring them back to England."

Isabel paused. "I will think about it."

"Endo, is this all right with you?"

"Yes, Sir Alexis."

Alexis thanked him and said he would leave him phone numbers and names of people in case he needed anything.

Alexis stood up and thanked him again, this time shaking his hand. Endo bowed very low and said goodnight.

The two of them lay in front of the fire drinking tea and talked all through the night. There were plans, details, a hundred things that had to be done before they flew off on Sunday.

At six in the morning they decided to go to bed and get a few hours of sleep because there was so much to do. They turned off the lights through the house as they made their way up to the bedroom. The bed had been turned down, and Alexis told her how happy he was to be sleeping with her in her room and that he would be the last man she would have in her bed.

He started to undress and Isabel went to the dressing room, returning with a hanger for him. He crawled into the bed and she went and hung his things up in her dressing room. Putting on a dressing gown, she returned to the bedroom and sat next to him.

He asked her if she had a couple of joints. She produced them and they smoked. After, he lifted her galabia over her head and told her to get into bed. They lay in each other's arms, and all the details of what had to be done just drifted away with the smoke.

He kissed her as she played with his body, rolling the covers off him to his knees to kiss his penis and beautiful large balls. He was only partially erect. She held him in her hands and fondled him and kissed his genitals again.

"I love you," Alexis whispered. "If you only knew how much I love you."

They lay together holding each other and not saying a word. Eventually they fell asleep.

When Isabel woke up she was alone. She dozed a little and then began to wonder where he was. She looked in the bathroom and dressing room. His suit was hanging up, so she knew that he had not left the house. But where would he be?

She washed, dressed in her raw silk galabia, put on her silver and amber necklace, made up her face and went back to the bedroom and drew the curtains open. She rang through to Endo and asked him to come to the bedroom. When he arrived the two of them made the bed together. She asked him where Alexis was. He told her that he was in the drawing room.

"Sir Alexis has asked me to tell him the moment you

are up," he said. "I am to begin the breakfast for three people."

Isabel was confused. "But, Endo, he has no clothes on."

Endo smiled and said, "Make no mistake, Miss Wells. He is a very organized man. He has something to wear."

She laughed and ran down the stairs towards the drawing room. She found him dressed in his camel-hair galabia, the same one he wore the time they were together in the pavilion at the palace on Roda Island. The dogs were sitting around his feet and all rushed towards her when she entered the room.

"Why didn't you wake me?" she asked.

"You were sleeping so soundly and there is so much for me to do, so I decided to come down here and make phone calls and try to get things organized. So many little details to be done, and quietly. We will be married in a civil ceremony and a Coptic ceremony. Do you mind marrying me twice?" He winked.

"Only twice?" Isabel pouted. "I would like to marry you every day!"

"But what about you?" Alexis frowned. "You are a Jewess. Does it upset you to be married in a religious ceremony that is not yours? You must tell me, darling. How do you feel about all this? I detest putting you through these things, but it is necessary. I want you solidly married to me for your protection as well as mine."

"Alexis," Isabel began, taking his hands. "I was born a Jewess, I will die a Jewess. I do not follow any one religion. I am happy to embrace your Coptic church, but you must know that I will never be any more a religious Copt than I am a Jew. You see, I am a very religious person when left free. I don't like organized religion."

"It is all a formality, but you do know that I love the Coptic world and come from an historically famous Coptic family. It also solves the problem of the Moslem part of me. You know that as long as I am attached to the Coptic church, I will never be able to rise politically in the service of my country. That ties in very much with what I want to do with my life without offending anyone." He smiled. "Thank you, darling. We have just jumped over what might have been quite a hurdle."

"Have you been up long?"

He looked at his watch. "Yes. I hope you don't mind. I

bathed and came down and gave instructions to Gamal and Endo about some things that they could be doing until you came down to take over. I told them that you would want all your clothes, all your personal things, anything that has to do with your writing. I could not tell them which of the things you might want from the house —the small objects, the books, the paintings. You must take everything that you think will make you happy to have around you."

"How can we get it all together, Alexis?"

"No problem. If we need more help, we will get it. The other thing, Isabel, is that I have been making calls to Cairo to set things up so we can be married at the beginning of the week—Wednesday, at the latest. The officials have to be notified and the supplies put on board. I found out what you must have. Your birth certificate and your passport. Have Endo bring them to me as soon as we have had breakfast. I hope it is all right with you, I called Alexander and asked him to come to breakfast. I said I would ring him back when you were up. I have not told him about us. I thought that we should tell him together. May I call him now?"

"Yes, of course. Listen, Alexis, after breakfast I think I should call my mother and sister."

"You know, I have been thinking about that, darling. No, I think the thing to do is for us to fly you to Athens in the morning. I will drive you into the city and meet them for a short visit, and then you can spend the day with them. I have so much to do in Cairo, it would be impossible for me to take the time now to stay on. We will invite them to come for a long visit when we are settled. I will send the plane for you the next day."

"No, Alexis, please. I don't want to stay the night in Athens; I want to be with you."

Alexis was pleased. "I will send the plane for you at seven in the evening, and we will sleep together in the house on Roda Island. Would you like that?"

"Oh, yes, that would be just wonderful."

"Well, that is that. Now let me call Alexander, and then after breakfast we will call my mother-in-law to say we are coming."

Suddenly everyone seemed to be very busy in different parts of the house. While Endo was putting the finishing touches to breakfast, Gamal entered the kitchen. Both men decided how Isabel should pack for her new life, agreeing that by the end of the day she would be incapable of doing anything. As it happened, they were right.

When the doorbell rang it was Gamal who let Alexander in and, before anyone could say anything, Alexander *knew* from the excitement charging through the house. After he escaped his reception from the dogs, he went to Alexis and Isabel, looked at the rings on her fingers and said, "Don't tell me, I know. You are getting married."

After he had agreed to act as the best man and father of the bride, the three of them went in to breakfast. Isabel teased him by saying he had brought it on himself. Alexander had done his job very well, and she would thank him all the days of her life for it.

They spoke about the details of the wedding. The more the men talked, the more nervous Isabel became. Alexis picked up on it. He told Alexander something in Arabic, and the subject was changed.

After breakfast they all went back to their tasks, and Alexis, walking Isabel back to the library, told her he thought it best if they spent their last night in London together at Claridges. It would give everyone at the house a chance to work without them underfoot.

"All you have to do is choose the dress you want for this evening and what you want to wear for traveling," Alexis declared. "You are not to think of another thing, agreed? Just pack your jewels and your makeup, or whatever ladies take. The rest will be on the plane. Gamal, Endo and Alexander will take care of everything."

"My heavens! You do get people working!" Isabel laughed. "What are you going to do?"

"Me? I am going to be taking care of you."

Endo interrupted them to tell Isabel that her mother had called collect while they were at breakfast. He hoped that it was all right; he had told her that she could not be disturbed at that moment and that Isabel would call back as soon as she was free. Isabel thanked him and turned her attention to gathering together her personal possessions for the journey.

IX

KATE WAS in a rage. It had been almost two hours since she placed the first call to London. Isabel had not returned the call. That lousy Chink probably never gave her the message, she decided.

She tried dialing through to London again. This was the fourth time. Isabel's line had been continuously busy. By God, Isabel was selfish. At last the telephone was ringing. Kate became even more furious because she had forgotten to call collect. Then she thought, *It was even better; let her feel guilty. She must have more money than I do, the way she spends it. Let her pay for the call, I will not. Let her feel guilty for her indifference.* Then, at last, the click—the receiver had been lifted. *It better not be that yellow peril.*

"Hello?" came a man's voice.

"Who is this?" Kate demanded.

"Who do you want to speak to, please?"

"What's your number?"

"What number do you want, madam?"

Kate became very annoyed and gave the number.

"Yes, madam, you have the correct number. Now, if you tell me who you would like to speak to, I may be able to help you."

"I want to speak to my daughter, that is who I want to speak to. And who are you anyway?"

Alexis put his hand over the receiver and said to Isabel, "You see, darling, you have me completely enslaved—now I am your secretary!"

The voice on the other end of the line kept on talking. Alexis interrupted and said, "I am so sorry, I did not get that. Who is calling?"

"Why don't you listen? This is a long-distance call. I want to speak to Isabel Wells. You tell her it's her mother on the telephone and to answer this call right now."

Alexis covered the mouthpiece of the phone and said, "Oh, dear, I have started off on the wrong foot. It is your mother. I believe she is angry with me. She was almost rude." He handed the telephone to Isabel.

She went over to the wing chair where he was sitting, took the telephone from him, sat on his lap, gave him a kiss and whispered, "I like having you as my slave." They both smiled, and he gave her a nudge to answer the phone call. He went back to writing some things down.

"Hello, Mother."

"Isabel?"

"Yes, Mother. How are you, Mother?"

"Isabel, do you know that I called you two hours ago? I bet that Chink never even bothered to give you the message. He is not as wonderful a servant as you think he is."

"Mother, he did give me the message."

"Don't you think you should tell him that when your mother calls he is to put me through? You certainly could not have been so busy that you were unable to spare three minutes on a long-distance call from your mother. Now just tell me, what was so important you could not answer my call?"

"Um . . . I was having breakfast."

"You were having breakfast! That was so important you couldn't talk to me? Well, pardon me, madam. Now who in the hell do you think you are? Who answered the telephone this time—not *another* servant? God, you have money to burn. Where did you get *this* one, in Egypt? I know he is foreign, he has a really ugly foreign accent. Honestly, dear, when are you going to come down to earth and deal in some realities? Isabel, you do try my nerves."

Alexis could not help but hear the entire conversation. It seemed that Mrs. Wells in Athens had a very loud voice and was very common. He could feel Isabel stiffen with anxiety. She had one arm around his shoulder and draped casually over his chest. He picked up her hand, turned it over and kissed the palm. Then, pulling her a little tighter to him, he picked up his pen and went on writing.

"Look, Isabel, I am not wasting my money on this call to discuss your bad manners. I am calling to tell you that I am arriving in Southampton two weeks from the day before yesterday. Darling, it will be lovely to see you. Just pick me up at the dock. All you have to do is call the Mediterranean Line and ask the time of the arrival of the ship, *Aphrodite,* the last port of call, Alexandria. You see, your mother can get to Egypt on her own, and I don't even have to lie about it."

"Oh, dear."

"What do you mean, 'Oh, dear'?"

"Well, now listen, Mother. I will not be in London two weeks from the day before yesterday. Something wonderful has happened, and I want to come to Athens tomorrow to see you and Ava and tell you all about it. I will come only for the day and would like to take you and Ava to lunch. I hope that is convenient?"

Kate was speechless with rage.

"Hello, Mother?"

"What do you mean that you will not be in Southampton to meet me? My plans are made. I am already packing."

Isabel started to laugh and said, "Look, dear, don't you think you are packing a bit soon? It must be days before the ship leaves."

"What do you mean, 'packing a bit soon'? Do you think that everyone does everything at the last minute like you? I happen to be very organized. I have a great deal of packing to do. If you cannot make the boat then just do me a favor, don't bother sending that Chink down there to get me. I'll find my own way up to London. I'll go to a hotel for a few days. I have no intention of staying alone in your house with that yellow thing. I suppose the one you brought from Egypt is as black as coal. Look, that is the best plan. Then, when you return, I will move in with you so we can have a holiday together."

"I do not think you understand, Mother. I have no idea when I will return to London. I will explain it all to you tomorrow over lunch. You are welcome to stay here in the house if you want to keep your plans and come to London for a holiday. I will not be here. We can go over all your plans tomorrow." By this time Isabel was losing control of her calm and gave a deep sigh.

Alexis felt it, put down his pencil and kissed her lightly on the mouth. He saw in her face a nervous anxiety, something he had never seen in her before, and did not like it. Isabel was holding the phone out and away from her ear and looking down at Alexis in slight despair while her mother went on.

"Change my plans? Have a holiday alone in London?

Live in a house with that sneaky, unreliable, filthy yellow midget? You really do make plans for me, don't you? Did it ever occur to you to cancel your plans? We made this arrangement only a few days ago, and you said nothing about leaving London. Tell me right now, why do you *always disappoint* me? Your *father* used to say you will be the *death* of me and you know, you *will*."

"Mother, lunch at one o'clock at the *Grande Bretagne*." Isabel sighed.

"Oh, just like that! Well, maybe it is not convenient for me at one o'clock, and besides, I hate the food at the *Grande Bretagne*."

"Where would you like to have lunch, and what time would it be convenient, or would you prefer me to call you back in half an hour and tell you my plans on the telephone? Those are your two choices. Which is it to be?"

"Look, darling, don't take that tone with me," Kate moaned. "You *know* that I made my plans and I am disappointed, but when we meet, maybe you can work it out. Sweetheart, I will meet you at one-thirty at the Hilton, downstairs in the Byzantium Room."

"Fine, Mother. Now would you please try and arrange it with Ava?"

"If you want to have lunch with Ava, then you had better spend the money and call her yourself. I am not going to get involved in a three-way thing. How long will you be here? Maybe if she cannot make lunch, she will make dinner."

"I will be gone before dinner. I am flying out at seven in the evening."

"Where are you going now? You must have money to throw away."

"Good-bye, Mother. I will see you tomorrow."

"Everything with you has to be a mystery. I am telling you right now, I am not canceling my plans, maybe you can cancel yours. You just think about that until we meet tomorrow. Isabel, I will see you tomorrow, but I have to tell you, I am not pleased, not pleased with you at all. I am changing nothing, and you had better face it. There have to be some changes made in *your* attitude. Good-bye."

Isabel handed the telephone to Alexis, who put it back

on the carriage. She said nothing, but her face said everything.

Alexis looked at her and asked, "Is it always like that?"

"Well, almost always."

"Oh, my dear, I am dreadfully sorry." He put his hand through the opening of her robe and fondled her breast with lovely, round movements. Then he bent his head down and put her nipple in his mouth. He sucked on it gently and then tucked it back under her robe and said, "Be happy, my darling."

They were interrupted by the telephone again. Isabel asked Alexis to answer it. A call from Cairo. She slid off his lap, motioning to him that she was going into the library to make lists.

When Alexis hung up the telephone he was delighted. If he were in Cairo Sunday afternoon at four o'clock, he could sign documents that would afford him a special license for marriage in a civil ceremony any time after Monday noon, anywhere he chose in Egypt. The High Priest of the Coptic church would arrange to have a simple five-minute service on Alexis's felucca which would make the marriage legal in the eyes of God. Now he could call his friend, the chief justice of Egypt, who would be certain to keep silent, and ask him to marry them on board his boat.

He went to Isabel and told her all was well. By Tuesday at sundown, she would be Lady Isabel Hyatt. There was more good news: With some luck they would be able to take a month, possibly five weeks; just the two of them in Upper Egypt.

Isabel was so happy. She went to him and said, "Oh, Alexis, I am making a mess of everything. I am confused and so happy and over-excited that I can not make one simple, sane decision. The news is wonderful. You are wonderful. However did you manage it all? I don't seem to be able to do anything. What should I do?"

"Do not do anything," he soothed. "There is no problem and you do not have to do anything. It will all be done. Just choose what you want to wear for dinner tonight and traveling. By Monday everything will be in Cairo and unpacked, ready for you to do whatever you want with your things. Now, put all these trivial matters out of your mind. There is one thing that I *will not have,* and that is you upset for no reason. I will not interfere with your family, but if you are going to Athens and will become upset, I would much prefer you to fly with me direct to Cairo. Now, do you think that you can handle them? Although I cannot really understand what there is to handle."

Isabel took a deep breath. "Look, Alexis, I am no longer upset. But I wanted to share this, the most happy time in my life, with the only family I have. If tomorrow they do not want to understand that, it will be their problem, not mine. I promise you, when I fly into Cairo, I will not be upset. I am not upset now; just embarrassed that you had to hear that dreadful conversation. For years it used to affect me, but it does not any longer. It just embarrasses me. You know, I am going to take the dogs out for a walk. Do you want to come?"

"No. Honestly, I must stay and finish making arrangements. I am happy for you to go out. I can see that all this has shaken you. Go for your walk and relax. When you come back, I will be dressed, and if you would like, we will go shopping, or for a drive into the country for lunch. There is one thing, darling. You *did* say that you would call your sister to invite her for lunch tomorrow."

"Oh, you are right; I had forgotten completely about it." Isabel laughed. "You *are* a good secretary!"

Alexis pretended to scowl. "Eh, yes, darling. I know that you are being so rushed by me, but those two! No, I do not think those two would ever understand!"

They both laughed, and Isabel said, "I think I will spare you a dose of the other one. I will call her from the bedroom."

He saw that the anxiety was gone from her face, and he knew that she was all right. She started to leave the room and he gave her a hard smack on the ass.

She yelped. "What was that for?"

"To show you I hadn't forgotten that secretary remark!" He grinned.

She gave him a rueful smile and left, rubbing her behind.

Ava answered the telephone in her usual calm, controlled, cautious voice. Her first words were, "I have already heard from Mother that you are coming into Athens for lunch tomorrow. Of course," she went on, "I will have lunch with you. As it happens, Alfred is going away for the day tomorrow afternoon. So it will be you, Mother and I. I would not miss that for the world. I think that it is a very good thing that we have a family talk. You know, you really are rotten to her. You upset her very much. She had made plans and arrangements, even sent letters to her family saying she was on her way to London. Why are you coming to Athens anyway?"

"Because I have something to tell you."

"Can't you tell us on the telephone? What is the big mystery about?"

"There is no big mystery, just a secret. There is no reason why I cannot tell you over the telephone. I am going to get married."

Ava could hardly believe her ears. She laughed uncontrollably over the wire.

"Why are you laughing?"

"Because I think it is very, very funny. You, married. I have never heard anything funnier." And she laughed loudly again.

Isabel held the receiver away from her ear. When her sister had got herself under control, she said, "Ava, I really do not see what is so funny. Millions of people do it. Why is it so funny if I do it?"

"Because I think it is very, very funny. You, married. I you have no idea what marriage is like. I shudder to think that you have fooled yourself enough into believing that you could hold together a marriage. You *know* you are too selfish to get married. I don't want to be rude, Isabel, but you do live in illusion and fantasy. Marriage is a two-way problem, that is all that marriage is. Forget it, Isabel. You will be divorced within six months. Marriage is not for you."

"Ava, I am going to take my chance," Isabel said patiently. "I am deeply in love, and I think he loves me as well."

"Ha!" said Ava. "Love, what has that to do with marriage? Oh, I see *now*. It is a moment of passion. You think that can last forever? And just who are you going to marry? One of those one-night stands of yours?"

"Ava, I think, as usual, you are going too far. You have never even met any of the men in my life."

"Look, Isabel, we have talked about the men in your life over the years, and they are always too young for you. They never have any money, they're irresponsible

and not reliable for anything. Painters, writers, business-
men, you've tried them all and you never made a relationship work. What makes you think you can do it now?
If you have picked one of your types to make a life with
because you are afraid of middle age and growing old
alone, you will see, he won't be there. Yes, you had better come to Athens so we can talk some sense into you.
Can you afford a husband? I doubt that you have found a
man who is going to take care of you. No, it is not for you,
Isabel. But, anyway, it has given me the laugh of the
morning. Where are we having lunch tomorrow? I can
hardly wait to hear it all."

"The Hilton at one-thirty."

"The Hilton? What an awful place to choose! Do we
have to go there?"

"Mother chose the place," Isabel said.

"Well, she would, wouldn't she? They make a fuss
over her when she goes there. Well, I suppose that I will
be able to find *something* to eat. Honestly, if we have to
eat in a hotel, you should have chosen the St. George.
Who goes to a hotel to dine? You know there are much
better restaurants around."

"Look, Ava, that is where we are going. The Hilton at
one-thirty."

"OK, but I hope you get more sensible. How long are
you staying? Mother says you are flying out tomorrow
night. Where are you flying to?"

"Cairo. I will tell you everything tomorrow. Bye, Ava."

After Isabel had returned from the walk with the dogs,
she and Alexis took a drive in the country, stopping for
lunch in Cookham. Then they went to see the Spencer
paintings and walked through the village to the church.
After that they drove back to London.

Before she left she laid out the things that she would
wear for dinner that evening and to travel in the next day.
Endo had emptied the safe, and all her jewels were in her
case except for her engagement and wedding rings, which
she had not taken off since Alexis had given them to her.
The passport and birth certificate had been given to Alexis.
Everything was sent on to Claridges. There was no need
to stop at Hill Street.

Alexis knocked at the door to the suite, and much to
Isabel's surprise, it was opened by Endo. It was a sweet

surprise: The dogs, Arthur and the three pussycats were all there, as well as Joanna and Joy. The two girls had been invited by Alexis for drinks because, as he put it, he was capturing her again to take her to Egypt for a while. He thought the girls would like to know all was well with their jobs and say *au revoir*. It was a lovely, happy, gay party. As they left, the two girls reassured Isabel that they would carry on, and she was not to worry, but to have a marvelous time. If there was a problem, Sir Alexis had given them Alexander Gordon-Spencer's number.

Both girls were entranced by the jewels on Isabel's fingers but were too polite to say anything. They made her feel very comfortable: She appreciated all the affection that these two wonderful helpers felt for her.

When they left, they each gave her a kiss on the cheek. Joy said, "Oh, we are so happy for you. He is such a *dish*, and so in love with you."

When they were gone she looked at Alexis, who had Honey Lamb and Desert Horse on his lap. On the sofa next to him was Rita, all four legs up in the air, cooing from the pleasure of having her tummy rubbed.

She thought that his gesture of having them all there was a sensitive, thoughtful thing to do, and she went to him, telling him so. She felt completely relaxed and happy.

Shortly after the girls left, Endo said good-bye and took the animals with him. Isabel made as little fuss about them as possible and went to dress.

Alexis was taking her to dinner as the guest of the two men from Damascus with whom he had arrived. She wore a full-length, black, silk jersey Chloë dress with a plunging V-neck and a halter top. It had a long slit up the front, and with every step she took, three-quarters of her black silk-stockinged legs in their high-heeled, black satin sandals, showed. She was splendid in a wickedly sexual way: The dress, and Isabel, set off all her diamonds magnificently.

When she came out of the bedroom, Alexis was overcome. He opened the slit of her dress and lifted it a few inches so that he could see what was holding up her stockings or if she had tights on.

The black silk stockings went to the top of her thighs and were held in place by a black garter belt that rested low on her stomach and across the lower part of her hips. Six black garters hung down from it, clipping onto the top of the stockings. Her beautiful vagina was framed out in the black underwear. He turned her around slowly, lifting her dress high, looking at her from the back. He snapped a black garter and ran his hand down over the silky roundness of her bottom, into the top of her black silk stockings. He would have liked to have taken her right there and then, but there was no time.

"Isabel, I find you so wicked, so sensual, I'm driven with desire to take you!" He pulled her up to him and kissed her, penetrating deep into her mouth.

The hosts and all the guests at dinner were a very gay party. They had a marvelous time, and Alexis was in fine form, laughing a great deal. Occasionally he would lean towards Isabel to translate a message from one of the non-English-speaking Arabs.

"They will be very embarrassed when they find out what is going to happen on Tuesday at sundown," he said. "I had to tell them that you were mine. Otherwise they would have made a play for you."

"I am sure that they asked you what I was like—what did you tell them?" Isabel asked innocently.

At that he put his arm around her shoulder and said, "I told them, 'It is not to be discussed, my friends. All I can tell you is she is sheer poetry.' " He laughed.

That night they made love again and again. In the morning they dressed and decided to go down to the dining room at Claridges for a grand English breakfast. Afterwards they walked directly to the car. Gamal had packed everything from the room upstairs and had gone ahead to the plane.

It was a bright, sunny day. London looked its best as they drove out to the airport. Isabel, understandably, felt uplifted. Her life, in such a short time, had changed so completely. She was no longer alone; someone wanted to care for her. And that someone was sitting next to her. It had come late to her, this chance for happiness, and yet she felt she had never been ready before now to take it.

She tucked her arm through Alexis's. He put down the newspaper that he had been glancing through and kissed her. They said nothing, secure in their happiness.

She watched the buildings flash by as they sped towards the airport. The sunlight caught the facets in her diamond, and the pure clear sparkles of light dazzled her. She held her hand up and looked at it. It winked back at her, as if to say, "I am alive and I am with you."

"Alexis," she said. "Look at my ring. It is so like a piece of a star." He held her hand and looked at the ring.

"Isabel, I would like to tell you about that gem. When I was in Paris and I wanted to buy you something, I was shown a wonderful selection of things, but nothing seemed right. Then in Van Cleef & Arpels it came to me why. I did not want to buy you just another beautiful gift. I wanted to buy you an engagement ring, and then I said to myself, *Fool, you have not the least intention of becoming engaged to that woman. You had better buy a wedding ring.* But, because I fell in love with you over six months ago, I brought you the engagement ring to remind you we have been together for a long time. I am so proud to see it on your finger. It is gorgeous, a symbol of how I feel about you, and I hope your wearing it is a symbol of how you feel about me. Does that sound overly romantic for an old man?"

She kissed him. "No, it's wonderful and I love you."

"By the way, Isabel, I have ordered a banana-colored suit to be married in." And they both began to laugh.

"Oh, Alexis, I have not even thought about it—what will I be married in?"

"All your clothes that you own will be hung up by the time you arrive in Cairo. You will find something lovely, I am sure. If not, go shopping on Monday. Besides, there is a freak heat wave in Athens straight through to the middle of Africa. So it will be very hot."

Shortly after that she walked up the stairs of Alexis's plane, and when she stepped into the main cabin, she could hardly believe what greeted her. Rita and Winston were leaping about and barking.

She was delighted. Alexis had a mischievous look on his face as well as a terrific broad smile. She threw her arms around him, kissed him and thanked him, telling him he was the most sensitive and tender, as well as thoughtful, man she had ever known.

The door opened from the dining room, and out walked Alexander. He kissed her and said, "Hello. You cannot leave without the best man."

They all sat down and got ready for takeoff. Alexis became organized, and said, "Isabel, these are the arrangements. Alexander and Gamal are going to accompany you in Athens."

Isabel began to protest when Alexis interrupted.

"Please, Isabel, do this the way I ask. Since it is impossible for me to make lunch with your family, and make the four o'clock rendezvous as well, to sign the necessary documents for our wedding, I would be happier if you allowed Alexander to accompany you. You do understand that I would much prefer to meet your family, but explain to them that we will all have a long visit after the wedding trip."

Isabel understood perfectly, and said, of course, whatever he wanted. Here she was again with Alexander playing nanny. Isabel found it extraordinary. Since the age of sixteen, she had always had to find her way alone, make every decision on her own. To have someone doing it for her, to have someone care for her, was wonderful.

When Alexis's jet touched down at Athens airport, Alexis, Alexander, Isabel and Gamal went down the stairs to a waiting car. While her escort entered the car, Alexis kissed Isabel good-bye, told her she looked lovely and said that he must love her very much to take Rita and Winston into Cairo with her.

He tucked her in the back of the car with Alexander and said, "Remember, the plane will be back for you to board at seven this evening." He then said a few things to Alexander in Arabic, patted Isabel on the knee and was gone.

She saw his plane taxi down the runway getting ready for takeoff. She was not the least bit sad, more proud of him and in love with him for the man he was. How could she be sad?

Lunch was not until one-thirty, and Alexander had a surprise for her. They drove to the house of a friend of Alexander's in the heart of Kolonaki, and minutes later he arrived back at the car with Katarina Syndamou, the world-renowned actress. She was a dynamic-looking Amazon of a woman; explosive and larger than life.

The two women liked each other at once. They were on their way to the Acropolis, closed to the public for the moment, but always open to Katarina. Katarina was every Greek's goddess, and to a goddess all was open in Greece.

The three of them walked through the ancient columns and stones. The unusual heat wave, in an October sky of cloudless deep rich blue, poured down on the three solitary figures roaming over antiquity. Quite spontaneously, rising to the dramatic, soulful, melodic, Katarina Syndamou recited from one of the great Euripidean tragedies. For Isabel it was more thrilling than either of the others could imagine. In all the years that she had been visiting Greece, and even during the years that she had lived there, she had never entered the Acropolis.

Today Isabel felt dressed for this long overdue occasion. She wore a white dress of common white cotton cheesecloth. It hung loose, with great kimono sleeves. In her ears were ancient Phoenician gold hoops. Her scarab necklace and the diamonds on her fingers sparkled like white fire. Her white lizard-skin, high-heeled open sandals clicked over the historic stones. She felt like an earthly goddess.

Before they left, an old Greek man with dark, wrinkled skin and a huge, white moustache took a black-and-white photograph of the three of them with his old box camera, painted in bright yellow enamel. He refused to take any money because of Katarina. It was a privilege to have heard her echoing through the Acropolis. No, he must pay her. He would deliver the photographs sometime within the next hour to the Hilton, down in the restaurant.

Being with Katarina Syndamou in the Acropolis, empty of the endless streams of tourists, with only Alexander and the old Greek photographer, on an unusually hot day at the end of October, was an experience that took Isabel out of the realms of reality and lifted her high into a spiritual world filled with sheer poetry. It was the sort of thing that happens once in a lifetime, and it would stay with her all her life.

As the three walked down the hill from the Acropolis, through the few trees giving a relief of shade every now and again, Isabel spoke the words of George Seferis:

*"We who set out on this pilgrimage
looked at the broken statues.
We forgot ourselves and said that life is not so easily
    lost
that death has unexplored paths
and its own particular justice;
that while we, still upright on our feet, are dying,
become brothers in stone*

> *united in hardness and weakness, the ancient dead*
> *have escaped the circle and risen again*
> *and smile in a strange silence."*

The chauffeur saw them approach and jumped out of the front seat, opening the door. The three people stepped into the air-conditioned interior, where nothing was said until they had passed Syntagma and were driving up Basilies Sophias to the Hilton. With the memory of the Acropolis still intense, they began to gather up their energies for yet another reality, the rest of the day and what it held for them.

At the hotel, they got out of the car one by one, and George, the doorman, gave them a resounding welcome. Then they made their way through the Hilton lobby and down to the Ta Nissa Room. Katarina was stopped constantly by people. She was very much loved by the Greeks and seemed to have a kind word for everyone.

As the three of them walked into the Ta Nissa Room, with Gamal behind them, Isabel thought to herself that this was a great mistake. Kate and Ava were going to see her come in with happy people whom they did not know, and they were going to be on the defensive. Well, it couldn't be helped now.

The maître d'hôtel greeted Katarina with all the fanfare that an actress of her stature gets in restaurants. Isabel and Alexander were introduced, and then Alexander took over.

"I believe that you have a reservation for Miss Wells, a table for three. Have her guests arrived?"

"Yes, sir, her guests are seated."

"You have a table reserved for me, Mr. Gordon-Spencer, close to Miss Wells's table?" he continued. "That one is for two."

"Yes, sir, we are ready for you. May I take your party to your tables?"

"Yes, and by the way, I would be pleased if you would allow my man here to wait for us in reception."

"Yes, with pleasure, sir."

Alexander slipped the man a very large tip and saw that Gamal was seated comfortably at a small table in the reception area. Then they were shown to their tables.

It was like the scene in the lobby, only magnified. They walked through the dining room, weaving in and out of the tables, while various men rose from their chairs to kiss Katarina's hand, and women stood up and kissed her on the cheek. Finally the entourage made their way to the windows where their tables were.

Kate and Ava were already seated and waiting. Isabel had waved to them when she saw them. Alexander's table was the first they approached, and so the two women said good-bye to each other, and Alexander said, "After you have finished your lunch, and you are ready to leave, we will be here at the table waiting for you. If I am gone, it will only be to take Katarina home, and then I will return here. Gamal is waiting should you decide to leave and go somewhere. Just tell him where you will be. I will come and pick you up. And, Isabel, if after you and your family have had lunch you would like to join us for coffee, I am delighted to invite you. Simply come and join us." He kissed her, and she went on to meet her mother and sister.

Isabel kissed Kate on the cheek and then slipped into the chair held back by the waiter. "Hi. I hope I have not kept you two waiting. It is so nice to see you. How are you, Ava? You're looking lovely."

"I did not know that Katarina Syndamou was a friend of yours," Ava said by way of an answer.

"Well, actually, she is not. She is a friend of Alexander's."

"And who is Alexander?"

"Alexander Gordon-Spencer. He is a close friend of Alexis Hyatt, and now he is a friend of mine."

"Well!" Ava fumed, "You really made an entrance, didn't you? You always have to have center stage, don't you?"

Ava had been doing all the talking, and Isabel thought to herself, *Oh, she is angry and holding it all back as usual.*

"She doesn't dress very well for a woman in her position, but what do you expect? You know how the Greeks are about taste," Ava hissed.

"We have just come from the . . ."

"Well, I suppose the fact that she is a great lady of the theater covers up a great many of her faults," Ava interrupted. "They say that she is going to retire, but I don't listen to the gossips. They say anything just to talk."

". . . the Acropolis was beaut——"

"All my life I have had the bad luck that people are always jealous of me," Ava continued. "My looks, my marriage, my home, my career—always the same problem—parasites who do nothing, always jealous. I am sure that she suffers from the same problem. Have you ever heard her Elektra? Oh, but come to think of it, you could not have appreciated it if you had, what with your bad Greek. You should have made more of an effort. Well, maybe now that she is your friend you will go to one of her performances."

"Isabel," Kate interjected.

"Yes, Mother?"

"Isabel, is *that* the man that I spoke to yesterday on your telephone? Is *that* your new servant?" Kate pointed, none too discreetly, to Gamal, sitting at his little table far across from them.

"No, Mother. He is the servant of Alexis, and Alexis is the man who you spoke to on the telephone yesterday."

"Since when do you travel with a strange man's servants around you? Just because you know one actress? Really, Isabel. Ava is right, you do try and hog the limelight. You are getting to be an actress yourself."

"Mother, I know it all looks strange to you, but please let me explain. Alexander, that is the man over there at the table with Katarina, and I, and that man, Gamal, flew in on an airplane this morning, and we are flying out of here at seven this evening. Since I was coming to lunch here, they decided to do the same, so that we would all stay relatively close together. Now, does that explain it all?"

With that Isabel called the headwaiter over and said, "We would like to order, please."

It was during the ordering of lunch that Ava first saw the diamonds on Isabel's hands. A minute later it was Kate who said, "Isabel Wells, let me see your hands."

Isabel could not help but laugh and very proudly put down her menu and showed the women her hands. The two women were nonplussed. Kate finally recovered herself and said, "Where did you get those?"

"Well, that is why I am here. I have something to tell you, but I'm sure that Ava already has."

"Ava has told me nothing. What were you supposed to tell me, Ava, and why haven't you?" Kate scolded.

"I have told you nothing because, for the moment, I

am not sure that there is anything to tell. If there is, then let Isabel find a way to explain this latest thing in her life. It has nothing to do with me, and frankly, I can't get enthusiastic over another one of her 'projects.' Well, Isabel, let's have the laugh of the day."

"I have no idea why Ava finds it so amusing, but the fact of the matter is that I am going to get married, and I would like to tell you everything. It is just wonderful and I am happier than I have ever been in my life."

Then the petty, inevitable questions began.

"How can you marry a man who you have only known for two weeks? Who is he? Oh, my God, he is an Arab! Oh, my God, he is half-Christian and half-Moslem? How do you know he really has money? Maybe he is a phony? Do you have to change your religion? What are you going to do about your American citizenship? Oh, Isabel, how could you do this to me? What will the family say? Is he very black, I mean brown? If your father was alive, he would put a stop to this. How old is he? Oh, he is so old! How many wives does he have?" And on and on and on it went.

Finally Isabel made it clear to Kate and Ava that she would marry somewhere in Egypt on Tuesday or Wednesday.

"Oh, so you come here like a princess with your three-ring circus, dripping in jewels, and simply announce that you are getting married in Egypt on Wednesday and Thursday," Kate attacked. "Did it ever occur to you to discuss it with your family?"

"Well, Mother, that is what I am doing here now, or trying to do, is more like it, and the wedding will be Tuesday or Wednesday, not Wednesday and Thursday."

"Stop interrupting me! What about *my* plans? Have you forgotten that you have a *commitment* to me?"

"I have a what?" Isabel gasped.

"What do you mean 'a what'? A commitment. I was coming to *live* with you. Did it ever occur to you that I don't want to change my plans? What am I supposed to do now? What am I supposed to do now?" Kate began to cry, with dry tears, at the table.

"Now you have done it, Isabel." Ava, on the attack. "For God's sake, Mother, pull yourself together. Leave it to you, Isabel, to pick a fine time to mess up everyone's lives."

"Upset everyone's lives? Mother coming to live with me?" Isabel managed. "Whatever are you two talking about? I come here to tell you that I am going to be married, that I am happier than I have ever been in my life. I want to share this with you both, and all I get is that I am messing up *your* lives. Are you both mad? Until this minute all I knew about Mother's plans was that she was going to spend a holiday in London with me, at her convenience, I might add. And as for you, Ava, how does my finding happiness with another human being mess up *your* life? Have neither of you any joy for *me?*"

"No one here is being practical at all," Ava said, ignoring her. "First of all, Mother is going to London. That is what she wants to do, and I think she should do it. And, I think that *you* should take the responsibility of making her *happy* in London."

Isabel felt as if she were on the edge of an abyss. She had just come to tell these women that she was marrying and was not going to be in London, and they were going on as if she had said nothing of the greatest change she would probably ever make in her entire life. They were ignoring it, almost as if it were a fantasy of hers.

"Ava, I don't think you realize that in a few days I am not going to be Isabel, neurotically trying to take care of herself, dying of guilt every day because she cannot take care of her family, but Lady Alexis Hyatt. A wife, married to a man out of a mutual passion and respect for one another. I am going to make this man as happy as he is making me happy. I am in love with him." She turned to her mother. "You and your trip to London, and whatever else you think I am messing up in your life, are going to have to face it. I am interested in nothing at the moment except making a happy life with this man."

As her mother began to argue, Isabel silenced her with a wave of her hand. "I am not going to London. You, Kate, are not coming to live with me. You never *could,* and you never *will.* Alexis asked me to invite you both, and Alfred, to come for a long stay with us in Egypt, after we are settled. When he extended that invitation, he was sure that you would like to share some of our happiness. If this dreadful luncheon is an example of your joy for us, I do not see how we could possibly extend such an invitation. Things have changed dramatically for me now. They could change for you also. We could have a settled, happy family, with a new member. This is something I have looked for, waited for, longed for, all my life: to find another human being with whom I feel complete. Is it so difficult for either one of you to wish me well in that? Not one *word* has come from either one of you wishing me happiness."

There was silence, and at this point the waiters brought the first course. The silence settled over the table like a Cape Cod fog. Isabel was surprised at herself for saying as much as she had. She picked up her fork and cut into the thick slice of grilled aubergine. She was very angry and shocked, not so much because of their lack of joy, but because of their meanness in not being able to enjoy her happiness. Isabel had pointed out to them all the horrific lack of love and simple affection between the three women. Isabel was forced to face the fact that she was no different from the other two. Her self-interest, her own happiness, were of prime importance to her. Another time, long ago, that was not so, but the years and years of Kate and Ava's domination and egoism had worn down to nothing her generosity towards them.

Isabel looked up from her plate at Kate, whose face was contorted with self-pity, anger, bitterness and rage. When their eyes met, Isabel saw Kate's face turn into a hard, mean mask from which the blood had drained.

"This is not the first time that you have done this to me, but it is the last time," Kate suddenly began. "I have loved you, adored you, given you everything, and you took everything and ran like a thief, and you are still running like a thief. You go to Egypt, you marry this man who has you under his power because he holds you sexually, pays you off with gems. You wait until a younger, sexier thing comes along, and he throws you in the street. Don't worry, your mother will take you in, just as she always has. Imagine!

"In love! Marry a man because you are in love! Disappointing *me* because you are in love with a man and want to make a life with him. You are smarter than I am. I lived a miserable forty years with your father. He was kind and good-natured and gave me everything he could, but there was no love. During that time someone did come along, but you never saw *me* running off, did you? I did not desert *you* because someone was satisfying me sexually, giving me gifts, paying attention to me. I did not abandon *you* and *my obligations* to *you*. I missed out my *whole life* because of *you*. You live with that!" She pounded the table with her fists. "You fly out today to your new husband and see what it is like to pick up after a man. To carry for him. To be dependent on him. To be dominated and enslaved by a man, for security, because you do not want to work anymore. That's what it is, you know. *Love!* Don't make me laugh! You have *no idea* what the word means. Be honest with yourself. You have never been able to love *anything* but *yourself* for very long. Well, I wish you all the luck in the world because, kid, you are going to need it. We are going to be in Egypt at the same time, you and I. But we won't see each other. I won't have *time* this trip, but give me your address, and I *might* send you a postcard."

Isabel was shattered. With a trembling hand she found a fountain pen in her handbag and a piece of paper. She wrote down the Sharia el Nil address and Alexis's name and handed it across the table to Kate.

Ava had sat there impassively taking it all in. The waiters served the second course to the silent ladies. Ava picked up her knife and fork and stabbed into her steak.

Kate pushed her plate angrily away from her and got up. "I am leaving. I have a great deal to do. You know, you are not the *only* one to make changes. New life, new friends, abandon the old. I am taking a leaf from your book of rules, and see how you like that!"

She stood there at the table and called the waiter over and asked for the bill. The waiter said, "I am sorry, madam. Is something wrong with the food?"

"Never mind the food, just give me the bill," she spat.

"The bill has been paid, madam."

With violently shaking hands she managed to open her purse and throw down five hundred drachmas on the table. Then she left.

Isabel sat there in silence as Ava ate her steak and salad. Slowly she felt herself grow calm once Kate was away from the table. She was so grateful that Alexis had not seen this, that he had been spared this horrible ordeal.

Ava turned to her and said, "You know that she let you off lightly? You are not going to make it, Isabel. You're weak, lazy. You have no discipline. You're luxury-loving and you're ruled by your senses. He will throw you out in six months, but then, you have your diamonds, haven't you? Vulgar, but at least worth something. You always did like to stand out, and with those diamonds, you sure do. But remember, you have to pay."

Isabel continued to chew her food, tasting only sawdust.

"I notice your new love isn't here. What were you afraid of?" Ava lashed on. "That we might show you up for what you are? A bully, a tyrant, a hustler; how else would you have been able to make your way in the world? And now with a track record like yours, you would lead me to believe he is so in love with you that he cannot wait to marry you after two weeks? That he adores you? That is all that you have ever wanted. Adoration and the center of attention—the spotlight—and now you think you have it. Well, I certainly wish you luck and look forward to seeing how you handle this. But now let's be practical. What are you going to do about Mother? Figure *something* out. You are a rich woman now, or will be in a few days, and it's about time you started paying back. She is all alone in this world and a miserable person, unfortunately very stupid as well, or she would never have ruined a life for you."

Suddenly Isabel looked straight up at Ava's hard face. For the first time in her life she noticed an added look on that face, a kind of venomous release achieved by the tongue-whipping she had just given Isabel. And strangely, Isabel thought with pity, Ava was now freed of a burden she had probably carried for all of their lives.

Ava said very calmly and icily to Isabel, "You know, I really do not like you. I never have liked you. I don't like anything you stand for, or anything you do. I consider you second-rate, and all these years I have pretended that you were first-rate. You're calculated and unattractive and very unfeminine. You are a freak. And now, with your big diamonds, and an unattractive Arab husband on the hook, you come here to Athens with a flashy entourage of flunkies, trying to impress us. Well, you don't. All my life I have had to suffer so you could be the center of attention. First as a child I watched you adored and loved, while I was forgotten in the background. When I ran away with my first new husband, I only then began to feel the luxury, the real luxury, of not trying to steal the show. You really don't think at this late stage in the game, that your marriage, no matter how successful the catch is, will impress me, do you? Because it never will. So why not save yourself a great deal of trouble later on, when it fails, and for-get marrying him? Collect what you can off him, and as soon as the passion dies, which never takes very long, you can go back to being alone. Believe me, it suits a selfish person like you, and then, of course, you will have Mother to make a life with. Well, do you agree? Surely you must see that I am right?" Ava ended a little lamely.

Isabel said, as calmly as possible, "All I see, Ava, is that you are mad and you are wrong. I am marrying Alexis Hyatt immediately, and we hope to spend the rest of our days together making love, in love, and sharing what love we have for each other with as many people as is possible and——"

Ava attacked instantly. "I have hated you since child-hood for this thing you hold so dear—love! This *fantasy* that is nothing but a word, and I hate you now for it. . . ."

It was at that moment that Isabel felt Alexander stand-ing behind her chair with his hand on her shoulder. Ava, so coolly hysterical, and going on in her icy, steady voice that mesmerized herself, never saw him. She saw only the object of her hatred and heard only the sound of her own voice.

Isabel was more shocked than surprised. Alexander put his hand firmly under her arm and half lifted her up; he pulled her chair back, and they left the table. Ava con-tinued in her icy, calm voice, telling the empty air how much she hated Isabel.

Alexander took Isabel as far as Gamal's table, and from there she was escorted by Gamal to the waiting car.

He then returned to the table where Ava was still spew-ing forth. He put his hand on her shoulder and very quietly and gently shook her. "Excuse me, but your sister has gone now, and I think your luncheon is over. May I take you to a taxi?"

Ava quickly recovered herself and drank down what was left of the wine in her glass. "That will not be neces-sary. I am quite capable of finding a taxi when I am ready to leave. For the moment, I would like to sit here quietly alone over another cup of coffee."

Alexander left Ava and went to the table where he had dined with Katarina. They left at once to join Isabel in the car.

As they made their way through the restaurant and up the stairs, Katarina said to Alexander, "Christ! That was theater! Such terrible things from that table! Such hatred, bitterness. There was no love. Alexander, those three women! Never will they flow together, never! You will see, Alexander; never will they meet again. Your friend Isabel has a good man, I hope? She will need a good man to wipe out a lifetime of that."

Katarina declined a lift with them, saying that she would walk to a friend who lived close by. Isabel got out of the car to say good-bye and thank her for such a marvelous morning. She apologized for cutting Katarina's lunch short.

Isabel had recovered and this put the party back in good form. As they were talking, the little old photographer arrived with the pictures from the Acropolis. They were marvelous and captured the spirit of the morning.

The two women kissed good-bye, and Katarina said, "Isabel, don't think of them anymore. You know the world is filled with women together with no love. It is just something you have to live with. I am not worried; I see love in you." And so they parted.

Alexander and Isabel made themselves comfortable in the back of the car, and Gamal got in the front with the chauffeur. She thought to herself about Alexis and how he had insisted that she be accompanied by these men, how, in fact, he had arranged everything to make it all easier for her. How had he guessed that it was going to be so bad? She wondered if it was not his strength that was helping her at this very moment.

It was Isabel, an embarrassed Isabel, who took control of the situation. "Alexander, you could not have had much of a lunch, and I only had a forkful of aubergine, which stuck in my throat. We have hours before the flight. Let's go down to Turkolimino and have a splendid afternoon eating fish and drinking retsina."

Just the thought of the old port with its many little fishing boats, the hundreds of little white-clothed tables sitting under the awnings near the water's edge, the baking sun overhead, cheered her up. There would be the Sunday Athenians out for a feast, all laughing and gay; the waiters running back and forth up and down the stairs to the restaurants on the other side of the road, balancing plates of *kalamarakia*, oysters, shrimps, *barbounia*, *glossa*, *salada horiataki horta* and *octopodi*. The smell of the olive oil, the lemons, the retsina, filled Isabel's imagination.

Alexander agreed it was a great idea, as he was fam-

ished. He squeezed her hand and said, "Let's get drunk!"
She gave him a grateful kiss on the cheek.

He told the driver where to take them, and said something to Gamal in Arabic, who immediately produced two joints. They lit up, and after a few puffs, both looked at each other and said together, "Fantastic."

"Alexander, this is just what's needed," Isabel said with a sigh. "I had no idea you smoked!"

Much too discreet to bring up the dreadful incident of the family reunion, Alexander remained silent on the subject. It was not until hours later, when they were up in the air and halfway to Cairo, that she asked him, "Please, Alexander, say nothing to Alexis. I do not want him upset for me. I have no doubts about what I am doing, and I am very happy and very much in love. I do not want him upset. It was only a bad hour out of what has been otherwise a wonderful day. The Acropolis and Katarina, all those hours at Turkolimino gorging ourselves and laughing and drinking with those amusing Greeks we met . . . Please, Alexander . . ."

Alexander put his hand out to stop her. "Isabel, please do not worry. Alexis will ask me, so I must say something. You must leave this with me. I will be most discreet and he will not be upset. He would not have sent us with you unless he suspected trouble."

He kissed her hand then and said, "You know I am very fond of you both. I know that you will be happy."

To himself Alexander thought it incredible that this lovely woman was about to marry one of the most eligible, interesting men in the world, without one kind word or blessing from her family. He knew that she was affected by the dreadful meeting, but he also knew that the love Alexis had given her made her very strong indeed.

He had a dreadful feeling that these two women were not through with her yet. Isabel behaved with a kind of innocence about them that he found frightening. If Alexander was concerned at all, it was that Isabel was terribly vulnerable, whether she knew it or not. Yes, he would have to tell Alexis, but in his own time, and his own words.

X

AVA SAT alone at the table while the waiters cleared away the uneaten food. After three brandies, she finished a cup of coffee and then called for the bill. She was told yet again by the headwaiter that the bill had been paid. She picked up the five hundred drachmas that Kate had thrown down on the table and none-too-steadily raised herself to her feet. She was on her way to see her mother. By God, she admired her.

Kate had two performances: the weak, pitiful, abused martyr was one, and the proud, vicious tiger was the other. There were variations on both themes. Ava found Kate the tiger a great deal more palatable.

When Kate opened the door there was no question in Ava's mind that the very vicious tiger was at work.

"I brought you your five hundred drachmas."

"I don't want it."

"Don't be ridiculous. Of course you want it," she said, putting it on the table. "What are you going to do?"

"What do you think I am going to do?" Kate growled. "I am not going to have my plans ruined because of Isabel. You can't tell me that Isabel has only known this man two weeks. She must have known for a long time she was going to marry him. Oh, I'm angry! It would have been a different matter had she said that she was seeing someone, had she confided in us. Had we *met* him."

"Isabel is not that special," Ava added. "There are millions more better than her. No, to receive diamonds of that quality for nothing, for two weeks in bed with a man! Who knows what they do in bed? Those Arabs are so strange, the whole world knows how they are with women! But, that's Isabel. She does what she wants anyway. She has to be taught a lesson."

"I am going to teach her one," Kate said. "Fortunately, my neighbor, the travel agent, tells me that I can fly to

253

Alexandria tomorrow morning to meet a cruise boat. I get my one day on the Nile, then I join the main ship that stops in Florida, North Carolina, New York and Southampton. It's a much longer cruise, and by the time it is over Isabel will have either gone through with this marriage, which I *doubt* after our luncheon *today,* or be back in London *alone* again. The way I see it, she will be in London, all apologies by the time I dock in New York. I will get off in New York, visit my brothers and sisters, and find out where she is and what she has done. If she has gone through with this ridiculous marriage, then I will stop in London for a few days and fly back here to my flat. And if she is alone, as I am sure she will be, I will join her as I'd planned all along. What do you think of that?"

"I think you should do what you want to do," Ava replied. "You know that you have always been welcome here, but I think that it is time you had a change. Travel around. I agree with you, it's time that she faced the responsibility of family. What time do you have to get your plane?"

"Eleven-thirty in the morning."

"Well, I will see to it that you get to the airport."

"Oh, darling, you do not have to do that. You are always so good and generous to me."

Ava smiled in agreement. "Of course I will take you. Now, do you need any help in packing?"

"No. Fortunately, I am not like your sister. I started packing four days ago. So I think I can manage everything by tomorrow morning. All I will have to do is get to the hairdressers as early as possible and then we can go. You know, Ava, this has given me a new lease on life. I like this. I like this just fine. This getting out and doing things my way. You will see, it will all work out."

Ava sat back and thought to herself: *I am going to enjoy this; I am going to enjoy watching both of you. You silly, foolish, stupid women, always going round in circles, spending money, getting nowhere, having nothing. No relationships, no success, just fantasies. Kate had her fantasies; Isabel had hers. But Ava is not going to pick up the pieces this time. Oh yes, I am going to enjoy every bit of this, and it could not have come at a better time for me. I will not have to go to Takis's dreary* pied à terre. *I will keep my mother's key and have my little romance here. Who knows, I may marry again before Isabel manages to crawl to the altar!*

"Listen, Mother, you give me the keys to this flat when I take you to the airport, and I will keep an eye on it for you. When you are ready to come back, you let me know, and I will meet you and give you back your keys."

"Oh, you are good, Ava! My God, you are a responsible, good daughter. Thank God I have you."

You stupid old whore, Ava thought. *You didn't always feel that way about me. It was always Isabel who got that speech.*

Ava left her mother and started walking home. There was no question in her mind that this entire charade of a marriage with a rich Egyptian was not out of love, but out of spite, simply to better the brilliant marriage that Ava had made.

She walked along at a very brisk pace, paying no attention to the burning hot sun. She saw two men give her the eye, and that cheered her up considerably.

Passing some of the tables in Kolonaki Square, she saw the old admiral. He stood up to greet her and kissed her hand. She started to flirt with him, but when he asked her to sit down, she said no, she had to be on her way, and swung herself more jauntily, in a sexier fashion, up through Kolonaki Square.

A couple of young Greek blades in their tight, tapered shirts and their cock-bulging trousers watched her. It made Ava feel very sexy, gathering admiration from those Greeks, young and old alike, who really enjoy their illicit fuck in the afternoon. Even if more dream about it than actually do it, she could always sense the afternoon sex hanging heavy in the hot air.

Ava walked through some of the narrow streets, and met a young *concierge* from one of the buildings near her house. He was a handsome young boy, and she flirted with him every day. She could see him become excited at the attention she paid him, and she reveled in her own power of attraction. She knew that he wanted her, that to him she was an unattainable goddess, so she tantalized him. Even to the point of "accidentally" bumping into him with her ass. He wanted her desperately but had not the courage even to touch her. She saw his hands tremble and then patted him on the cheek; the poor boy almost

came in his pants. Satisfied, she moved away from him
with a friendly wave.

When she arrived home there was no one there, but
she had known that there would not be. The house was
cool, quiet. It did not seem to calm her down very much.
She went to her bedroom and undressed. She walked
through the house naked, looking at herself wherever she
could catch her reflection. Then into the bathroom to run
a bath, and while the tub was filling, she looked at herself in the full-length mirror. Her figure was very good,
much better than Isabel's, and she was so firm and limber.

There was something youngish about her and her figure, not voluptuous like Isabel. The voluptuous, sluttish,
animalistic kind of look was just common and vulgar. She
could tell by all the men that wanted her on the way
home, and Takis—how he wanted her—that the slight,
feminine coquette was still the winner.

Still looking in the mirror that was misty now from the
steam, she arched her back and pushed her pelvis forward. She opened the lips of her vagina and looked at
herself, thinking of Isabel's diamonds and how she might
have got them. What did she let the man do to her? She
knew that she must have received them for fucking, for
all *sorts* of obscene sexual acts. You don't get diamonds
for love. You get them for lust.

You get nothing for love.

Ava admired herself in the mirror, which she now
wiped down to see her image better. She saw her nipples,
big ones and pointed, and she knew that they were de-
sirable. She pulled one of them, squeezed it. It was supposed to do something for you, arouse you. She squeezed
it again, but did not much like the pain, so she stopped.
Then she lifted her leg very high and pressed her foot
against the wall and looked at her genitals again. She
wanted to see how she looked with a cock inside her. She
wanted to feel it and see the expression on her face feeling it. She became obsessed with the idea of seeing something penetrate her and how she looked that way, what
her expression was like. What could she put inside her?
What was the same size as Takis? She ran around picking
up things. A perfume bottle, too large. Syringe of a
douche bag, too thin. A cucumber from the fridge was too
obscene, too big, too depraved. The courgettes were too

small. She was frantic. Then she saw Alfred's deodorant, a cock-shaped, fluted glass bottle about an inch in diameter, and about eight inches long. She surely could get half of it in her and see the rest sticking out. She washed it with hot water, then cold, with disinfectant, more hot water, lukewarm water, then soapy water and finally rinsed it. At last she thought it sterile enough to enter her.

She went back to the mirror, put up her leg, and spread herself open. First she inserted Nivea cream and worked it in well with her fingers. She almost gave up the idea, it all seemed so disgusting. But her desire to see herself in the mirror overcame her revulsion and she very, very slowly pushed in Alfred's bottle of deodorant. Oh, it looked wonderful. She moved it in and out, watching herself dispassionately. How wonderfully sexual and beautiful she looked, she thought. A lovely position. Not everyone would be able to keep that position and that balance. She walked around, with it sticking out of her and thought she looked just as dignified that way as well. Then she pulled it out, washed it four or five times and put it back on the shelf.

Back at the mirror she examined herself again as she thought of Isabel's diamonds and then of Takis. Takis was very rich too, and when she got him she would not accept diamonds. They were vulgar. No, she would opt for property.

The telephone began ringing just as Ava was drying herself off. She wrapped a towel around herself and ran into the living room and picked it up. It was Takis. He was free for an hour, and he knew that Alfred was away. Could he come by and see her?

She teased him, saying that it was impossible. They must wait a couple of days; then she would have a surprise for him: a secret place where no one would find them.

She had him dreadfully excited on the telephone; she could tell by the passion in his voice. When she put the receiver down and looked in the mirror, she saw the pretty, flirtatious Ava with an old Greek man on a string. She felt a thrill go through her body and then smiled: Her thoughts had made her come ever so lightly.

That evening, when Alfred arrived home, he found Ava in an over-excited mood. He instinctively knew that something was very wrong. Being a man of peace, and know-

ing his wife very well, he asked no questions, happily
following her every wish. After a few drinks together the
two went out to dinner. Halfway through their meal,
Takis and his wife, Evangalia, and an old bachelor friend
of Takis's arrived in the same restaurant. Ava was annoyed when she saw them come in but said nothing. Of
course they joined them.

Ava dismissed her annoyance, and was at her very best.
During the gay and happy night they decided that, because of the freak heat wave, they would all go to Marathon for a picnic lunch and a swim the next day. Ava
would take along her writing box so she could work on an
article for the *Reader's Digest* while the other four played
bridge.

The endless arrangements that Greeks get into about a
midday excursion went on, and finally it was settled.
Takis would pick up Ava at 10:45 A.M., along with a
hamper filled with crushed ice and wine and a portable
bar. Takis would tuck it all away in the boot of his car,
along with the food that had been supplied by Evangalia.
He proudly announced that there would still be room in
the enormous boot of the shiny new Mercedes for Mrs.
Wells's luggage, as he insisted on taking her and Ava to
the airport. That done, he would pick up the others at the
Piccolo in Kolonaki at noon. Of course, what was not announced was that the arrangements allowed the possibility
of a quick fuck with Ava, or at least some time for the
two of them to be alone and make some plans for a midday fuck in the near future. The ever-generous Takis
liked Kate and was happy to see her off. What he would
not realize as he drove them to the airport was that although Kate hid it, she knew Ava very well. The moment
that the car pulled up in front of her flat, with Ava in the
front seat and Takis running out for the luggage, she
would know that *this* was the reason why Ava was en-
couraging her to go away and this was why she was so
pleased to care for her flat. Ava was about to launch an
affair with this old and trusted friend, and she wanted her
mother out of the way.

At the airport Kate would kiss her quickly good-bye,
trying not to hit her for cheating on Alfred, and then,
"Mother dear, you have forgotten to give me the key."

"Oh, so I have. Well, never mind, I don't want to

bother you, sweetheart. The flat is closed up. There is no need for you to go there."

"Don't be silly, dear. Give me the key."

"No, honestly, there is no need."

"I insist."

"You insist?"

"Yes, I insist."

Kate would see a mean iciness come into Ava's face as she held out her open palm. Kate would be furious, on the verge of tears. She would want to hit her but would not dare. "Now, give me the key."

In her obvious anger she would throw it into Ava's outstretched hand and miss. Ava would bend down and pick it up.

The last thing that Kate would say to Ava would be, "Ava, don't use my flat as a whorehouse, use your own," and with tears in her eyes, she would walk away towards customs.

But now it was 2:15 Monday morning. Ava was in her nightdress, lying next to Alfred, who had made love to her and was now in a deep, comfortable sleep. Ava had nothing but affection for Alfred and respect for his money. If it were possible for her to have any hatred at all for Alfred, it would be because night after night he slept on like an innocent baby from the moment his head hit the pillow, while she remained the tortured insomniac.

Oh, she *would* sleep, but no more than three or four hours a night. Tonight, the party over and Alfred asleep, all attention was cut off. She had no one but herself to lie with in bed.

Now Isabel's diamonds flashed before Ava's eyes. Suddenly the hatred and resentment came back. Ava knew that she would never, *never* accept the fact that Isabel might marry. All that she could see in the quiet of the dark room was the sparkle of those diamonds.

They were a symbol of material wealth, of security that Isabel now had. The one thing that Ava had all her adult life to hold over Isabel was security. Now those diamonds were flashing like warning lights to Ava. A new kind of security for Isabel weakened Ava. She did not like that at all.

She tossed and turned. It was terribly hot. She kicked off the sheet, went for a drink of water, returned to the bed and lay on her side, away from Alfred, then on her back, staring up at the ceiling. She tossed and turned and still Alfred slept. Back on her side again, she leaned on her elbow and watched him breathing in the dark. She could have strangled him.

It was six in the morning before she finally fell into a light, nervous sleep. By half past eight she was sitting at the dining table having her second cup of coffee.

Alfred sat across from his wife and meticulously peeled an orange. He knew by the shrillness of her voice and her incessant chatter that she had had a bad night. He offered Ava a piece of orange. She took a segment, and they talked about the clothes they would wear. It was finally decided that he would not swim and that he would wear his gray flannel trousers; a beige short-sleeved, open-necked shirt; a small scarf of red and navy blue Thai silk in a tiny pattern of *fleur de lis* tied jauntily at his neck; and his navy blue blazer with its antique sterling silver admiral's button.

Ava finally decided to wear a black bikini and over it a pink-and-white polka dot, two-piece dress that buttoned down the front. Alfred would put her robe, bath towel and all her other bits and pieces that she used for sunning, such as a hat, sun glasses, oil, bath cap and, of course, a mirror, in a large basket ready to be put with the picnic things in the boot of Takis's car.

Alfred asked her about Kate and her forthcoming trip. Not one word had been said about Isabel and her visit the day before. Very subtly he asked how the luncheon went and if Isabel was well.

"Yes, Isabel was well," Ava said.

"Did you all enjoy your lunch?"

"No, we certainly did not. The food was bad and Isabel thinks that she is going to get married."

"Really? That is very exciting. Who is she going to marry?"

"That does not bear discussion, Alfred. It is probably another of her fantasies. She arrived at the table dripping in diamonds and had an entourage provided by some Arab. The one she says she's going to marry. She does not intend to be in London when Mother is going to be there, and she is in Cairo at this very moment. When I receive a telegram saying that she is married, then I will believe it, and not until then. Alfred, it honestly does not bear talking about. You know Isabel is never going to marry, and if she does, how long will it last? I did my best to make her face the fact that she will never be able to sustain a marriage. Let's hope she listened."

"But, Ava, I've never, ever heard Isabel talk about marriage before," Alfred pointed out. "I'm sure she would not go into it lightly. If she is contemplating it, then she must be very sure of the relationship. If she was not, she would never have flown in here yesterday to tell you. Who is the man?"

"Well, I do not know about the marriage bit, but he *is* obviously keeping her. It's some Egyptian called Alexis Hyatt. Some dreadful Arab."

"Oh, no, Ava." Alfred laughed. "I believe you have that just a little wrong. If he is *Sir* Alexis Hyatt then we are going to have in the family one of the most important figures in the Middle East. He is not just a rich little Arab, but a highly cultured man; very intelligent, a most honorable person, a great connoisseur. I'm surprised you've never heard of him."

Ava went pale. "It can't be, Alfred. Are you sure that he is the same man?"

"Well, unless there are two with the exact same name. How amazing! To think that he might be part of the family. Ava, you would like him very much."

"Alfred, stop getting excited. I tell you, it is never going to come off. Never in a million years. You will see, it will never come to anything."

"Well, I hope for Isabel's sake that it does. He would certainly give her an interesting life and he looks to be a handsome, dashing man."

"How do you know that, Alfred?" she quietly asked.

"Because recently I saw a picture of him in *Time*. About two weeks ago, I think. I may still have the copy." He went into his study.

Rage rapidly mounted inside Ava. Why was Alfred so enthusiastic? It was something that was not going to happen anyway. If he was that important, it was impossible. Isabel would not be able to handle it. Why would he want Isabel? What was even more upsetting was that she knew Alfred was always correct about his facts—which meant that Sir Alexis Hyatt was really something.

Oh, that Isabel! She had even managed to disrupt Ava's day with Alfred with her carryings-on. Oh, God, maybe he won't find that old *Time,* maybe Ava would not have to see him.

It was at that point that Alfred came in and took a chair next to Ava, thumbing through the old magazine. There it was, on the top half of the page, a black-and-white photograph of two men. One was King Khalid of Saudi Arabia. The other was handsome, with a broad smile and a pair of mischievous eyes set in a very handsome face. The caption under the picture read: "Sir Alexis Hyatt, the world's Middle Eastern Ambassador of good will."

Ava's reaction was killing: He was handsome, rich, middle-aged, intelligent and respected the world over. And her sister was going to marry him. It was just not possible. And the usually very calm Alfred was actually excited for his sister-in-law.

"Fascinating, just fascinating, a very interesting man," Ava muttered. "I do not think that it can be him. Of course, it is just possible, but we will see. If we ever get to meet him, and *if* he is still around in a few weeks' time."

Alfred saw the glint in Ava's eye and closed the magazine slowly. "When are they marrying?"

"Oh, I don't know. She said something about today, or tomorrow. It's all very secretive. Look, Alfred, if he is all that important, then what is the secret? No, no, we had better just forget the whole thing until we are sure."

"Ava, *where* are they marrying?"

"In Cairo."

"Aren't you thrilled for her? Don't you think we should send a telegram or something?"

"No, I certainly do not. If it is such a secret, then we will do nothing. That is, supposing that there *is* a wedding, which is still in doubt. None of us was invited to it anyway. Now I am off to dress. I must be ready for Takis. It was so nice of him to offer to take Mother to the airport. I'll see you at the Piccolo at noon."

When Alfred had gone off to his attorney for a meeting, Ava poured herself a triple shot of whiskey, throwing it back in one swallow. She was trembling with rage. It couldn't be true? She closed her eyes and the warm surge of the alcohol in her blood lifted her spirits immediately. She opened her eyes slowly and examined her face in the mirror above the bar. It was all right, she was still there, still beautiful. She felt better, much better.

She gave a few instructions to the maid and that made her life yet again more real. She went into the bedroom to dress, and to think about Kate, now rushing around getting her hair, her feet, her fingernails all done up for her trip and her new life with Isabel. She suddenly realized how naive Kate was. *Well*, thought Ava, *I am out of it. Let them fight it out between them.*

The party of five—Alfred, Ava, Evangalia, Takis and his bachelor friend, Philipos—were ensconced on a lovely and quiet spit of land. The road went around the great burial mound in Marathon and then parallel to the sea. From the road to the water there was a small forest of shady, twisted pine trees. They had parked the car under the pines and carried all the things. Beyond the little forest they came to a finger of land crowned with a pine-clad hill high above the sea.

To the right of the little hill there ran a freshwater river. It had a strong current that pulled far out into the salt water. It ran deep, and you could see the change of color as the salt and fresh water mixed almost as far away as your eye could see. To the left of the headland and all down the coast there was a sand beach from the end of the pines to the water's edge.

They could hear the faint sounds of other people coming from that end of the beach but saw no one. They were all delighted with the spot and set up their table and chairs to dine and later play cards.

Ava made a claim on a little hill just above the rest of the party. She spread out her blanket, sun things and the writing-box, with her many drafts of the *Reader's Digest* article.

She took a cloth-covered hanger from the basket and hung up her dress on a low branch of one of the pine trees. There was a heavy carpet of brown pine needles making her hill very soft, if impossible to walk on without sandals. It was very, very hot. Too hot at that time to sunbathe.

To protect herself, Ava wore a great straw hat and a sheer cotton white shirt that came down to her thighs. Afterwards she went down from her private little world to join everyone for a drink.

The table had been set up in the coolest spot and was weighted down with food. The little bar was set up and busy. It was a pleasant, happy affair, particularly as Ava was the center of attention.

She was, after all, the only one in the group who had a figure and a little turned-up nose and was agile enough to bend over without hearing the bones creak. She flitted around the men, flirting and teasing like a girl of sixteen.

She bounced herself on Takis's lap, knowing very well that he could feel the separation of the cheeks of her ass, and the movement of the outer lips of her vagina through the scant bikini. Ava knew he would be maddened with desire to take her, and, of course, that was impossible.

Next she made an attempt to play with Philipos. He was not at all interested in her. He had a penchant for *young* girls. A woman of twenty was past her prime for him. He was simply not interested in making a life with one woman. All that was, of course, a challenge for Ava.

When she dropped onto Philipos's lap and tried to tease him, he took his thumb and forefinger and pinched her so hard on the ass that she screamed and jumped off. Ava stayed away from him for the rest of the picnic.

She treated Takis's wife, Evangalia, like her grandmother. The more she flirted, teased and threw her good body around, the more ancient and decrepit and grandmotherly she treated Evangalia.

After they had all eaten and drunk too much, they decided to take a walk along the beach before they settled down into an afternoon of cards. Takis asked Ava if she would swim, and she agreed. He told the others to start down the beach; he wanted to make sure that Ava swam on the sea side. They would catch up with the rest of the party later. As Ava and Takis walked, he explained about the river—the Narcissus.

He showed her that the surface was almost without a ripple, as it ran quietly. No more than two feet below the still water, he said, there was a frightening undercurrent formed by the underwater caverns that ran across the bed of the river. The cracks in the riverbed had opened and forced a great tunnel of swift, sweet water far out to sea.

Now Takis showed Ava why it was called the Narcissus. When you bent over the surface of the river, you could see a perfect reflection of yourself. They walked upstream a way. Takis rolled up his trousers and took off his shoes and socks. He got down on his knees and knelt over the water's edge. Sure enough there he was, a perfect image of himself. As clear as a silver-backed mirror. Ava knelt down next to him and was enchanted at the picture of them both there together. They kissed, and as they kissed they watched.

They went wading very carefully. Takis warned that there was a small shelf of sand before it dropped off into deep water. When the water was up to Ava's calves, she felt her toes hang over the edge of the sand shelf. She leaned over and there she was again. A perfect portrait of Ava. She was enchanted with it. She raised one arm and it waved back at her. She waved both arms and they waved back. She smiled and loved the smile of the laughing lady in the water. She saw the adoration in the eyes of the reflection.

Takis became fired up, because Ava was bending over with her rear end up to him. In that position the bikini looked even briefer. He lifted the sheer cotton shirt and pulled down the bikini, saying, "Don't move." But she did, straightening up, and turning round to face him. She started for the shore and, just at the edge of the sand where she was sure to be safe, she pulled down her bikini. Takis bent down to kiss her vagina. She teased him, pushing herself into his face. She could see the others way off in the distance, with their backs to them, and walking in the opposite direction, so she had no fear.

Suddenly Takis told her he did not want her that way. He wanted to fuck her right up the ass. He spun her quickly around and bent her over.

Ava became wildly frightened. She pulled up her bikini and started running down the beach. No man had ever done that to her, and no man ever would. Takis was a filthy old fool, but she could tell that he was trainable. When he called after her, she ran back to him again, saying, "No, no, not here. Don't be silly, not here."

He could hardly keep his hands off her and smacked her hard on the ass he so wanted a couple of times.

She put her arm through his and said, "No, stop that, we must join the others. If we want to have a wonderful affair, we must be very discreet."

Takis liked that idea. He gave in, and they caught up with the others.

Ava walked back on the arm of Alfred, saying what a nice day it was. Then, after the walk, the four cardplayers sat down for their game. Everyone was terribly concerned

that Ava not feel left out. No, no, she was very happy
with herself. She would go up on her little hill and join
them later for coffee and cake.

Ava walked up to her well-arranged little haven on the
tiny hill. There was a small breeze, a hot breeze, as if
someone had opened an oven door. Yet, in the warm air,
her pink polka dot dress was turning and moving. She
looked at it and thought: *It is me without me, dancing in
the air,* and was enchanted.

First she arranged herself in the sun, but that was much
too hot. Then she moved to the shade and decided to
work on her writing. She settled down but could not keep
her mind on it. She closed the box after only a few minutes and decided to do some exercises.

She stretched and moved her disciplined body. It was
hard work but always rewarding. Once she started on her
program of exercises, there was no stopping. Heat or no
heat, she completed them, then collapsed down next to the
writing-box, exhausted. She decided that if she went in for
a swim, she would be revived.

She all but dragged herself down the little hill, along
the beach and into the sea and was indeed revived. After
her swim she felt energy again in her body and went all
wet and dripping to visit the cardplayers. She sprinkled
them with the salt water, and pushed her wet body up
against Takis's chair so that he could feel her through his
back. She ran her wet arms over Alfred's cheeks to cool
him down, but she ignored Philipos and Evangalia. She
looked at the various hands being held and managed to
drip water over their cards, making very indiscreet re-
marks about the hands being played. In general, Ava
made a fuss and disturbed them.

As the cardplayers paid her no attention nor had any
reaction, she went to the portable bar and poured herself
a double Scotch, drank it down and announced that she
was going to her haven on the hill and that she was not to
be disturbed for coffee; she was going to have a sleep.

She lay down and drank in that wonderful feeling of
the sun sucking up the wet, penetrating the skin and melt-
ing out the nerves of her body. She moved her body under
the sun and felt glorious.

She thought about Kate but then decided that there
really was not much to think about except that she would
hear soon enough that Kate was restless, that the cruise

was a mistake, that Egypt was filthy and that she hated her family in America. She was sure to return to Athens, but all that would take at least a few weeks, maybe a couple of months even. Who was to know? By that time her affair with Takis would be well secured. No, there really was not much to think about Kate, for the moment anyway.

It was Ava's conscious intention not to think about Kate.

As she lay there, baking now in the hot sun, Isabel appeared in her thoughts. Ava could not help but wonder what Isabel was doing. Was she getting ready to be married? Was she being married at that moment? Was she being fucked at that moment for more diamonds? Was she back in London after realizing what a mistake she had nearly made?

What if Alfred was right and this kind of man did love her? Isabel would have pulled off a coup. Ava could not bear Isabel's pretense of loving. The *diamonds* were why she was involved. It had *nothing* to do with loving. It was that basic dishonesty of Isabel's that irritated Ava beyond reason. That nonsense about love.

Ava felt herself growing restless again. She realized that she simply did not want Isabel's marriage and new life to happen. She jumped up from her blanket, bored with sunning herself and thinking of her sister; angry about the time she had wasted. She went to the writing-box and took out a few typewritten pages; she would sit in the sun and read them. Ava saw and heard the cardplayers through the pine trees. She pitied them for their dull, boring lives.

Realizing how important she was always put Ava in a better mood. She lay down on her stomach, her head and shoulders stretched over the edge of the little hill that hung over the Narcissus. With her two arms stretched out into space and holding her papers in her hands, she began reading.

After the first paragraph she stopped to think over what she had just read. She thought it perfect, and while she was lying there, she stretched her body and her arms even further out. She looked down, and far below her she could see herself and the white paper that she held in her right hand looking up at her, reflecting off the water. It would have been much more clear if she had been closer

to the water. She waved and could see the movement far
below.

There was a small verge directly below her about five
feet above the river, just large enough to lie on and
stretch out over the water. Here she would see the perfect
portrait of herself.

She tucked the white paper in the back of her bikini
and made her way carefully down the bank to the verge.
She brushed the ledge clean with her feet and lay down
on it. She looked. There she was.

Her head, her hair, her face, her eyes, nose, mouth,
neck, shoulders. She stretched out her arms, making all
sorts of gestures, and was delighted to see them motion
back to her.

The river was clear, pure, translucent. Ava looked up
and down the Narcissus and then far out to the sea as it
glistened in the sun.

She gently moved further off the verge and over the top
of the water. The closer she came the better she could see
every detail of herself. She lay there gazing, enraptured,
into the silver reflection hour after hour. She began a conversation with this beautiful woman looking up at her;
they went on talking, and she fell in love, more in love
with her because of the beauty, the intelligence, all shining
back at her. Ava and her reflection talked away the boring people, the cracked and faulted world. They narrowed
it down to past friends, family and eventually to Kate and
Isabel. After them the moment of ultimate truth hit Ava.
There were only two people left in the world. They were
Ava and this incredible beauty looking up at her from the
river.

She moved still closer to kiss this beautiful girl, her
friend, her lover. How could Ava possess her and yet not
possess her? At last in a second's terrible anguish Ava
saw that it was this grief that was destroying her.

She reached out and touched the cheek of the beauty
looking up at her. She slid slowly off the verge and on top
of the beautiful girl smiling up at her. Their lips met and
the river covered them over. There was hardly a splash
and they were gone.

The search party included eighteen policemen and looked
until dark. The following day they continued, along with a
motor launch following the river out to sea, hoping to find

the body. They began at dawn and stopped at one that afternoon. The search was abandoned. The body was never found.

Alfred was inconsolable. Under heavy sedation he was watched constantly by his friends, Takis and Evangalia. There was no way for him to contact Kate. He would have to wait to hear from her. And Isabel—he would send a cable not to Isabel, but to Sir Alexis Hyatt, in the hope that he would break the news to her at the right moment.

It was doubly difficult for Alfred because they never recovered the body. He would never have her laid to rest in the earth. There were moments when he could not believe that she was not just out at the hairdressers, or the dressmakers, or in the library doing research on one of her little projects. Her belief in herself was so complete, the adoration she had for herself was so enormous, that to see her just disappear without a trace was doubly horrifying.

He could no longer face their sterile, large, empty flat, with all of her things neatly tucked away in cupboards. He packed a bag and moved into the Hilton to wait for Kate's return or word from Isabel. He would wait for them to come and pick up what was left of Ava, her clothes.

But only a few days after Ava's death he suddenly found himself surrounded by friends and relatives who somehow across the years had seemed to have disappeared out of his life without a trace. There was not a day that went by but an old schoolfriend, an acquaintance, a casual cards companion, a distant relative, would call upon him and sweep him back into a sociable life again. Within a few weeks Ava's disappearance from his life was not even noticed by him. Indeed, he realized, it was almost a relief.

The enormous pressure of Ava had been on him for almost twenty years. Now he was relaxed and enjoyed a new kind of freedom. A few weeks later, astonishingly, Alfred would only have one worry—that Ava might be found alive somewhere.

What had kept him with her for those twenty years? Twenty years! A lifetime. He had made believe that it was love, but now he knew that it was not. What he could not know was that her vanity and narcissism had in the end destroyed her, just as it had almost destroyed him.

One day Alfred caught himself looking in the mirror as he knotted his tie, and realized that for the first time in years, he was feeling more secure, more confident in himself and his abilities.

These days he often went to have a drink in Kolonaki and sit with his paper, as millions of Greeks did, to watch the women go by. For the first time in years he thought about fucking them, taking them ruthlessly, purely for sexual reasons, but he never did. He now became a charming, more amusing, more sociable Alfred. He liked the way he felt, and he liked what people saw. If he now thought of Ava at all, it was that it was too bad that she was not there to see his new success as himself.

Behind his back all the Greeks who knew him were saying that the best thing that woman ever did for him was to disappear; they had their friend back again. As for Ava, now that she was gone, all that they could feel was relief in her absence.

XI

A VERY angry, trembling, hot, over-excited Kate dragged herself through customs at Athens airport and into the waiting-lounge for her flight to Egypt. She sat there with her hand-luggage, chocolates and magazines piled around her, a tired, bitter old lady on the verge of tears, but strong enough and more than angry enough to bite back.

Nothing ever went as Kate wanted it to go. Here she was supposedly flying to Alexandria, and there was no direct flight. Now she would have to fly into Cairo. Well, at least she could mail a postcard from Cairo airport. The very thought of Isabel receiving a postcard from her, mailed in Cairo—Isabel's precious new city—lifted Kate out of her self-pity. Throwing Isabel into a state of guilt always helped cheer her a little.

She opened her bag and took out her handkerchief and her Yardley smelling salts. After wiping her face, drenched in perspiration, she took a deep whiff of them to revive herself.

She had an hour before her plane took off for Cairo, but Kate liked being early for everything. She started to flip through a magazine that Takis had bought her. She thought him kind, but stupid to get himself involved with Ava. Well, the hell with them, who cares anyway? She flipped through a few more pages of the magazine, but could not concentrate.

Her attention kept wandering back to the events of the last twenty-four hours. She was very, very angry at both her girls, but more so at Isabel. The only good thing she could think of that had come out of that luncheon was that she behaved correctly with Isabel. On her arrival in New York, she was sure there would be a letter of apology and an invitation from Isabel to stay with her in London. She knew there was one thing that Isabel could not bear and that was total rejection from her mother. Kate always knew that she could devastate her daughter, and now she would punish Isabel for what she had done.

By the time Isabel arrived in her lover's arms in Cairo she would have faced the reality of this hateful marriage. Kate made up her mind to be magnanimous about Isabel's latest mistake. She would never again mention that dreadful luncheon. All Isabel had to do was return to London and be finished with that filthy Arab.

For the moment, however, Kate was very angry. Her mind went back to the moment when she had left the Hilton, walking home to her flat. She was very lucky that she had found her young neighbor, the travel agent. Kate could never understand why strangers, neighbors and friends were all so good and considerate towards her, while her children were so short-tempered and unloving.

This sweet young boy, Stephano, the travel agent, for whom she had been baking Toll House cookies for the last few months, would do anything for her. When he heard that she must be on the day trip on the Nile, he dressed and went down to Syntagma, opened his office and made contact with the ship, ran around and prepared tickets, typed up information for what she had to do, arranged everything.

While little Stephano was doing all that for her, she worked like a fiend to complete her packing. Her hand-luggage had almost killed her as she heaved it around through customs. It was filled with her twelve place settings of silver flatwear, her Victorian silver tea service and all the jewelry that she had, which was not worth much, but weighed a great deal.

She knew that it was too much to travel with, especially in this heat, but she would not leave it behind. She did not want to go to Isabel's without her own things. Her main problem at the moment was that it was all too heavy for her to carry from the lounge across the tarmac, and oh, my God, she had to drag it up all those stairs to the airplane and down again in Cairo as well. *Well,* thought Kate, *by then I will have found someone to befriend a courageous old lady with heavy hand-luggage.*

Sitting there among the debris of her life, Kate decided that she needed a nice hot cup of tea. To her surprise, just as she was wanting it, one of the waiters came to clear away the dirty dishes from a nearby table. She gave him the money, and he said he would bring the tea at once. Things were looking up for Kate. The fact that she was able to obtain a cup of tea without the horrors and struggles of trying to catch a Greek waiter was an omen that things were getting better.

She was feeling more alert by now. She sat back and pulled out the little typewritten itinerary sweet Stephano had given her. But the moment that she tried to study it, she realized that she was not quite calm enough to digest the details. Her mind flashed back to that luncheon of the day before.

Again she saw Isabel and her diamonds. That had to be the largest diamond that she had ever seen. And Isabel's face! That face of contentment, softness, laughter as she put her hands forward to show them her jewelry!

As Kate sat there in Athens airport, staring into space, she told herself: *Face it, your Isabel is a whore.* How could her eldest daughter even imagine going to bed with an Arab?

Kate knew that men sometimes *got* to Isabel, men like that painter. That horrible, handsome American painter. Yes, Isabel really did have a problem. Kate shuddered. Maybe she *liked* sex.

Kate suddenly could not understand what had happened across the years. Why her two daughters would not obey her every wish. She should have been more demanding as a mother. They should have been *made* to obey her. Well, by the time this trip was over, they would both have been put in their places.

She would write a letter to each telling them where she was and how they could contact her. After all, she was a woman of stature, a mother who deserved respect from her children, and she would have it. Every mother she knew was coddled by her children. Only Kate was lonely and did not get enough attention; only she had suffered her many illnesses in silence. Well, those days were over.

The young waiter brought her tea and she sipped it, thinking that she had gained a great deal of control over herself. She laughed at Isabel and that ridiculous entourage of hers, that dramatic entrance to tell her such big news of a wedding.

She took another sip of tea, thinking to herself how upset Isabel must have been when she had to fly to her lover without anyone's blessings. Well, if she could do nothing properly, why should she expect blessings? It was not that Kate did not wish her well. She wanted *nothing* but the best for her children.

Kate's thoughts were interrupted by Stephano. I surely hope he got it all planned correctly, thought Kate. Sweet, but who knows how bright he is?

Stephano stood before his friend, Mrs. Wells, with two orchids in a clear cellophane box. He had come to wish her a happy holiday and help her to the plane with her hand-luggage.

Kate could hardly believe it. How sweet of him! All those Toll House cookies had paid off. She made room for him next to her, patting him on the cheek, telling him that he was like a grandson to her. She managed a few tears of appreciation and a sniffle as she pinned the orchids to the bolero jacket of her cream-and-navy-blue-striped seersucker outfit.

He should not have wasted his money on an old lady, she told him. Better he should buy some young girl flowers. Oh, he was such a good boy! Oh, how she would miss him! Oh, if she was only twenty years old she would never let him get away!

He was very flattered and puffed up to the occasion, telling her he had some good news. She did not have to travel alone. There were two more people, a husband and wife, who were joining her cruise ship. She would have friends from the beginning of her journey. He would go and have them paged and introduce everyone.

The little travel agent scampered off to find her traveling companions. Eventually he returned, and when Kate saw him approach, she became furious. Who asked him to stick his nose in her business anyway. She surely did not need a pair of old fogies like that hanging over her head. They must be at least eighty!

The travel agent was beside himself with joy. To think that he was lucky enough to find an American couple from the Midwest to keep Kate company.

Kate could have smacked him one right in the face. He was a nice boy, but why didn't he mind his own business? She listened as Mr. and Mrs. Malcolm Nesbitt from Ogalala, South Dakota, were introduced to her. Oh, my luck, thought Kate, Midwestern farmers. They will be so boring. Whatever are they doing on a trip like this?

It was worse when it was explained by Mr. Nesbitt that the reason they were flying on to meet the cruise ship was that he had been taken ill in Athens and so had missed the sailing. *Do I need this?* thought Kate. *I am on holiday; haven't I got enough to worry about?*

The enthusiastic Stephano explained to the Nesbitts that Kate lived in Athens, but was an American lady from Massachusetts. They thought that was courageous of her, to live in a foreign country. Oh, my, she was so cosmopolitan. They were just farm folks. This was the first time that they had been out of their country ever. Why, they had never even been to Massachusetts, but would be happy to get back to the good old USA.

The Nesbitts only had one small nightcase between them and so were loaded down with Kate's sterling silver as they clambered up to the plane. Once aboard and settled in the airplane, Kate felt suddenly exhausted, short of breath, and could not stop perspiring. Her dress was wet through as water kept dripping off her body. She called the stewardess for a glass of water and took half a dozen different pills: to settle her stomach, for her nerves, for her headache. But there was nothing that she could take to settle her turbulent emotions about stepping on the ground in Cairo.

She started to torture herself. Should she call Isabel from the airport? Should she even go and *see* Isabel? After all, she did have the address. She decided to stick to the original plan: send one card from Cairo airport and one from Alexandria, then sail out at noon the next day on the *Aphrodite,* with twelve hundred other passengers, to have a wonderful time.

Let Isabel die of guilt. Imagine being in the same city as your mother and not seeing her, and supposedly a few days before you are to be married. Imagine allowing your mother to deal with those foreigners, to travel alone in a hostile country while you are being kept in diamonds by a rich Egyptian? No! Isabel would get nothing but the card. Let her die of guilt. Well, maybe not die, but at least let her suffer plenty.

Kate closed her eyes and relaxed, trying to put her mind at rest, but torn between hate and love, she lashed herself on. She remembered the time when Isabel was a good young girl. Oh, how Kate had adored her, when she had her darling under control. Where did it all go wrong? Why did she hate her now?

Was it because she got interested in boys? That was what was wrong now. She was interested in this Arab. How could Kate have missed up until now the fact that Isabel was a slut?

It was impossible to meet a man and marry him two weeks later. It was impossible to have been given diamonds that size after two weeks. It was impossible to think of living in an Arab country. It was impossible to *marry* an Arab. It was impossible for Isabel to marry and live with a man after so many years of living alone.

Kate would be the first to bless a marriage for Isabel if she could find a nice, plain, simple, Jewish widower. Someone that Kate, at least, could understand; that she could accept. But no, everything Isabel did was a means of excluding Kate from her life.

By the time the stewardess brought lunch around, Kate was feeling a great deal better. She had even begun to chat with the Nesbitts sitting across the aisle from her. She learned that they were not going to take the boat down to Alexandria. Mr. Nesbitt only wanted to get back to the cruise ship and his own cabin. They would travel back with the man sent to meet them, and after they had taken Kate to her Nile cruise boat, they would continue the journey by car to the ship. They did not want her to worry about all her luggage: They would be extra protection.

What a lucky break for her: She did not have to be bored by them, and they would be taking care of her belongings. Oh yes, things were sorting themselves out for Kate.

The temperature was 104 degrees in the shade when they landed at Cairo airport. Kate found it unbearable. It bounced off the black tarmac, up through her feet. It shot down in huge bolts from the sky above.

But somehow she pushed through the heat, forward into the terminal.

The terminal was even hotter. There was not a puff of air. It was filthy; what windows there were could hardly be seen through for the dirt on them. The smell of it, oh, God, what a smell! A combination of onion, disinfectant and unwashed-body odors.

Everyone looked sinister to her except the Nesbitts. Mr. Nesbitt in his drip-dry, powder-blue and white plaid jacket, powder-blue Dacron slacks and his $18.95 Hush Puppies. And, Mrs. Nesbitt—for the first time in her life Kate had nothing but admiration for those eighty-pound wonders of crinkled skin and brittle bones, those pure, kindly faces who would never say "fuck" even if they had a mouth full of it. Pure, clean, cotton-trouser-suited Mrs. Nesbitt, with her medium-blue-rinsed hair, all done up in its tight little curls. She could have kissed her right there and then for being Mrs. I AM AMERICA, SENIOR CITIZEN. They may be wrinkled, old, and slightly decrepit, but, when she looked at them she heard "The Star-Spangled Banner" in a decadent, dirty, smelly Egypt.

Customs was a nightmare. Suddenly it occurred to Kate that it would be impossible for her if they opened her luggage and found all that silver. Oh God, why did she drag it along? She remembered Isabel telling her about never taking gold or silver in any quantity through customs of different countries without declaring it. Oh God, on the plane she had written on the landing card "Nothing to Declare"! She had thought it was none of their business what she had with her. Now she began to panic, her heart began to beat faster and then she thought *The hell with them! What will they do with an old woman like me? They will not get my sterling silver. I sweated plenty to get it and keep it across the years, and no Arab will beat me out of it.*

She saw the semblance of a line forming to go through and then, towards the middle, she spotted a group of about twenty-five American drip-dry tourists with name tags on them, all bunched together like cattle. She pushed the Nesbitts quickly and told them to move in with the others; it was their only chance to get out of there fast. She was sure that the tourist party would be passed through without a single case being opened. They were so typical that customs could not be bothered.

The Nesbitts considered her a world traveler and would have done anything that she told them to do. After passport clearance, they elbowed their way into the middle of the group. Since all American tourists in group tours look the same, even the people in the group thought the three belonged to them.

Sure enough, Kate the world traveler was correct. The customs men wanted their lunch and siesta and so pushed the whole group through with one wave of the hand. Not one piece of luggage was opened. Kate felt in control again. She gathered the Nesbitts and all her luggage, and at last they made their way to the ship's officer who held a sign reading *Aphrodite*.

While a porter took all the luggage, off they went through the terminal to the car waiting outside. Just as they were approaching the exit doors, Kate grabbed the officer's arm and announced she had to buy a postcard. He told her there were postcards on board ship, but she insisted she had to mail a postcard from the Cairo airport.

He told her to wait right there, he would go with her, but first he had to put the Nesbitts in the car and see that the luggage was stored in the trunk. Kate dragged herself through the terminal with the young man helping her along. She could find no postcard and became hysterical.

The young man promised that he would be sure that she had a postcard once she arrived in Alexandria. He would see to it himself; she must not be distressed; after all, it was only a postcard.

No, it was not *only* a postcard, Kate shrieked. If she did not have the postcard, then what was she doing there in the first place? No, she must find one. In the midst of her anxiety, she saw a young American girl leaning on her luggage writing postcards. Kate ran to her, and begged the girl to sell her one. The girl said she would be pleased to give her one.

It was a picture of a mummy stretched out on a marble slab. A three-thousand-year-old somebody whose name Kate could not pronounce. It was not very attractive, a body all wrapped up in those dirty old bandages, but it could not be helped. From what Kate could see of Egypt, it was not very pretty anyway.

With a horribly shaking hand she wrote: "Isabel, just passing through Cairo. Didn't have time to call you. Am with friends, we find Egypt fascinating. Not nearly as hot as you said it was. Must go now, the boat is waiting. Having a wonderful time, hope you are. You can write care of the ship, New York. Love you, Mother."

She gave the girl a dollar and said that she was not feeling at all well, would she do an old lady a kindness and put it in the postbox over there since it already had a stamp on it. The young girl refused the dollar bill and said she would be glad to post it, but when the girl took the card Kate panicked. She did not think that the girl looked very responsible, and so grabbed the postcard from her, saying, "Never mind, dear. I will post it myself."

There were protests from the ship's officer as well as the young girl, but Kate ignored them and struck out to the far side of the terminal and the postbox. They watched her push her way to the box and back again to where they were standing.

Kate was an exhausted, nervous mess, but triumphant. She thanked the girl again for the card, and when the young lady made an effort to give Kate back the dollar bill, Kate said, "Never mind, kid, you keep it, buy yourself a soda," and grabbed the officer's arm. He rushed her along to the waiting car and the wilting Nesbitts.

She sat in the front seat with the driver as they headed towards Heliopolis and Cairo. The plan was to drive through the heart of Cairo, pointing out a few sights *en route,* then on to Giza and the Pyramids. It would have to be a quick look in order to make the rendezvous with the Nile cruise boat sailing down through the delta, to Alexandria. They would not leave without Kate on board, and with that obligation in mind, the young Greek officer from the *Aphrodite* was doing his best for them. Laboriously, but with charm, he recited to them from a small guide book. The weary, exhausted senior citizens could not have cared less. They did not know what they were doing there in the first place, and each wished silently that he or she had had the courage to stay at home.

The first great Pharaonic statue that they saw was the

Ramses II, surrounded by its fountains. The heat and dirt
of the city impressed themselves on the trio much more
than any old *Ramses II* did. The car weaved, swerved,
shot in and out and kept pushing through the traffic at
top speed. The Egyptian Museum was pointed out to
them from the outside, but the car never stopped, and
who wanted it to anyway? They passed by the Nile Hilton
and even that looked shopworn. On they went along the
Corniche, through Garden City. Kate thought it began to
look a bit better. It was more green, maybe even a bit
more cool. The many parks and flowers made it look a
little less dirty. There were grand-looking residences and
not many people on the streets now.

They crossed the Sayala Bridge to Roda Island, and
soon after they passed by a large, beautiful, walled-in estate, set in a vast, tropical, romantic garden. Kate leaned
out of the window and tried to catch a breath of air, but
there was just plain, dead heat, not at all refreshing. She
pulled her head in just in time to escape decapitation by a
plum-colored Rolls Royce passing them. She saw a driver
in the front seat and a very handsome man sitting in the
back. There was hardly any traffic on the road and they
followed behind the Rolls until it slowed down and took
a left in through a pair of huge open gates. As the car
passed they saw several servants pushing the gates closed
after it. Kate strained herself to lean out of the window,
trying to see more.

The young ship's officer told them that it was a small
private palace; a museum that was open to the public a
few days a week when the owner was not in residence.
Maybe they were lucky and had just seen him.

Big deal, thought Kate. What could that man ever do for
me?

The young officer kept reading from his little tourist
book about the house and its history. Kate could not be
bothered to listen and so missed the owner's name—Sir
Alexis Hyatt.

Their car left it all far behind as it crossed over the El
Gama's Bridge. Now the young man was terribly excited;
he wanted them to look at the beautiful feluccas sailing
up and down the Nile. They were crossing the longest
river in the world. Kate barely looked at it. She reached in
her handbag for another whiff of smelling salts. She

sniffed deeply, choked a bit, then pulled herself together and seemed more revived.

As she passed the little oval bottle of lavender salts to Mrs. Nesbitt, she thought about the handsome man in the plum-colored Rolls Royce going into what looked like a Garden of Eden. It was all too unreal, a bit like the Arabian Nights with dirt. She thought about him, and her mind wandered to what kind of a wife a man like that would have. She would be a beautiful young girl, you could be sure. A twenty-year-old at the most. Isabel would never find a man like that. She was too old and much too worldly. Poor Isabel! Well, she should have found herself a good husband when she was young. A man like the one that Kate just saw does not give diamonds. Ugh, how stupid Isabel was.

They made a left turn off the bridge and went up the Sharia el Nil. Riding alongside the Nile, Kate looked down and saw a huge, beautiful felucca. There were many servants and seamen on the deck, and she could see that it was being loaded. It was getting ready for a trip. She saw two dogs that reminded her of Isabel's nasty pets, lying in the shade of a box on the deck, and supplies disappearing into the hold below. Just as their car passed the stern of the boat, she saw a beautiful striped canopy, something like a wedding *huppah,* she thought. A servant was wrapping the poles of the canopy in garlands of green leaves. She saw more action going on in that one boat than she had seen anywhere since she landed in Egypt. If she had turned around to watch she would have seen the last of the loading, the small gangplank taken away, the sails catch the tiny, hot wind and her daughter Isabel's wedding felucca sail for Memphis. But she did not turn around to look.

No one had spoken in the car for quite some time, as they were all too exhausted. The car continued straight up along the Nile to another section called Imbaba. Just before they came to the Imbaba Bridge, the car stopped. Down below, the Nile cruise boat waited for Kate Wells.

XII

WHEN THE plum-colored Rolls Royce had passed the car near the entrance to Alexis's house on Roda Island, nearly decapitating some foolish tourist hanging out the window, Alexis had been thinking about Isabel, whom he loved more than he ever had dreamt possible. The new dimension that she added to his life left him in awe at the wonder of being alive.

The night before, when the plane had arrived from Athens, he had not been there to meet it. Isabel and Alexander had gone straight from the airport to the house, which had been all lit up and made ready for them. While Isabel was getting settled into the Roda Island house, Alexis was in his study at Sharia el Nil working very hard on all the arrangements for their marriage on Tuesday.

That Sunday night he had met Isabel and Alexander for a light supper. Alexander had told Alexis about the unfortunate luncheon in Athens. There was almost no need for Alexis to be told. He'd had a feeling when he heard Mrs. Wells's voice, that nothing good would come from Isabel's effort to share her joy with those two women.

Alexander left soon after supper and was driven to the Sharia el Nil house, where he was staying. Alexis and Isabel saw him off in the car and then walked through the gardens together.

It was extremely hot even at that time of night. The two said very little to each other. Somewhere deep in the garden, with the night sounds playing for them, the heavy heat and the scent of jasmine and roses, new mown grass and lilies, he took her in his arms and kissed her.

She was wearing a white, wide-pleated silk dress with shoestring straps. It was tied at the waist with a soft silk sash of the same color and material. She also wore the

scarab necklace, his first gift to her, and her diamond
rings, his latest gift to her.

The lights from the house lit up the patch of open grass
where they stood. She stood on tiptoe in her white, high-
heeled sandals and started kissing the top of his forehead,
down over his face, to his mouth. She unbuttoned his
shirt and sucked on his nipples while he undid his trousers and dropped them, then slipped off his shirt. She
bent low and slowly removed his underpants, rubbing her
face over his stiff cock. She opened her mouth and ran
her tongue over, and then up and down along the under-
part of it. Taking his delicious balls in her mouth, she
rolled them around, making them all wet.

He untied her belt and pulled the fine silk dress over the
top of her head. Down they went onto the sweet-smelling
grass. She lay over him with her face between his legs and
sucked on him as tenderly, as lovingly, as sensually as possible. He played with her clitoris and put his tongue deep
inside her. She kept coming with strong orgasms, and then
they came together with an equally high intensity.

They lay in the grass. The coolness of the earth beneath
them was yet another sensuous natural carpet for them to
experience. He stroked her hair and kissed her. She told
him, as he held her, that there was never a moment in the
day when she was not ready for him, when she did not
want him, when she did not want to make love to him.
The tears ran from her eyes, and she wept, not from sorrow or joy, but simply from the relief that all the years
without him were over.

He was sitting up in the grass, and when she told him
that, he was so moved that he picked her up and, putting
her on his naked lap, rocked her and told her that she was
the most wonderful woman he had ever known and that
they would spend the rest of their lives with no less desire
than they had for each other at that moment. And in her
heart she knew that he was right.

He pinched her playfully and said, "Let's go for a
swim."

They grabbed their clothes and walked naked to the
pool. They swam together. He loved the way her wet skin
glistened, and he made love to her again in the water.
They slipped on the terrycloth robes that were lying there
waiting for them and walked to the other side of the garden to the love pavilion.

Gamal was there waiting. A hookah was lit and they smoked the best Lebanese gold. They were very high when Alexis told Gamal they would spend the night there, and for him to wake them in the morning.

The two of them spoke of their plans and the wedding. He told her all was well for them; they would be married at five in the afternoon, on Tuesday.

He found her wet and ready, wanting him again. He kissed her and played with her nipples and told her that before the evening was out, she would come many times from different sensations and one that she had never known before. They found different, exciting positions and things to do to each other. Undreamt-of fantasies were created, and it was all sublime. They never stopped until they were utterly spent.

Holding her in his arms, he saw that she was asleep. With a soft wet cloth smelling of orange blossoms, he washed them both clean. She did not wake and he held her in his arms. Eventually he dozed off.

When he woke in the morning, it was to the sound of the birds and Isabel riding his morning erection, her tits moving over his face. He had no idea how long she had been doing it, but he could not hold back one moment more and sucked on her nipple as he shot high up into her. They rolled over on their sides, and he said, "Good morning. It is Monday and I am going to marry you tomorrow."

After that they put their robes on and went for a swim. They had breakfast at the pool and talked about their plans for the day and some details about the wedding.

Isabel knew what she would wear but refused to tell him. "All right," he said. "I have a surprise for you as well."

Isabel told him that she would like to stay on the grounds of the Roda house and get herself and her things together, maybe even work on her latest novel.

It seemed like a fine idea. They would part for the day, and he would work at the Sharia el Nil house, have lunch with his mother and bring her back to Isabel for tea.

Suddenly Alexis looked embarrassed about something and Isabel sensed it at once, asking him what was wrong. Well, he hoped she did not think him a fool, but after he took his mother back home, he would like to return to her with Alexander for an early dinner and leave her before midnight. He was in fact superstitious about seeing her on the day of their wedding, before the ceremony. They laughed about it and agreed not to see each other after midnight until she was brought to his boat by Alexander.

Isabel made it clear that she thought he and Alexander were going to have a stag party in a whorehouse. Alexis said yes, they certainly were. He asked her if she wanted him to send her a few men for her last night as a *bachelor lady*. She said that she would think about it and let him know what she wanted for the evening.

Isabel was delighted with all the plans, and one of the main reasons was that the less they were seen together, the less chance there was of people finding out about their marriage and their being caught up in a mountain of good-wishes. This was to be their own personal matter, and they wanted to keep it just that way.

She also thought it extremely sensitive and touching of Alexis not to include too much of his mother in their plans. She knew it was so as not to embarrass her about the absence of her own family.

Late that afternoon Alexis rejoined Isabel, and they walked together to the pavilion where they were to have tea. They saw the tiny, slight figure of Madame Hyatt playing with the tame white doves. Gamal and her personal servant, Abdul, stood close by with baskets of feed for them. Madame Hyatt loved her son Alexis beyond measure but never had imposed her wishes on him. All the same, she was overjoyed that he had found love in this woman, Isabel Wells. The very first time they had met, Madame Hyatt knew that her son would be happy with Isabel. Yet she had refrained from mentioning it to Alexis, wisely letting nature take its course.

The three kissed and Madame Hyatt thanked them for asking her to tea. They sat on the cushions and Isabel told her about what she had been doing to get ready for her wedding trip. Madame Hyatt told Isabel to call on her if she needed the least little thing. Isabel said that she thought she had everything under control.

She spoke of the dress she would wear to the ceremony, one that she had never worn before. She told how she had seen it in Paris and, feeling extremely extravagant, had gone in and bought it. Now, at last, she had no need to feel guilty about the dress.

The only thing that she had not worked out was how to get her hair done without appearing at the Hilton salon.

Madame Hyatt said that was easy, she would handle it and what time did Isabel want her hairdresser there?

That settled, Isabel said, "How wonderful! Now I have nothing to worry about." She was quite sure that between Juju, Maryka, Doreya, Gamal—not to mention Alexander—she would make it to the altar. She told Madame Hyatt that it was more help than she had ever had in her life and that she felt like a princess.

Madame Hyatt answered her by saying, "In another time, Isabel, you would have carried that title." She smiled as her man and Gamal brought in the tea.

The two men carried in a magnificent table decorated with full-blown garden roses of various colors. There were ornate silver baskets and pedestal dishes filled with cakes, small sandwiches and sweets. The silver tea service was French baroque silver of the finest and rarest quality, and the cups and saucers were *Sèvres,* once belonging to the Empress Josephine.

Isabel was comfortable and aware that Alexis's mother not only approved of her, but meant her to be happy as well. She felt a moment of embarrassment for the way her own family had behaved.

At one point during the tea party, Madame Hyatt called her servant and whispered something in his ear. When Abdul returned, he carried with him a large parcel. It was obvious by its shape that it was a framed painting. It was her gift to Alexis.

A second servant handed a box to Madame Hyatt which she gave to Isabel, telling her that it was her wedding present. She wanted Isabel to know how much she welcomed her to the family, and explained that the gift was something that had been in their family for a very long time. She had never been prepared to hand it down to anyone until this very day.

Isabel, deeply touched, kissed her warmly in thanks. Both she and Alexis wanted to share the opening of the gifts with Madame Hyatt and finally won her approval to do so. Alexis opened his first.

It was an oil painting by Modigliani entitled *Reclining Nude.* He had fallen in love with it from the very first day that he saw it. It was a superb example of the artist's work. He was overwhelmed by his mother's generosity in parting with it and told her that it would indeed sail with them up the Nile. He would hang it in their bedroom on board the boat. He thanked his mother and kissed her hand.

Isabel thought it wonderful. She had never seen it before, except when it was once photographed for a book. She was delighted for Alexis, who went to her and said, "Now let's see what Mama has given you."

Isabel first removed the white roses and stephanotis from the parcel, then the white satin bow and at last the paper. It was a royal-blue velvet jeweler's box of considerable size. Isabel, very excited, suddenly flushed with embarrassment, and Alexis wondered what was going through her mind but was too sensitive to ask. He was sure that she was thinking of her family and thought that his mother's generosity and kindness were a sad contrast to how her own mother had behaved. He put his arm around her and kissed her, saying, "Shall we open it together?" She was near to tears as she looked up and said, "Yes, please, let's."

They lifted the lid of the large velvet box, and there, lying on the molded velvet interior was a magnificent rope of blue-white diamonds. The rope itself was made of platinum, and each diamond set into the rope was round, weighing about four carats. The length of the rope must have been about thirty inches. It was so brilliantly crafted that all one could see were the diamonds, and when Isabel slipped it over her head it lay on her neck and across her breast. Alexis lifted the empty interior of the velvet box. He had seen his mother wear these jewels all of his life, so he knew that there was something else inside. He handed the box to Isabel, who gasped in astonishment. There was a second rope of yellow diamonds set in pure gold. It was the same length as the first. He put them over her head and arranged them on her breasts and kissed her.

"Now, darling," he said, "you lift that second empty tray; there is still another one."

She could hardly believe it possible, but she did lift the empty tray, and there was the third necklace: a platinum rope again, but this time the diamonds were pale pink. When the three strands of diamonds were around her neck, their beauty was dazzling. She held them in her hands and watched them sparkle with the mixture of their colors.

Madame Hyatt told her how lovely she looked in them and how proud she was to pass them on to her. Isabel was told about them, for they were famous the world over. Called the Saladin Diamonds, they had been passed on down through Madame Hyatt's family through the ages. They were worn originally by the great Saladin himself and then given to his favorite concubine, who later became his favorite wife. The necklaces had traveled to many exhibitions around the world but had never been imitated.

Such a rare and historical gift left Isabel speechless. In her wildest dreams she could never have imagined such opulence, such treasures to be part of her life. One of the servants had brought a large hand mirror for her to see herself in, and now she stood and looked at the Saladin Diamonds around her neck.

She went and sat next to Madame Hyatt and, with a break in her voice that she could not hide, thanked the elderly woman for accepting her into the family, for giving birth to such a son and for such generosity of spirit.

"Spoken like a princess," Alexis laughed.

Isabel kept the necklaces on all through tea and was surprised at how easy it was to wear them. How nonchalant one can be with treasures when they belong to you, she thought.

After tea they walked Madame Hyatt to her car. She wished them happiness, said that she would see them on their return, and hoped that God would be with them.

They watched her car drive away, and when it was gone, Alexis put his arm around her and said, "Come, let me show you some more rooms in the palace. I will show you one that Mama loves."

After passing through several courtyards, they went into a lovely reception room. Its walls were of filigreed white marble. Next they walked up a winding marble staircase into an octagon-shaped reception hall. Alexis pushed open a pair of solid silver, carved doors, and they entered the original hammam, where the wives and concubines of his ancestors used to bathe.

The entire room was inlaid in several shades of pink marble. The sunken pool, with its stairs going down into it on four sides, was filled with scented water on which floated fresh flowers. There were beautiful slim columns around the pool and the wonderfully ornate, pierced screens of marble that the ladies used for privacy. There were elegant white marble chaises everywhere with heavy,

pink-and-white striped silk cushions upon them. The
whole room looked as if it were made of pink-and-white
sugar icing. There were palm trees and skylights and the
sheerest of shining white silk which hung on a pink marble pole that stretched between a few of the columns. The
curtain of silk, so fine, moved from the merest motion of
the air in the room.

It was a dream. As Isabel stood there, she told Alexis
she could almost hear the tinkling laughter of the plump
and beautiful odalisques as they lounged about, their servants pampering and caring for them. She could see the
lovely ladies being washed in the pool, and imagined the
sultan entering to choose who he wanted for that night;
the eunuchs dashing about . . . Oh, how fantastic it must
have been.

"Yes," Alexis said and smiled. He was the sultan, and
she was his odalisque. He undressed her and laid her on
one of the white marble chaises. He sat down next to
her and stroked her hair. She was naked but for her magnificent jewels: the diamonds in her ears and on her fingers and the Saladin Diamonds from his mother around
her neck.

He told her he was saving himself for a debauched,
depraved last evening as a bachelor and that he would
play with her, bring her to orgasm, as long as she liked
but that he would not make love to her, much as he
wanted to. He kissed her, and then he slipped one of the
ropes of diamonds from her neck. He moved his mouth to
her nipples, then with one hand, his fingers deep inside
her, he stretched her open and slowly stuffed the diamonds high up into her. When they were all inside, he
moved them round again and again until the sensation
was so exciting for Isabel that she came in heavy spasms.
He could actually hear the diamonds swishing around inside her. He lifted her head off the chaise, folded her
close to him and, kissing her passionately, pulled the
necklace with one sharp tug. Isabel screamed as the diamonds came out of her all wet and sparkling.

He draped the rope of diamonds back over her head
and held a worn-out Isabel in his arms. She watched him
suck each one of the stones clean. She rested against him,
and all she could think of was that she wanted him, she
wanted to be where only he had ever been able to put

her. He looked at her and knew; she did not have to say a thing, for her sexuality was oozing out of her.

He whispered in her ear, "I will arrange something for you tonight. Now stand up." From his pocket he drew a pair of silver balls. He showed them to her, and then he gently laid her on her back, while she watched him insert them inside her. He kissed her and told her to get up and walk about a little and she would come. She would come all the time she had them in, for they would move around, giving her light orgasms.

He told her that if she decided to have a man tonight she must remove them, or have the man remove them, or Juju or Maryka. As she walked he laughed as he saw her flush from the new sensation of them. She heard them click together, or at least she imagined she heard them as they roamed around inside her.

Isabel sat next to him and put her tits in his mouth. Alexis raised her and played with her cunt balls. She came and came.

They stayed in the hammam for a very long time. He held her in his arms, playing with her jewels and her nipples as they talked. He told her how much he loved her and how happy she had made him. He wanted to know, did she have everything she wanted?

More than she had ever dreamed of having with any man, Isabel replied. As they lay there quietly in each other's arms, Isabel, floating on a river of orgasms, thought of Kate, who, unknown to Isabel, was at that very moment sailing down the Nile to Alexandria.

She thought of Ava, her only sister: *I am so sorry you would not let me share my happiness with you. Oh, Ava, my spoiled little sister, maybe one day you will let me.* But of course Ava would never let her. Ava, with her great love for herself, was flushed out to the sea. At that precise moment Isabel flowed with orgasms of life like a river. Three women. Three rivers.

She wafted nude in a fantasy world made real and vital by the very love that these two people exchanged with each other. Isabel lay there with her man in a state of constant flow—lust instilled with tenderness. She tried to conjure up Kate and Ava, the two women who had been her family all of her life until this man had come along. She could not. They were gone. That they had disappeared, and she could not find them, did not distress her in the least, but only surprised her and filled her, momentarily, with sorrow.

After being a wanderer, all alone out in the world for most of her life, she had come home. Alexis, holding her in his arms, suddenly felt a surge of pity for Isabel, pity for the price she must have had to pay to become the delicious, wonderful woman that she now was. He kissed her deeply; moments later Alexis told her it was time to go. He stood her up and dressed her.

He would not let her do a thing. He slipped her high-heeled shoes back on her feet, and then, when she stood, so beautiful and radiant, he kissed her. With his arm around her, they started walking through the palace. They had gone about a hundred yards when Isabel suddenly stopped. Alexis looked at her and at the pale blush of pink on her face. He started to laugh and said, "You have come, haven't you?"

Isabel was ridiculously embarrassed to think that just through walking she could have such a strong orgasm. Alexis laughed at her again, and he took her by the elbow, watching her closely as they walked down the stairs, enjoying every minute of it.

It was an extraordinary sensation, so sensual, the constant coming. Isabel kept imagining a little click when the balls inside her came together. When they arrived in the ground-floor drawing room, Alexander was already there with a cold glass of champagne in his hand. He kissed Isabel hello and told her how ravishing she looked. He recognized the Saladin Diamonds and said, "Oh, my, Madame Hyatt has certainly done you proud. Are you very happy?"

"Alexander, I am so happy I think I am a little frightened," Isabel blurted. "You will get me to him on time tomorrow, won't you, Alexander?"

He touched her cheek and said, "You must worry about nothing, it is all arranged. Just leave it to Uncle Alexander."

They dined together, and half an hour before midnight Isabel began teasing them about their depraved, debauched night in the whorehouses of Cairo. Alexander asked if she was jealous. She thought about it and replied that all she wanted was for Alexis to be happy, and that she hoped he would have the most sexual, sensual, debauched, depraved evening possible. She was just glad she was not going to be there to see it, for she might murder the women.

Much to her surprise Alexis teased her in front of Alexander, saying that he had arranged for five of the best well-hung men in Cairo to call on Isabel that night. What she did with them was up to her. She could turn them away, or she could have them all. They were her slaves for the night and would do anything she wanted.

Alexander asked him if he was jealous. No, Alexis said and smiled. As a matter of fact, he was very aroused by the idea and, unlike Isabel, he would not mind watching and even joining in, because he knew that it would take all five of them to do the job that he alone could do with her.

They all laughed at his vanity, and Isabel, not wanting to let him get away with it, decided to leave him worried. "Well," she said. "We might just have to find out if that is true, mightn't we?"

"Oh, she has got you wondering now, old boy." Alexander laughed.

What each one did the night before they were to be married, neither of them ever knew. Alexis and Gamal paid the men before they entered Isabel's room. The servant waited outside her door in case he was needed or she was in any danger, but other than that, Alexis knew nothing else about her night and never asked. As for Isabel, well, only Alexander could have told her what had happened, but she never asked.

At ten minutes to twelve she saw both men off. When Alexis left her, he whispered in her ear, "Remember, remove the silver balls." He kissed her and said, "I will see you on board the *Mamounia*."

When the two men drove off to their rendezvous, Alexander asked, "Do you think she will take the studs tonight?"

Alexis turned to him and said, "Let's just say that I have taken out a few insurance policies, and I would be very surprised if she did."

"Insurance policies?"

"Yes," and from his pocket he took the beige suede pouch that had held the silver cunt balls, opened it, and held it upside down over his open palm to show Alexander that it was empty.

Alexander roared with laughter and said, "You know, old boy, you are a very clever devil."

"Alexander, it is not a matter of cleverness. It must be seven months now since I first laid eyes on her, but I knew even then that I wanted to be with her for the rest of my life. It was that old cliché that people always talk about but think never really happens. Love at first sight, a chemistry that happens between two people. Just talking about her makes me love her all the more. She is the most wonderful, sensual, intelligent, soulful woman I have ever met and having her near me adds something to my life."

Alexander was touched by the passion and love that his friend had for this woman, and was happy for him. From a box next to him on the car seat he removed two opium pipes; they lit them and smoked as they were driven on to what Alexander called his "secret palace."

Mrs. Nesbitt tried to persuade Kate not to take the Nile cruise down to Alexandria. She told her in the nicest way that Kate looked very tired, even a bit overwrought, and that although one would think that the heat would make her look flushed, she was decidedly pale.

The young ship's officer explained that the Nesbitts and he would drive straight through to Alexandria; they would take the delta road part of the way and then switch to the desert road. It would be interesting and in three and a half hours they would be in the heart of the city. In four hours at the latest, she could be in her air-conditioned cabin aboard the luxury liner *Aphrodite*.

Kate told them she was determined to take the overnight trip down the Nile. She would have plenty of time to rest and sleep once the great ship had sailed from the port at noon the next day.

There was nothing that Kate's traveling companions could do to change her mind. With much reluctance, she allowed them to take control of all her luggage including her sterling silver. The small overnight case that she had packed stayed with her, and after yet another reassurance from the Nesbitts that her things would be safe with them, she said good-bye and started down the stone stairs to the slip where the yacht and its thirty-five passengers waited to cast off. A steward from the yacht took Kate's nightcase and started up the gangway, helping her along.

Before she could even turn around, the gangplank had been removed, and the yacht started to pull away into the mainstream of river. There were three sharp blasts from the ship's horn as Kate was greeted by the recreation officer of the *Aphrodite*, who was in charge of the tourists on their way back to the mother ship.

Oh, thank God for little blessings! Billy Buckley, the recreation officer, was a twenty-two-year-old football player from the University of Wisconsin. A big, tall, broad-shouldered, handsome, blond American kid with dimples in his cheeks, and a mouth full of perfect white teeth. He gave her a "rah-rah" welcome and told her not to worry about a thing. He was there to see that she had a good time. He would have her case put in her cabin. When Kate said she could do it herself, he said, "Listen, doll, you wouldn't want to go down there now, it's like a boiler room. I'll see that the case is put away while you go sit under that nice striped canopy and have tea with all the others. This is tea-time in Cairo. Isn't it exciting?"

Kate was utterly exhausted. All resistance gone, she said, "Do what you want. I could use a cup of tea."

He led her out to the many little tables jammed together. Kate was appalled. It was a geriatrics' holiday cruise, and she certainly did not see herself as part of it. She was maneuvered in and out of the tables to one close to the rails at the very rear of the deck. There were three other women seated, and they all looked like carbon copies of Mrs. Nesbitt. A hot cup of sweet mint tea was brought to her, and there were cakes and sandwiches on the table. Best of all was that, although it was sweltering hot, they were, mercifully, out of the sun.

Kate could barely get the cup to her lips, her hands were trembling so. One of the women very kindly offered her a small, battery-driven white plastic fan the size of a flashlight. Kate did not even have the energy to reach for it. Finally the lady reached over and placed it near Kate, aiming it up to her face.

There was a crackling sound, and over the loudspeaker came Billy Buckley's voice, telling them they were now passing under the Imbaba Bridge. About half of the geriatric tea party stayed where they were, too tired even to chance another step, but the rest tottered to the rail at his command.

Kate seemed a great deal better once she had finished

her tea and, suddenly feeling hungry, she had another cup brought to her and then put a few sandwiches on her plate. She realized as she ate that she was very hungry indeed. It was growing ever-so-slightly cooler now.

It was hard to believe that she had had her hair done only that morning. She thought about her darling Ava on her picnic, and said to herself as she looked at her watch: *Eh, if I know my daughter, she is bored with everyone by now, even Takis. She is off by herself, giving herself a lecture about how superior she is to everyone around her. Well, good luck to her, maybe she is.*

Kate took herself away from the table and went to the railing of the yacht. She looked at Cairo as they sailed between the banks of the river. She looked down over the side into the water and watched it swirl around. Suddenly she saw Ava's face in the foam. She knew that she was imagining it, but it was such a clear image looking up at her through the river. Kate blinked her eyes and looked again. The swirling foam had flattened out, and Ava had disappeared.

Oh, for Christ's sake, now I am seeing things, Kate thought. She was feeling sick to her stomach and suddenly had a severe attack of heartburn. She thought to herself: *I am so over-tired that my mind is playing tricks. Oh, that Ava, she haunts me always, ever since she was a child. I will be believing in ghosts next.*

She spat in the river and decided to go and lie down in her cabin. Maybe if she freshened up a bit it would make her feel better. She was wet through with perspiration, dirty from the road, tired with a terrible headache, and on top of all that, she realized suddenly, she was going to be seasick.

Billy Buckley came to her rescue just as she was about to faint in the corridor while looking for her cabin. He informed her that the air-conditioning had broken down.

When Kate was finally seated on one chair, her feet put up on another, and her smelling salts found and used, she seemed revived. She told Billy to go and get her case at once, that she had no intention of going down to that hellhole again. The heat was so oppressive and the smell of disinfectant mixed with the sour smell of vomit so strong, it would have knocked anyone out. He then received a lecture and reprimand for even thinking anyone could sleep in a cabin in such conditions.

You silly old bat, Billy thought, *you are absolutely right, and it's just as well you did not see the cabin. Four people in a ten-by-twelve-foot space would have really thrown you.* He returned with a towel filled with ice and plonked it on top of Kate's head.

She grabbed it and said, "For God's sake, Billy, watch my hairdo."

He lifted her hair, not even thinking about what she had just said, and smacked the ice-towel onto the back of her neck. He patted her on the shoulder and left her holding the ice on various parts of her body.

When she was revived enough, Kate found a corner at the rear of the deck and assembled a place for herself. She had a chair to sit in, a chair for her feet, one to the right of her for her overnight case and one to the left of her for her handbag. Covered by the canopy and next to the ship's rail, she was as comfortable as she ever could be. She had a clear view of the riverbank, a little breeze off the water and at least an element of privacy from the others.

The city of Cairo was slowly left behind. There was just a smattering of shacks amidst the vegetation along the banks of the river. It was luscious and green, all rural, all peasant country. Except for the lingering effects from the pitch and roll of the motor launch that made her so very sick to her stomach, the constant pain that she had in her chest, and a dizziness, Kate thought she was feeling better.

She closed her eyes and tried desperately to relax and lose some of the tension and exhaustion that was weighing so heavily upon her. Occasionally she would open her eyes to glance at the late afternoon sunset. Once when she opened her eyes she saw her fellow tourists having a revolting dinner of seven courses, which they wolfed down.

Kate had weak tea and some biscuits, but they made her feel even sicker. Just the smell of food turned her stomach. She was close to the rail and ready to retch several times, but she held back, using willpower. She was a stubborn and vindictive old lady. She was going to control as much of her mind and body as she could during this trip. Every time she felt herself slip into heavier nausea or felt a deeper pain in her chest, she thought of Isabel and the lesson she was teaching her. She thought of Isabel and how she had to be punished. She thought of Isabel and how she hated her.

Kate no longer knew why she hated Isabel. All she could think of was that at last, after years of pretending that she didn't hate her daughter, she could now admit that she did.

While Billy Buckley had his thirty-five passengers playing "Simon Says" on the longest, most romantic river in the world, Kate's mind wandered on about the hate she had for Isabel. Isabel would not take her with her. Isabel left her behind. Isabel made a life for herself. Isabel could create things from nothing and be successful at it. She was admired by people. Her Isabel had even made history out in that vast world. She had remained free and independent.

Why shouldn't Isabel be enslaved like everyone else? Kate knew that there was only one thing that enslaved Isabel and that was guilt. Not as long as Kate lived would she allow Isabel to rid herself of it, for it was the one hold she would always have on her daughter.

The red-hot sun had gone down now. Along the bank of the river, scruffy little children in torn and patched galabias waved at Kate. They ran along, trying to keep up with the boat. Peasant ladies, draped in their black dresses and veils, waved like the children to the strangers passing by. The boat moved closer to Alexandria.

Now it was black, black night, and the sky was shot full of stars. There was even a moon, a big, perfect, white half-moon. Kate was looking at her watch. She could hardly believe it. Eleven o'clock and they were serving food again. Her ancient traveling companions were still on their feet, now drinking hot tea, coffee and milk and eating biscuits and sandwiches. She settled for weak tea again and tried another biscuit.

Billy Buckley came over to her and asked if she was feeling better. He thought she did not look at all well. She had been awfully still and quiet and had not demanded anything. In his experience as a group guide that did not seem right.

Kate told Billy that she was all right. He slipped a pillow under the back of her head. It made her a little more comfortable and she thanked him, saying, "Go away, Billy, I'm fine, just thinking about my daughter."

Again she began to fantasize about Isabel. For the very first time since this whole insane journey of hers had started, and she had seen Isabel in Athens and received the news that her daughter was going to marry, Kate at last considered the possibility that Isabel might go through with it.

Her imagination took flight and she saw Isabel giving herself in a strange exotic ceremony. Dozens of Arab men in flowing long black robes were all around her, while a few dark, black-draped women off in a corner watched.

Isabel herself was all draped and veiled in black except for her breasts, which protruded through two round holes in her dress. She had diamonds, huge diamonds, on all her fingers.

Kate tried to conjure up what the man looked like. He looked like, like, who? Oh, yes, she remembered the look of an Arab man. He would look like that awful oil sheikh from Saudi Arabia. She remembered how he looked from all the pictures of him in the paper.

He would take her to a big house with lots of servants and keep her there, just for his own sexual needs. He would give her no money but shower her with presents.

For the first time in her life Kate saw her daughter, Isabel, ask even for the very bread that went into her mouth, or a dress for her body, all because of this man. Isabel beaten down and made dependent on this man. Why would she do it? Because this man dominated her sexually? The slut! *That* is why she did it. Oh, my God, she made herself a slave, that stupid, stupid girl. She was free all of her life, earned her own money, and now she makes herself a slave for a man!

Kate became hysterically agitated. In her warped imagination, she hated her daughter Isabel even more. *I only hope that when she tries to get away, he does not let her go. He'll know how to keep her. I hope he beats her. I hope he whips her. I hope he gives her all the whippings that I never did. The minute that she tries to be independent, stubborn, an individual, he will take a whip out and let her have it.*

Kate became strangely excited by the idea of a man whipping her daughter. The thought that he would punish her because she wanted to leave him, wanted her freedom, was just.

When she opened her eyes most of the passengers had gone downstairs to their hot, smelly cells to try and get a few hours' sleep. A few just sat all night in their upright chairs.

When her eyes were open, reality of a sort came back to her. The heat, the constant threat of seasickness and the state of her emotions, as well as the pain in her chest, all merged into exhaustion, and finally Kate fell into a restless sleep.

The sun was just coming up when she felt the most terrifying pain across her chest. It was as if someone had taken a sharp knife and driven it into her heart. The pain woke her out of a deep sleep. She screamed as loud as she could, and gasping for breath, she grabbed for her chest. The people on deck jumped up and ran towards her. She opened her eyes and the pain subsided. There was just a horrible soreness as if someone had beaten her around the chest. There were tears in her eyes. She whispered to please bring her a drink of water so she could take a pill. She told them she had been deep in a horrible nightmare and that it had frightened her; the next thing she knew she was screaming.

Someone brought her a glass of water and she took her pill, asking them to please just leave her alone, she would be all right. Kate closed her eyes and the nausea came on her fast. She struggled up from her chair, went to the rail and vomited violently.

The sun came up and it became light, hot and then bright. Kate made it the few steps back to her chair and, with tears of pain from her own wretchedness, she sat there looking across the river to the bank, where life was beginning to stir. With a great deal of effort, she put her feet up on the chair opposite her and lay back. She closed her eyes, and in a while she felt a little better. She would take it very easy onboard the *Aphrodite*. This was a very hard trip, but she was sure in the end it would be well worth it.

At eight in the morning all the tables were set for breakfast, and the senior citizens, none the worse for wear, streamed to the tables. The smell of fried eggs and coffee, combined with the chatter of the blue-haired travelers, made Kate even more miserable. All she could think was: *I am sick enough to die. Will this river trip never end?*

Once the realization came to Kate of just how miserable and ill she was, real fear set in. After all the years of imaginary heart attacks, Kate realized that she had suffered the real thing a few hours before. She was still in pain, but she knew that as much as she wanted to be taken care of, she dared not make too much of it until they were off the river and on the *Aphrodite*. Once out to sea, she would then let them put her in the sick bay.

There was no way that she would allow them to discover how bad she was, for fear that they would put her in the hospital at Alexandria. The last thing on earth she wanted was to be in Egypt and have Isabel find out she had not had a wonderful holiday for herself. There would be good doctors aboard the liner. They would have a fine sick bay, what with all these old cronies. She would be fine once she was out of the Egyptian waters on her way to America.

She took stock and decided she could brave it all the way to the ship. She would take it easy and pretend it was all a severe case of seasickness and dysentery.

Billy Buckley was standing over her. He had a tray, and on it was a glass of orange juice, a poached egg on toast and a cup of tea. He very gently put the tray down on her lap.

"Oh, Billy, I know that you are trying to help. You are a good boy, but please, darling, go play 'Simple Simon' over there."

"It's 'Simon Says,' Mrs. Wells."

"OK, Billy, go play 'Simon Says' over there. I couldn't eat a thing."

"I think you should, Mrs. Wells. You have been so seasick that I think if you made an effort to put something in your stomach, it will give you a little energy. Look, there will be a bus when we land to take us to the *Aphrodite*, but you need to have some energy so we can get you on that bus. You want to see a little of Alexandria, don't you, on the way to the port?"

"Listen, Billy, I don't care if I never see a thing of Alexandria. Don't worry about me, I will drag myself onto that bus, and once I am off this crappy river I will be my old self again."

In the end they made a compromise. Billy's dimples and sparkling white teeth, his open and good nature, got Kate to eat part of the egg on toast and drink most of the tea. It seemed to stay down this time, and she thought, *I will be just fine when I get on that nice big ship. Two days and I will be up and around and bored with all these old bags.*

In the early hours of the morning Kate did manage to get out of her chair, even spoke sweetly to a few of the blue-haired ladies and took a small walk on deck. She never strayed very far from the little niche she had made for herself and eventually went back, sat down, and put her feet up.

If there was anything good she could say about the trip, it was that at least she was out of the city, and it was nice to see all the fresh greenery along the banks of the Nile. So far as Kate Wells was concerned, all the Arabs could keep their country. She had seen plenty of it, and it was less than nothing. The romantic Nile, you could keep it. Leave it to Isabel to end up the rich wife of a man who would make her live in a country riddled with disease, poverty and heat. That is *if* she got married, or was going to get married.

An hour outside Alexandria, the delta cruise ship passed a village along the bank of the river. It was no different from any other village, except that the people were walking along in some sort of procession. Kate watched them trail along the path. There were a dozen people sitting on an old wooden flat cart. It was being drawn by an emaciated ox, or some sort of animal like that. The animal was draped in garlands of colored flowers, half fresh, half plastic. Around its head it had a wreath of green leaves. The people were all laughing and playing.

Kate tried to look away. After all, they were just another bunch of peasants, but something kept drawing her eyes back to them. It was their joy and happiness, their open sweet smiles for such miserably poor, disease-ridden people.

Billy Buckley stopped by and said, "Isn't it nice? We have even seen a wedding along the way."

Kate looked and did not think it was nice, but was mesmerized by them, their innocence, their joy for this one happy day. After the boat had left them far behind, Kate kept thinking of the little procession, and her mind started slipping back to her own problems.

How had she come to this? Sailing down the Nile, in the heat of the day, all on her own. Sailing down a river going where? How could it be? Kate had two daughters, they were her family. Then, how was it that Kate was all alone?

Soon her confused emotions mounted to hysteria, and

that was the worst thing that could happen to her. Every nerve in her body went taut with anxiety over her plight, and her damaged heart started pumping hard. Her daughters! She had given up her life for her two daughters.

Ava had everything she wanted and for years had reveled in her financial security and her doting husband. How was it Kate never had that? She knew way down deep in her heart what an unloving, self-centered daughter Ava was. She had seen her cover it up for years by playing the coquette and using her money as advantageously as possible. But Ava had a life of her own, and the rest of the world didn't matter, including Kate.

Now, after all the years of pretending insecurity, that selfish Isabel was also eliminating Kate. Ava and Isabel would have lives of their own and financial security, the two things that Kate had never managed to attain in her life.

She thought of the wedding procession again. Maybe today was the day that *Isabel* was going to get married. Maybe somewhere in this crazy country she was having a wedding party. It then struck Kate that if that were true, then on the biggest, happiest day of Isabel's life she had eliminated her mother. Her daughter was getting married while Kate was making the hundredth, probably the *thousandth* attempt at bravely making a life for herself in a world of people who could not care less. God, she was tired of it, tired of pretending, of lying, of cheating herself, and everyone else.

The boat tied up at a small dock on the outskirts of the city. Billy Buckley picked up her things and helped her to the bus. Kate used every drop of willpower she had to keep the dynamic pain in her chest under control. She made up her face and settled herself in the bus for the ride through Alexandria.

It was Kate in her best performance. She used her sick energy to charm every person on that bus. She took a keen interest in every sight that was pointed out to her, and when her fellow passengers were critical of the filth, the crumbling buildings, the heat and the humidity, the disease, the flies, the human shit in the streets, it was she who chided them for not accepting the facts of the world. In this way she hung on, waiting only to make it to her

cabin and her bed, where she would lie between clean
sheets and rest.

Like everything else on this journey, the bus trip
seemed endless, but eventually they arrived. The *Aphrodite* was a great ocean-going ship and it looked to Kate
like Paradise in dock.

The smoke was belching out of her two enormous
stacks, and several gangways, like long tongues, reached
out from the different decks. People were hanging over
the rails, and as the old men and women filed off the bus,
weary and exhausted, they received a cheer from their
shipmates who had remained aboard. With a new surge of
energy they trundled up the ramps as quickly as they
could. Kate was among them and Billy Buckley was not
far behind her.

There were three blasts from the whistle on board ship
—that wonderful sound that means "we are heading out
to sea"—and as soon as the gangways were empty, they
were pulled away and the open rails quickly clicked shut.
Before Kate had even found a seat, the S.S. *Aphrodite*
was sailing out of the port of Alexandria.

Kate felt relief the moment she stepped aboard. Everyone seemed so happy, and everything was so spanking
white and clean. Kate looked at the deck and thought to
herself how one could eat off the floor. The crew, which
was mostly Greek, was a joy to see in their white and
blues, and the few Americans among them were, like Billy
Buckley, rushing around making everyone comfortable.

Once on board, Kate went to a deck chair, where she
remained for the sailing. An hour out to sea, Billy arrived
with the cabin steward and Kate was ushered to her stateroom. There was music coming through the loudspeakers.
Bing Crosby crooned across the decks, through every hall.
Oh, God, it was nice to hear Bing. "When you wish upon
a star . . . bump, bump, bump, bump . . ." went Bing.
Oh, God, it was nice to hear him. The stateroom was far
more than Kate had imagined it would be for the money.
Ah! Little Stephano, you did come through for me.

With the help of the cabin steward she unpacked and
made herself comfortable. Within an hour she had managed to bathe and slip between the nice cool sheets,
dressed in a fresh nightgown. In her air-conditioned cabin
she was comfortable at last.

She ordered a proper lunch, even though she was sure

she would not be able to manage it all. It was wheeled in by the waiter, who raised the side flaps of the trolley and presto! there it was, a perfect little round dining table with a crisp white cloth and yellow tea roses in a silver bowl. She slipped on a dressing gown while still in bed and weakly moved over to the chair that was held out for her by the waiter. From underneath the table, he removed the dishes that Kate had ordered and served her lunch.

Kate found herself making a supreme effort to charm the waiter. After all, he had to serve her all the way to New York. The effort was too much, and halfway through the meal, she suddenly felt terribly tired and just barely made it back to bed. She managed to ring for the waiter, who removed the table.

All through the afternoon Kate lay in her bed making resolutions. She would have the best holiday ever on board once she was well again. The river was forgotten, all her hatred for her two daughters gone, and Kate again was making plans to live with Isabel once she had completed this holiday.

On Tuesday afternoon at 5:38, aboard the S.S. *Aphrodite,* somewhere at sea, and eight minutes after her daughter Isabel was married on the river Nile, Kate Wells had her second heart seizure. It was nowhere near as severe as the attack she'd suffered on the Nile cruiser. Kate knew the moment that it hit her what it was. It took nearly an hour before she had some relief from the pain, and although her breathing was labored and she still had considerable discomfort, her mind was clear.

After forty-five minutes of hanging somewhere close to death, Kate saw her whole miserable life run before her like one big, bad movie. So many people came across her screen. Her mother, father, Sam, her sisters, brothers, friends, Isabel, Ava, the admiral, her miseries and her unhappinesses. It all ran out before her, and Kate was able to see what her life had been. She was quite ready to give it up. She knew that she would never see the end of this voyage.

It was from exhaustion, not by choice, that Kate gave up her fight for life. Her heart was so badly damaged that she knew that she was going to die. The only thing that she could think about was the relief that her daughters would not be there. Now that she knew that she was going to leave the world, she would at least do it on her terms, or as close to her terms as she could manage. She would die among strangers, alone, and that was just fine with her. She had always done better with strangers. After all, what was there to say to her daughters? They were going to live.

Kate had thought that as long as Isabel was alone, there was always the hope that Kate could win her over and live her life. It was only after realizing how severely wounded she was that Kate accepted that it would never be.

Kate managed to ring for the cabin steward and asked him to bring Billy Buckley to her at once. It was Billy who wrote out Kate Wells's last will and testament. The cabin steward and first officer were witnesses and a notary made it all legal. Only after that was done, the document sealed in an envelope and handed over to the captain to be opened upon her death, did Kate allow the ship's doctor to examine her.

Kate hung on for three more days. There were two doctors, four nurses and an excellent sick bay with the best equipment to help save Kate, but she had been as good as dead from the massive heart seizure she'd suffered on the river, en route to Alexandria.

The captain and his first officer, the doctor and two nurses were the attendants at two o'clock in the morning, somewhere in the Atlantic Ocean, under a sky full of stars, when Katharine Anne Wells was buried at sea.

The captain followed her last will and testament to the letter. She was buried, as she had requested, before her family were notified. Her belongings on the *Aphrodite* would be stored in New York and released to her elder daughter upon her arrival there. A telegram was sent to Miss Isabel Wells, c/o Sir Alexis Hyatt in Cairo.

It read: "This is to notify you that Mrs. Katharine Anne Wells was buried at sea in the early hours of the morning of Saturday November 1 somewhere in the Atlantic Ocean. She died of a massive heart attack. Her last will and testament asked that you be notified after her burial. All her possessions are to be given to Miss Wells upon her arrival at our offices in New York. The S.S. *Aphrodite* docks at Pier 57 on November 22. We regret having to send you this news. Signed, Captain Panos Papastamati S.S. *Aphrodite*, at sea."

XIII

THE SUN was streaming into the room when Isabel opened
her eyes on the morning of her wedding day. Someone
had drawn back the mosquito netting while she slept. She
lazily moved herself up the pillows and looked around
what was still the most beautiful room in which she had
ever spent any length of time. The antiquity of it, the del-
icacy of the craftsmanship, the peace, the beauty, and yes,
even the smell of it, enveloped Isabel.

She saw at one end of the room, near the cupboards,
Maryka, Doreya and Gamal whispering among themselves
softly as they assembled cases and packed clothes. She
saw her galabia lying across the bed, picked it up and
slipped it over her head, then raised herself up to a sitting
position. Isabel moved almost in slow motion and ever so
silently. She felt strangely beautiful, amazingly happy; she
felt different, and could not understand it at all. It was as
if a great burden had been removed from her life.

She watched the three people at their work, assembling
her trousseau. She wanted to say good morning but was
powerless to do so. She slipped her hands out from under
the covers and saw the diamonds on her fingers sparkling
up at her; oh, they were beautiful. "Alexis, I love you,"
she murmured.

Almost quietly, she said good morning and then sat
back. The three left their tasks and went round to the bed,
all happy smiles. Gamal carried a large, round, flattish
basket. Alexis's three devoted servants threw rose petals
and jasmine blossoms over her bed and around her. They
wished her the sweetest of life and the happiest of days.
Isabel could not stop smiling and laughing because of the
touching gesture. There were petals everywhere, and
when she scooped them up in her hands and threw them
up in the air, they rained down all over her. Gamal went
to the telephone while the three women played with the

blossoms. He went back to his work after telling Isabel that he had ordered breakfast to be brought.

Isabel slipped ever so gently from her bed to go into the bathroom, and when she returned to the room she just as carefully slipped back under the coverlet into her bed of blossoms. Ordinarily, she would have checked on everything, but she seemed to be floating on some sort of magic love carpet. It was so nice not to have to be in control. She played with the petals, running her fingers through them again and again.

Gamal brought a box over to her. It was wrapped in yellow paper and had many thin ribbons of the same color all tied together in a vast bow. On top of the bow were pinned fresh, fully blown, yellow roses. There was a letter in a cream-colored envelope slipped under the bow.

"From Sir Alexis for when you are awake," Gamal intoned. He left her with the dress-box and went back to his work.

She opened the letter first and read: "My darling, not seeing you until this afternoon does not mean I cannot write to you. I hope you had a good night and woke up happy and as much in love with me as I am with you.

"Here is a little something for you to wear for our first night together, and it is just that, since every night with you is a first night.

"Alexander will be with you all day, and bring you to me. I think of you with love as I always have from the first moment I saw you. Alexis."

Isabel carefully removed the roses, and she inhaled their scent. She put the flowers among the other blossoms on her bed. Then she untied the ribbons and opened the box.

A chocolate-brown nightdress of the most exquisite Belgian lace, with shoestring straps, a low-cut front, narrow waist and slits up the sides lay inside. She took note that the lace was designed in such a way that both her nipples and the darker pink skin around them would lie bare, exposed through the lace like the center of a flower with its stamen.

Under the nightdress was a peignoir of the same chocolate-brown-colored lace, with long, bell-shaped sleeves in an exquisite cut, very full and trailing in the back, tying low in the front under the bust. Pinned at the fastening was an English Georgian dragonfly with a wingspan of about five inches. The wings were of diamonds and the body was of Cabouchon rubies. The whole thing was utterly gorgeous.

She lay there looking at it all and running her fingers through her flower bed. It was like some wonderful fairy tale. The only strange part was that she was so at ease with it all. It was as if she had been like this all of her life and had just woken up to it after a bad dream of years of merely sexual relationships, loneliness and the working life.

There was a tap at the door and Gamal opened it. In walked Alexander, followed by two servants who carried in a breakfast table set for two. The table was placed close to her, and a chair was drawn up for Alexander.

Alexander told her that it was his day now. He had her all to himself from now until he delivered her to her bridegroom, and he intended to make the most of it. He was arranging a special wedding lunch for her at the pool, but since it was a secret wedding they would be the only two guests.

Alexander was dressed in his pajamas and a very smart dressing gown. He looked extremely handsome and dapper with his small silk handkerchief poking out of his pocket. He told her she was not to ask one word about the night before, and he would ask her nothing; all she need know was that they were going to have an easy day because he was feeling fragile.

Over breakfast he told her that a car would take her cases to the boat. The plan was for her to spend the morning relaxing in bed while he had a few hours sleep. They would have a relatively early lunch at the pool, and afterwards Doreya, Maryka and Juju, her handmaidens, would be waiting in the hammam to make her ready for her groom. He would deliver her into their hands, and when he returned, she would be dressed and coiffed for her wedding. Then the two of them would drive to Memphis and board the *Mamounia* there.

"He is something, your Alexis. He has planned the loveliest way to be married. By the time we are aboard all the officials will be there ready and waiting. We will sail up the Nile during the ceremony. There will be a quick and light refreshment for the officials and then we will be set ashore, where cars will be waiting for us to whisk us back into Cairo while you cut loose for Abu Simbel. Not bad

for your first wedding, old girl." He went round the table
and kissed her on the cheek, then continued, "Isabel, I
have brought you a little something as a wedding present
from acting father, nanny and friend of the bride. My
wedding gift to you both, my real wedding gift, is waiting
for you on the *Mamounia*. This is really only a token of
how happy I am for you."

Isabel was deeply touched. She removed the red wrappings and opened the Cartier box. Inside were three hair
clips of diamonds. One was in the shape of a star about an
inch-and-a-quarter across, another was a crescent moon
about the same size and the third one a flower. They were
exquisite, and she immediately asked him to pass the hand
mirror so she could place them in her hair.

They were a fun gift, because once they were pinned in
her chestnut-brown hair, they sparkled and were very special, decorative and amusing rather than extravagant and
overly elegant. They were things she could wear a great
deal, and she was delighted with them. She made her way
out of bed and went around to Alexander, bent down and
kissed him in thanks.

He put his cup down, and while kissing Isabel, her galabia opened, exposing her breast. Alexander slipped his
hand inside her robe. With his other hand he held her face
by the chin, close to his and said, "Shush, I have something to say. If you had not fallen in love with Alexis, and
if he had not declared himself, I would have tried for you
myself." He ran his thumb over her nipple and kissed her
on the lips very gently, then went on, "I love Alexis and I
love you. I want you to know that. I will be your friend
for always."

With both his hands now, and very quickly, before she
realized what was happening, he lifted her breast to his
mouth and kissed and sucked her nipple. Before she could
even pull away he tucked it back in her galabia, took her
on his lap, lifted her face to his and said, "Please do not be
angry with me, it will not happen again. But I wanted you
to know." He kissed her lovingly and touched her cheek
again.

Isabel thought it was rather bad manners and would
have made an issue about it, except that she knew that Alexander Gordon-Spencer was being honest: He did love
her. He loved them both. He and Alexis would be in that

not uncommon situation: two friends in love with the same woman.

She knew that Alexander understood that she would never have an affair with him. They were two mature people who knew the rules of the game. She was sure that was why he had told her, so that she would know exactly how he felt, and appreciate it, use it, play with it, as *he* would play with being in love with his best friend's wife. Isabel was almost sure that if Alexis did not already know, then he would very soon. It looked like they were going to be a *threesome*.

There was no reason to make an issue. Alexander wanted her but would never have her. Instead he would love her always. She took herself off his lap and stood there, not knowing what to say.

He lifted the coverlet to the bed and told her to get back in. "You are to have a lazy and lovely day. It is my treat today until I give you away. I am in charge."

She slipped into bed and pulled the light coverlet over her legs. He scooped up handfuls of the petals from where they had fallen when he had moved the coverlet and showered her with them.

She was laughing, and as she looked up into his face, he bent down and kissed her on the forehead. "It is all right, isn't it? My love for you is to give you more pleasure, not to make you unhappy. I will never abuse it, you have my word for that. You do understand, I hope."

"It is all right, Alexander," Isabel murmured. "Thank you for loving me. I will never abuse it either."

"Ah, that is good. Now we both know where we stand and that makes it perfect." He sat down and poured more coffee, then buttered another *broiche* and offered it to her. When she refused, he said, "Open your mouth," and fed it to her.

They laughed, and all through their breakfast conversation they talked about many things. He told her that he had a penchant for whores and that he derived great pleasure as a voyeur. She must understand that as much as he would like to have her sexually, he enjoyed watching her and Alexis and their life together; he was not a masochist.

"As a matter of fact," he told her, "you might just as well know that I am more a sadist than a masochist. So, my dear, you must never worry that your love for Alexis will make me suffer."

Eventually he left her, saying that he expected her at the pool for a swim before lunch, which was to be at one o'clock.

After Alexander had left Isabel's bedroom, she remained in bed luxuriating in her own laziness. Never had she felt so pampered and spoiled, decadent and depraved. She thought of Alexis and the fact that this was his life, the life that he had always lived. She thought of all the good and constructive things that he had done and still did for so many people. He was living proof that with love for yourself, confidence of who and what you are, and knowledge of what you want in life, you can accomplish great things.

Her mind drifted between the rose petals and jasmine blossoms to her Meredith Montagues and how much she enjoyed writing them. In her new life she would be able to carry on with her writing as Alexis pursued his work. How lucky she was that writing could be done anywhere and would never interfere with Alexis's work or plans.

She thought about Kate and Ava, about herself and her relationships with them. When there was the chance of offering them a rose, she had, but they refused even to take the scent. Still, Isabel had never given up on them. Now that there were flowers in such abundance in her life, she would try again. Surely Ava and Kate would not refuse her now?

Thinking about them usually depressed her, but today, lying among the cushions and blossoms, she had none of those feelings. She just knew that Kate and Ava, wherever they were, would never change. If any change had taken place, it was that she herself was no longer pushing to be accepted. At last someone had seen her and her worth. Thank Alexis for that.

The very thought of Alexis, and what he had done for her by accepting her exactly as she was, made her feel warm and wet inside. She wanted to open her legs and be there waiting for him. She turned on her side, tucked the pillow under her cheek, and thought about how much she loved him. She dozed off. When she woke she saw the last of her cases being taken from the room.

Eventually Isabel left her bed and changed into a lightweight, simple cotton galabia. Taking a white, one-piece swimsuit with her, she went down to the pool.

There was no one there, so she went into the bath

house, changed into her suit and dived in. Slowly she swam the length of the pool a few times. The water felt like liquid satin. She lifted herself out of the pool and took off her wet suit, slipping again into the galabia. She stretched out on a chaise under the striped awning.

She heard a splash and opened her eyes to see Alexander swimming. He remained in the water for about fifteen minutes, floating on his back. When he had had enough, he took the chaise next to her, telling her that the swim had done him good, he was quite revived. After lunch, when he had delivered her to the hammam, he might go down and have a sauna and a sleep so that he would be in top form for giving her away.

He asked if she was nervous. All that she could answer was that she was beyond being nervous. "After all, what can happen, Alexander? At the very worst he can jilt me, and then I will go back to my old life. I have always done the best that I could with what I have. I suppose that I would do the same again."

He touched her wet hair, laughing. "You silly thing, he is not going to jilt you."

"Well, then, there is nothing for me to be nervous about, is there? Listen, Alexander, if we start talking about him and me, I'll get nervous and over-excited. So what say we while away our time with a little gin rummy before lunch?"

"Brilliant, old girl, only we play for money, right?"

"Oh, surely not! You know what a rotten gambler I am. No money."

"Oh, I had forgotten. Well then, *I* will play for money and what will *you* play for?"

"Well, what can I play for?" Isabel asked.

"I will play for fifty pence a point, and, let's see . . . you play for . . . Ah, I know! If you lose, because it's your wedding day, I will be generous. I will let you get off easily. But remember, in the future, if we gamble together and you can't bear to play for money, you will have to pay some forfeit as the loser. Agreed?"

"Agreed, as long as it is not anything that is harmful or repugnant. Do *you* agree, Alexander?"

He laughed at her. "You do not know me very well, my dear. I told you that I love you, and so I would *never* ask you to do anything that is repulsive or repugnant. But, to ease your mind and doubts, I agree. You will learn about me in time."

Isabel felt uneasy.

Her mind slipped off, and she wondered if as a forfeit one day Alexander would ask her to do something sexual. Expose herself to him, perhaps?

He rose from the chaise, and she started to get up to go to the round table under the umbrella to play, but before she could, Alexander picked her up in his arms, took her to the pool side, and said, "You are a very naughty girl, Isabel. You are thinking dirty things about me, were you not?"

"Alexander, put me down!" she scolded. "Yes, I was thinking dirty things! I was only wondering!" She could not help but smile as he had caught her.

"Isabel, you do not believe me when I tell you that I love you and that we are going to be friends. You silly woman, you have two men in love with you, and what happens is all up to you. I will tell you only once more that I will never press you. Now, for thinking the wrong things——" and he dropped her in the pool and walked away, calling to a servant to bring the cards.

How extraordinary, Isabel thought, and an old friend of hers came to mind. He used to say that a man is always in love "when the woman is on top of the relationship."

By the time Isabel had climbed out of the pool, and had returned from the bath house, where she'd changed her wet clothes, Alexander was waiting for her at the table. The cards were already dealt out when she sat down and said that she was going to beat him into a pulp.

By the time the gin rummy players broke for lunch she was far behind in the game. He teased her continually about the delicious forfeit he was thinking up for her.

Gamal came to announce lunch at the table set on the other side of the pool. Alexander put his arm around Isabel as they walked along and asked her if she was having a happy day. She told Alexander that she was. Very.

The luncheon was a delight. Alexander was at his most amusing, with many anecdotes about the Arab world and his experiences in it. He was a true Arabist, an Englishman who loved the Arab world and knew how to deal with it and enjoy it.

He laughed and told Isabel that she now had the best of both worlds. He told her how he was sexually oriented as an Englishman, but orientalized in sexuality like an Arab. They spoke about sex in the East. He was sure that she was learning quickly that the most important thing about sex that was never learned in the West was how amusing, entertaining, and pleasurable it was.

In the West we agonize too much and do not enjoy sex enough. Did she not agree? Yes, Isabel did.

The food they ate while talking about all this was sublime. First, they had heaped plates of ice-cold black Beluga caviar with lemon squeezed over it. Paper-thin brown bread that had been toasted to a crisp and spread with sweet butter. None of the other trimmings usually fussed about with the best Beluga. They used fine antique wooden Russian spoons, made for eating caviar. There was ice-cold Roderer Cristal—the champagne in which Alexander always indulged himself, pouring only a tiny amount for Isabel. Enough for his utterly charming and sensitive toast to her on her wedding day. He told her that she could have as much caviar as she wanted but no more alcohol and no dope before the wedding. He was to deliver her to Alexis calm, collected, sober and relaxed. Alexis wanted her to enjoy every minute of her wedding day not under alcohol or drugs but under the sheer excitement of each other.

After the caviar there was a cold lobster bisque which was absolutely delicious, and after that, cracked Alaskan crab, ice-cold and served with perfect mayonnaise. There were cold, fat, white asparagus with lemon squeezed over them and then a salad of Belgian endive. For dessert there were fresh, peeled figs covered with fresh cream, and afterwards, hot, sweet coffee.

Alexander looked at his watch and asked Isabel to stroll with him through the gardens to the house. It was time for him to deliver her to the hammam, and her attendants, Doreya, Maryka and Juju, who would bathe her. A man would be there to do her hair. There was to be a special treat: a divine masseur.

Alexander told Isabel she must give her body to this man. He was Alexander's own masseur, and he was especially good for ladies about to be married. "If you have any nerves or knots, Isabel, he will iron them out."

She said that she had no nerves, that she was feeling fine. He stopped her in the path, where they were surrounded by an abundance of huge red hibiscus, all in bloom on their great bushes. He held her very tight to him, his palm spread against the center of her back, and moved it around slowly. Then he moved it up over her shoulder blades to the back of her neck and then made his way down to her waist, to the very crack of her ass.

"No, my dear," he said as he felt her tremble. "You only think you are calm and completely relaxed. I can feel that you have a slight anxiety, are a wee bit tense. You can tell when a person is insecure or frightened—for that matter you can tell when a person is feeling strong and powerful—simply by the way that they move. The very being, the soul of oneself, is hidden but expressed through the body in the most far-reaching ways. The body speaks, Isabel, although you do not know it."

Alexander felt her tense up ever so slightly, and he said, "You see, do not be ridiculous," and gave her a gentle slap on her ass. "Do not be foolish. I want to deliver you to Alexis completely relaxed, and if you are tense, you are going to be sexually tense."

"Alexander, if I was not nervous before, you certainly are making me nervous now!" Isabel muttered.

He laughed at her and said, "Stop acting so Western. For Christ's sake, pull yourself together. Everyone there is ready and waiting to prepare you for your husband. They are Eastern ladies, you know, who will practically make you a virgin for your wedding night."

"Well, that will take some doing, Alexander." She laughed.

"Well, it may be not as difficult as you think. All I say is that I would love to be there to watch. I understand that you have been sent an amazing old woman who knows about such things. She is supposed to have the most incredibly tiny, soft hands, and is instructed to do something divine to you for tonight. I do not want to give anything away, but only to prepare you for what is to come. No anxieties and nerves are necessary; you are to enjoy every minute of it. There is not one in a million women who is lucky enough to be prepared for a wedding as you will be today."

Isabel knew that he was only half teasing her and was grateful that he was happy enough about it all. He looked at his watch again and said, "There are only two and a half hours before you are to be bathed, dressed, and ready to step into that car. Since you do not have to do a single thing except lie back and enjoy it, I would say you are going to have a very nice afternoon!"

He then changed the subject as they walked through the courtyards towards the hammam. When he pushed the silver doors open, the soft pink marble and diaphanous white silk curtains came alive.

Juju came forward, all smiles. She had not yet seen Isabel that day. From the small basket that she carried, she threw fresh jasmine blossoms. In Arabic and French she welcomed the bride. Isabel and Alexander laughed as they picked jasmine blossoms from their hair.

Juju led them to one of the marble chaises near the huge sunken bath. Maryka brought them tall crystal goblets of lemonade with crushed mint. Alexander sat sipping the refreshing drink, saying to Isabel that he would stay only a few minutes.

It was all so civilized, Isabel marveled. That was one of the things that was so fantastic, how civilized everyone around her seemed to be. The hysteria and twisted emotions that she had learned to accept and live with were missing. Was the world sweeter and more loving, or was it just her?

She saw at the other side of the sunken bath a high marble table and standing next to it, Sahid, the only other man in the hammam. Alexander spoke to him in Arabic, then introduced him to Isabel. She actually had met him the night before. He was one of the men that had been sent to her by Alexis. Neither one of them acknowledged that they had ever seen the other before.

After Alexander had dismissed Sahid, who said that he would wait for her at the high table, Isabel asked Alexander what he had told him.

"I told him that I wanted you absolutely relaxed. That he was to work on you until he was sure there was not a drop of tension left in you, or I would cut his balls off. They would be enormous, don't you think?"

She gave him a friendly slap and said that she would not know. To herself she thought, *Alexander, I wonder if you know that they are enormous, and big and black, and that his cock is the longest, broadest and with the most amazing knob on it I have ever seen.*

When Sahid had entered her room the night before, with four other men, and they assembled themselves naked before her, only saying that they had been sent by

Sir Alexis, it was Sahid who understood what was called
for and how to behave. It did not, however, deter him
from going erect to such proportions that she thought
about him long after the men had left.

It was Maryka who went over to Alexander and very
sweetly said, "Mr. Alexander, we know you. There is
nothing for you to watch here today." Giggling, she pulled
him up and led him from the hammam.

He was no sooner out the door than the ladies took
over. There was much to do. They removed Isabel's
galabia and led her to Sahid, who helped her up onto
the table. Someone tied her hair up in a rose-colored
chiffon scarf. He started working on her body. She was
lying on her stomach as he started on the back of her
ears, then moved his magnificent hands to the two low
lobes at the bottom of her head and the top of her neck.

Although she had been sure that she was relaxed, Sahid
was working anxieties out of her that she had not even
known were there. He worked under her armpits and the
inside of her breasts, then both sides of her body to her
waist and the center of her back. He was, as Alexander
had said, remarkable.

He rubbed scented oils into the mound of her ass. He
worked first one cheek and then the other. He moved the
muscles around in a circular motion, and then he spread
the cheeks apart and worked around her anus, rubbing
the oils in.

Isabel was as relaxed and as high as if she had smoked
four joints of the best hash. She felt his finger entering
and massaging the very inside of her once-tight anus. She
could only moan softly from the pleasure of it and the
release of yet another tension she had not known she had
had. She was not sure, but she thought that she felt herself come. Sahid moved to the top of her thighs, the back
of her knees and then down to her toes.

When he was ready, he never even asked her to turn
over but lifted her up as if she were a matchstick to place
her on her back. She opened her eyes to see this huge,
strong, black man standing over her and closed them
again as she felt his hands working the under part of her
chin, and her neck.

When he came to Isabel's breasts, he had a way with
his fingers that, of course, aroused her. Somehow he made
her nipples longer, much more protruding than they had

ever been. When he was done working on one breast, he summoned Maryka and Juju, who had been standing at either side of the table all through the massage. Maryka bent her head down and sucked in a certain way on the nipple, stretching it a little bit longer each time. When Sahid was ready, he called Juju, and together the two women played with Isabel's breasts.

Sahid moved down to Isabel's stomach, to knead it, while she lay there completely relaxed. The three people worked away on her. She was now having continual small orgasms and just lay there and let herself come.

Sahid worked away on the inside of her thighs and down her legs, between her toes. He spoke to the girls, who left off sucking at his instruction. Going to her breasts, he put the flats of his hands over each of her nipples and stayed that way for nearly a minute. He was now able to lengthen the nipples and took some salve and rubbed it into them and over the dark area around them.

Isabel's body glistened from the oils and herbs that he had rubbed into her. She smelled wonderful. He walked behind her head and, taking her chin in his hands, he moved her head round and round, manipulating her neck until she felt still more tension leave her body. He moved his hands from her neck, down over her shoulders and then slowly over her arms, then stood away from the table and said, "Madam, you should sleep now for a few minutes, I think."

Isabel thanked him and he left. She lay there dozing until some time later when she heard whispers. She opened her eyes and saw Juju and Maryka with a very tiny old woman standing over her. She felt the two girls spread her legs apart. She was so relaxed that for a minute she almost felt as if she had been drugged. Maybe she had been, by something in the ointments that had been rubbed into her body? No, she decided. She was simply drugged by the lack of tension within her.

Doreya went to her and touched her cheek. She told Isabel that the woman was there to wash her and prepare her for her wedding night. Juju and Maryka raised Isabel's legs, holding them comfortably high and away from her. Doreya put cushions underneath her and each of the girls, with their free hands, held Isabel's cunt lips wide open.

Isabel, who had been ashamed of her body and exposing it all of her life, could not believe that there she lay, all relaxed, not caring who did what to her. She was now happy with herself and her body. Why had it taken so many years for her to be free?

The little old woman went to Isabel and spoke to her in Arabic. Doreya translated. The old woman told Isabel that she would go into her with her hand. Isabel saw that they were the tiniest, softest hands she had ever seen, almost the hands of a child. The woman explained that she would go all the way up inside Isabel, that she would take her uterus, her very womb, in her hand and massage it. Isabel would have much pleasure. Isabel was not to worry and was to come all she wanted. Isabel was not the first woman she had prepared for a man. If she came, fine, and if she wanted to come more she had only to ask Doreya, who would suck on her clitoris. "We are all women here and want only to give you pleasure."

After the old woman had massaged her sexual and reproductive organs and the walls of her vagina, she would then wash Isabel and dry her. She would finally go in again with a special ointment. Isabel was not to be frightened when she felt herself contract considerably. The ointment, the woman explained, would make her very small for her wedding night.

Isabel lay there, completely submissive. She was not so sure that she wanted to be small for her wedding night, but at the moment she was past resisting.

The first time the small, soft hand of the woman went up her cunt, she was so filled with her own wetness and was so open and ready to be penetrated that the little woman was able to push through her juices and high up into Isabel with no problem whatsoever. Isabel could feel her juices running out along the woman's wrist and down her arm as the fingers worked caressingly inside her. It was the most extraordinary, wonderful, soothing sensation that she had ever felt. The woman was magnificent. Her hand and wrist were not much thicker or bigger than the largest cock that had been in Isabel, and she was most clever and adept at her work, managing it with no pain to Isabel at all.

To have one's dark recesses kissed and rubbed with kindness was the dream of every woman. It was the most rare and wonderful pleasure; Isabel could not help but come in the most relaxed and euphoric way.

She actually felt the woman's tiny fingers go into the very opening at the neck of the uterus to massage and squeeze it. The woman pulled her hand out, and it was wet up to her forearm. She went to a bowl to wash her hands and arms, then returned to Isabel with a sponge, scented water and a syringe, quite large, which she inserted into Isabel. By squeezing the rubber bulb on the end, she washed her with soothing herbal water.

Isabel was told how to contract her vagina until all the water was pulled high up inside her. Then, as she relaxed, the water was expelled. Isabel had very strong muscular control in her vagina, and so she was able to suck the fluid high in and push it out in great spurts, washing herself beautifully and pleasing the old woman.

The woman's fingers were like feathers as she spread the ointment inside Isabel. This time there was more difficulty for the woman because the vagina, all washed clean and dried, was more contracted. In a few minutes, after the woman had withdrawn her hand, Isabel felt her insides contract even more as her vagina grew smaller. It was a strange sensation. Her outer lips were rubbed with a different ointment, as was her clitoris. Isabel jumped with excitement; her clitoris was that sensitive. The old woman smiled and said something in Arabic. All the girls laughed.

Juju whispered in Isabel's ear that the old woman had said she was lovely and that she would have a wedding night as if she had never had a man in her life. Sir Alexis would be very pleased. When Isabel was being opened up, she would think of how remarkable the old woman was. They all laughed, including Isabel.

Juju now checked Isabel's nipples, and she was delighted because they were still almost a quarter of an inch long and staying out that way. She said to Isabel, "Sir Alexis will be very happy tonight, Madam; Sahid is a very clever man."

Isabel now turned over and the old woman did her expertise on Isabel's anus. When she had finished, she wished Isabel happiness and then left the hammam.

Isabel felt wonderful. Every bit of her body was at ease. It was as if she were coming down from some amazing trip. She felt wonderful, happy and ready to go.

Juju and Maryka shed their clothes, led Isabel into the bath and began washing her. At one point Isabel began to laugh. She could not help but smile to herself as she thought, *oh, Ava, would you not die of anger if you were to see this scene? And Kate, you silly old thing, could you accept this? If only I could persuade you both to share this happily with me and enjoy your lives for once.*

Isabel felt quite childish and broke away from the girls to swim across the bath. They grabbed her, and in their broken English told her that there was no time to play, or she would be late for her wedding.

They took her from the bath, dried her off, scented her body and felt very proud when they saw that her nipples were indeed longer, and staying that way. They rubbed more ointment into them until it was absorbed. When she was dried thoroughly, she slipped on her galabia and then sat on one of the chaises with her feet up. The door was opened and at last came the hairdresser, the manicurist and the pedicurist to do their work.

After Alexander had left Isabel in the hammam, he went on to the guestroom that he always used when he was at the Roda house. Everything that he had told Isabel was true. He was in love with her. He did not know how or when it had happened, but sometime during her first visit to Cairo he saw a change in her—a sensuality that reached out to him, and he found himself fascinated in a way that he had never known before.

He had been tempted to stay and watch everything that was being done to her for her wedding day. He had no jealousy in him about Alexis being the one whom she was marrying. He was a strong man and would never torture himself for one second if he could not have something.

As he walked to his room, he thought of the little old woman and how she would open Isabel wide, only to tighten her. Just the thought of making Isabel scream with passion from his caresses aroused him. The thought of filling her with semen, working on her sexually in various erotic ways, aroused him even more.

He wanted to sleep, but he wanted a woman as well. That in itself was incredible after the night that he and Alexis had just had together. He thought of that whore and how Alexis and he had fucked her. She was incredible to be able to take both of them into her at the same time. It was fantastic their both coming in one cunt at the same moment. He wondered if one day he and Alexis would do it to Isabel.

Ah, the sensual Isabel . . . Yes, he would have to call for a woman.

As soon as Alexander was in his room, he spoke with the madam of his favorite bordello and told her what he wanted in an hour's time and where and how to send her to him. He then undressed and went to sleep.

Gamal arrived with the girl and a tray of hot, sweet coffee an hour later. He looked the girl over and then said, "Gamal, come back for her in an hour." After Gamal left, Alexander sipped his coffee and had the girl undress.

By the time he had the girl dress herself again, he had taken her in every way that he had wanted to take Isabel. He was not only a well-versed lover but a clever one as well. He even made the whore beg to be fucked by him.

Later Alexander was dressed in his best, light-weight, gray pin-striped Saville Row suit, his Lobb shoes, Turnbull & Asser shirt and a perfect French tie as he paced back and forth through the huge entrance hall of the Roda house. The car was waiting outside. He had sent a servant twice to hurry Isabel along. Alexander could see up the grand wide curving staircase to the balcony above where Gamal stood outside Isabel's bedroom door, waiting for her to emerge.

At last he saw Gamal move and the door open. Isabel hurried along the balcony and down the stairs. She was simply ravishing. Her chestnut-brown hair, shining like silk, was parted in the center and swept back softly away from her face, falling in soft, large billows down around her shoulders. Somewhere down low, around the nape of the neck, stuck in among the waves and curls, were the three little diamond hair clips that he had given her. Her makeup was exquisite: She looked soft and sensual, yet fresh and young, and her eyes, with their pale lavender shadow, looked bigger and more soulful. In them was a twinkle of such happiness that just looking at her made Alexander smile. She swiftly and elegantly traveled down the stairs.

Her dress was the color of the Sahara sand. It was an antique Fortuny, pleated silk dress and moved perfectly

with every step she took. It was a sheer piece of soft
sculpture in flight. On her feet were sand-colored, high-
heeled, open, braided, suede sandals. Her ruby-red toe-
nails and fingernails were accents of sensuality and part
of her outfit.

In her ears she wore diamond earrings and on her fingers, the magnificent diamond rings. Around her neck
were the Saladin Diamonds, all three strands of them, and
close to her neck, on the rim of her dress, she wore her
diamond bumblebee. She was more than ravishing. She
was transfigured.

Alexander thought her wedding dress the most beautiful he had ever seen in his life. He hoped that she would
not be too warm. Although the heat was cooling down at
this hour, it was still a very hot day. Then he noticed in
her hand an ivory-handled, ribbed fan of fine, sand-
colored silk and a Cameron compact and knew that she
was prepared to handle the heat.

Alexander watched every move she made and wondered how this beautiful, sensuous, intelligent Isabel was
going to manage to keep out of the limelight once the
marriage was common knowledge and international society focused on her. He went to meet her at the bottom
of the stairs, and when she asked if he thought she looked
all right, he could not help but laugh. He kissed her on
the cheek and told her that she was more than all right.

He tucked his arm under hers and they started through
the front door. On the veranda, a chauffeur whom she
had not seen before went down the stairs and opened the
door to the long, large, comfortable Rolls Royce. It was a
dark, rich olive-green.

As soon as Isabel got into the car, she noticed them.
The tiny Lalique vases in brackets at each end of the
seat, filled with miniature lotus flowers and trailing white,
heavy-scented jasmine. The interior of the car was in
white glove leather. On the seat was a large cushion of
the same leather, which Alexander picked up to tuck behind her. It had the initials I.W.H. elaborately and intricately embroidered in olive-green silk.

As they drove away, Isabel saw the entire staff of the
Roda house line up in salutation along the path to the
gates. It was a sweet gesture, and she rolled down the window and smiled at them as she passed.

Alexander laughed and rolled the window up, saying,

"You had better stay cool. It is twenty miles to Memphis."

Isabel sat back and turned to face Alexander. She stretched her long legs out and put them up on the little upholstered footstool. "My, I think this is the most luxurious of Alexis's cars. Beautiful isn't it? It seems to just purr along, and the air-conditioner is so silent, one hardly realizes it is on."

"I am sure Alexis will be pleased that you like it," Alexander grinned. "Why not pull on that little handle attached to the back of the front seat?"

Isabel did, and enchantingly, a perfect little desk of burl walnut appeared. Inlaid in the top were the initials I.W.H. in silver and gold.

"It is beautiful, Alexander! And how sweet! He had my initials put on the desk-top. What an extraordinary thing to do."

Alexander told her to look in the panel that pulled out from the center of the back of the front seat. She pulled the knob, and out slid a charming small bookcase with a dictionary and one of each of her Meredith Montagues. Tucked into the corner of the little car library was a vertical drawer. She opened it, and inside was an envelope addressed to her in Alexis's handwriting. Quickly she opened it, suddenly wanting him very much. It read:

"My darling, the man driving the car is called Anwar, he is your own personal chauffeur and the car that is carrying you to me is my wedding gift to you. I hope you are happy with it. Love, Alexis."

Isabel sat silent with pleasure. She handed the letter to Alexander and continued looking at all the intricate details of the car.

She folded everything back into the seat and said, "I am getting too excited. He does spoil me terribly. I don't think I should see any more for now."

Alexander bent forward and put away her letter, took her hand and kissed it. He reached over across from him, and from the back of the front seat a little door dropped down. He offered her a nonalcoholic drink. She said no, she was fine. From the little bar, he poured himself a Scotch and soda. He closed up the bar and set his glass in the built-in niche next to him.

He sipped his drink and they talked as Isabel's Rolls Royce glided on its way to Memphis. It could not have been a more perfect day. The heat outside the air-cooled Rolls was going down as rapidly as the sun. The sky was clear and blue and the air was extraordinarily translucent. Everything on the road to Memphis was lush and green, with vast groves of great tall palm trees. The city with all its concrete and noise was left far behind by the time they arrived in Memphis. They had passed through a few little villages and had seen Egyptian country life, with its simple fellahin and their carts and oxen; farm people tilling the soil richer than any other soil in the world.

Then there was Memphis. Before they drove into the village, she saw in the distance the chain of step pyramids of Sakkara. Sakkara is the City of the Dead. The necropolis contains over fourteen pyramids of mastabas and tombs, along with art objects and engravings dating from the Thirtieth Dynasty. It was there that the oldest mummy and the oldest papyrus were found. These pyramids predated those of Giza.

Alexander told her that he would take her there, for he knew Sakkara very well, and the museum archaeologists would be more than happy to show her things that were rarely seen. For example, the Scrapeum, the most curious tomb of the whole necropolis. It was dedicated to Apis the Ox, and the animal was mummified in exactly the same ceremonial fashion as a human being.

"We will talk to Alexis," said Alexander, "and arrange something wonderful, because Sakkara is something very special that he knows well. It was Alexis who taught me to love Sakkara as he does."

And then, suddenly, they were there in the center of the ancient city of Memphis.

Memphis was the City of the Living, as Sakkara was the City of the Dead. There was something about it that Isabel liked at once. On a site in Memphis there is a simple building with a long flight of stairs going up one side of it to a balcony. When Isabel and Alexander arrived at that site, there were no bus tours and no tourists, just a few of the local dragomen who were standing around talking.

"I have a surprise for you," said Alexander. "There is something wonderful here. It will take only a few minutes, and it is something special to see on the way to your wedding and the trip up the Nile."

They left the air-conditioned car and went up the flight of stairs, after being greeted by the dragomen, who all seemed to know Alexander. The doors were thrown open, and they looked down upon the enormous, magnificent, recumbent figure of Ramses II. It was breathtaking, just lying there under a shelter, in this sleepy little village, all that was left of a great dynasty.

Isabel walked the length of the platform with Alexander, looking down upon Ramses. She noticed Alexander look at his watch and smile, and then she knew that they must go. He stopped her, saying no, there was a little more time, and so she kept looking down and studying the colossal sculpture, one of the world's greatest works of art.

She could hear many men talking and a great deal of laughter outside. Other people must have arrived. It was then that Alexander put his arm around her, and the two of them strolled out of the shelter and started down the stairs to the waiting car.

She saw that twenty or thirty villagers had gathered around six magnificently draped and decorated camels and their drivers. She could not believe it. It was Ishta and her keeper, Hosni, and Alexis's camels and drivers from Giza.

"Oh, Alexander, what a surprise, how divine!"

"I cannot take credit for this. It was Alexis. They have come from the desert to escort you from Memphis to the boat. He told me you had a camel escort of sorts when you first arrived in Cairo, and now you have another."

Isabel was almost on the verge of tears at the lovingness of it all, the immense effort that was continually being made to make her happy. She went with Alexander and spoke to the men. They expressed elaborate congratulations through Alexander to Isabel. She went to Ishta and greeted her, seeing she had the great silver neckpiece that she had bought for her happily dangling from her neck.

The head dragoman went to Isabel and extended his good wishes on behalf of himself and the village. He called out an order to someone in the group and, within seconds, two fellahin, draped in black, their eyes heavy with kohl and sweet smiles on their lips, ran up to her in their bare feet and gave her a few pale pink, full-blown roses. They had been nibbled by insects, and were rusted around the edges, but they were from some country garden around Memphis, and the gesture was so sweet that Isabel only saw them as the more special for that. She took them in her hands, and everyone broke out in smiles and chatter.

The dragoman spoke through Alexander and told Isabel that he was touched that she should come to them on the way to her wedding to see Ramses. They knew that the boat was waiting for her and were proud to have a look at the bride who was so beautiful. As the head man of the village, could he please offer a gesture of affection from them all? He handed her from the palm of his hand a small faïence statue of the god Bes. He was very longwinded and flowery in his speech, and she was amused at his pride and touched by his kindness. She thanked him.

Alexander warned her that she had better move because the village was really awake now with the excitement of the wedding. They went quickly into her car. The six riders mounted the decorated camels, and the villagers all milled around as the camels went into position, three on either side of the car. The entourage left the village. It was a happy, gay sight to see. The contrasts of the old and new were fantastic. The sleek, long, green Rolls, purring along with the camels riding close to it as an escort, made its way down a wide dirt road that led to the very bank of the Nile. The villagers were all trailing on foot behind.

Isabel was laughing and felt so joyful as she watched the riders and heard the *hup, hup, hup,* as they drove the beasts on. There was the sound of the men calling out flowery wishes for joy and happiness to the bride as they trotted along close to her car and waved to her. There were sweet songs coming up from the local villagers and their children as well. It was, she thought, all something out of the Arabian Nights.

The tinkling of the camels' bells, the sound of their decorations, were another kind of music that mixed with the dull, thudding sound of their hooves on the sand road.

Alexander was amused, and translated some of the things that the drivers were calling out as they escorted her to her bridegroom. Such things as the beauty of the bride, the sweetness of the day, the joy she would have in the night. They spoke of Egypt and how it would love her and be good to her. Then they called out things about the bridegroom: how he would be kindness itself to the bride and how he would provide for her. How he was a strong man among men. Then they became more bold and spoke of his virility and how he would satisfy her and keep her locked up and full of his seed always.

Alexander laughed and looked at her, bent over and kissed her on the cheek. Taking the Saladin Diamonds in his hands, he played with them and said, "My dear, it is like taking a queen to her wedding."

The road suddenly seemed to come to an end, and the car and camels stopped in a cloud of flying sand. There were a few children waiting at the end of the road and at the beginning of a six-foot-wide path that had been cut through the undergrowth. Boards had been laid, and kilims overlapping each other covered them.

Isabel could see, fifty yards away down the carpeted path, the sails of the felucca at its mooring. The village children in their torn and tattered clothes, with bare, dirty feet and smiling, dirty and scabby faces, peered at her from a distance, all laughing and giggling.

Isabel opened up her compact and did a final check on her face in the small, beveled mirror. She dabbed some powder on her nose and made some adjustments to her hair, closed the compact and, looking at Alexander, said, "Well, this is it."

The two of them left the air-conditioned car. They saw Alexis coming up the path from the felucca. Isabel passed the drivers and the seated camels and thanked them very much. Then she went on to meet Alexis.

She saw his eyes fill with tears over the sheer beauty of her. He thought her magnificent in all her jewels and the Fortuny dress. Her face shone and her soul came forth through her eyes just as he had seen it the first time he saw her in Chicago. He tried to contain himself, to hold back in front of all the people, but he could not help it. He simply gathered her in his arms and kissed her.

Up rose little chuckling noises from the men standing around, sighs from the black-draped ladies and giggles from the children. Alexis got himself under control. "It is not quite right you know. I am supposed to be more cool. But you are so beautiful, I could not help myself."

Isabel looked at this handsome man whom she loved so much and burst into peals of laughter. He was wearing a banana-colored suit for the wedding.

"Yes, I told you I would," he said, laughing, and they

stood facing each other. How clever of him to do something like that, she thought. Something so amusing and intimate, a joke only known between them. It made it all a
bit less serious, their heavy love for each other and the
coming ceremonies.

"Isabel, take off your diamond wedding band and give
it to Alexander." Alexis then gave Alexander a small jew-
elers' box with the ceremonial gold wedding bands, telling
him that when they were called for during the ceremony,
those were the right rings to produce.

He turned to Isabel and told her that during the actual
ceremony each of them would slip a ring on the other's
finger, but he was not a man to wear a wedding band, and
so they had been designed to go as guards on either side
of the diamond wedding ring that now lay in Alexander's
pocket. Alexander would take Alexis's ring back to Cairo
and have it made to the proper size for her.

Just then two servants came up from the boat and
across the kilims with trays of soft fruit drinks and sweet
cakes for the camel drivers, villagers and children standing all around them. Alexis whispered something to Alexander, who said, "Well, old boy, this is it," and the three
friends, Isabel in between the two men, walked down the
kilims to the felucca.

Little children who lived nearby brought forth armfuls
of long-stemmed flowers—Nile flowers, wild field flowers
—and ran in front of the three with smiles and much
laughter and strewed their path of kilims with the blossoms.

Isabel wondered how on earth Alexis had managed all
this.

Later she learned that he owned the farms and mooring
and most of Memphis and that these were actually his
people, as their fathers before them had been and their
fathers before them and on it went, far back into history.

Alexis stepped into the felucca first, helping Isabel, who
was backed up by Alexander. He took her by the waist
and swung her down to the deck. When he felt her breasts
against his chest, he whispered, "I would like to take you
in front of all of them, right now, and forget the ceremony, but I want you to be my wife more."

He put her down, and as he did, a sexual passion
seemed to rage in him for her. He wanted her so much at

that moment that all he could think of was how divine it would be to rape her.

Alexander stepped in between them at that moment and took Isabel by the arm. Alexis kissed her hand, and leaving them, he went forward and stood under the canopy of flowers. The bride and the best man walked arm in arm, slowly, to imaginary music, towards the bow of the felucca.

Isabel was taken aback yet again. It was simple, but exquisite. She saw four poles decorated with green leaves and white camellias. They held up a canopy of palm fronds and white lilies, heavy with scent. Trailing down from the canopy were stephanotis and jasmine.

Alexander felt her surprise. He whispered in her ear, "Alexis thought that there should be at least one Jewish thing about this wedding, hence your *huppah,* darling." They smiled at one another.

The boat seemed to be filled with men. Alexander introduced her to the chief justice of Egypt, who was performing the civil ceremony, and then the High Priest of the Coptic Church, who was a most regal and very pure-looking man. He looked at Isabel in more of a stern than friendly manner. There was also a scribe who sat at a small table with two chairs in front of it. The table was covered with half a dozen seals and stamps and many papers.

Under the canopy of flowers were a pair of high-backed wicker chairs with arms. Casually draped over each was a cloth of gold embroidered with silver pomegranates and a cloth of silver embroidered with golden poppies. Standing in front of the chairs, to the left, was Alexis.

Alexander walked Isabel to the canopy, where Alexis stepped forward and took her hand, leading her the few steps to the chairs. They both sat down. They smiled and chatted to one another while Alexander went to the scribe and recorded the details necessary for the ceremony to take place. That done, he and the chief justice asked them to rise, and suddenly it was all terribly official. The chief justice had trimmed the ceremony down to no more than three minutes, but to Isabel they were the longest three minutes of her life.

The chief justice asked Alexis to take Isabel's hand, and for the first time, she panicked. He felt her hand begin to tremble and held it as tight as he could, hoping to reassure her. Alexis looked down into her face and was almost frightened, for it was as if some great shadow were passing over her.

While the chief justice was performing the ceremony, Isabel gave a great sigh, almost a sob, and then a few tears trickled out of the corners of her eyes. A moment later the life and sparkle flooded back into them again, and she smiled at Alexis just as the chief justice asked Alexander for the rings.

When Alexis kissed her, she looked into his face and found him so handsome in his banana-colored suit, the best suit she had ever seen, with his tie of dark brown, heavy raw silk. He smiled, and the first thing that she said to her husband was, "I never dreamt I could be in love with a man in a banana-colored suit, but I am. Imagine! Enough to marry one! Oh, I do love you," and they kissed.

The chief justice shook Alexis's hand and kissed the bride's hand. Alexander said, "None of that for me," and kissed Isabel on the lips. The High Priest came forward and asked them to be seated as husband and wife under the canopy so that he could take them and put them in the arms of God through the Coptic Church of Egypt.

The two of them sat together, holding hands and looking at each other. The priest performed a two-minute service in the form of a blessing, and then it was over. They were married by the law of the land and the law of God. He congratulated them, and they stood up. Isabel Wells, a Jewish girl from Massachusetts, was married on the Nile in Egypt to the most eligible man in the Middle East.

They thanked him and Isabel mentioned that the priest did not look very happy.

"No, he is not," Alexis said. "He would have liked to carry on for about an hour and a half, giving us the works. Well, I could not have stood that, and, I am sure, neither could you." He put his arm around her and said, "Well, we are married in any event, my love."

They went over to the scribe and sat down to sign paper after paper. Alexander and the chief justice signed as witnesses and at last the scribe stamped and sealed the papers with a flourish.

They stood up, and Alexis said, "Please, everyone, come." To Isabel he said, "We must offer our guests some refreshment before they leave." Isabel had not realized how terribly nervous and excited she must have been, because it was only after she left the canopy a married woman that she realized that they were sailing up the Nile and evidently had been from the time they had boarded the felucca. What had happened was that as soon as the bride was aboard they had cast off into the mainstream of the river.

Gamal stepped forward, wished Isabel well, and they all left the bow of the felucca and went astern, where a lovely table had been set with champagne, caviar and oysters. In the center of the table was a very small three-tiered wedding cake, all iced in white, and on the top was a crystal vase filled with yellow orchids. A breeze had come up and the felucca was sailing with considerable speed. It was Alexander who served the champagne. Alexis plucked a flower from the vase on top of the cake and slipped the stem of the little yellow orchid through the pin under her diamond bumblebee, saying, "Darling, you have no flower on for your wedding." He looked deeply into her eyes and asked if she was all right.

"Yes, I am fine." She smiled up at him.

"You know, you frightened me for a minute during the ceremony. I was afraid that you might pass out or change your mind. It was a good thing I set sail."

"I do not know what happened to me, Alexis. I was fine and then suddenly I felt some life just drain out of me. I have no idea what it was, but then I felt my life flow back into me again. So strange, I cannot imagine what came over me, darling, but I am fine now."

He looked at her finger and the very slim gold ring on it. "When they are all gone, we will take our rings off and read what I have had written inside them, but not now."

Just then Alexander caught them looking at the wedding bands and went over to return the diamond wedding ring to Isabel by slipping it on her finger. At that moment Alexis was distracted by the High Priest. As he slipped the ring onto Isabel's finger, Alexander whispered, "Now I have married you as well," and kissed her on the cheek.

Alexis overheard and teased Alexander, saying, "Yes, my friend, you have. I do not mind sharing her with you, Alexander. After all, you did bring her to me." He then went back to his conversation with the priest, who spoke no English.

Isabel chatted on with Alexander and the chief justice,

who was a charming man, and very amusing about the
fact that he was concerned that he would now have to go
home and explain to his wife that he had just married
Alexis to a beautiful American woman, and why he had
kept the secret, even from her. He finally said, "How does
a man tell his wife he could not confide in her because she
is the most outrageous of all the Cairo gossips? How long
must I keep silent about it?"

Isabel told him he had to ask Alexis. They sailed up
river for about forty-five minutes, and then the felucca
moved into a new, makeshift mooring. Close by, two cars
were parked: One was the plum-colored Rolls and the
other a black Mercedes 600. The chauffeurs stood next to
the cars, waiting for the guests to disembark so that they
could drive them back to Cairo.

Once the felucca came to a stop next to the dock, the
guests all said good-bye very quickly. Within minutes, the
felucca set sail for Upper Egypt.

Alexis, in all the excitement, had forgotten to cut the
wedding cake. He laughed at the idea that he was nervous
enough that all should go well that he forgot something.
"Never mind, darling," he said. "The wedding cake is for
us. We will cut it together tonight."

They walked to the center of the felucca where, on a
raised section of the deck, there were soft silk Oriental
carpets and heavy cushions. There were small ivory-inlaid
tables and a magnificent old brass brazier with a conical
top.

Alexis went first up the steps and then pulled Isabel up
to him. He touched her nipple through her dress as they
fell upon the cushions.

Gamal arrived with an ice bucket and a bottle of chilled
champagne. A hookah was already lit. The smell of the
Indonesian grass reached Isabel even before she drew on
the pipe.

They rested with arms around each other on the cushions. From the raised deck they had a wonderful view of
the river.

They smoked and kissed, and Alexis told her how much
he loved her and how happy he was to have her as his
wife. He fondled her breast and pulled on her nipples
through the silk Fortuny dress. He slipped his hand under
her dress and was surprised and pleased when he found
her so tight he could not get in. He pushed one finger high

into her and felt her divine tightness. He was able to move his finger in and out easily because she was so wet.

"Oh, my dear, tonight you will be loved like you have never been before. The old woman has done well by us for our wedding night. We will have a delicious time opening you back to your normal size. How did it feel when I was touching you?"

"Alexis," Isabel asked. "What has she done to me? Every part of me is ten times more sensitive to your touch. When you were simply playing with my labia, I had to bite the inside of my cheek not to scream from passion."

Alexis teased her, saying that all the city of Memphis would be thinking about the beautiful bride in her sparkling jewels tonight. That the men would be thinking of ways that they would take her, the women would have endless discussions among themselves about her cunt and then about the size of his cock.

"About my cunt? Alexis, you are exaggerating. Why ever would they think about my cunt?"

"Oh, my dear, among Egyptian women of the village class the curiosity would be high. They would be very interested in your cunt and what it looked like and what had been done to it. You know, all of the women you have seen have been circumcised. Their clitorises have been removed."

"Alexis, I know that it is done occasionally, but surely not to all women?"

"No, not all women, but ninety percent of them. And in the villages you can be sure it is one hundred percent. Here in Egypt we have three forms of circumcision for women. The mildest is known as sunna, the tip is removed and the labia minora. The next stage involves taking a bigger piece of the clitoris. But the most dramatic of all is what they call the Pharaonic method—total removal of the clitoris and the labia minora. The vagina is then stitched up. Some of the Sudanese tribes do this with thorns, leaving only a small opening for menstruation and urination. On the wedding night the bridegroom rips the thorns out and then fucks his lady, if she can take it.

"Don't look so appalled, darling, most of the women in Egypt have suffered the milder method of sunna and it is done when they are between the ages of six and ten. Now you understand why they will all be wondering what your cunt is like."

Alexis bent over and kissed her tenderly, and said, "Actually, I would love them to see it because it is so divine—the color, the size. Your clitoris, so sensitive and lovely, and how you are always wet. Yes, if I were to show you to them, to go down on you and they were to see the pleasure that you get, that would do more to reform the practice of circumcision in Egypt than all the campaigns at work!"

He laughed at her and pinched her nipple and said, "Let them wonder and have a good time thinking about us. Tonight is, after all, our night, and I hope the whole world is as happy as we are."

She unzipped his fly, bent her head down and took Alexis in her mouth and sucked on him for a few seconds, tenderly. When she stopped, he said, "More, more," and she laughed and said, "No, darling, no more. I do not want to get lipstick on your banana-colored trousers."

With much difficulty, she managed to put his tumescent cock back into his trousers and zip him up. She snuggled up next to him, and he said, "I will get you tonight and make you pay for teasing me like that."

They lay there quietly in each other's arms listening to the sounds of the river, the distant sounds of birds and cicadas coming from the bank, the occasional order being given from below somewhere on the felucca.

Suddenly Alexis sat bolt upright and struck his forehead. "A wedding picture! We do not have a wedding picture. Shall we have one of us lying here among the cushions in all our wedding clothes?"

"Oh, that is a good idea."

He clapped his hands and called for Gamal to bring a camera. He pulled her up and arranged some cushions the way he thought they would look best. He used Gamal as a stand-in while he set up the camera. When he had everything just as he wanted it, then Gamal and he switched places and Gamal punched the button.

"There we are, darling, our first picture together." Alexis smiled. He slapped Isabel on the ass. "Now let's go down below and get out of our wedding clothes."

There was one huge room below the main deck, and it was quite amazing. It stretched from the center of the felucca to the stern. It was a bedroom-cum-sitting-room with a huge bed that could have slept four. The bed was covered with a mustard-yellow kilim. It was very old, worn almost thin in places, and the pattern was a big and bold geometric, very beautiful and very rare. The cushions thrown on it were oversize and covered with other kilims in shades of yellow and white, with a strong accent of terracotta color.

The walls of the room were of white linen, and the carpet on the floor was a huge, red, antique Bokhara. One of the walls was a cupboard made of antique mushrabiya in its naturally dark wood color. There was also a white marble desk, quite large, with a walnut-and-cane chair for it, and a pair of easy chairs, covered in the same white linen as the walls. Above the bed hung the Modigliani nude, given to Alexis by his mother.

Isabel told Alexis that she thought the room was superb. He smiled and began to undress her, saying that there was something else about the room: It was air-conditioned and sound-proofed. "So, my darling, you will be able to scream to your heart's content when I beat you, and no one will ever hear. Come! I think I will make love to you."

Alexis had removed the Saladin necklaces and dropped them on the bed and now he undid the bumblebee and dropped that on the bed, too. He took the diamonds from her ears and lifted the Fortuny dress over her head. He looked at his wife and folded her in his arms, tight against him, telling her how lovely he found her.

It was true, Isabel knew. The girls had elongated her nipples a quarter to a half inch. She could see from the way that Alexis looked at them that he liked that very much. He took one in his mouth and sucked on it, telling her how much he liked her nipples that way, and that she must work to keep them like that. Would she do that for him?

Yes, she would do that for him. Isabel smiled. She stood on the bed as he requested. He opened the lips of her vagina and put his tongue on her clitoris, moving it round and round. He sat on the bed and she lowered herself above his face. With his tongue he went into her, then he pulled her down on his lap.

"Tonight, darling, I will take you like an Arab man takes his virgin," he murmured. "We will wait for now, but tonight, after I have broken you in, then I will do wonderful things to you. You will have a little pain, I think, because you are so tight, but you can pretend you are a virgin. We will make love all night and before you sleep, you will know that you are not. I will never let you sleep until you feel like a spent, satiated whore. Will you like that?"

Isabel was completely spellbound. When they kissed, she knew that Alexis was, as well.

They both changed their clothes. He put on a simple white cotton galabia, and Isabel put on her tobacco raw-silk one, and the great silver and amber necklace that he had given her. In her ears she put the Phoenician gold loops. Alexis rang for Gamal, who was instructed to gather up the jewels on the bed and put them in the safe. He sent Isabel with Gamal so she could learn to open it and be able to take what she wanted from it, when she pleased. After, Gamal remained behind and put their things away while they went to explore.

The felucca was a large one, very traditional in style, and about seventy years old. It was brilliantly fitted out. It did not look like a luxury boat, but rather like a simple, large, working craft of the Nile. The crew of four wore no uniform of any kind, but simple cotton galabias and white turbans. As extra hands, Alexis had brought Gamal and Doreya to serve them. The crew's quarters were in the lower level, up in the bow of the felucca and completely away from Alexis and Isabel.

The deck was sectioned off into a dining area and the raised section. The dining area was out in the open, and since it hardly ever rained, there was little problem about that. When it did rain, there was a canopy that could be pulled across on cables. Today there was an extra addition on the deck, the flowered *huppah*.

When they looked at the *huppah* and its flowers, they both decided to have a large double bed made up under it for their first night as man and wife. Alexis called Gamal and told him. Just as the servant was leaving, he was called back and given more instructions. Gamal disappeared down in the bow of the boat.

A few minutes later, up out of nowhere rushed Winston and Rita. They had been hidden away in Gamal's cabin. They barked and howled and jumped and leaped all over the couple. Isabel was overjoyed.

"Now, darling, with all that noise, you are sure to think you are at home," Alexis kidded.

She kissed him and said he was wonderful. He replied by saying that he knew that, and if he needed any proof, keeping those two dogs was it. "By God, they are spoiled, Isabel. Will you spoil me as much?"

She said, "Yes, but only in bed."

They lay among the cushions and talked. The sun went down and suddenly it was dark. Gamal and Doreya had lit the candles in the old pierced-copper and glass lanterns so that the felucca was lit up in soft yellow candlelight.

Alexis suggested to Isabel that she go downstairs and put on her chocolate-brown lace nightdress and peignoir. "They are going to set all the food out in a buffet for us, and we will serve ourselves. They are going to drop anchor a bit further up near a village where they know the boat will be safe. The crew, all the crew, including Doreya and Gamal, will take the dinghy and row ashore to celebrate our wedding. They will not come back until the early morning so that we can have our wedding night alone on the felucca."

"Just the two of us is perfect!" Isabel exclaimed. "I would love that."

"And the dogs, of course?" Alexis teased.

"Yes, and the dogs, of course," she agreed, laughing, and went below to change.

The bathroom aboard the felucca was large and included a bathtub for two, a dressing room and a pair of washbasins. The fittings were white, while the entire bathroom was in beige travertine marble. All the towels were mustard-yellow and there were kilims on the marble floor.

After she had bathed and put on fresh makeup, she slipped into the magnificent nightdress he had bought her for this night.

Isabel looked at herself in it and realized what great erotic feelings and fantasies Alexis must have about her. The nightgown was elegant but evoked a feeling of base sexuality. Her nipples and the dark flesh around them protruded through the openings in the lace, and the slits up the side exposed her thighs, hips and legs. It was, without question, a nightdress to tantalize the sexual appetites of a man. When she put the peignoir over it and pinned the diamond dragonfly at the closing under her breasts, she realized that she did not feel like Isabel at all, but like some sexual object designed, prepared and ready for her man to use.

She was deeply excited. This would be a night of pure sexuality. Tonight she would use Alexis as the sexual animal that he was, and together they would reach new heights, as husband and wife.

She sighed and went to the safe for her diamond earrings. She would wear them this evening.

When Alexis came for her, she was looking out of the oversized portholes to the banks of the river. She could see fires twinkling in the distances.

He looked at her and said, "I cannot believe we have done it, and you are my wife."

He could not help but take each of her nipples in his hands and roll them around with his fingers. Then they went up on deck together.

The felucca looked an absolute dream. It was totally silent on board except for the sounds of the Nile lapping up against the boat, and Rita and Winston, who were on the raised deck lying among the cushions, snoring away.

The deck was lit by lanterns, and under the *huppah* of flowers a large bed had been made and covered in silk embroideries. It looked like the most magnificent four-poster bed in the world with its canopy of glorious flowers above.

Towards the stern of the boat a sumptuous table had been laid. There were quail in a casserole of rice, several different salads and fruits, along with cheeses and baked ham. And for dessert—the wedding cake.

When they cut their wedding cake, both their hands were on the knife. They repeated their vows exactly as they had under the *huppah,* only hours before. She knew then that he loved her in a way that she had never been loved. It was all that she had ever wanted.

They kissed each other, their mouths tasting of the sweet and rich wedding cake. They went up and lay among the cushions on the raised deck. They found set on one of the small ivory-inlaid tables a jug of hot, sweet coffee, and a pair of small cups on a tray. Alexis poured for them, and they sipped and smiled at each other lovingly.

He leaned back, took a box from one of the tables and prepared a few lines of coke. They sniffed them and floated off together as the boat rocked them gently. Occasionally they could hear laughter above the cicadas' symphony, somewhere in the distance. They lay on their backs looking up at a ceiling of stars, like diamonds thrown helter-skelter on black velvet.

They were silent now for a very long time. He pulled

her up to her feet, undid the dragonfly and took off the peignoir. He undid his kaftan and dropped it where they were standing. He picked up a large box from among the cushions and put one arm around her waist; they started down the stairs. He moved his hand from her waist to the cheek of her ass and walked her that way to the bed under the huppah.

He put the large box and the small box of coke down among the cushions and looked at her, taking her in his arms. His cock was huge and erect. With one hand around it, he lifted it and offered it to her; with the other he held his scrotum.

She dropped to her knees, ready to make love to him, but he caught her as she was going down and he lifted her. She could feel his erection pushing against her, he held her so tight to him.

"No, do nothing now," he told her. "I want to take you, make love to you, be tender and cruel to you and keep doing it for a long time. You must not touch me yet. Later, much later, I will give myself to you. It will be different for you tonight. You will be very tight. I will play on you, work on you, open you wide again."

He took the little box of coke and put his fingers in it and rubbed it on her nipples and then put a bit on the tip of her tongue. It made her feel instantly sexier as he went down and sucked the coke off her nipples. All the time his hands were moving over her hindquarters, separating them and pushing them together. Finally he lifted her nightdress over her head and then caught her breasts as they fell into the palms of his hands.

He put his finger inside her, and she was wet. He pushed up as high as he could and found her very tight. Reaching over to the large box, he took out a small jar of cream, and rubbed it high up into her vagina.

Isabel was longing to have him. She knew her smallness excited him so that he grew to even larger proportions. She could feel the throbbing of his blood pumping in his penis.

Alexis moved himself slowly along the outside of her genitals and then between the wet and slippery lips. Finally he dipped the very tip of it into the small opening of her vagina. She was amazed at how small the opening was. She wanted him so much, but now she was afraid that he would never get it into her. He was tender with her about it and treated her as if she were a virgin bride. He slowly managed to get the head of his cock inside her.

With his arms under her armpits, he drew her up towards him, her legs high up now on his shoulders. He kissed her, and when he saw her passion rising, he let her down gently on the cushions. Then, pulling her legs even higher on his shoulders, he felt her wet orgasm running over the knob of his cock. Suddenly he rammed as hard as he could up through her, and she screamed from the pain.

Although Isabel had screamed, at that very same moment she was flooded with an enormous orgasm. That first scream was not the only one that came from the felucca that night. It was as if she had been a virgin. Whatever the old woman had done, she had done well for the both of them. Alexis had her many times. They slept in between and were never satiated.

The sun came up and the lanterns were still burning when Alexis lay looking at the sleeping Isabel. He wanted to see the sun rise on the Nile with his wife, and so he woke her by gently spreading her legs and licking her like a pussycat.

She woke from his tongue and lazily sat up. She kissed him good morning while he slipped her nightgown over her head. He lifted her breasts and adjusted them in her gown by drawing the nipples into the holes cut through the lace. Then he cupped her breasts in his hands and smiled at her. He found her peignoir where they had dropped it the night before, and he helped her on with it.

She took his kaftan and dressed him, tying the strings on the side. Then they went together to the bow of the felucca and, stepping up on the small raised platform, sat on some cushions and watched the sun rise.

They heard the sounds of early morning—birds, and the rustling of small animals on the banks of the river. Far up the Nile, in the magnificent sunrise, they saw a felucca in full sail. The sun was up about half an hour when they heard voices and turned to see the dinghy coming towards the *Mamounia* with the crew, Gamal and Doreya.

Alexis said, "Come, let's pick up our things from under the canopy and go to bed below."

She picked up the cocaine box, and in the larger box he put the jars of ointments and the other accessories they had used. He noticed a few bloodstains on the cushions, and for all his Western education, the Arab in him came out and he felt a kind of pride. He quickly turned Isabel away from seeing them, but it was too late.

Isabel looked at him and said, "We have to be the most depraved, debauched couple in the world," and had the good grace to blush.

"Yes, aren't we lucky!" Alexis roared.

They laughed and then hurried down to the cabin before everyone arrived on board.

Isabel was awake, that is, her mind was awake, but her body was asleep, and her eyes were still closed. She was feeling very lazy and sensual. She felt herself moving up and down and round and round with her pelvis, hardly moving the rest of her body. She opened her eyes and realized that she was moving with Alexis's cock. She closed her eyes again and reached out her arms to pull him against her. They kissed, and he said, "Good morning, my lady wife."

Isabel opened her eyes again and smiled up at him. They rolled together on their sides and faced each other as he kept pumping in and out. He had her coming now in stronger orgasms, could wait no longer himself. He let go and flooded her. Isabel squeezed hard on him, and he felt himself held there by her. They kissed while they were together like that and then lay there and dozed.

Much later Alexis woke and unfolded himself from Isabel and went into the bathroom. He ran the bath and filled it with a wonderful scent and soap bubbles while he shaved. Later he went back to kiss Isabel awake, then dragged her out of bed and into the double bathtub with him. She had only just enough time to wrap a towel around her hair and brush her teeth while Alexis ordered breakfast for them.

When they finally went up on deck and were greeted by some of the crew and Gamal, they realized they had slept the day away. It was five in the afternoon. They sat in their simple white galabias on the beautiful felucca that was in full sail, making great speed up the Nile. Isabel adored the movement of the boat, and loved watching the crew at work. They were all smiles and happy to be traveling up the river.

When she spoke about it to Alexis, he said, "You cannot imagine how proud they are to be taking us on our wedding trip. They love the Nile and the felucca and are very proud of their skills. It is the epitome, the peak, to be taking the new lady of the house on her first trip, and her wedding trip at that, on the river."

She left Alexis at the table and wandered around the boat. She found a place for herself up on the right-hand side, in the bow, and watched them plough through the river. She could see the banks on either side and the view straight ahead. Her mind drifted off, thinking of nothing. She just went with the rhythm of the boat and the beauty of her life.

In time she went back to Alexis and poured herself another cup of coffee. He was smiling over the gossip of the night before told to him by Gamal. The servants had all had a wonderful time at his wedding party on the shore. There was a great deal of dancing, feasting with the village people and lovemaking with the paid women sent to them by Alexis.

Alexis told all this to Isabel and then said, "You have no idea how proud they are of our passion."

"Passion?" Isabel began to blush. "What do they know of our passion?"

Alexis laughed and said, "Yes, my dear, passion. Every time you let out a scream, which, by the way, resounded over the water, it was a sign of how successful the marriage would be." He patted her on the cheek and said, "Never mind, Gamal has been with me a long time and he knows everything, darling. But we will not allow them to see everything."

Seeing Isabel's embarrassment, he was quick to add, "They heard me scream as well, and knew then that we would be happy always. It seems that our passion fired quite an orgy among our crew."

Just then Gamal arrived with a silver tray. On it were half a dozen letters. Alexis picked them up, and Isabel asked how they had got there.

"They were brought aboard by Alexander yesterday," he explained. "I gave instructions only to send post that will keep me abreast of things going on but do not need my attention."

He took an antique, Islamic, inlaid gold-and-bronze letter opener and opened some envelopes, reading the letters as he went on chatting with Isabel. Then in the middle of the pile he found Kate's postcard to Isabel. Alexis did not read it, but when he picked it up, an ominous feeling went through him. He handed it to Isabel, saying, "Darling, this one is for you."

Isabel read the postcard. When she finished, she handed it to him, saying, "My mother is incorrigible."

Alexis was puzzled by the card. He found Kate's actions extraordinary. He asked Isabel, "Why did she send this calculated and, I might add, very unattractive card, instead of calling us?"

"Alexis, do not even begin to try to understand." Isabel groaned. "It is all done to keep me feeling guilty. I am afraid that in the last act of her life, she will still be trying to make me feel guilty for something I cannot give her or do for her. Just leave it to Kate to find me, even in the middle of the Nile on my first day as your wife, not to send love, but to make some strange point."

"My dear Isabel, she is far more clever in her sickness than that. The card arrived yesterday, on our wedding day. Please, let us not think about it. You are not upset, are you?"

"No, Alexis, she is far away by now. I cannot explain it, but it is almost as if some mad woman I have heard about does these things. For the first time in my life, I don't even think of Kate my mother being alive any more. Do you know, since I stepped on this boat with you, I haven't even thought of her. Do you know, Alexis, this is the first time in my life that twenty-four hours have passed without my even thinking of her once! Not only does she not affect me, but she no longer exists. I only wish, for her own sake, that she would stop and lie back and enjoy the rest of her life. But she will not. All I can do now is not think about her anymore." With that, Isabel began to cry softly.

Alexis was very angry. There was something so unhealthy, so destructive, so unloving about the postcard from Kate. He remembered her voice on the telephone and wondered why this woman, whom he had not even met, so upset him.

Alexis had never been involved with anyone as common as Kate Wells. He did not want to pursue it with Isabel, but he hoped that it *was* true that she no longer existed for Isabel. As far as Alexis Hyatt was concerned, a woman like that had no place in his world *or* his wife's. He would in time make that very clear, not to Isabel, but to his mother-in-law.

He pulled Isabel down and sat her next to him. Isabel put her arm around him and kissed him on the cheek. As she did, she picked up the postcard and balled it up in her fist, then tossed it into the wind.

Together they went forward and he pointed things out to her about the river. He called for a pair of very powerful binoculars and they saw the wild flowers on the bank and tiny birds that had been hiding from the sun and were now coming out. He had a map brought for them and he laid it out so that they could follow every kilometer of the trip.

Their cruise was the sort that lovers dream about all of their lives. They made love whenever and wherever they wanted. They slept, they spoke and they learned a great deal about each other. The more they learned, the happier they were. They visited tiny little villages, spoke to the people and rode out to almost unknown and certainly unseen pyramids.

They stopped only if they would not be involved with large communities. Wherever they went, it was a country of endless beauty and monumental surprises. They traveled in luxury and were welcomed everywhere with warmth and hospitality.

When Isabel went ashore with Alexis on their archaeological excursions or to the villages where she was sent to sit with the women, she wore long thin cotton dresses in order not to offend anyone. They were like loose smocks, with long, full sleeves. She usually wore her silver-and-amber necklaces and covered herself with fantastic, barbaric-looking, antique silver and cornelian jewelry, such as is worn by the women of the desert tribes of Arabia. They were all gifts that Alexis kept pulling out of nowhere and presenting to her.

She covered her long, chestnut-colored hair with floppy straw hats, or colored chiffon scarves. She wore open sandals and rolled up her sleeves when it was the proper thing to do. Alexis was proud of her sensitivity to the customs of his country.

News went fast up the Nile, and after a while the felucca was eagerly awaited in every village. They were made welcome everywhere by the country people, who were proud to present their great sights of antiquity. The people laid feasts of simple food for the couple, and after they had left, Alexis always took note of what the villages needed the most, later arranging for such things to be sent.

After they left Malawi, they docked for two days to see the Northern Tombs, the Royal Tombs. The men of the village made a large feast for them and performed country dances, and there was much laughter. Isabel began to realize that these people knew Alexis well. He later explained that his family on his father's side were great landowners in that part of the desert for hundreds and hundreds of years. Wherever they traveled, he would be well known.

The next mooring was at El Qusiya, where Alexis told Isabel to pack a few things, because they would sleep on shore for two or three days. The felucca docked and Isabel could see a place had been cleared for them along the bank. There were about a dozen village people standing about, and, to Isabel's astonishment, there they were— Alexis's six camels and their drivers, all waiting.

She looked at Alexis, who was laughing at her surprise; he was delighted with himself. She could hardly resist it and went up to Alexis and kissed him. Her enthusiasm for all that he did fired him as it always did. He looked around, and seeing everyone busy docking, he quickly slipped his hand under her dress as he stood just slightly behind her. He played with her and kissed her at the same time on her lips, saying to her, "I am having the most wonderful time of my life. I will thank you every day as long as I live with my love."

He kissed her again, and as he did, he put three fingers into her and moved them around; she closed her eyes for a second and sighed with the pleasure that he induced. When he felt her come all over his fingers, he wanted her right there and then. She saw through his trousers that he was hard and just how much he did want her.

They forgot about everything happening around them for the moment and just vibrated their sexuality at each other. His fingers lingered and played with her insides, and he sighed heavily with passion for her. She wanted to go down on him right there and then, make love to him and take him in her mouth, but they both knew that their desire had to wait. He stepped back and took a handkerchief from his pocket to wipe his hands. "A pity, darling. I would love to lick my fingers, but I think people might think that a bit strange!"

They both laughed and, arm in arm, walked over to the table where he had spread out their map to show her where they were. He explained, "Listen, darling, there is an old rattletrap of a car that is at your disposal. It belongs to one of the village elders, and he would be delighted for you to ride in it to the monastery and the necropolis at Mira. I will ride with the men on camels and meet you there, unless you want to go on Ishta. It is only a few miles to the monastery, but I think it would be more fun for you to go out by car accompanied by Doreya, and then from the monastery to ride through the desert with us to the Rocky Tombs."

She went down and changed into a pair of long, wide, cotton trousers that looked like a divided skirt and a voluminous cotton shirt which hung over the trousers with huge loose sleeves, and over it she tied a soft sash of the same material. It was the color of putty, and her great silver-and-amber necklaces and silver earrings made her look as if she belonged there.

She was at a loss about what to do with her hair. Alexis watched her as she finished putting on her sandals. He told her he found her perfect as always and called for Doreya, who pinned Isabel's hair up and wound a turban of white cotton over it, leaving one long end draped over her shoulder and down her front. On the side of the turban she pinned a great silver-and-amber broach and then showed Isabel how to drape the long end of the turban over the bottom half of her face and hook it onto the brooch. A sort of yashmak in case the sand started to get up her nose and in her mouth.

Alexis wore a white open shirt of finest batiste cotton and a pair of white cotton trousers. They were held in place by a brown alligator belt. Around his neck he tied a red-and-white cotton scarf, and she laughed at him and said, "You learned that from John Wayne, now, didn't you?"

He laughed and said, "Darling, my ancestors were wearing scarves to keep the sand out of their mouths long before your people massacred all the Indians," and smacked her on her bottom.

He went to the mirror and put on his old, battered, white Panama hat that had come long ago from Herbert Johnson in London. She looked at him and thought. *My God, he cuts a dashing figure, my husband does,* and smiled at him. She also thought to herself how clever he was to have chosen that kind of outfit rather than to have done himself up as the Arab sheikh on his camel.

Doreya and Isabel rode to the monastery in the desert, jostled around in the old mongrel of a car, after they had seen the men ride off on the camels. Doreya did her best to make Isabel understand that Alexis was a very important man in the district of Asyut. There were literally thousands of people in the area who looked to him as a leader. Isabel was very proud of him and loved watching him ride with the men.

The belt of green close to the Nile was so fertile, but then suddenly it stopped and they rode through the desert to the necropolis of Myra. It was wonderful to see the monastery rise up out of nowhere in the sand, and long before entering it, one felt a serenity, a sense of purity, that was uplifting. Isabel felt its vastness and the excitement of being a guest in the history of mankind. The silence was all around them.

By the time they left the monastery, it was very late in the day, and Isabel mounted Ishta with little difficulty. Hosni rode on one side of her and Alexis on the other. Isabel was comfortable riding and pleased that she was not feeling the waves of sickness she had experienced a few times on other occasions when she had been on a camel. The desert was so clean and smooth with its patterns of rippling waves made by the wind. The endless changing color of it, with the shadows and the sun. Its emptiness enveloped her, and she was almost swallowed up by the atmosphere. No one spoke as they rode almost three hours at a slow pace to their camp.

When night was almost upon them they caught sight of three open fires and three great, sprawling, black Bedouin tents.

The camp was primitive and wonderful, but Isabel was very tired and hot, dusty and very thirsty. Doreya came forward and brushed some of the sand from her and then removed her turban.

Alexis came to her, and smiling broadly, he said, "You are wonderful. I am so proud of you and your enthusiasm for my country," and as he spoke, he walked her into one of the tents, pulling the hairpins from her hair and arranging it as it fell to her shoulders.

The tent was very simple, with many cushions scattered

over the kilims covering the sand; lanterns were lit. From
the entrance of the tent they could see many people outside: camel drivers with their camels sitting around the
fire and being tended to, visitors from the villages close to
the camp who brought fruits, cakes and sweets, flat bread
and village goat cheese.

Isabel stayed in her tent while Alexis went to sit in the
guest tent and have coffee with the men and talk. It was
exciting and at the same time clever of him to let her
taste desert life with him alone. Doreya brought brass
troughs of water for her to wash in, a long, ruby-red, fine
wool dress that was cut low in the front and back, and a
shawl to match, with a deep, silk fringe, to protect her
from the cool night air. On her neck she put the scarab
necklace. She made up her face and lay among the cushions, resting and watching Alexis and the people across
from her, a hundred yards away.

She drank hot, sweet tea and nibbled on some bread
and cheese, and waited. In time Alexis came to her and
told her she was looking divine. Doreya brought him
fresh water to bathe in and a black, fine wool galabia
trimmed in gold. The flaps to the tent had been dropped
and Doreya, acting as his valet, helped him to undress,
bathe and change. Isabel watched them. He was in a
wonderful mood and very busy giving instructions to
Doreya as she washed him.

When he was dressed he pulled Isabel up off the cushions, telling her he found her ravishing in the red. He
covered her exposed front by draping the shawl around
her and said it would be best to keep it that way until
they were alone together.

Isabel took note that he did not touch her again once
the tent flaps were opened. They went in to supper and
sat down together. Only after they were seated did all the
guests, all men, enter the tent and sit down. As Alexis introduced her to them each stood up, bowed and said
something in Arabic to her and sat down again.

They ate delicious lamb and rice and bowls of hot
moulihaya. Then some sweet cakes. After about an
hour and a half, Doreya went to Isabel and whispered in
her ear that Alexis wanted her to retire. She got up and
no one, not even Alexis, paid any attention to her leaving.
She understood and made her exit discreetly.

It was another hour and a half before Alexis went to

her. All he said as he undressed was, "You were a great success, darling. I am sure they will all go looking for red dresses for their favorite wives now. Did you enjoy the evening?"

"It was fantastic, Alexis, but I did feel I was intruding because I know that women are not ordinarily at dinners like that."

"Well, you behaved perfectly and I adore you and I will not wait one more minute. I want you." Alexis seemed so different that night in the desert. More wild, not brutal, but maybe more primitive and fierce in his passion for her.

She loved his wildness and reacted to it but tried to control her own passion because she was afraid people might hear her outside.

He slapped her gently but strong enough for her to know that it was a reprimand, saying, "Never hold back with me. Never! You let go as loud as you like and as much as you want. It is part of our whole love, your never holding back. I do not care who hears us, it is your very passion, and the life that constantly flows from you that enthralls me."

Then he kept driving into her, until she lost control in a huge wave of orgasm. Her scream was followed shortly by his.

Never in her life had Isabel wanted sex more. She felt such an animal with Alexis. He always like to take her in the morning, but *this* morning, she climbed on *him*. Now it was her turn: She wanted to take him in the desert. She drove him mad with her cunt as he had driven her mad the night before until they lay in each other's arms and decided, laughing, that they were disgusting. Two lovers of their age with such passion!

Finally they dressed and went out for breakfast very early in the morning. They spent a second night in the desert, broke camp on the third day and traveled a good distance up the desert in those three days. The *Mamounia* was docked and waiting to carry on up the Nile. An old, battered car took them from the camp through the desert and into the lovely green belt close to the Nile.

The moment they were on board the crew went to work pulling up sails. Orders were called, and the wind filled the sails almost at once. They looked at each other with smiles, but said nothing. There was no need to articulate their happiness.

They were on their way when they went down and bathed together. Very tired, they climbed into bed and fell fast asleep.

It was the next morning, while Alexis was shaving and Isabel had gone up on deck, when Gamal went to his master. They spoke, and then Gamal handed him two cablegrams that had been brought to the boat by one of Alexis's agents.

The first cablegram that Alexis read was from Alfred More, in Athens, informing Isabel of the circumstances concerning her sister Ava's death by drowning. Alexis put down the cablegram and opened the other one; it was from the S.S. *Aphrodite,* and detailed Kate's death. He put both cablegrams in the pocket of his robe and finished shaving.

Once in the bedroom, he lay down on the bed. He was thinking of Isabel and how bruised her heart would be when she heard the news that her mother and sister had died so quickly and so closely without ever resolving their relationship with her.

He knew how happy Isabel was with him. How ironic that these two tragedies should happen almost at the same time, on her happiest day, her wedding day. Alexis felt a deep sorrow for Isabel, and this last burden she must bear from her family.

This sorrow certainly ended any spiritual separation and estrangement which might have existed between Alexis and Isabel, for, as he lay there thinking about it all, he was aware of guilt for the first time in his life. Previously, this force in his wife's life had been foreign to him.

He could now understand and detest it. This tragedy would only bring him and Isabel closer. They would pity each other for the burden now laid upon them and love each other more for it. If their bodies were already united by pleasure, now their souls could be united, in pain.

Those two extraordinary women who had kept Isabel anxious, unhappy, and unfulfilled all of her life, through death would bring her love. The more barriers their tragic lives interposed between the lovers, the stronger the impulse would be for the couple to love each other.

Alexis lay there quietly for a very long time. Finally he

made a decision. He would carry the burden of this monstrous situation by keeping it to himself. He would tell her when they reached Abu Simbel. It would be soon enough for the horrors of the outside world to come in on them.

And so the weeks passed, and Alexis and Isabel did fall more and more in love with each other. They spent their days and nights in sexual communion, and their souls began to meet.

On this sublime journey up the Nile, destiny was playing an extraordinary role in their lives. The Nile, this magnificent river under whose spell Isabel had fallen and on which she was reborn. Every time Alexis made love to her, she died for that split-second with every orgasm.

They lost track of time and spent their days and nights with whatever and whoever came before them. They sometimes sat at night by fires in the desert, not far from the moored felucca and spoke to primitive people of their life and their world.

By this time the intense love they felt allowed them to talk to each other from their souls and hearts. It was a new revelation for both of them. They may have loved passionately, but they also loved gaily and lightly.

Once Alexis turned her over on deck and entered her from behind, sure that the crew could not see them. Once, in the dark of the night, while they sat with three village men talking under the stars, Isabel, sure that they could not see, unzipped his trousers and took him in her mouth as he talked to the men.

They were naughty lovers. Risks became part of their sexual play. They had each other for their own amusement as well as their passion and their love.

Isabel thought of nothing but took every hour and every day as it came. Then they were there. They had sailed 768 miles up the Nile, and had reached Abu Simbel, the most colossal of all the temples of Egypt. The preservation and setting were unbelievable. The temple was carved out of the side of a sandstone cliff facing east, to let the rising sun penetrate the inner sanctuary.

It was exactly at sunrise that the *Mamounia* sailed before Abu Simbel. Alexis and Isabel were standing on the raised deck as the temple lit up with the day. A felucca pulled up close to the anchored *Mamounia,* and on

board were two old friends of Alexis. One was the head
man of Upper Egypt, a grand old fellow with great white
flowing robes and a huge white turban. He carried the
staff of Upper Egypt, a sign of his authority. He shook the
staff at Alexis, shouting out, "Welcome to you and your
bride. You will be my guests, Alexis, I will take you to
Abu Simbel this time."

Word had been sent weeks before about their eventual
arrival, and since Alexis had been instrumental in saving the temple, there was nothing that they would not do
to make him and his bride welcome.

With the old man was another old friend. He was one
of the archaeologists responsible for the moving and preservation of Abu Simbel.

Alexis was delighted to see the old man, said to be in
his ninety-eighth year. He had adored and known him all
of his life. He whispered to Isabel that this was one of the
great characters of his country, a brave, courageous man
of the desert.

Isabel had on a long smock of rough white cheesecloth,
cut with a round neckline that went to just below her
collar bone. She had on her Bedouin silver-and-amber
necklace. Her hair hung down around her shoulders and
she wore a wide-brimmed Panama hat that kept her face
and shoulders out of the sun.

They changed feluccas among endless instructions from
everyone on how she should jump on board. Eventually
she became frozen with fear until Gamal took over. He
simply threw her across into Alexis's arms.

"You silly thing, why ever did you not jump? You will
always be safe with me." Alexis smiled at her and put
her down.

She was introduced to the handsome, dark, wrinkled
ancient man, Hamouda, and the archaeologist, Nassim.
Several women, all draped in their black robes and covered with gold jewelry, hovered around and presented her
with armfuls of flowers. They giggled and smiled at her
and took her off to one side when Alexis was swept up by
the old man and Nassim. After coffee they sailed straight
for the temple.

Two days and one night of celebrations arranged by
Hamouda were held in their honor. As if by magic, a full,
pure white moon appeared over Abu Simbel, and dozens

of feluccas brought guests to the very foot of the temple where a temporary dock had been made.

The temple, measured from the facade to the innermost chamber, was over two hundred feet long. The first room had a ceiling supported by eight columns faced with huge statues of Ramses II in the pose of the god Osiris. The ceiling and walls were magnificently decorated, and the colors in most places were still brilliant.

It was in this first room that huge tables had been set up and laden with flowers and silver platters of food. The entire temple was lit by torchlight.

There were a hundred guests invited to honor the wedding couple, and everyone sat on the carpets that had been laid over the floor of the vast echoing space, now filled with flowers and laughter for this night. Mountains of fruits, pigeons, huge fish from the Nile and meats roasted with herbs were passed around the table endlessly.

Hamouda outdid himself. It was a reception almost unimaginable in splendor. He sat Isabel next to him and Alexis on his other side. Isabel had dressed magnificently for the occasion. She wore all of her jewels, including the Saladin Diamonds, over a long, paper-thin, white cotton evening dress that was completely accordion-pleated. When she walked into the temple, people gasped. Her dress was not unlike some seen in the ancient paintings on the tomb walls. Her hair was freshly washed and seemed to light up from the glow that her jewels gave. She was dazzling as she floated through the temple, meeting everyone.

Hamouda jabbered on to her all through the evening, but since she understood nothing she just kept smiling and nodding. Three-quarters of the way through the evening, he reached out and touched the Saladin Diamonds and in so doing, touched her nipple. Both she and Alexis noticed it. Alexis could not help but smile, and he gave her a sign not to make a fuss. She understood, although she did wonder when Hamouda turned to Alexis, who roared with laughter over what the old man said.

After the meal, which went on for hours and hours, there were exquisite folk and belly dancers. Then it was over.

After all the thanks and good-byes were made, they sailed away on the *Mamounia*. The felucca was in the mainstream of the river when the sun began inching its way off the Nile, across the sand, and up the temple walls. They stood again, arm in arm, as they sailed away, this time towards Cairo and home, and watched Abu Simbel come alive again in the light of another day.

Then later that day Alexis asked Isabel to sit with him among the cushions on the raised deck. They spoke of the wonders of their trip and decided to have their dinner served to them up there on small tables.

They dined on tiny birds that had been shot somewhere along the green belt of the Nile and presented to them by a village elder. They had been stuffed with grapes and were served on a bed of rice with a green salad. There was fresh yogurt from a village nearby, with bananas and tangerines for dessert. It was yet another delicious meal and an end to yet another marvelous day.

After Gamal and Doreya had been dismissed, the couple lingered over their coffee, and Alexis lit up a couple of strong joints for them. The deck was lit by the usual lanterns and candles. They listened to the sounds of the Nile that they were quite used to now, although they received the same pleasure that they always did.

Alexis drew Isabel close to him and unbuttoned the tiny gold buttons on the galabia she had on. His fingers moved slowly, almost tenderly, as he exposed her breasts and played with her nipples. When he felt her completely relaxed and sighing from the pleasure that he was giving her, he pulled her close to him.

She slipped her hand under the galabia that he wore and fondled his balls and penis, which was only semi-erect.

He widened his legs and she was then able to hold his testicles in her cupped hands. She loved feeling the weight of them. She kissed him, and he told her how much he loved her.

They lay there like that, just petting each other lovingly, and he lit up two more joints for them. They finished them and, completely relaxed, listened to the night. Isabel had her arms around Alexis's waist and her head resting on his chest. He gently, very slowly covered her breasts. That was when he told her about her mother and sister, ending with his promise to show her the horrid cables at another time.

Ava and her mother. Both dead. All the obsession over

the years about her mother's funeral . . . and now there would be none.

Alexis saw the blood drain from her face, and for a moment he thought she was going to faint. He called for Gamal and gave some orders; at the same time he drew from his pocket a vial with some liquid in it that he held under her nose. It seemed to bring a little color back into her face. Gamal appeared with some whiskey, which Alexis told her to drink. She refused, and Alexis said very firmly, "I said, drink it down, all of it."

Isabel did as she was told, and then, with a deep sigh, she looked at him. "My father always said, ever since I was a child, that I would be the death of my mother, and I was, you know."

Still holding her in his arms, he was shocked to find her body had gone very cold. He rubbed her hands and arms.

She looked at him, and the tears just poured out of her eyes. "Oh, God, how did we make such a mess of it all? Why didn't we help each other, love each other, why did we make such a mess of it? The waste, I cannot forgive myself for the waste. We lost each other because of the little things. Why did we make such a mess of it all, why?"

Alexis didn't speak, he just let her cry it out. It was not very long before she fell asleep.

When she awoke a few hours later, she was still in his arms. He was smoking a joint and looking up at the stars. He asked her if she was better, and she said yes, she felt calmer. He passed the joint to her, and she smoked and asked him to please take her down to bed.

When they were in the bedroom they undressed and slipped into the bed. He took her in his arms and made tender love to her. At some point her passivity stopped, and she began to make love to him. She kissed him gently, and their lovemaking that night turned from tenderness to wild passion, then to animal lust, and then back to deep tenderness. They never stopped until she was exhausted and fell asleep in his arms. She was all relaxed and floppy like a little rag doll, and he held her close until he too slept.

When he woke in the morning he went to the bathroom and bathed, shaved and dressed. Then he went back to the sleeping Isabel and, lying down next to her, took her in his arms to wake her up. He offered her a large glass of mango juice that had been brought in by Gamal, and while she drank it slowly, he poured them both some hot black coffee.

"How do you feel?" he asked.

"I have a terrific headache, and I feel quite confused, but calm."

He picked up two tablets from the silver tray that her mango juice had been brought in on. "Well, darling, first things first," he said and handed them to her.

She went into the bathroom, and when she returned, she had bathed and looked a little less confused. She climbed back into the bed next to him.

"Do you feel well enough to talk a little about it?" he began.

"Yes."

He poured fresh cups of coffee for them and handed her a soft roll on a plate with some butter and marmalade. "Isabel, I want to tell you that those cables came three and a half weeks ago. I made the decision not to tell you because I could not see that there was anything we could do then. Your mother's ship has now docked in New York, and there are things for us to do. I want you to know how sorry I am and that I feel in my heart a great pity about all this."

"Alexis, the one thing I wanted was to spare you the problems of my family," Isabel said, and sighed. "I don't think I can bear you to be involved in any more of this than you are. It is my problem; actually, it is the end of my problem. I must think and work out what to do. Oh, I am so sorry it has all been laid on you. I wanted to give you only pleasure, and this is what I have saddled on you even before the honeymoon is over." She began to cry.

"Isabel, listen to me. It has drawn us *closer* together, my knowing all this, because I have suffered *for* you. But, darling, I think, for lack of any other word, you must forget the *ghosts* of these two women. Darling, if you do not, in time they will come back and torture you as they did in life. This tragedy has happened at the beginning of a new life for both of us, and I do not intend it to linger on. I have a plan. I think we should fly into Cairo for a few days and then on to Athens to see your brother-in-law for a day. Then, I think we should go on to New York. I don't want to question your feelings, but I think we must bury these women in the only way that their deaths have allowed us to and then get in with *our* lives. Does that make sense to you?"

"Yes, I think it does." Isabel nodded. "Alexis, something strange happened, and I want to tell you about it. You see, I let them die out of my life during that terrible luncheon in Athens. Now that they are really dead my guilt is gone. The reality of never being able to resolve our relationships is a defeat that I can accept, I think. But you are so right, I will never know until I bury the ghosts. I wonder how I would have faced all this without you."

He kissed her forehead and then the tip of her nose and smiled. "We will be all right, my darling. Do not look so worried. We will do this burying as painlessly as possible."

He looked at his watch and said, "In an hour's time we will dock and be driven to a small airfield a few miles out in the desert. A plane has been waiting for us for two days now. We will be in Sharia el Nil, your new home, in time for lunch."

He kissed her and told her to dress. She need take nothing with her but her jewels and whatever things she would want in New York that were aboard the felucca.

He watched Isabel walk around the room naked as she gathered her things together and made up her face. She put her diamonds on her fingers, her scarab necklace around her throat, which he fastened for her, and the Phoenician gold hoops through her ears. On her wrists she put her ancient gold bangles. She slipped her feet into high-heeled sandals and went to reach for a beautiful, thin, sand-colored, handwoven cotton shift with heavy, soft, slub yarns of the same color going through it.

He walked up behind her and stopped her. She felt his naked body and his heavy cock standing high against his belly as he hugged her, taking her breasts in his hands. She turned round, and Alexis told her how much he enjoyed watching her dress and bejewel herself. She kissed him tenderly on the lips and said, "I thought you were all dressed and ready to go. Now I want to dress you with me."

His desire for her, his virility, always excited her, even now, because it had nothing to do with the outside elements, not even the presence of death that seemed to be in her thoughts at the moment.

He lifted her by the waist, and with one of her hands, she took him and he went high up into her. He saw her eyes go liquid with passion, and when he lifted her off and she stood before him, his cock glistened with the wetness of her. How they handled each other, what they did to each other, almost drove them mad with passion until they could bear it no more and drained each other dry.

Whatever she may have felt about the deaths that had occupied her mind, he knew she would not be able to sublimate, and taking her the way that he did, he knew that he would release her tension. He was clever about her and he knew it. That was why he had not taken her tenderly and gently, but violently. He left her with bite marks deeper than she had ever had before and welts across her bottom that he kissed. He fucked her so long and so hard and she came so much; and still he would not stop until she begged him to.

Afterwards they lay together in each other's arms, both exhausted. While they rested and regained their strength, he was, at last, at ease about her sorrow, for he knew that he had broken even the barrier of the deaths. He broke it through the act of love, and she knew why he did it and was deeply grateful to him for it. She kissed him tenderly and finally said, "I think we should dress again and go. I am ready to bury the ghosts if you are."

They said their farewells to everyone on board and gave their thanks to the crew. Walking to the plane across the primitive sand-covered runway, Isabel realized that the unpleasantness they were going to go through now had nothing to do with their lives and how they would live out the rest of their days. She loved Alexis, at that very moment, more for not allowing her to wallow in self-pity. Kate and Ava were gone. It was over.

As Alexis followed her up the steps of the plane, he gave her a light smack on her bottom. She turned to him, smiling, and said, "Remember! Your turn might come. There may be a day when I will have to love *you* into life again, and I will." She caressed his cheeks, turned and hurried up the steps.

Alexis sighed deeply and thought to himself, *She is the only woman in the world for me.*

The pilot, after taking off, circled back. They flew low over the *Mamounia* and buzzed it. It was already in the mainstream of the river and homeward bound.

Tears came into Isabel's eyes, and she said, "Alexis, those were the happiest days of my life. Thank you, darling."

The Lear jet followed the Nile to Cairo. The jet flew very low so that she could see the river all the way home.

XIV

"NEW YORK is a city built on rock and one-liners," Isabel exclaimed. "It is kept going on adrenaline. If you are low on adrenaline and you cannot get your one-liners together, you had better get out of town. They say it is tough, rough and violent and it is. It is called the Big Apple and the Baked Apple. Actually, I see it as one enormous apple strudel, the richest, the most delicious, fattening apple strudel in the world, served up with a bowl of heavy whipped cream. Now, if you can afford to eat it, you can live well and happy in New York, because it is a city like no other city in the world. One has to be very rich, a millionaire. Or better still, a multimillionaire: very young, student young, *enthusiastic* student young. No in-between. It is rotten for children and old people.

"If you are born in New York, you usually end up being a smart-ass who thinks that Los Angeles, California, is built on sunshine and low IQ's. If you are born in Manhattan, you're a high-class New Yorker; in Brooklyn, a Jewish intellectual of distinction; in the Bronx, you have to struggle harder for distinction, a great deal harder; in Queens, you had better move if you want distinction.

"It is a city filled and supported by institutions. Museums and department stores, universities and department stores, hospitals and department stores, the United Nations and Bloomingdale's. What is left is divided between big corporations, lawyers and means of communication such as the telephone company, and master classes in EST.

"Some say it is very Jewish, but it was once very Irish,

and times change; the potato latke and the knish are being replaced by the soul food of the black and the Span-
ish beans of the Puerto Ricans. It has the best Chinese
food, Japanese food, Italian food and seafood in the
world, but the worst French food. The coffee is terrific,
but it is impossible to find a decent cup of tea. You can
buy anything and everything in New York. It has better
theater, dance, art and literature. You could also die of
culture shock if you are not prepared. You could also die
of loneliness if you are not very bright, rich, well-read,
amusing, beautiful, successful and read every word of the
New York Times on Sunday."

Alexis bent over his wife Isabel and laughed. "You're
bright, you're terrific at the one-liner, as you have just
demonstrated, you're beautiful, you are now a million-
airess, and you are married to me. I think you are going
to have a great time in New York, in spite of the unpleas-
ant tasks ahead."

"I agree," said Alexander. Isabel put her arm around
Alexis, and they looked out of the window of the helicop-
ter as they flew lower than the tops of some of the buildings, through the steel and glass canyons to the landing
deck.

They were, by now, over the East River Terminal. The
vast towers of concrete and steel shone with electric light
through all the glass running up and down their facades.
Honeycombs of people, buzzing like bees working for
their lives. They began to spiral down and plumped themselves on the ground like a duck hitting on a lily pad.

A few minutes later they were riding up Park Avenue
in a maroon Rolls Royce lined inside in beige leather. It
was an early day in December and it was very gray. There
was that wonderful nip in the air that told you that
Christmas was not very far away.

Isabel watched the people hurrying up and down the
streets. The women looking terrific, if not a little terrifying, as all New York women always did. Just a little too
well turned out, a little too well shod (didn't their heels
ever run down?), uncreasable, wrinkle-proof. They were
smart, chic, professional women of New York, whether in
the bed, the office, playing mother, mistress, executive
wife or liberated super-swinger.

The streets were filled too with the successful New
York male. They all seemed much taller; their suits well

cut and fitted: Their light-weight overcoats with too much style. Their hair too well cut and blow-dried to perfection. It was image, all image, obsessively calculated image. One wondered—for what? The New York man was now wearing his hair longer (but unfortunately his trousers still too short). There was even the occasional white sock to be seen inching its way between the dark trouser and the black shoe. But as Isabel watched them, she felt their *freshness*. They looked clean, honest and neat. They looked packaged—the American dream with a cock. They all looked married but on the lookout for a good fuck on the side.

It suddenly occurred to Isabel that she was riding up Park Avenue with her husband. She turned away from the window and looked at him. Alexis smiled at her and said, "Is it strange for you to return to your country with a husband from the desert?"

"It is not so much strange, Alexis, as it is different. Everything in my life since I met you is so different."

As Alexander chuckled, Isabel thought about Kate and Ava. They were all the family she'd had until she'd met Alexis, only a little more than a month ago. Now they were both gone. Nothing was at all the same.

One thing that had certainly not changed was the Sherry Netherland. They were received warmly by the manager, who shook Alexis's hand and patted Alexander on the shoulder. The elevator took them directly to Sir Alexis's suite.

The suite was on the thirty-second floor and extremely handsome. There was the main drawing room, which was enormous and had one of the little turrets of glass suspended over Fifth Avenue. There was a banquette built in all around it with soft cushions in a bold, bright flower pattern. One could curl up in this little glass cage hung over Fifth Avenue and watch the city and the park.

There was a lovely fire going in the yellow-and-white marble Louis XV fireplace. The furniture, two huge sofas facing each other, was covered in beige damask. There were dozens of white lilies on the coffee table. All the furniture was rich-looking but easy and comfortable. There were six large Bergères covered in cream-colored raw silk. The walls were painted white, and the Aubusson carpet was of the palest shades of iced greens, blues and creams, with a strong touch of peach.

The paintings were sublime. There was a magnificent, dark and rich Soutine of considerable size over the fireplace. It was a brooding painting with a life of its own. She recognized a superb Gauguin and then realized that these were Alexis's paintings. Although he had said nothing, she now knew that this was his New York residence.

Alexis helped Isabel off with her coat. He walked to the little turret, where they stood together as he said, "I have given you Cairo and Upper Egypt, and now I am going to give you New York."

He then led her by the hand through the rest of the rooms. In addition to the drawing room, there was a small but very charming dining room. Done in shades of yellow, it was a room in which no more than six could dine. There was a small kitchen, more like a butler's pantry, but that was all that was necessary since the superb hotel's service was available to them at all times. Next was a smaller sitting room with a large and beautiful boule desk with a worn black-leather top. The room was of a rich brown walnut French *boiserie*. All the furniture was covered in a pale coffee-colored silk velvet, and there were rough white scatter cushions for color. There was a wing chair behind the desk, covered in a seventeenth-century tapestry, and the draperies were white, lined in silk velvet, the same material as the furniture. The paintings were four large and wonderful Mirós that sang to you and made the room come alive and vibrant. Very chic, very New York.

There was a huge master bedroom and a dressing room and bath. The bath was marvelous, obviously done in the early thirties, with green onyx bathtubs, very deep as well as wide. The basins were of the same onyx, and all the taps were sterling silver.

There were two more guest bedrooms and baths, and just off the paneled sitting room was a small but charming library. A circular room, its book-covered walls alternated with floor-to-ceiling windows. It was a view of New York that was spectacular.

The library's floor was white marble with a dark green vein. Thick, fluffy polar-bear skins were scattered about. There was a chaise longue covered in a magnificent old Bokhara of ruby reds in great roundels. The chaise sat in the window section with the best view. In the center of the room, there was a white marble desk on a pedestal base of bronze dolphins.

The top of the desk held a typewriter, dictaphone, pads and pencils, dictionaries and a telephone. Behind the desk was a high-back Queen Anne wing chair covered in white cotton, with heavy slub yarns making an interesting rough texture.

"I thought you might like to use this room as your own little study when we are here in New York," Alexis said, from behind her. "You must, of course, change anything in it that does not please you." He pondered a moment. "As a matter of fact, Isabel, you must change anything in *any* of our houses that you do not like. We could re-do them *together*. But will this do for the moment?"

"Oh, yes, darling, it certainly will do!" Isabel smiled.

They went back to the drawing room, where they found Alexander sitting with a drink in his hand. Alexis and Isabel offered him one of the guest rooms for as long as he would be in New York, but he declined, saying that he had made arrangements for a small suite on the floor below them.

The two men spoke of some people that they wanted to see while in New York. Alexis and Isabel accepted Alexander's invitation to dine. He then kissed Isabel and left.

Alexis had made arrangements to conduct his work from the city for as long as Isabel felt she needed to be in the United States to finalize her family affairs. He'd told her that it was important to him that they should not leave before Isabel had buried all the ghosts. He had brought his secretary form Sharia el Nil, and Gamal, to serve him; Maryka and Juju to serve Isabel.

Doreya had been left in Athens to help Alfred dispose of Ava's things and close up their home. Alexis had offered her services to Alfred when he saw how upset Isabel was at the thought of going through her sister's things.

Alexis saw a certain kind of indifference in Alfred about Ava and her death. He'd found it extraordinary that Alfred had left the house just as Ava had. He was clearly waiting for her mother or sister to come along and empty it.

All things considered, Alexis thought that Alfred was a gentleman who had made the day as painless as possible.

He had met their plane at the airport and they all drove to lunch together at the *Grande Bretagne*. It was

not a strained lunch by any means, and finally, over coffee, Alfred spoke briefly of Ava and how he could not
bring himself to arrange a service for her that he was
sure she would have snickered at.

Tears had come into his eyes as he looked at Isabel
knowingly, saying, "I only hope that she can find peace
at last."

With that he had put the keys to the closed-up flat in
Kolonaki on the table and said, "You are her only living
relative. You take all her things."

Both Isabel and Alexis had expected him to do that,
which was why they had brought Doreya along to take
over. Alexis was anxious not to have Isabel too involved,
so when Isabel explained that her wish was that Ava's
things, including all her jewelry, be packed and given to
an orphanage in Patras, he was greatly relieved. Ava's
ghost was about to be buried once and for all.

If only Alfred had not said to Isabel, "Ava would be
very angry at us for giving her things to mere peasants. I
think she always thought that you would die first. Her
things were precious to her, and she always spoke of them
as to be sacrificed only if you had a fatal illness and there
was no one to care for you. She saw them as your insurance policy, because you were not a success, and had no
husband to support you. You know what a responsible
person she was. In a way, at least she was spared your
happiness. You cheated her of her martyrdom."

Alexis thought of those words now as he sat in the
drawing room. He thought of how pale Isabel had gone,
how she'd never said a word to Alfred, and how she'd
held the palm of her hand over her heart for a few minutes, as if in great pain.

Alexis poured himself another drink and offered one to
Isabel, who said no. He went and sat beside her, and she
snuggled up next to him after kicking off her shoes and
tucking her feet beneath her. They stayed that way for a
long time without speaking.

Alexis went on thinking about her, and his heart went
out to her with pity and love. He thought of her eyes and
how they had filled with tears after she had said good-bye
to Alfred and Doreya. He had taken her hand to help
her into their car so as to start back to the airport and
their plane. It had been ice-cold and trembling. What
could he say? He said nothing.

The car had been moving for a few moments when she had turned to him and said, "Please, Alexis, I cannot go like this. I must do something for her. It will only take ten minutes."

They'd driven back, past the *Grande Bretagne,* to the very beginning of Basilies Sophias, where there were dozens of little flower stalls. Isabel had the driver stop, and she asked Alexis for money. It was the very first time she had done that. He gave it to her, and she went with the driver to several stalls, buying armfuls of flowers. They put them in the trunk of the Mercedes.

She then told the driver to take them to the Tomb of the Fallen Warriors, and Alexis watched her cross the empty marble pavings with her arms full of the rich and colorful flowers. The driver followed a few paces behind, loaded down with more blossoms. She arranged all the flowers along the steps at the base of the statue of the warrior. She did it meticulously and then stood back and looked at it for a few minutes before returning to Alexis.

She slipped her arm through his and said, "You did not know her, Alexis. She was a fighter, a warrior. She deserves some tribute from me. I always brought her flowers. I would like to think I am doing this for her now, but I am not so sure. Perhaps I am doing it for me. Can you understand that?" And then Isabel said, "Please Alexis, let's get out of Athens as soon as possible."

And they did.

In the days that followed their arrival in New York, many things happened to the Hyatts. A gamut of emotions was run by the two of them, but it was always made a little bit easier by the presence of their friend Alexander.

Isabel took each day as it came and dealt with it accordingly. It was because she handled herself this way that she was able to cope with it all so admirably.

Alexis used the paneled sitting room as an office where he did most of the work with his secretary. Isabel had the small library. She was delighted to be able to work on the outline of a new Meredith Montague with all the events going on around her.

There was an endless stream of telephone calls, all handled adeptly by the secretary. Alexis did have some important meetings: The Ford Foundation, a UNESCO conference, dinner with the Rockefellers, a visit to the

United Nations for lunch with the leaders of the Arab
bloc.

There were invitations galore for both of them. All New
York and its international diplomatic and political corps
wanted to meet the new Lady Hyatt. Over their last cup
of coffee in the morning, it became a habit to go over the
list of invitations extended the day before. They went over
them seriously, each always willing to accept to please the
other, and always it ended with them both laughing and
deciding to dine together alone, or with Alexander or with
one or two of Alexis's friends with whom they really
wanted to be.

Since Alexis was a master at delegating, he seemed
never to be ruffled with arrangements or meetings taking
place. There was always more than enough time to spend
with Isabel quietly and alone.

Isabel took everything in her stride, but could not help
thinking how naive she was concerning her role as Alexis's
wife. They talked about it together, and he was marvelous, telling her he wanted her first for himself. She was his
private life and love. The social demands made upon
them need never be filled unless they both agreed.

He was extremely enthusiastic when he met her American publisher and thrilled when she signed a contract for
four more books. They would be delivered one a year for
the next four years.

Two days after they'd arrived and recovered from jet
lag, Alexis announced that he was taking her on a little
shopping expedition. Isabel hated shopping and told him
laughingly that she would agree to go only if he would
take her to one of her favorite restaurants for lunch. He
accepted, and as he walked her past Bergdorf's and into
Van Cleef & Arpels, he put his arm around her and said,
"You did not think I was taking you to a department
store, did you? Darling, I detest crowds."

There really was not that much shopping to do. He
bought her a pair of perfect matched Burmese rubies,
Cabouchon and about the size of robins' eggs. They were
set in a circle of splendid blue-white diamonds. He kissed
her when he saw them on her ears and said, "I thought,
darling, that you might like them for evenings. Ever since
I saw you in a red dress, I could think of buying you nothing but rubies."

They had them sent round to the hotel, and then the

two strolled down Fifth Avenue to Myako's, one of Isabel's really favorite restaurants. It was the first Japanese
restaurant in New York and was just as she had remembered it. In an old brownstone on East Fifty-sixth Street,
the restaurant was heavy with dark paneling, simple and
beautiful. The food was divine, and the atmosphere was
more like dining in a Japanese home than a restaurant.

They ate from dozens of small bowls of wonderful food,
drank hot saki and talked about her love for him, his generosity and her rubies. They were the last people to leave.

When they were on the street again, going back to the
hotel, he whispered in her ear, "I am going to take you
home and fuck you for the rest of the afternoon."

She whispered back laughingly, "What a nice idea! But
promise to hold off until after you have opened your wedding present which, with some luck, should be there waiting for you."

He looked delighted and asked what it was. Isabel gave
him a smack on the arm and said, "You must wait! You
are not the only one in this family capable of giving surprises!"

Alexis took her by the elbow and rushed her up the
avenue. They were as happy with their life together in
New York as they had been in London, Cairo and Upper
Egypt. As they entered the lobby of the Sherry Netherland, Alexis stopped Isabel and said, "It is wonderful being with you here in New York. There will be so many
things to do together. But first, do you feel up to seeing the
captain of the *Aphrodite*? I think it would be best if we
saw him in the next few days, don't you?"

"I think you are right, it would be a good idea to see
him as soon as possible," Isabel agreed. "Would you be
free to come with me and help me tomorrow, or the next
day?"

"Fine, darling. Leave the details to me."

They were let into the apartment by Gamal. Alexis
spotted the package on the coffee table at once.

Isabel went and picked it up, saying, "This, darling, is
my wedding gift to you. I hope that it pleases you."

He kissed her and then took the large package,
wrapped in a shiny, dark brown paper and tied with a
white ribbon bow. There was an envelope tucked under
the bow.

Alexis, for all his maturity and suaveness, was suddenly

like a small boy. He led Isabel to a place on the sofa.
They sat close together as he opened the envelope.

Moved by what Isabel had written, he put the envelope
down and took her in his arms. He first brushed his cheek
against hers, then his lips against her cheek, and then he
kissed her, almost trembling with passion for her. He
kissed her again, and he could feel her reacting to him. He
ran his hands over her breasts and then put himself under
control. He told her to order some tea while he opened
his gift.

Alexis found it absolutely extraordinary. It was the
most beautiful pornographic picture book ever made, and
one of the rarest books in the world. A signed edition, one
of five, of the great painter and printmaker, the Japanese
Utamaro. The bound book was a series of thirty-two exquisite colored prints, each one more exciting than the
last. Kitagawa Utamaro was born in 1753 and died in
1806; his book of pornography was made when he was
thirty-five years old, in his prime.

Picasso, who had one of the editions, is said to have
considered it one of his favorite possessions and spent
many hours looking at it, gathering enormous inspiration.
There was another edition in King Farouk's collection of
pornography, which had been one of the finest and largest
private collections in the world.

This copy had been purchased from a private collector
in Paris. The seller wanted to remain anonymous, but
both Alexis and Isabel did some guessing and thought that
it might have come from André Malraux's library. Of the
remaining editions, one was in London and the other in
the United States, both owned by museums.

It was a rare and marvelous object to receive as a wedding gift from one's wife. Alexis was obviously overwhelmed by it. They looked together through the first five
of the prints until Gamal brought in the tea. Alexis
thanked him and told him not to disturb them until he was
called.

They drank tea and looked at the next print. It was the
purest pornographic art, absolutely so beautiful that it
fired one not only sexually but aesthetically as well. The
colors, the patterns, the textures drawn, were magnificent.
To see a woman's cunt drawn to such perfection, its color
of deep pink and shadings from pale rose to dark ma-
genta, made one look deep into it and think of an orchid.

The expression of ecstasy on the man's face, as his tongue reached down into the beautifully formed cunt, was tantalizingly sexual and a miracle of art and desire.

They looked at two more pages and Alexis told Isabel that he adored the book. How exquisite an expression of sexuality it was, and how clever she was to have been able to find it.

He turned to another page: a painting of two men fucking a geisha who was dressed in a checked and flowered kimono that was draped open only where she was being used.

It was outrageously sexual and unutterably beautiful. Alexis could hold back no longer.

He turned to Isabel, threw her down on the sofa and lifted her skirt up. He spread her legs wide, telling her that he wanted to look and play with her as they looked at the pictures. Before they closed the book that afternoon, he had taken her in every position depicted.

Instead of being exhausted and worn-out from their hours of love play, they were very happy. They dressed again, and Isabel lay stretched out on the sofa, her head in Alexis's lap. He rang Alexander, asking him to come see Isabel's wedding gift if he was free.

The minute that Alexander entered the room, he knew from the atmosphere that they had had an orgy. He laughed at them and told them that he resented being called down after they had done everything to each other. He sat down and looked through the magnificent treasure on the table.

Alexis decided to keep the book on the boule desk in his sitting room, and Isabel laughed, asking what he would do if his secretary or some of his business associates looked through it. He said he would be delighted, for it would be good for everyone to be able to see such delicious things.

The next morning Isabel had a meeting with her American publisher. When she returned, the two men, Alexis and Alexander, were talking over business in the sitting room. Alexander stayed on for lunch with them in the yellow dining room. While they waited for it to be brought up and served, they opened a bottle of Roderer Cristal and talked about some people that they had met at the restaurant where they'd all dined the night before.

Lunch was delicious, a gay and amusing meal, as all

meals seemed to be when the three of them were together. Isabel could see now how very close her husband and his best friend were. It was over coffee that Alexis suddenly turned serious and said to Isabel, "Darling, the captain of the *Aphrodite* and the ship's doctor should be waiting by now in the drawing room. Alexander knows that they are here and I have asked him to stay. He is our best friend, and if he can help in any way, he would like to."

Isabel was taken by surprise, just the way Alexis had planned it. All she could say was, "Well then, let us not keep them waiting."

Alexis thought that it was going to be a difficult and upsetting meeting, but he never imagined how horrific it would turn out to be. They heard from the captain and the doctor what had actually happened and were handed the written report about Kate's arrival, behavior and her heart attack on the Nile. Alexis read the last will and testament and the doctor's report and death certificate, and turned to Isabel, asking her permission to pass them over to Alexander to read.

After Alexander had finished reading the documents, he turned to the captain and doctor and said, "Gentlemen, is it your concern that we might litigate against your company and you as individuals for executing the last will and testament of Mrs. Wells?"

It was the captain who spoke up. In the kindest way possible he said that he was under pressure from a dying woman to respect her last wishes. That it was only after the event that he realized the possibility of legal action by the family. He hoped that Sir Alexis and Lady Hyatt would not follow that course, since he was at the time acting in the best interests of his dying passenger.

It was Alexis who said, "We have no intention of doing anything except seeing you this afternoon and taking possession of Mrs. Wells's things as she asked in her will. You may rest assured, gentlemen, that after this meeting, the incident will be closed."

Isabel had been listening to everything and had finally composed herself enough to ask for the documents so that she might read them.

"Isabel, your mother is gone," Alexander said. "I honestly think that it is not important for you to read them. It is more important for you to forget them."

She realized Alexander was right: It would do no good

for her to mull over circumstances. She could see the pattern emerging of how Kate had manipulated herself and everyone else into the situation. It was her ultimate bid for attention.

Alexis squeezed her hand. She still looked very pale.

Isabel turned to Captain Papastamati and said, "Thank you very much for coming to see me and for all that you did for my mother. It only remains for me to take possession of her things. Where are they?"

"My instructions, Lady Hyatt, those that were left in the will, are to deliver them to you and you only. I have had them taken out of storage. They can be delivered to you within the hour or sent anywhere you desire."

"Please have them sent here."

Isabel signed ten documents, realizing why Alexander had been asked to stay.

Alexis stroked her hair and said, "Alexander and I have read everything. These documents are simply releases freeing the shipping company, the captain and the doctors who buried your mother in the manner that they did, of all responsibility. They are quite in order and I think it best that you sign them. We have no desire to cause these people any further trouble."

He handed her his fountain pen and, with a trembling hand, she signed wherever she was told. Ten documents, ten signatures. It was over.

Alexis thanked the men for everything they had done to make Kate's last hours as comfortable as possible. He sent Isabel off to lie down while he offered the men a drink. Just as Isabel was stretching out on the bed, Gamal arrived saying that Sir Alexis had sent her two tablets to take with a glass of water. She took the pills, feeling quite numb and exhausted.

Isabel could not sleep. She lay there wide-awake thinking about her mother's funeral. The real funeral. The one that had happened aboard the S.S. *Aphrodite*. Not one of the fantasy funerals that she had spent so many years thinking and worrying about.

Then her thoughts went to her cousin, Natalie. Oh, God, she must tell Natalie, and then it suddenly occurred to her that Alexis was right, there *were* things to be done. Her mother's sisters and brothers had to be told.

Her mind drifted and she began to imagine Kate's funeral in the middle of the Atlantic Ocean in the early hours of the morning. Maybe it was all untrue, all a dream, a fantasy. She would wake up and there would be Kate, and Ava, and letters, and telephone calls, and postcards, and the lies, and the guilt, and more guilt. No, unreal as it all seemed, it was true. They were both dead and gone. Isabel would have hoped for a last sign of kindness, of love, but in her heart she knew she would never find one.

It was little over an hour before Alexis went to her. He opened the curtains and sat down on the bed next to her.

"How are you feeling?"

"Unhappy, and depressed and thoroughly sorry for myself. Almost as sorry as I am feeling for Kate and Ava," Isabel said. "I do not want to cry, or maybe it is more that I cannot cry."

There was a tap on the open door. It was Alexander. He went to the two of them sitting on the bed. Isabel pulled herself up on the pillow, and when she did, Alexander stroked her hair and said, "Go repair your face, and you, Alexis, go pull out that silver whiskey flask of yours. I have a horse and carriage downstairs. We are going out to get some fresh air. This is all too depressing. I do not mean to be flippant about this, Isabel, dear heart, but they were a bad lot in life, and they are a bad lot in death. That is the truth. Now come, you two. I think the three of us could do with seeing some life around us." He clapped his hands, and Alexis, with a look of thanks to his friend, jumped up. He went to get Gamal to fill the flask.

Isabel pulled a comb through her hair, put some rouge on her cheeks, added a touch of lipstick, and then the three of them went down to the waiting horse and carriage that had trotted over from the fountain in front of the Plaza Hotel.

There was no question about it, Alexander's idea was inspired. From Fifth Avenue, they turned into the park. They swigged whiskey from the silver flask, and the city moved their heads and hearts again. It was a sweet, crazy afternoon. They were all three a little tipsy and maybe trying a little too hard to forget about Kate and her death, but whatever it was that drove them on, in time they were laughing and chatting.

They came out of the park and their carriage passed the Guggenheim Museum. Alexis called out to the cabbie to stop, and they went in to see the current exhibition. Then their horse trotted them down the avenue and out across to Madison, and Alexis pulled out three joints. They lit up and smoked their way down the street and window-shopped.

Like three naughty, happy-go-lucky, rich children, they stopped along the avenue whenever there was something they fancied. Alexander started off by dashing into one of those elegant boutiques, to come out with a magnificent Patagonian-fox car robe backed in beige felt. That went to Isabel with a kiss. "It is really for your Rolls," he said. "But we can cover ourselves with it now; it is getting a bit nippy."

The three of them snuggled together under the fur rug as the carriage rolled them down toward Fifty-seventh Street. There were ties for the men from Alexander Shields, and big fat cigars from an exclusive tobacconist on Fifty-seventh Street.

It was mad and extravagant and perfect. There was a fabulous new lynx coat for Isabel, because Alexis said she needed a coat with sleeves and the window dresser was draping one just at the right moment in Henri Bendel's window. There was the most enormous box of handmade white chocolates with real cream centers, flown in daily from Belgium, from the Godiva Shop at the St. Regis, because suddenly the joints they had been smoking had given Alexander a desperate sweet tooth.

A window display of the newest handmade fishing rods for fly-fishing stopped them at once, and twenty minutes later, the carriage had three rods carefully packed along with the proper waders and the latest book on fly-fishing.

When they stopped for a red light, it was Isabel who spotted a magnificent vicuna sports jacket in Brooks Brothers' window and insisted that Alexis should try it on. He loved it and they bought it. Time was running out for them, but they did manage to make Saks on Fifth Avenue fifteen minutes before closing and, sticking to the ground floor, they purchased an enormous bottle of Norell perfume, handkerchiefs for the men, a Gucci silk scarf for Isabel and a pair of black fishnet stockings, spotted by Alexander, which Alexis bought for Isabel.

The bells rang, the immaculate dust sheets came out and the store closed. A good thing too, for now they could barely get into their carriage, which was looking more like a goods wagon. The three of them laughed when they looked at their cabbie, who had an enormous Havana cigar stuck in his mouth and was searching through the huge box of chocolates trying to find one he wanted.

Then it was on to drinks at the Carlyle, where Pierre, the wine steward, instantly produced a magnum of Bollinger '69, and Alexander made a date with a Southern belle just seconds before her fiancé arrived. Tentatively Alexis suggested the opera, but Alexander said no, as the Bollinger sparkled. "What we need tonight is some of New York's finest luxuries."

"Wonderful," said Isabel, picking up her lynx coat, pouring the last of the champagne into a glass, sweeping out into Seventy-sixth Street and presenting it to a no longer startled driver. Gratefully, he thundered off down Park Avenue to El Parador for dinner. As they jolted along, they laughed and lit up joints. At El Parador, the elegant and handsome Carlos was delighted to greet them and, as usual, offered them a perfect table, the most divine Mexican food and, of course, the best margaritas in the world.

The horse and carriage had been paid off at El Parador and the driver turned back to the Sherry Netherland, where he delivered the packages to the doorman and a note instructing that the Rolls be sent to wait for them.

By this time the Rotten Apple was not merely the Big Apple, it was the Apple Strudel—whipped cream and all. They were having a fantastic time and joined in a conversation with two Texans who were as big and as bold and as colorful as their state.

They left El Parador very high, and as they were about to get into the waiting Rolls, a woman in smart tweeds and brogues with the face of an elderly angel, screamed at them, "You miserable, mother-fucking, capitalistic perverts!"

Alexander smiled sweetly at her and said, "How perceptive of you, madam!"

Driving uptown they smoked a little more and snorted some coke. They were all flying high, wide and handsome.

It was time for Studio 54, and naturally, they didn't have to wait in line. When they arrived, the chain was removed and they passed through. It was wild that night. The light show, the snowstorm, the dazzling effects. Pretty girls, beautiful girls, young girls, smart, snappy-looking chicks, all high-stepping. And Isabel joined in. They were all turned on fast and stayed that way.

Men on the make, handsome New York blades with money, more without, smart, well-dressed, dirty old men acting like dirty old men, and the handsome gigolos seemed to be everywhere. Gay boys kissing and cruising, two men sucking on a spaced-out chick's tits and a coked-up French rock singer with an enormous cock, beating off in the upper balcony, were just a few of the side-shows. Isabel and Alexis were fascinated. They all went onto the floor and danced, danced, danced. Isabel, to Alexis's delight, found herself with four handsome men; the two Texans, as she soon noticed, were lovers.

They left long after the sun was up and rode down to the Fulton Fish Market and the Battery and watched New York come back to life again.

Despite the coke, they were starving, so the Rolls slid uptown to Barney Greengrass's and they ate bagels and lox, scrambled eggs and slices of sturgeon and drank lots of black coffee. They ate, and as they ate they listened to the babble around them.

"So, how did you make out last night, Abe?"

"So, who made out, forty-six years old and she's playing the Virgin Mary. I said, 'Sylvia, you wanna fuck?' She, said, 'What kind of question is that to ask a lady?' So already I knew I was in trouble. So I said, 'All right, already, so you don't wanna fuck, come on, I'll take you home.' She says to me, 'Look, Abe, we don't have to go home, we could talk, try and communicate,' so I said, 'Look, Sylvia, what's to talk about? I talk all day, I communicate all day, at night I like to keep quiet and fuck.' Then she laid it on me. 'Abe, have you ever heard of EST?' So I said, 'EST? EST? What's that? Some kind of perfume?' "

Isabel laughed, and the laughter, deep draughts of it, came to her like a tonic. She nudged Alexis to listen.

The waiter was standing there poised, ready to take an order at another nearby table. Isabel, Alexis and Alexander switched their ears to that table.

"Good morning, Mr. Vinklebaum, and good morning to you, young lady."

"Good morning," said the young lady.

"Vell, Mr. Vinklebaum, vat's it to be this morning? The usual?"

"Yeah, Lester."

"Scrambled eggs with fried onions and lox, bagels toasted with a side order of cream cheese, coffee with milk. OK, and, you, vat'll it be for the little lady?"

"I'll have a soft-boiled egg, please, three minutes, and a ryvita, no butter and tea."

The waiter looked at her as if she were insane. Mr. Winklebaum looked at his lady and said, "Jesus, Mary-Louise," and turned to the waiter and said, "Lester, she will have coffee with milk, a toasted bagel and lox, no butter, but cream cheese, forget the soft-boiled egg."

"Right, Mr. Vinklebaum."

When the waiter had left, the curly-black-haired young man turned to his young lady, an exquisite, doll-like blonde. A beauty with a vacant, almost dumb look on her face, who spoke in a soft, almost breathless kind of whisper.

"Mary-Louise, how many times do I have to tell you that you don't come to Barney Greengrass's to eat a three-minute, soft-boiled egg. A three-minute, soft-boiled egg you eat at home. Do you understand?"

"Yes, Irving."

"Mary-Louise, why are you fidgeting; stop fidgeting."

"I'm nervous."

"Nervous? Christ, what have you got to be nervous about, doll?"

"Well, as long as you asked, Irving, it makes me very nervous every time I have to leave the house early in the morning like this, hide all my clothes and pretend that I don't exist. Irving, you are going to have to tell your mother about me some day. Irving, it is three years now, surely she must know that we live together?"

"Listen, Mary-Louise, with my mother, she only knows what she wants to know."

"Well, as long as you asked, Irving, I don't think it is very fair to me. It makes me so upset, this. It is going to drive me to a head-shrinker. Irving, are you going to marry me or aren't you? I would just like to know. I am tired of pretending I don't hear your mother on the telephone when she calls and asks if you are still going out with that 'filthy *shiksa*.' I don't think she should call me a filthy *shiksa*. I am very clean. She says *shiksa* like it is some terrible dirty word."

"Look, Mary-Louise, to my mother *shiksa* is a dirty

word. Listen, baby, we talked about marriage before. You don't want to go through that hassle, honey; you would have to study for years to become Jewish, because, you know, I could never marry a girl who was not Jewish. Then you would have to go through that business of changing your name."

"Changing my name, what business? Every girl changes her name when she gets married, silly."

"Not their first name, Mary-Louise."

"Why would I have to change my first name, Irving?"

"How can you even ask such a question? How could you go through life with a name like Mary-Louise Winklebaum? No, you would have to change your first name, and then you would not be my Mary-Louise any more. Listen, we are very happy the way we are now. Eat your bagel and lox. After all, you would not want to lose your identity, would you?"

And with that subject closed, the young man, very annoyed with his doll-like beauty, snapped open *Women's Wear Daily* and began to read as he shoveled forkfuls of a Barney Greengrass's special into his mouth.

They called for the bill. As they waited to pay, they saw Irving leave, and watched Mary-Louise, with big tears in her eyes, ask the waiter for an Alka Seltzer. And, at last, the Rolls purred back to the Sherry Netherland.

Just as silently, Isabel and Alexis undressed and collapsed into bed to fall asleep in each other's arms. They slept until ten o'clock that night. When they awoke, they made love, then bathed and went back to bed again. They ordered a light supper. It was served to them in bed on trays, and then they watched television. Then they went back to sleep again.

Two days later, Alexander left them to return to London. He had a few minutes alone with Isabel, and it was then that she thanked him for all that he had done and especially for taking them out that day in the carriage. She told him that she loved him very much.

He kissed her hand and said, "That is what you are supposed to do. I told you that you would like having two men in love with you." Then he kissed her good-bye with great tenderness, as he held her very close to him.

As chance would have it, a long time would pass before the three of them would be together again. They talked often on the telephone and surprise gifts arrived and were sent between them, but they did not see each other; their lives changed.

Kate's belongings were delivered and unpacked in one of the guest rooms for Isabel's inspection. One day, Isabel finally plucked up the courage and went to the room. The ever-faithful Gamal had the room locked, and so Isabel had to ask for the key. He gave it to her and went to Alexis, who was in his office with his secretary.

By the time Alexis arrived at the room, Isabel had picked up one or two small things and looked at them. All the silver was spread out, all of Kate's dearest possessions. How many times had she said that she only polished them and cared for them in order to give them to her children after she was gone?

She was weeping uncontrollably when Alexis came to her. All she kept saying was, "Get it out, Alexis, I never want to see it all again, get it out."

Alexis was frightened. He took her to the bedroom, undressed her and put her to bed with the help of Juju. She was put under sedation and slept all that afternoon and through the night. When she woke up the next morning, she told Alexis how sorry she was for having lost control but that she really did not want to see the things again, they had no meaning but that of pain. Just things. Kate's last stab.

All the things that Kate dragged with her to her death were finally packed up and sent to the home for the aged in the town where they had lived in Massachusetts, the town where her father was buried, the place where her mother thought that she would always end her days.

Notes were duly written to the remaining family members and sent to them at addresses found in Kate's address book, except for cousin Natalie, whom Isabel planned to go and see. The notes were composed by the secretary, giving the details of Kate's death and a box number where they could write if they had any further questions. They were signed by the secretary for Isabel, as she had not been in touch with the family for well over twenty years, and after great thought she decided that a death was no reason to start now.

At long last it was over. Isabel had buried her ghosts.

XV

THE WIND was pushing the rain with such force that it all but blasted the windows of the little glass turret where Isable sat looking out over New York and the cold, wet December day.

Warm, cosy, well protected, she liked looking out at the storm and the sparkling lights in all the millions of windows. It was only four in the afternoon but dark. It was exciting because it was the dark of bad weather, not the dark of night. At any time it could stop, just the right gust of wind and the day would be back.

Isabel was sitting with her feet up on the brightly colored banquette, one side of her body pressed tight against the cold window. There were moments when she could feel the pressure of the rain as it hit the glass. She had pad and pencil and was making notes for her new novel.

She did not hear the doorbell, or Gamal let Alexis in. He called to her and when he found her, he kissed her hello and told her to stay where she was, he was wet through to his bones and would take a hot shower and return to her shortly.

When he did return, he was in his camel-hair galabia, smelling of some wonderful men's soap, looking handsome and happy. Behind him trailed Gamal with a tea tray which he put down on the table in the center of the glass turret.

"I love finding you here like this," Alexis said. "I adore it when I see you working on one of your books, all calm, warm, comfortable. I like having you all protected here in your little glass cage. I am mad for you, you know."

She made room for him close to her on the banquette, as he went on. "I have just come from a meeting where I sat with England's prime minister and an Arab king. I listened to them as they went on and on, and suddenly I thought of you and wanted you. They were being so foolish and boring and completely on the wrong track, and there I was, thinking of you. That you are mine and you were home here, waiting for me."

"Oh, Alexis, I always want to be with you." She kissed him, and his arms went around her, and then his hands moved to her breasts. She kissed him again and then said, "What finally happened?"

He poured two cups of tea and handed one to Isabel. "Well, they could not even get a dialogue together, never mind a solution, because there is a basic lack of understanding of the problems. The issues are very great, indeed, and not defined in a simple and clear manner. They want me to step in and negotiate for them and to help assemble the other Arab leaders involved. If I will help them, they are sure that they can solve this present crisis before it flares up into what could be a potentially very dangerous situation."

"And will you?"

"I told them that I would think about it. That I would let them know." He took Isabel in his arms again and unbuttoned the opening of her galabia.

She stopped him and said, "I love you, and I want to *make* love to you, right now."

She lifted his galabia, slipped down off the banquette onto her knees, and took him in her mouth. She made love to him while the wind and rain beat against the windows.

When it was over, he helped her up off her knees and walked her over to the sofa, where he removed her galabia. He laid her down, putting cushions under her head and shoulders so that she was comfortable and could watch him as he put his head between her legs and made love to her.

They drank from each other that afternoon and then lay on the floor in front of the open fire in each other's arms. The soft cushions were tucked under their heads, and the Patagonian-fox car rug that usually lay draped on one end of the sofa covered them. Underneath it they were naked and together.

Alexis lay there relaxed and completely content. Isabel leaned on her elbow and looked at him while they talked about their lives together.

His eyes were closed. She whispered, "Alexis?"

"Mmmmm."

"Alexis, you know that if you want to take on this job, I can do my work anywhere we go. It does not have to be New York, or London. I can make a life working and waiting for you anywhere that you are. I only need a suitcase of books, some paper, and I will be happy. Very happy, if I can be part of your life."

Alexis's eyes were open now, and he gazed at Isabel as she went on, "I am not blind, darling. I have seen the cables from all over the world congratulating you on your new happiness in taking a wife. There has not been one head of state who has not sent a message. Whatever you want to do, I am coming with you. I am ready to get on with our life together, and all that it has in store for us."

Alexis said nothing. He just stroked her hair and listened to her.

"If you have the time," Isabel continued, "there is something I would like to do. It would be very nice for me if we could go to Massachusetts for a few days. I would like to show you some of the beautiful places that I loved when I was young and that have influenced my life. I would like to walk along a deserted beach with you on the Cape; I'd like to show you the New England of my youth. I'd like to see it again myself, and maybe then I will be able to leave America, remembering it only for the beautiful and good things that it gave me. It would be so nice to leave those places again just because I wanted to go and not because I was running away. Do you think we might have time to do it? Would you like that?"

"I would like that very much. I think it is a really wonderful idea," Alexis said softly.

"I would only like to see one person. My cousin Natalie, for a lunch. She lives in a wonderfully small town. You see, darling, I always wanted to go back. I loved Massachusetts. I loved New England. The leaves and the colors in the fall and the snow in the winter. I loved to swim in the Atlantic Ocean in the summer. I liked the people. Oh, Alexis! If we go, I would only need one day here after our return to gather books and do a little shopping. Then I will be ready to leave for the most remote part of the world, or the Sharia el Nil house, or aboard the *Mamounia*. We can do whatever you want to do. I want to be part of your life and back you up as you have backed me up. You are a delicious, wonderful man, very

special, and I love you, and I want to help you and add
to your life always."

Alexis removed the fox robe and she saw that he was
very hard and very big. He opened her legs, and he very
gently and slowly pushed himself high up inside her. They
made love for a long time and slowly. Just before he was
ready to come, he managed to pull her tightly to his chest,
and while he was still deep inside her he said, "Tomorrow
morning we will buy a map, plan a wonderful tour of
your New England and leave after lunch." Then he laid
her down on the cushions and came into her. He did not
withdraw, but stayed inside her, and they lay together
there on their sides, facing each other. He reached down
and pulled the Patagonian fox up and over them.

"With you all life begins," he whispered. "Every time
I am with you, all life begins."

They lay there not talking any more but just looking at
each other and feeling their skins touching under the
cover.

Some time later there was a knock at the door. Alexis
checked that all was decent and then told Gamal to come
in. The servant spoke to him in Arabic as he went around
picking up the galabias and handing them to Alexis and
Isabel. Alexis's secretary wanted to come in to have a
word: He was holding a call from Egypt's president.

Gamal brought the telephone and put it on the floor
next to Alexis. The two remained where they were,
stretched out in front of the fire.

Isabel started to pull away from Alexis, who stretched
his arm out and pulled her back close to him. They smiled
at each other and he told Gamal to bring his secretary in.

There was a great deal of talk in Arabic between the
two men, and finally Alexis held his hand up for the secretary to be silent. He turned to Isabel and said, "He has
called for three reasons. To congratulate us, to say he
wants to hold a reception in our honor upon our return
and to ask me to please help them, having had a call
from the king that I met this afternoon. Shall we say ten
days from now, in Baghdad?"

Isabel kissed him and said, "Ten days from now in
Baghdad."

They both turned at the same time when they heard a
sigh of relief from Alexis's secretary. The three of them

smiled. Sir Alexis picked up the telephone and spoke to the president of his country.

The seaplane's motors were being revved up when Isabel and Alexis hurried down to board the plane. The captain saw them, cut the motors and went through to meet them. He stepped out onto the landing, shook hands with Alexis, was introduced to Isabel, and the three boarded the plane and sat down. The co-pilot came out to join them around a table in the main cabin. Then they went over the maps that Alexis and Isabel had worked on that morning.

Since the plane was a twelve-seater, and there were only two people traveling, the main cabin had been rearranged. Some of the chairs had been removed and a table set up for their comfort.

The co-pilot asked after their luggage, and both very proudly told him that all they had was the one small Louis Vuitton duffle bag, which he promptly stowed away. He brought coffee for the four of them and they went over the route together.

The two men went forward and started revving the motors again. They needed a good deal of power to charge up the East River, clear the Fifty-ninth Street Bridge and get airborne.

Isabel stood up to take her jacket off, and Alexis moved his hand over her buttock.

She turned around. He looked at her and said, "The moment that I saw that suit in the window, I knew it was for you." He had bought it for her that morning, having seen it on the way home from the map shop.

The mocha-colored suede trousers fit tightly over her behind, cut like men's, with a fly front. The suede was so fine and soft that the trousers hung like the best gabardine. With this was a beige silk blouse with balloon sleeves tight to the wrist and an open collar like a man's shirt, with small mother-of-pearl buttons. A suede vest that matched reached just below the waist. The jacket had sleeves and a waistband of thick, chocolate-brown, knitted wool. A hidden zip fastener did up the front. It had no collar, but a knitted wool scarf went with it. The main body of the jacket was a mocha-colored, natural ranch mink. She wore shiny, dark brown leather cowboy boots which went high up on her legs under the trousers. She wore her hair loose and casual, as she always did, and antique gold hoops in her ears. Her gold bangles were on her arm and her diamonds on her fingers. She looked stunning.

"You spoil me, you know, and I love it." Isabel laughed. "I love every single minute of it." She sat on his lap and kissed him. He pinched her and told her to go and buckle herself into the seat.

The pilot announced over the intercom that they were ready to take off. The seaplane shimmied and shook until Isabel thought that it was going to break in two before it charged up the East River. It was terrifically exciting, masses of water spraying the plane everywhere, so much so that one could hardly see out of the windows. Then, after what seemed like an eternity, she felt them lift off the river, climb and they were away.

They were so far up the East River now that they circled over Yankee Stadium, then followed the river back down to the Battery and saw it empty into the upper New York Bay. Now they struck out over Coney Island and Rockaway Beach Park towards Fire Island.

Isabel was delighted and very happy to be out of New York City. With the map spread out in front of them and the real thing not far below them, Isabel told Alexis all about Fire Island. For Isabel, it was still one of the best stretches of beach in the world, and she was really happy to see it.

Isabel tried to explain how crazy life was there during the season, and how wonderful it was off season. Alexis laughed at her descriptions and thought it looked a magnificent piece of beach. He was surprised at how closely people lived together.

He liked Southampton and East Hampton even more. She pointed out Montauk Point, and then told him how much fun it was for her to show him all this and how brilliant he was to think of going by seaplane.

When they flew over Block Island and Fishers Island, she told him all about her summers spent on the Connecticut shore. New London, Old Lyme, Old Saybrook. She told him about how summer life changed along the coast.

From Block Island they struck out for Martha's Vineyard and Edgartown, where they would spend their first night. Isabel regaled Alexis with stories of what it was to live a summer life in New England. She told him about being a teenager and lying on the beach from seven in the morning until seven in the evening, sunning and swimming, and knitting argyle socks for her boyfriend because that was the fad that year.

She told him about the other things, as her mind drifted back. The summer playhouses dotting the coast; the open-air concerts and the dance festivals. Then there was the summer food, the clams, oysters, lobsters and crabs; the fish chowders and the flounder and haddock and cod.

She told how she loved the sand dunes, and the shells along the beach, and the driftwood after a storm. Then there was the ocean glass: old pieces of bottles washed smooth and into strange shapes by the ocean. There were the clumps of high, dried-out grass that grew out on the sand dunes in patches, the blankets, and the smell of the baby oil and hot sand. Isabel had not remembered those things for years.

They circled over Martha's Vineyard, and it was almost dark when they checked into the Harborside Inn. It had changed little in the twenty years since she had stayed there. It was the same wooden whaling captains' houses linked together, and there were open fires, and the smell of burning hickory wood and beeswax furniture polish. The rag rugs on the floor and the antique New England furniture were a delight to see after so many years.

Their room was large and beautiful and overlooked the harbor. There was a great, deep, four-poster bed, draped in crisp, white cotton eyelet with a ruffle of the same material around the canopy. There was a patchwork quilt in the pattern known as "wedding ring" for the bedcover. There was a rocking chair, an antique cradle, chests of drawers and flower chintz curtains. It was a grand, elegant, old New England room.

They went down and walked around Edgartown and went into the few shops still open, where they spoke to people who were friendly and kind about giving information.

Their first day out of New York had been a glorious one, and the weather held for them the second day as well. They rented a car, and Alexis was impressed with the unspoiled beauty of the island.

They'd taken a picnic with them, and had it down on the beach, where they built a bonfire out of the driftwood they had collected. It was deserted, with high sand dunes that protected them from the road. They loved being there alone together, with the ocean and the sun and the slight nip of coming winter in the air. When Isabel stood up to throw another piece of driftwood on the fire, Alexis stood behind and put his arms around her to unzip her fly.

"Alexis, no, someone will see us."

"Not if you stand still just as you are, facing the ocean. From the road no one can see us; if someone comes by, they will think, 'There are two lovers looking out at the water,' and we are."

"Well, if we get caught, you get us out of it!" She laughed and said, "Darling, hurry, I long to have you inside me."

He pushed her trousers down around the top of her thighs and he had her bend over slightly. He pounded into her with the same force as the waves pounding onto the beach, and they watched the white foam as they crashed together in their own foaming orgasm.

When it was over for them, he withdrew and spun her around and held her tight to him. He kissed her passionately as he pulled her trousers up and then zipped up the fly. He pulled her down on their picnic blanket close to the fire and said, "You are disgustingly sexy, thank God!"

They remained in Edgartown another night, and early the next morning he woke her and took her down to the harbor where he had been having a talk with an old sailor called Bill. They went sailing and after lunch flew out on the seaplane for Cape Cod.

They flew along the ocean side of the Cape. It was beautiful with its bays and inlets and the fallen colored leaves mixed with the scrubby, but still luscious, green pines. They put down at South Orleans, on Pleasant Bay.

There were more wonderful days when they explored Truro and Wellfleet, then Provincetown, old, filthy, ramshackle to the point of being sublime. They ate lobster and New England clam chowder, blueberry muffins and home fried potatoes and green salads with Roquefort dressing, which absolutely appalled Alexis. But he did admit that they were eating the best seafood he had ever had in his life.

They flew out after two days, and he told her what a good time he was having and that her New England was lovely. "But, darling," he said, "you know that you were already grown up when you sought out these places."

She wondered what he meant by that.

They routed themselves across Nantucket Sound, and then the top end of Buzzards Bay, and on down, past Newport. Alexis liked that very much. They flew low over the great houses and sprawling gardens perched on cliffs above the stormy ocean.

They followed the coast of Rhode Island into the coast of Connecticut. The plane wove in and out along the coast, and she showed Alexis the charming small towns. They then turned away from the coast and flew up the Connecticut River.

Isabel was following the map and putting old familiar names to the towns that she saw below. There it was, Windsor and Windsor Locks and Suffield—how many thousands of times had she driven through those places, most of the time unhappy? And there was Enfield and Thompsonville and Longmeadow, beautiful Longmeadow. There below now was Agawam, Springfield and West Springfield, Westfield and Chicopee. All this she pointed out to Alexis, and he watched her and listened to her tell about them, but in the telling, he was finding out more about Isabel.

They were over Holyoke now, and from there they cut away from the river because they had a plan. They were on their way to Stockbridge. There, waiting in an eighteenth-century inn was a room, and down by Stockbridge Lake was Alexis's chauffeur waiting for them, just as instructed, with the Rolls.

They taxied over to the car and Isabel and Alexis left the plane. It would be waiting in two days' time for them at the spot they had pointed out on the Connecticut River between Springfield and Longmeadow. They need not rush, the pilots would wait as many days as necessary for the Hyatts.

Stockbridge, a jewel of a town, was where Natalie lived. It was also where Norman Rockwell had lived, and so many of its people and places looked like his magazine covers. It was plunk in the center of the prettiest part of the Berkshire Mountains in Massachusetts.

Isabel called Natalie and went to see her without Alexis. She broke the news of the deaths to Natalie, who was horrified, never dreaming anyone died anywhere except in their own bed or in a hospital, and there was *always* a body to bury. She said how grateful she was that Isabel had made the effort to come and see her, and was thrilled that Isabel had found someone to make a life with and was married. She recovered enough to have lunch with Isabel and Alexis, and did not mention the tragedy again.

From Stockbridge they went to Williamstown and its fine, small museum, which Alexis was delighted to see. They went to Pittsfield, Greenfield, Adams and North Adams and then made their way down to Great Barrington, through Lee and Lenox, over to Otis. They cut across country so she could show him Amherst and Smith College, and they stayed at Wiggins Tavern.

They drove back down along the Connecticut River to a home town which she hardly recognized. Most of the city had been swept away by a great urban renewal project which never came off. Now it was a wilderness of parking lots. She had once thought it one of the nicest cities in the world to grow up in, if you had to grow up in a city. Now it was nothing but a shell. A dirty, miserable, depressing shell of what it had been.

In her tour around the city she had them pass by the house that she was born and brought up in. It was a small, Cape Cod, cottage-type house, white with blue shutters. It should have looked charming and quaint with its white picket fence running around it, but it didn't. It was shabby and tiny and worn-out looking, and it had crab grass everywhere.

The Rolls purred by the house, and she never even told Alexis that it was the house that she had run away from, because when she looked at the house and was about to tell him, it was not the house that stopped her, but the memories. The unhappy memories and the final running away. So they drove past it.

They stayed in the best hotel in town, which was depressing beyond belief, and in bed that night, after they had made love, they talked about the look of the town and all that they had seen.

Alexis said, "Martha's Vineyard is the American dream come true, darling. Your hometown is the American dream gone bad. Do not be upset, it happens."

The next day Isabel and Alexis went to a completely restored New England village an hour's drive away.

Sturbridge Village was in pretty countryside and kept and lived in just as it was in the 1700's, when the pilgrims settled there. There were country stores and craftsmen working, and everyone wore costumes of the period. There was a tiny museum which Alexis found charming.

At the inn they had an excellent lunch of corn chowder, turkey with all the trimmings, sweet potatoes, and vegetables like yellow summer squash and pumpkin, which Alexis had never before eaten. For dessert he had lemon chiffon pie with whipped cream on top.

They strolled around the village again and he bought her some small mementos. It was all pleasantly charming, and at one point they looked at one another and wondered what they were doing there.

They took small, winding country roads as they made their way back towards Springfield and the seaplane that was waiting for them. It was a pretty day, but the leaves were all down off the trees, and their wonderful bright colors were now faded and rusty. They were just dead leaves. It was beginning to smell as if winter was just around the corner.

They leisurely drove through the small towns of Brookfield and Warren and Ware. They followed a river from Ware through West Warren and a place called Thorndike. Suddenly there appeared another river on the other side of the country road. The ride was lovely. A river on either side of an almost deserted country road that was banked thick with dark green ferns and great tall trees.

The road kept winding its way downhill, until suddenly the two small rivers rushing around the occasional boulder were especially pretty. There were the sounds of rushing water and rustling leaves as the light wind moved them about. Around another curve, and about a quarter of a mile away, they could see a small town at the bottom of the hill. Alexis had the car stop and instructed the driver to wait for them in the village just beyond the bridge.

They walked arm in arm through the leaves towards the small hump-backed stone bridge that led into the center of town. It was more like a village; you could see it all from where they were. They watched the Rolls disappear, and then they walked in silence, just listening to nature all around them.

Just as they were about thirty yards from the bridge

they saw a third, small, swift river coming from another direction. They walked onto the bridge and stopped in the middle of it to look down into the water.

"I like your New England," Alexis said. "Thank you, darling, for taking me with you on your pilgrimage."

"Oh, Alexis, I did not know it was a pilgrimage."

"Yes, darling, I feel like we *have* been on a pilgrimage. If nothing lies at the end of it, I can only say that the traveling has been worthwhile."

"You have known this all along, haven't you?" Isabel whispered.

He put his arm around her waist, and she her arm around his, and together they walked over the bridge, listening to the roar of the three rivers rushing along underneath them. At the end of the bridge there was a very neat, white sign with the crest of the State of Massachusetts emblazoned on it.

It said: WELCOME TO THREE RIVERS, MASSACHUSETTS, POPULATION . . . and the numbers had been wiped out.

Isabel looked up at Alexis and said, "The circle has come full round: Three Rivers, Massachusetts, is where Kate was born, and I have never been here before."

"You know, darling, there is a great deal of mysticism in a pilgrimage."

The two walked on in silence for a few minutes and then Isabel looked up at Alexis and said, "What does one wear in Baghdad this time of year?"

A smile broke out on Alexis's face, and he roared with laughter and said, "I will buy you something new for Baghdad."

Slowly a smile crept over Isabel's face, and she said, "Come on, I'll race you to the car!"

COPING, LOVING and SUCCEEDING

Ballantine has everything to help the modern woman in today's world.

AL-2ª

Women of all ages can look and feel their best

with these bestselling guides to wardrobe, weight loss, exercise and skin care.